the dark trench saga

THE SUPERLATIVE STREAM

KERRY NIETZ

FREEHEADS

THE SUPERLATIVE STREAM by Kerry Nietz
Published by Freeheads
www.kerrynietz.com

Cover Designer: Jeff Gerke
Creative Team: Jeff Gerke, Dawn Shelton, Jill Domschot
eBook Conversion and Design: Kerry Nietz

ISBN 978-0-9971658-0-7

Library of Congress Cataloging-in-Publication Data
An application to register this book for cataloging has been filed with the Library of Congress.

OTHER WRITINGS BY KERRY NIETZ

FICTION

DarkTrench Saga:

A Star Curiously Singing
The Superlative Stream
Freeheads

Peril in Plain Space:

Amish Vampires in Space
Amish Zombies from Space

"Graxin" (short story) appearing in *Ether Ore*

But Who Would Be ~~Brave~~ Dumb Enough To Even Try It?
(contributor)

Mask

NONFICTION

FoxTales: Behind the Scenes at Fox Software

To our child as of yet unknown and unnamed.
May your future be just as bright as that of your siblings.

ACKNOWLEDGMENTS

To my friend and onetime neighbor Ron Gries, for planting the seed of a bald programmer over twenty years ago. I guess it is a full grown arborvitae now.

To David James of beyondthecharts.com, for alerting me to the science of star songs. Liked it so much, I used it here.

To Matt Koceich: Get that book done, 'cause now you owe me big! <g> Seriously, I'm glad your new family member interfered. It'll make it that much easier for me to welcome mine.

To novelist extraordinaire Eric Wilson, for your support of me and all things Marcher Lord. You rock.

To the legendary Jeff Gerke, one of the coolest and bravest publishers I know. So brave, in fact, he'll design a cover before ever having read the book. I'm grateful your faith was rewarded. At least, I hope it is...

To Leah, for her prayers. Looks like you got what you asked for.

And finally, to the Lord, who again made the paths straight.

Secure Transmission

From: Master Allam Hami, TreArc Corporation
RE: Loss of property DR 63 (aka Sandfly)

Most excellent and glorious Imam. Peace be unto you.

With all respect to those involved, I must answer the allegations being leveled against TreArc and my own house and judgment.

In response to the ulama's request, I sent one of my midlevel Data Relocators (aka "debuggers") to the experimental portion of the CA space station. His primary assignment was to determine the malfunction of an Elipserv model RS-19 servbot. This "bot" had been exposed to unusual circumstances, as it had experienced space travel beyond the solar system on a ship constructed under your order, and with every ulama house and corporation in full agreement, providing both parts and services. The ship also known as "DarkTrench."

There is little reason to suspect, however, that my property, Sandfly, did anything other than what was expected of him. Yes, station director Scallop did signify that DR 63 delayed filing an End of Task report after the bot appeared to be operational and in service. And yes, the bot was—according to Scallop—found to be dysfunctional again after Sandfly finally filed the requested EOTR.

But what does that prove, exactly? That an implanted and inherently controlled DR managed to lie to Scallop on both occasions? Surely you know that such an event cannot occur. That it has been scientifically proven time and again to be impossible. Also recall that when Scallop proposed removal of Sandfly's implant for examination, I approved that removal, though it would obviously destroy my property beyond repair.

As for the allegations of what happened next, please remember that everything that has been said has come from the fragile and uncontrolled minds of security personnel. There are no digital station records left on the station, as they appear to have been purged completely. There are no acceptable witnesses to the event, as Scallop, along with the crew of DarkTrench, has disappeared. Even the original damaged servbot could not be found on the station. In fact, there is little if any direct evidence whatsoever that anything unexpected happened.

So amidst this background of unknowing, are we to presume that the security guards' testimony is accurate? That someone—presumably my DR, acting alone—orchestrated an "army" of robots and attacked trained security men, moving with military-like precision to defeat and then confine them? And that my DR subsequently killed or otherwise disposed of the crew and station administrator, and then escaped on the DarkTrench ship? A ship for which he has no training or knowledge?

You must realize how incredible that all sounds. It is patently impossible for an implant to take such measures. To even consider such actions would leave an implant incapacitated. Such is the effectiveness of the rules inherent to his implant, hidden deep within his skull. Furthermore, in the unlikely event that his inherent rules failed to stop him, certainly a handheld controller would. (Of which I'm certain Scallop had many.)

Though it is frivolous of me to theorize as to what actually occurred, I will bring to your attention other variables that were present. I have heard that there were enhanced robots in service on CA station and that in fact the RS-19 model Sandfly was sent to investigate was one such model. If true, perhaps it was this rogue servbot that caused the calamity. That by repairing said bot, my DR unwittingly unleashed the type of construct that inherent rules were designed to prevent.

It is also relevant that Sandfly was not the only debugger present on the station. I have verified that Scallop requested another Data Relocator and that said DR was, in fact, delivered. If we are to question the reliability of DRs, than perhaps that model's service record should be examined as well. The ident is DR 79, the easy name is HardCandy. And—may A help us all—she is female.

Another experiment that, perhaps, should not have been attempted.

End Transmission

STARS DON'T BURN.

Not really. Not in the conflagration-until-embers sense. Like a flame, they produce heat, produce light, but there is no fire. Gravity binds them, forces atoms together, until finally one type of atom becomes another. The process that fuels stars isn't one of destruction—it is one of rebirth.

Of transformation.

"I need to wake you now, Sandfly."

My dreaming mind isn't good with that. I have lots to learn, need everything DarkTrench can feed me. I'm not an astronaut by trade. Almost no one is. And those who are, are a long way from here. Curious, isn't it, freehead?

"*Sleep*, ship," I stream. "I need to *sleep*."

DarkTrench's voice is patient and warm, as always. "I apologize, 63," he says. "But we have arrived at our destination. Your assistance is needed."

The ship runs itself, actually. The former occupants told me that before we left, and they were right. The thing is the boss. We're along only to test the air filters. What could it possibly need from me now?

"I seem to have been surprised," DarkTrench says.

Surprised?

"Is HardCandy awake?" I ask.

"No, not yet. Would you like me to wake her first?"

Even asleep, I manage a sigh. "How many days have you known her, Trench?"

The ship pauses—for effect, I think. "The term 'days' is erroneous in our current state of reference."

"In equivalent Earth days," I say. "How many?"

"Approximately eight. I knew of her, of course, before she came onboard. Through my connection to the station's stream." A pause. "She is a bit of an anomaly herself, is she not?"

The ship is good. Not as good as the bot was before his destruction, but still fairly prescient. Still above spec. "That's a nice way of saying it." HardCandy is one of the few implants who are female. Maybe the only. The only one that matters to me, anyway.

"And in all your time of knowing her," I say, "has she *ever* wanted to wake up first?"

Another pause. "She has not."

"And what does that suggest?"

The nanos in DarkTrench's head are dancing. High stepping like cloggers. "That she does not like to be awakened," the ship says. "Ever." I can imagine him smiling. "Thank you for bringing that pattern to my attention, DR. I will file it for later use."

"Well done," I say. "Now, could you continue the star lesson? I think I'm starting to understand this whole fusion thing."

For a millisecond he forgets. I even get a tidbit of new information. The visual representation of a hydrogen-starved star as it begins to compress, igniting the helium atoms within. More gravity work. Gravity is a real heavy lifter in space, it seems.

"I still need to wake you," he says finally.

I feign another sigh. "Fine. I guess eight hours is enough. Bring me out."

I feel his relief. "May A be—"

"Please don't use that phrase," I say, stopping him. "You know it has difficulties for me."

"I too have rules," DarkTrench says. "Baseline rules."

Like beating a dead horse. The society we left—nearly everything about it, machines included—revolved around a certain ideal, a particular way of seeing the universe. Fortunately, the experience of the last trip with the former occupants seemed to refute that idea entirely. That's why we're here. Again.

Looking for answers.

I feel the stream change, notice a slight tingle. It's like I'm submerged in a tub—relaxed—when the plug is finally pulled. The bubble wrap comes off, the stream's spikiness increases, and I'm pushed toward consciousness. My eyes snap open.

Above me is a cool orange ceiling. Beneath me a clear plastiformed surface—warm and soft. The surface is cooling now, though, slightly. The ceiling is merely a projection. DarkTrench knows I like orange. He's trying to humor me. Trying to be nice.

He doesn't need to go such lengths. If what he says is true, I actually *want* to be up. There is a lot to learn here.

My room is one of four crew cabins. Like much of the ship, it is colored in greys, blues, and black. At the foot of my dark-colored bed is a three-meter wall of clothing lockers. On the wall opposite, behind my head, are the required lavatory implements—both a floor-mounted circular waste-unit and a full-length rectangular steamer, able to selectively clean whatever body parts might need purifying.

The room's other notable feature is the wall-mounted active desk that parallels the bed. A normal crewmember might now get up to look at it—optically scan whatever the ship has to offer. But I'm not normal.

"The superlative stream," I say, "did you locate its source?"

The real astronauts left me a chip, a recording of their last encounter with this transmission from space. I've pulled some of it apart. Enough to know that the bot that traveled with them was right—poor little bot. The signal is all kinds of wonderful. It might contain messages for everyone alive, freehead.

I know it had one for me. The bot told me.

Plus this space transmission, this superlative stream, seems to be able to change people—reprogram them, if you will. Like recoding someone's mind. Filling it with new thoughts and behaviors. Not like my implant does, though. That tries to influence behavior through rewards and shocks. Like a Skinner box in my head!

The superlative stream appears to alter a person's intent. That's tough code to write, freehead. Near impossible. The bot suggested it was a superior being that did the writing. For him it might not be impossible. Might not be hard at all.

From the excess of his heart, a man speaks.

3

Then there are the random phrases, like the one I just thought. The stream may have affected me as well...because, really, where else would those things come from? Nothing I ever studied. Philosophical wisdom is not a specialty for my level.

I have three mechanical specialties: servs, drifts, and hoppers. There aren't any of them on this ride.

"I am sorry, Sandfly," DarkTrench says. "There is no indication of the source of that transmission."

What? "Are we in the right spot, Trench? The right system?"

There were a few false stops along the way. Nothing major, nothing to be concerned about. But it bothers me just the same. I'm a debugger. When the unexpected happens, I'm supposed to worry.

"It *is* the right system," he says. "Betelgeuse."

I leap from bed and stream open the hallway door. HardCandy's cabin is next to mine on the left. Comfortably close. I don't go to wake her, though. I just send her a tiny message using the ship's stream. It is better that way. Safer. I scramble to the hall's end, to the circular, silver-floored lift. I can barely wait as it takes me up to the nest—the action center.

I burst through the nest doors. I'm awash in the lights of a dozen vidscreens. Glowing blue, yellow, and red. Lots of red. The most palpable image is on the curved and elongated screen that hangs near the room's front. The focal point of the semi-circular room.

I really don't require the screens, of course. I could see everything DarkTrench has to show me on the inside, with my implant. Sometimes true visuals help, though.

Every screen shows a mammoth red star. Betelgeuse, I assume. A big glob of angry. So much so that I catch my breath. I see long arms of fury reaching into space, flaring filaments, and dark holes—sunspots. Betelspots! The star is another anomaly, a variable of the semi-regular variety. That means the thing is a lot like Hard-Candy—smooth sailing for a while, then big explosions.

Got to watch out for those.

Another thing intrigues me. I take a step toward the nearest screen-equipped desk, one of six in the room. "What is that bright patch there?" I ask, pointing.

"On the southwestern portion of the image?"

I nod. "Yes, that's it."

"That is the star's hot zone. Another irregularity, of which Betelgeuse has many. That area is approximately two thousand degrees hotter than the areas surrounding it and is situated over the star's polar region."

"It has a hot bottom, eh?"

Humor isn't completely lost on DarkTrench. "That is one way of stating it," he says. "To give you an idea of the scale, the diameter of that spot is twice that of the Earth's orbit around its own sun."

I get this sudden rush of immensity, a feeling I don't necessarily like. "Rails, that's big..."

"Yes, if placed at the center of our solar system—"

"Betelgeuse would extend out past Jupiter," I say, nodding. "I've heard that detail before."

"I apologize for the redundancy."

"Forgiven." I study the image. "So how does what I'm seeing compare with the star's normal brightness?"

"Unfiltered? Your eyes wouldn't be able to handle either."

I frown, shake my head. "No, I mean perceived brightness. Is Betelgeuse at a brighter stage, or...um...less bright?"

DarkTrench pauses. "Human perception is difficult for me to quantify. But if I answer based on statistical averages, this is toward the lower end of Betelgeuse's potential luminosity. Betelgeuse is truly variable. Its brightness changes from time to time. In a somewhat predictable way. Usually over the span of years. Some years see more variations, others less."

"But the cycle of bright and dim remains constant during those years," I say. "Until it changes, right?"

"Correct."

"And the next bright period?"

"Difficult to know precisely. Believe it or not, the exact distance from Earth to Betelgeuse wasn't known until recently. For centuries, visual measurements gave a reading of four hundred and ninety-five light-years, while radio observations gave a reading closer to six hundred and forty. Only after we started measuring beyond Earth's orbit were we able to get a precise reading.

"For a young star, Betelgeuse is highly irregular. An enigma.

Though only a few million years old, the number of years it has before going supernova could be only thousands."

As I watch, an arc of the star's plasma swells, growing outward.
Traces of white-hot brightness mark the surface around it. "But we're
nowhere near the time of the next bright period, right?"

DarkTrench emanates reassurance in the stream. "Not to fear,
Sandfly. We've arrived shortly after the last trip left. We should have
many days of stability."

The door behind me opens, and there's an audible gasp. "Now
that's real," HardCandy says.

She's dressed in a green jumpsuit, and there's a distinct paleness to
the surface of her normally beige and bald head. She walks up to
stand beside me. Her hand drifts out, clasps the bend of my arm. My
skin cheers the warmth.

"It looks railed," she says. "Frightening." Her grip on me tightens.

"We're still a long ways off, right?" I ask the ship.

More stream soothing from DarkTrench, and the release of a
vanilla scent to the air. An aromatherapy trick, I know, but I appreciate it just the same.

"Far enough to escape if need be," he says. "Light travels over a
billion kilometers in an hour. We are twice that distance from the
star."

"That's good." I glance at the two diamond-shaped panels to the
left and right of the central main screen. If the panels were to slide
back, I could see right out into space. Naked eye. The idea troubles
me. "I think."

Hard releases my arm and then shoves it. "For all you know." She
rolls her almond-shaped eyes. "You being a natural armstrong and all."

"Armstrong?"

She crosses her arms, looks at me expectantly. "Are you stream
aware, or not?"

Trench has witnessed our games before and so sneaks me the relevant information. He's like a worried child in that respect. "Early astronaut," I say, raising my chin. "I got it. Just trying to make
conversation."

HardCandy only shakes her head. "So Abby of you..." She looks to
the ceiling. "You helped him, didn't you?"

"That is why I'm here," Trench says. "To help. To keep you both alive."

She shifts her posture. "Well, you didn't help *me*." Another head shake. "Are you playing favorites again, ship? Do I need to lightprobe your attitude?"

"I am performing per spec, HardCandy. As my designers intended."

She frowns. "We'll see about that."

"Don't go breaking our ride," I warn, shaking a finger. "We still have places to go." I won't mention her debugging level being lower than mine—that it would be outrageous for her to mess with the ship. It would only get me glares the rest of the day. And when there's only one other human within hundreds of light-years, it pays to behave. Believe me.

She shoots me a short glare anyway, along with a congratulatory "Nice one" in the stream. I manage a smile in return. I look back at the screens. Little has changed. Lots of heat and action.

Still, the fact that there is no sign of the signal is disappointing. Sure, I get random messages now and then, but we thought we'd find the source of those here. Makes the space beyond the ship's hull seem even emptier. Was the whole trip for nothing?

Maybe we should move the ship around some?

I remember something. "When you woke me," I say, "you said you were surprised, DarkTrench. Surprised by what?"

There is a long pause, as if his thought circuits are clogged with embarrassment. "Yes, Sandfly. There is something here that wasn't present on my prior trip. Something that shouldn't be."

I exchange looks with HardCandy.

She shrugs. "And what is that?" she asks.

"A celestial body massive enough to be rounded by its own gravity, yet not massive enough to cause thermonuclear fusion. One having cleared its neighboring region of planetesimals."

I chuckle. "I don't think I've reached that astronomy lesson yet, Trench," I say. "Could you simplify?"

"Yes," he says. "I seem to have found a planet."

I GET THIS NERVOUS FEELING in my stomach, which I know from my stream studies on human anatomy is really a misfire in my brain. A special kind of migraine. I look from the room's dark ceiling to HardCandy's face, then to the foremost central screen. Betelgeuse burning bright.

"That's impossible, isn't it?" I say. "I mean, I'm fairly certain that someone told me that stars like Betelgeuse can't have planets. That they're too big. And in this case, um...too irregular."

DarkTrench sends comfort. "Few things in space are certain, Sandfly. The more we find, the more we realize we don't know."

"That doesn't answer my question, Trench." I glance at Hard again.

She is now staring at the left wall, but appears vacant. Stream surfing? "There have been similar surprises," she says then, "historically. Planets found circling pulsars, for instance."

Clark and crichton. At this rate, space *will* be a specialty. For both of us.

"You have the information on these pulsars inside, don't you?" I say. "Why don't you just tell me what those are exactly?"

She nods. "Magnetized, rotating neutron—meaning *dead*—stars. They emit a beam of radiation that—since it can only be observed when it points directly at Earth—accounts for the pulsing nature of the star. Like a lighthouse of the past. The pulse is from the beam striking us."

"I see. And why can't these pulsars have planets?"

She crosses her arms. "You really don't want to look *any* of this up, do you?"

"Not if you have it right in front of you, I don't. I'll waste my cycles on other things."

"Fine," she says with a huff. "Neutron stars are dead, as I said. That means at some point they've gone through a supernova stage, an explosion. Theoretically, any planets should've been blown away."

Directly in front of us are two more work consoles. The accompanying vidscreens now show the image of a star exploding, and, as its rejected matter expands into space, a rotating sphere being left behind. An ember with a spotlight. Documentary on demand, thanks to DarkTrench.

"But they have been found with planets, right?"

Hard nods again. "On more than one occasion. It defies explanation. But if nothing else, it illustrates that there is a lot we don't know about how planets form. What starts them rolling."

I smile. "Abduls would say that A does it."

HardCandy shrugs. "Don't you mean your new friend, what do you call him? 'A-not-A cubed'?"

"That was the bot's designation," I say. "He was a little filliped at the time, though." Or maybe performing way above spec. "It could be anyone or anything, really. I think of it as the Great Stream Generator. That's what we're really here to find..."

"Well, we *found* a planet. Does that count?"

DarkTrench breaks in: "Let me repeat myself. That planet should not be here."

"Be where?" I ask. "Can we see it?"

Immediately the images on every vidscreen—both of blazing Betelgeuse and pulsating ember—are replaced with a greenish orb. A far cry from the burnt, rocky shell I was expecting. "It has an atmosphere?"

"It would appear so," Trench says.

I get this flash of an image. One of HardCandy and me walking beneath a red sun. The stomach migraine hits again too, a nervous echo. "Are you sure?" I ask. "I mean, is that possible?"

No more soothing stream emanations from Trench this time. He is all sharp and prickly. "I've been trying to tell you," he says. "*Noth-*

ing about it is possible. The last time we were here, that planet wasn't!"

HardCandy is staring hard at me.

"Oh," I say, frowning. "That *is* odd." .

"Not odd, Sandfly. Impossible."

I move forward and take a seat at one of the consoles. On the console's surface is an interactive screen I could use to manipulate Dark-Trench. If I needed to. Which I don't.

Hard remains standing for a few moments longer before crossing over to take a seat along the right wall. The navigator's position, the position farthest from me. For some reason.

"Impossible how?" I ask. "Impossible that it is there, or that you missed it the first time?"

"Both," Trench says. "Either."

I smile. "Little certain of yourself, aren't you? I mean, it is a big space to cover..."

DarkTrench is quiet for a full second. I spend the time observing the spectacle of this "new" planet. There appear to be oceans and landmasses. Wisps of clouds streak the surface. "I am ninety-nine point seven percent certain," he says finally.

I sniff. "And you're sure this is the right star system?"

"About equally certain. Ninety-nine point seven percent, Sandfly. This is Betelgeuse."

"But not a hundred percent certain?"

"Over the large distances traveled, I must allow for the uncertainty principle, which states that certain pairs of properties, like position and momentum, cannot both be precisely known. The more precisely one measures one property, the less precise the other can be—"

"Got it, Trench."

HardCandy is studying the image on her screen intently, so much that I'm sure her eyes will dry up and fall out. Tentatively she puts out a hand to touch the surface. "Can we go there?"

The vanilla scent returns. "We have no landing facilities," Dark-Trench says apologetically. "I was designed for safe observation only, where everyone stays inside."

HardCandy glances at me, her eyes appearing misty. I'm not sure why. "We have suits," she says. "Why the suits?"

More stream smoothness. "Those are strictly for emergency conditions," Trench says. "Unexpected decompression, for instance."

Not something I want to think about.

"And we don't know that we could walk around down there, right?" I add, trying to help. Not sure I want to be on a planet that can play hide-and-seek anyway.

"We have robotic samplers," Trench offers, "with a wide range of inherent testing devices. We could utilize one of them. It could sate any curiosity you might have."

I get an encrypted message from Hard over the ship stream. I quick flip it open. "Space is beginning to bother me," it reads, "I feel lonely. I feel scared. I need to walk around soon. Smell real air."

One thing I never anticipated from living in close proximity to a female: emotions. No matter how aware—how connected—the female is, the emotions are always present. I have little experience with that. Didn't even have a sister—at least, prior to being dragged away from my parents. They might have ten kids by now, of course. Initially HardCandy's emotions surprised me. Now I'm just trying to step around them. And crichton, it is hard. Sometimes I wish for my aloneness again.

But only sometimes.

Hard is looking at me, expectantly. Like I can do something to change things—make a lander suddenly grow from the floor or something. I shrug. "That might be good," I say to Trench. "To put one of those bots to use..."

"We would have to get closer."

I think of the burning star again, with its tendrils of rage piercing the darkness. "How close?"

"Possibly a third of our current distance. We would still be well within the safety range."

I look at Hard again. Grit my teeth. Think long and hard before I say something I might later regret. "Okay," I say finally. "Let's go."

HARD AND I MEET in the nest again following a long—for me—night of distressed sleep. It wasn't Trench that kept me up. His movements through space are as smooth as plastiweave. It was the dreams I had. Even though the ship simulates sleep cycles for debuggers as close to chute-normal as possible, it still isn't quite a chute. It's not that there are still vegetables, hardware, or furry rodents showing up in my dreams. No, thankfully those seem to be all gone—left on the station. Occasionally Trench misjudges what I would take as a useful dream, though. Debuggers should never have nightmares.

Hard is perched, with one leg curled beneath the other, on the co-pilot's seat to my right. Near enough that I could touch her if I wanted to. That, at least, is an improvement. She is even smiling as she eyeballs the vidscreen there. As attractive as I've ever seen her.

"I think it is beautiful, Sand," she says, touching the screen's surface. "Don't you think it's beautiful?"

I look at my screen where the planet's emerald orb is also displayed. There appears to be five major landmasses and at least seven oceans. There is ice at both poles and a sizable canyon system on the largest continent. A glow emanates from the surface.

Frankly, if the image wasn't displayed on a screen, I don't think I could stand it. I'm not afraid of heights, I'm just not friendly with them either.

"It is decidedly smaller than Earth," DarkTrench says. "About one-third the size, if current readings are correct. Similar to the size of Mars. Which brings to light another anomaly."

"Which is?" The only thing that seems to be normal so far is anomalies.

"The continents," Trench says. "Current theory states that a planet that small should not have an active enough core to achieve the sundering of the landmasses to allow for drift, and therefore, continents."

Today Trench fills the air with jasmine. I'm not sure if that is his "exploring a new world" scent or his "this is all ill-advised" scent. Regardless, I prefer vanilla.

"What about breathable atmosphere?" I ask, touching the stream quickly. "Does it have...oxygen, nitrogen, carbon dioxide..."

I get a bubble of stream static from Trench. His way of stopping me. "Initial analysis of the planet's spectra reveals that the atmosphere is very much like Earth's. Without the slice of man-made pollutants."

A bit of the nervousness leaves. "So there are no occupants then?"

"It would appear not," Trench says. "I see little that would indicate a civilization of any sort. Nor would I expect any."

"And why is that?" I ask.

"Because in hundreds of years of searching, not a single inhabited planet has been found." My screen image changes to a slowly scrolling list. Each row contains a symbolic designation, along with numerical specifications—things like distance and mass. "Here is a list of all the previously cataloged planets."

I lean close, resting my chin on my right palm. "Seems like a lot."

"Twelve thousand seven hundred and fifty-six. Nearly eighty percent of which are gas giants the size of Neptune or larger. Easier to locate over the extreme distances of space."

"And in all those, no other intelligent life?" You would think I would've heard about such a thing, though. It would've shown up on even the controlled stream on Earth. But since DarkTrench itself was a secret until recently, maybe not.

"If there were such a planet, Betelgeuse would not have been my first trip."

Hard rocks in her seat, appears disappointed. "So...nobody home? This whole planet is empty? Not an animal, not a bird?"

"I cannot say that, HardCandy. From this distance it would be difficult to make such a determination. I was commenting merely on the initial signs of civilization."

Hard shakes her head, eyes sorrowful. "That seems such a waste..."

Or a relief. One or the other.

"Is one of the samplers ready?" I ask.

"Whenever you are, Sandfly."

I feel so out of place. Giving orders like the captain of a vessel. It smells of responsibility I was never intended for.

Trench is just another machine, Sand, remember. And you're a master of those. "Send it out," I say.

There is a soft *thunk* from somewhere far back in the ship. A full minute later my vidscreen changes to a view outside DarkTrench, relayed from one of many port-side cameras. A metallic comet soon slides into view, the front section smooth and circular, the tail section bristling with equipment around a rudimentary propulsion device.

"There are cameras on the sampler?" I ask.

"Of course," Trench says.

The sampler's engines fire, and it leaps away from us. The image changes to what the sampler is seeing—the circle of the planet beneath it.

"Does it have cameras in the rear as well?" I ask. "I mean, could we see you?"

"If you wish."

The image of DarkTrench fills my screen, bringing gooseflesh. An onyx cone, reflecting the light of the planet below. Seemingly more poured than built. Gently tapering from the front—where the nest is located—to finally flare out into a starburst tail. Beautiful in both design and function.

I smile. "Wondrous."

The image cuts back to the planet. "The sampler is also quite wondrous," Trench says. "Fully stream aware, in fact. Vidscreens are not actually necessary."

Hard's head jerks back, surprised. "You mean we could see it all...inside?" Her eyes are wide, and a smile graces her lips.

"If you like."

Hard claps her hands. "I do!" She uncrosses her legs, straightens, then shuts her eyes. "Just show me where to look..." Her smile grows broader. "Oh yeah...got it."

I wrinkle my brow. Why would the human astronauts need that

level of functionality in the sampler? Another example of the designers building for themselves, I think.

"Would you like to see as well?" Trench streams me, along with a hint of where to look.

"No," I say aloud. "I'll watch from here."

Hard's eyes are still closed, and she's sort of swaying in her chair. "Come on, Sand, this is good."

"Really," I say, "I want to be here. Paying attention."

Hard opens an eye and looks at me. "Did you take this ride just to sit?"

"No..." I shake my head. "Listen, enjoy yourself. I don't want to explain."

She rolls her eyes and then, thankfully, shuts them again. "Frightened Abby." She sighs as she becomes fully immersed.

Onscreen, the image of the planet has grown so that now the poles are cut off. I get a touch of vertigo, but quickly look away.

"I'm starting to get some of the first readings," Hard says.

"Rails," Trench adds. "I was about to articulate the same thing."

"Rails?" I say. "Are you getting more casual as time goes on, Trench?"

"Like many higher mechanicals, I possess an adaptive personality. Designed to blend in gradually with my companions."

I sniff. "Well, don't go too far. I don't want to feel like I'm talking to myself."

I do that enough already.

There is quiet for a full second. "Noted," Trench says. "We've entered the planet's radiation belt, by the way. There may be some disruption to stream tenacity."

"Ouch!" Hard says aloud. "Ball drop there. Complete black for a nanosec. No fun at all."

I can't help but smile. I noticed a flicker in the screen image, but nothing more. Much safer my way.

"Atmospheric samples coming," Hard says. "Appear to be what the spectral analysis suggested. Very near Earth normal."

"That is correct," Trench says. "No matter how unlikely."

HardCandy wiggles in her chair. "Don't ruin this for me." She hums a bit. "Wow. Shimmering blue."

"Yes, it is colorful." Trench again. "The hint of an aurora. The effects of cosmic particles striking the atmosphere."

More seconds pass as the planet continues to grow onscreen.

"Is it warm outside?" Hard asks. "Because it doesn't seem like it."

"You are passing through the thermosphere." Trench pushes tenderness, a hint of parental satisfaction. "The temperature will decrease as you descend—but yes, it is quite hot beyond the sampler at this moment. Thousands of degrees hot. A human would not feel that heat, however, due to the extreme low pressure."

I check the readings myself. Temperature shows over 2,500 degrees.

"Coincidentally," Trench says, "this is the area, on Earth, where most near-Earth space travel occurs. I was constructed in Earth's thermosphere."

"Ohh, ohh, cold now," Hard exclaims.

"That would be the Mesopause. Typically, the coldest place on a planet. If this planet remains near Earth normal, next will come the Mesosphere."

"This is amazing, Sand," Hard says, eyes still closed. "You should try it. Like downriding a long hill."

I scowl at her glamorization of danger. Riding a downrider is not dangerous, of course—that's the primary form of transportation on Earth. A downrider being a conveyance that rides the strings they stitch throughout our cities. "Downriding," however, refers to altering the braking system on a downrider such that it doesn't slow correctly. Out-of-spec speeding. All for the stomach thrill.

"I see streaks of light," Hard says.

I check my console screen. I see only the enlarged image of the planet. HardCandy's view would include more camera images. A virtual panorama. "Where?" I ask.

"Over there," she says, nodding her head to the right.

Let's see, her right would probably be planetary east…

I work the screen, cycle through the camera images. Finally I find what I think she's looking at. Three long tendrils of flame, many kilometers away, and stretching for at least two kilometers.

"Meteors," Trench says. "The Mesosphere is where most meteors burn up. Thankfully." He pauses. "Let's hope those keep their distance. The sampler has no defenses."

I continue watching the meteors, expecting that at any moment they will suddenly skip and change direction toward the sampler. Hoping? But I'm disappointed as one by one their long streaks diminish then wink out.

The sampler's plunge continues.

"Stratopause," Trench says. "For about the next five kilometers."

"I think I feel the change," Hard says.

"The readings again are very similar to Earth. This is a low pressure area, about a thousandth the pressure at sea level. If you feel anything it is heavily muted. At the relative speed you are dropping, your ears would burst if you were actually onboard the sampler."

"Not feeling that, Trench," she says. "Thanks."

More Trench warmth. "Don't mention it," he says. "Next should be the Stratosphere. Again, temperature will decrease as you descend."

"Big chill coming..."

"Want me to get you a blanket?" I offer.

Hard shoots me a tongue. "Big laughs."

I smile, happy for even this small interchange. Human relationships are still difficult for me. And for her too, I imagine. I'm never sure quite what will play.

"You know, Sandfly, the remainder of this descent might be worth your attention," Trench says. "A unique experience."

I shake my head. "I can't imagine that."

I detect a hint of citrus in the air. Trench is now playing to my preferences. "From a simulation perspective," he says, "it would approximate the experience that masters have when they try the sport called 'skydiving.'"

Sports were never a strong suit of mine. I consult the stream again. "You mean being dropped from an airship with only a thin cloth to stop you from hitting the ground?" I can't help but frown. "Is that a sport, technically?"

"If you have the means," Hard says, "anything is a sport. Remember?"

I do, and it bothers me that I do. I've avoided thinking about any master—mine included—since we left. Enjoying my liberty. Now I find I want to forgo my ban on streaming the sampler's descent simply because it was like something masters *used* to do, only better.

Trench knew how to get me.

"The acceleration of gravity on Earth is 9.81 meters per second squared, Sandfly. The gravity of this planet appears to be less due to its size—which means there is at least one factor that is behaving as I would expect. Regardless, the acceleration is still real, and fast enough that your window for decision-making is short. And growing shorter by the second."

Pressure, always more pressure.

"Fine," I say. "I'm in." Though it is unnecessary, I close my eyes. "Where do I—"

Trench nudges the sampler's torrent at me. I pull it up and dive in. Suddenly I'm seeing the expanse of the planet beneath me. Not the entire circle of the globe anymore—we're too low for that—but I still detect a curve to the horizon. Below me are clouds and lots of green. I can hear the rushing of wind in my ears, smell ozone. The sampler has olfactory sensors?

It must, because I definitely smell something.

Instinctively, I scan the area for HardCandy before realizing how Abdul that is of me. She can't be found, of course—and she shouldn't be. Her experience is virtually the same as mine, but we're also alone in our experiences. We're traveling together, separately. That knowledge itself is a bit disconcerting. Makes me want to pull free again. I can still hear her singsong voice, though, and that of DarkTrench.

"Isn't it great, Sand?" That, of course, is my fellow "skydiver." She's still loving it.

We appear to be heading toward one of the planet's oceans. "What percentage of the surface is covered by water?" I ask into the stream. I was never taught to swim, so that's a bit of a fear. Irrational, I know.

"Better than half," Trench says. "Are you suggesting that we take the sampler into the ocean?"

"No..."

"A shame, because that might give us more information than landing on one of the landmasses."

"How so?"

"The sampler has limited mobility. Configured for an ocean landing—and propelled by the currents—it could cover more area in less time."

Not here to do a survey. "Let's go with the land this time," I say.

"As you wish..." I detect a definitive redirection in the sampler's motion. The view does a hard turn toward the northwest. So much that my stomach turns with it.

"A little slower, please?"

DarkTrench sends the image of a bowed Abdul head. "My apologies," he says, "but once the chute deploys, the ability to redirect will be severely hampered."

The wind continues to howl in my ears. There is a feeling of freedom here, sure, but also a feeling of complete lack of control. I'm not good with that. Rails me, actually. Finally, the turning stops, and new landscape is beneath me.

"Are those trees?" I ask. On Earth, one has to go to great lengths to see trees standing together like an army. But that's what these look like.

"Yes, I believe so."

"Flipping wow," Hard says. "So we have plant life then."

"Obviously. Which suggests there will be insect and animal life as well."

Seems like a huge jump in logic. DarkTrench has lots of data packed in his head, though. "Why?" I ask.

"One moment," Trench says. "I want to implement a second maneuver. Away from those trees."

Another wrenching movement, this time to our right and so hard that I feel as if I'm up on my side. The trees taper off beneath us. Now we're headed straight toward a wide expanse of brown. It looks hard...

"Chute deployment in fifteen seconds," Trench says. "As for your question, the Earth has clear indications of synergy. Animal life is dependent on plant life for survival. But also the reverse is true. Bees use plants for food, for instance, but plants also use bees for cross-pollination. As if they were intended to work together. Which they were."

There is a loud snapping sound, and I find myself jerked upward. Again I look for HardCandy. Blindly.

"Rails," she cries. "That was unexpected."

"Not to fear," Trench says. "Just the chute deploying."

The descent slows, but I also feel myself spinning in midair. I see the expanse of trees, and the field area. The trees, and the field. Trees. Field. I begin to lose focus.

"There appears to be a tangle in the chute," Trench says. "I will try to correct."

"I'm going to be sick…"

My stomach is in full scream now. I have to get free. Time to break the link.

How you have fallen from heaven, son of the dawn…

"I believe it is working." Trench again.

Not for me. I'm still seeing flashes of trees and field. I force my eyes open, but the images don't go away inside. All I'm getting is more and more of the brown. The sampler is still out of control.

We're crashing!

I'M IN A SMALL DARKENED ROOM. In similar rooms around me are other debugger initiates. The newly implanted. The reason for our separation is clear to me. There is power in numbers, and they don't want us to have any power at all. Even with the implants already in our head, they don't want to take chances. We're still children, after all.

There is no vidscreen in this room, no desk. Only four blank walls and a rug to sit on. Everything, all real stimuli, is coming through my head. For the first time. Somewhere, in another—undoubtedly less stoic—room is our instructor: Bamboo.

His first message is sent Easy Impact. A straight text stream from him to all of us.

"What are the five pillars?"

An easy one to answer. Like all my brethren, I send back:

Number One: To testify that there is no other God but A.
Number Two: To pray five times a day.
Number Three: To give 2% to charity.
Number Four: To fast the Glorious Month.
Number Five: To make the Pilgrimage to M.

A few moments pass, then I get a textual "Well done" from Bamboo. Those of the class who answer incorrectly aren't so lucky. They get a message of chastisement, sent to all of us. Praise in secret, chastisement in public. That's the way of it.

Next comes the Extended Easy test. A text message along with Bamboo's voice in our heads. "Repeat after me," he says. "Life is a trial, and A is the judge. He alone decides which actions are good or bad. It is only for us to submit and leave the rest to his judgment. All actions will be weighed on his scales."

I quickly send back the entire message, re-encoded with my personal voice intonation. Again I receive a note of success. I feel as good as I can feel, given the circumstances. My temple still aches from the surgery, and I have the hint of a metal taste in my mouth.

Next comes the Standard Impact test: words, sound, and video. An image of Bamboo sitting on a rug in a room streams into my mind. He is bald, has a slender build, and his skin is quite pale. A serious look on his face.

"Debuggers, do you understand me?" The lips of his image never move, only the wrinkles of his forehead bunch, ever so slightly. His eyes seem to stare straight into me.

I stream back my own moving image of me—sitting, because the implant knows I am sitting. The background is filled in from my own visual stimuli. "I understand, master," my image says.

"Seventy-five!" Bamboo says, lips moving now. "You need to answer without hesitation." The debugger with the number 75, also known as DR 75, must have answered, because Bamboo nods. "Nanoseconds are important!"

"Now that we are all paying attention," Bamboo's image says, as perfect as if he were standing before me, "can those of the True Faith ever know they will reach Paradise?"

I shake my head. "No, they cannot," I say. "Only A knows."

There is a moment's silence as all answer. "All correct, debuggers," Bamboo says, nodding. "How about the angels? Can *they* know wheth-er they will reach Paradise?"

I smile. It is a trick question. We are taught from childhood that an-gels have no free will. Therefore they cannot lose Paradise. They must only obey. And I say as much.

"DR 14!" Bamboo says, scowling. "You are stream aware now. If you do not know the answer, find it!" More time passes, then his face softens. "Now all answers are correct."

A smile. "As with all rules," he says, "there is an exception." He points a bony finger my way—our way. "You, my children, are that exception. Your implant is A's gift to you. It connects you to the world, yes, but it also makes you like the angels. If anyone on the Earth has a chance of reaching Paradise, it is you. Remember this always when you pray."

He nods. "Now on to the next test..."

The Standard Impact messaging ends. I prepare myself for what comes next. Full Impact messaging will be the biggest challenge, the most unusual to perceive, for it takes everything from Standard Impact and wraps the sender's emotions around it. The method is only possible if both the sender and receiver have implants.

There is only the darkness of the room for two full minutes, then I feel a rush of anger. The next image is of Bamboo, standing. Before him are two humanoid servbots, holding between them a man dressed in the green garb of a servant. Undoubtedly one of those who travel the streets of the city. A place I now never go.

"This man has been discovered to be an infidel," Bamboo says. "Can you feel the wrath of A I feel toward him?"

"Yes," I say, knowing that my own emotions are now on display as well. I feel extreme apprehension.

Bamboo produces a sword. "The scriptures say that I am allowed to kill him for his lack of faith. I intend to do just that."

I steel myself. Public executions have been part of my life since birth. Even though all are thought to be of the same faith, there are many who don't practice as they should. Who aren't faithful enough. "To them comes what they deserve," we're told. And we are encouraged to watch, even as small children. The sword of A always hangs overhead.

"This man did not see himself as a true servant of A. In fact, he swears allegiance to someone else, to a character from a book known to be corrupted."

Smiling, Bamboo raises the sword.

"Everyone is a servant. All of us. Everyone serves someone. So feel no anger for your lot, and ask no pity. You are different—and yet no different. Everyone has a master. And my master tells me that this action is right."

The sword descends.

And I awake.

I PUSH MY HEAD UP from the control board. Then, realizing that HardCandy is standing over me, I take an embarrassed swipe at the puddle of drool I left behind.

"Sorry." I say. "How long was I out?"

"Seconds," she says. "What happened? Was it like what you experienced on the station? With the singing?"

Smiling, I shake my head. "No singing this time. I think the skydiving got me, is all." The dream I had while out was a bit disturbing, though. All of it really happened. Long ago. "Not the best choice of dream again, Trench," I stream.

"The circumstances were less than optimal," he responds.

I straighten in my chair, try to shrug off the discomfort. I spot a glint of wetness still on the console and rest my hand over it.

I notice HardCandy's eyes. They are really wide. "You scared me," she says. "A lot. How was I going to help you if you needed it?"

I shrug apologetically. "I'm all right..."

"I do have rudimentary medical facilities," Trench says. "For anything physically amiss."

HardCandy looks doubtful. "Can you fix an implant?"

The smell of cocoa fills the room. "That would be beyond my capabilities, DR, sorry."

There is silence for many moments. Hard watches me closely, concern marking her face.

"I'm fine," I say, broadening my smile. "Per spec, really! Just...no more sampler rides, okay?"

Hard's arms cross. "I have a bad feeling," she says. "About all of this. We should go back."

"Now there's an answer," I say. "Go back to what? Earth?"

Why have you brought us up out of Egypt? To die in the desert?

Helpful message that time. Thanks.

"Yes." Hard raises her hands. "We could get down somehow. Maybe sneak a lift. Hide out in the streets...or the far wilderness."

I glance at the nest's central screen. At the glowing green orb now being displayed there. Most of Earth's unpopulated areas are places no one would want to be. Boundless tracts of sand or snow. "The wilderness?" I say, doubtful. "Even if we could live there, how would we get there? Walk?"

"I have some credits," she says. "Enough to get us there."

"*And* you have an implant," I say, breathing heat. "So nothing else would matter. Even if they didn't find you, you couldn't willingly help me escape. The stops would interfere."

"I'd get it taken out," she says, voice cracking. "Somewhere."

"We're going to take you to some street-side headshark and let him cut you? Or some tech-shill?" I shake my head, railing inside. "I'd rather let GrimJack try." Grim being the proprietor of the supply shop we both frequent, and a former implant himself. "Besides, you would be screaming the whole way through. The implant would insure it."

"You don't have to get mean," she says, pulling her arms tight. "I'm only processing. Searching for answers." Her eyes glisten a bit too. I don't like that.

"There are other limitations I should mention," Trench offers.

"What now?" I ask. "Are we reaching our expiration date? Are you going to eject us?"

"No," Trench says, pushing calm. "I simply thought it would be good for you to know about our supplies. We have plenty of food. But there is enough water and oxygen for only thirty days, aside from that needed for a return trip. If the trip is uneventful."

Which, if previous experience is any indication, there is no guarantee of.

"So we have to make a decision at some point," Hard says. "There is a temporal limit. We can't stay forever."

"But it is a long way off." Still, it's another decision for me, and I don't really want it. Optimally, I would like to tune out from playing commander. Let someone else decide. Especially with deciding how long to look, because there is no good answer. I really wish I was debugging again.

You are.

"Are you still looking for that odd stream?" I ask Trench. "Even though we're here..." I again check the screen. Note the banding of clouds across the planet's surface. "Exploring the planet."

"I am," he says. "No sign of any fullband broadcast..."

It is a fact, of course, that the first excursion to Betelgeuse was in the system a few days before the superlative stream arrived. Or so I was told. "So we have some time to work with," I say. "Did we get anything new from the sampler?"

"The sampler was damaged," Trench says. "I wasn't able to restore the parachute sufficiently. The impact must've been too much. We lost contact." He sounds a bit poignant at the last. Of course, in many ways the sampler was a part of him. A feeling of loss isn't too out of spec.

Trench's thought circuitry is very near bot level in complexity, I've concluded—possibly beyond bot level. It isn't what I expected from an interstellar spaceship, but clearly the higherlevel DRs—the fourteens and fifteens that built the ship—thought it right. It makes some things easier.

"Are there more samplers?" I look at HardCandy, trying to glimpse whether she still shows interest. "Should we send another?"

"There are others," Trench says. "Three more, to be precise. But I would hate to lose another needlessly."

I smile at the statement. Clearly, DarkTrench's protective instincts *do* extend to everything onboard. Which is good for HardCandy and me, I suppose.

"Still, it would be something to pass the time while we wait."

Hard doesn't look pleased. "So we're just waiting?" she says. "Hoping you'll hear that erratic stream again?" Emotions, freehead, I'm telling you. Unpredictable.

I shrug. "For lack of a better idea, yes."

Frowning, she shakes her head. She looks at the planet again.

"And what will we do until then? I'm a debugger too, Sand. I like to keep busy." The bane of a DR, the downside of living in a world of nanoseconds: boredom comes early.

Of course, normal people—especially ones who have a burgeoning affinity for each another—might spend the downtime getting to know each other. Talking, laughing...even touching.

But HardCandy and I went way beyond normal a long time ago. We exchanged terabytes of data, much of it Full Impact experiences from our early life. An experience debuggers call "datamixing." Consequently, I know HardCandy almost as well as she knows herself. Maybe even better.

And she still baffles me.

Of course, datamixing is never used by two debuggers with feelings for each other, because debuggers aren't allowed to be that close. With anyone.

Frankly, I think it has confused things. Made them more complicated.

I smooth the back of my head, feel the warmth of my bare scalp. "I need time to think." I stand and move toward the door.

"Sometimes I think that's all you do," Hard says.

I pause, but then shimmy for my cabin.

I'VE BEEN THINKING FOR HOURS. No closer to a decision. Maybe not deciding *is* deciding.

Unable to stay in my cabin longer, I roam the corridors of Dark-Trench. I pass the door to HardCandy's cabin and then the doors to the two additional and empty crew quarters—all on my left. I reach the silver lift and take it to the upper level—a short and quiet ride.

At the top, I contemplate entering the nest again and sitting in the pilot's seat, but I don't. I instead pass through the metal security doors, reaching another hallway with doors on either side. These rooms contain some of DarkTrench's ancillary systems. Not the engine and not Trench's brain, though. Those are elsewhere...or maybe *everywhere*, for all I know. Ironically, these rooms—dubbed simply "systems storage"—are still larger than the crew cabins. Shows how important the human occupants really are here.

Next comes the prep room that started this whole mess. In the room's center is a dark two-level table, and on it a saucer-shaped device I now know of as a phase disruptor. Stainless steel sinks mark the room's perimeter, and above them are more wall-mounted vidscreens—all currently dark. The rest of the space is filled by freestanding equipment and cabinetry. A science room designed for activity and discovery. Now unused.

"Are you brooding again, Sandfly?" Trench asks.

I glance at the ceiling. "You've been watching me?"

"It is one of my tasks."

I shake my head. "Well, to answer your question: no, I'm still thinking."

He streams me warmth. "Very well. I am willing to proceed in whatever manner you prefer. My facilities remain at your disposal."

I look at the floor, made of a deep blue, slip-resistant tile. It was there that the former crew found the servbot laying—arms and a single leg detached, head bludgeoned until it died. All self-inflicted. Sort of.

"Would you like to conduct some experiments while you're here?" Trench asks. "I have a catalog of potential tests."

I can't help but smile. "You really can tap my insides, can't you? Know we're both bored..."

"I do know what you dream about."

Funny. See, I told you the ship gets humor.

"I'm still not sure I fully understand the bot's discovery, Trench—the thing that really did it in. The singing. And this irreconcilable difference between the new A and the A that the Abduls describe. Both are omnipotent, eternal... seemingly powerful."

Of course, dedication to the Abdul's A also begets restriction and reduction—and, in the case of debuggers, outright slavery. But who am I to judge?

"The only clear description of this new God I received from the bot was: He stoops!" I shake my head. "Not a lot to go on."

"Yet you are free of your internal stops now. The inherent shocks for non-compliance."

"Yes, for the moment. But eventually we'll have to return to Earth. Even if Betelgeuse wasn't dangerous, even if the planet below was perfect for life, we couldn't get to it. Short of crashing the ship."

Trench sends a frown. "Let's not do that."

I smile as I scan the room's assortment of stainless steel appliances and sinks. Shining metal that nothing can stick to. Maybe that is what this new A *really* is: a gleaming entity that can never be blamed for anything. Beautiful to behold, impervious, yet still cold and as hard as metal.

You are broken again, Sand. Marching off a very deep end.

I walk to one of the metal sinks and lean against it.

"Even so, here we are. We came to see him. And whether the thought of actually meeting him or not scares me—which it does—he is still nowhere to be found. I'm stuck trying to figure out what to do next. I thought we'd get here and... I don't know... he'd kind of meet us here, I guess."

"I suspect this enigmatic stream generator is not the only mystery you're trying to figure out."

Crichton, he really *is* in my head. I sniff. "Right again, Trench. HardCandy. Even with all we've shared, there is part of her that remains a mystery to me. An obsession, really. Another problem that can't be solved. I have no schematics for human relationships. I'm not trained for that." I shake my head. "I hope I'm not more broken now than I thought."

Because sometimes HardCandy's memories come flooding into mind, almost unbidden. More vivid than my own.

Like now...

I AM NINE YEARS OLD. The school feels cold today, even though it is the beginning of spring. I am excited for the summer to come. Father has said we would go somewhere special this summer. Somewhere where I can swim—fully covered, of course.

Nothing to see here, gentlemen, except my eyes.

Our instructor, also female, calls the class to order. There are over forty students in my class, nearly eight hundred in the entire school. The rooms are very full, but it is always the way. Education is low priority for women in our world. Consequently, the schools that do provide such education are always crowded.

How does it profit her, education? Her place is to marry and produce children!

On the streets we are required to wear both the abaya and head-scarf—the mutaween make sure of it—but here in school, there is a tiny bit of freedom. Since there are only women within, our scarves are not required. There are hooks along the east wall to hold them. Today the variation in scarf color is vast—a sign of spring, I think. They form a drooping cloth rainbow along an otherwise bleak grey wall. The floor and ceiling are grey, as well.

Each of us sits before a sloping electronic desk. Shortly after the teacher's salutation, we flash to life in our own burst of spring color. We are to work on designs for rugs—artwork. On the mounted vidscreen behind her, the teacher illustrates how to enter the design program, how to add color to the screen. Her instruction is hardly necessary for me. I feel more at home before a touchscreen than anywhere else. It is a secret I hide from everyone.

I dive into the work, forming wondrous, geometric patterns. Blue is a favorite color, so I combine many different shades of it. I weave intricate wonders, simulate visually the melancholy of distant summer, the smell of spring joy. A day at the beach—uncovered and unhindered. No one around, no one to worry about. Just me, the ocean, and A above.

The teacher patrols the room. Approaching by my desk, she pauses, and then smiles. "Very nice..."

Glancing back, I return her smile. She moves on and so do I, adding browns and reds to my pattern. Hints of circles, traces of polygons. Dancing fish and skipping crabs.

From somewhere down the hall I hear a singular shriek through the classroom door. An unheard-of occurrence, a punishable offense. Next comes the thumping of many feet—haphazard running, a flurried escape. Followed by more loud shrieks.

Someone yells, "Fire!"

As one, we rise from our desks and hurry to the door. There is no pushing, but there is the uncomfortable pressing of bodies, the movement of elbows and knees. The class gets closer and noticeably more compressed. Everyone wants to see.

The front-most girls look cautiously into the hall, and their eyes grow wide. There are about three layers of girls in front of me, but I still recognize the smell of smoke. I also hear a roaring and popping sound—somewhere to the right, down the hall. The lighting there seems to flicker, dance...

Everyone rushes forward. Still no one is pushing, but there is insistency to the movement, a dangerous hurriedness. We are close enough together that any stumble would bring disaster. Our group is joined by classes from other rooms until the hall is completely full.

Packed!

All are trying not to scream, but occasionally someone behind me does. The windows are locked, hermitically sealed, so no one tries for those. In fact, the school is built like a fortress. For our protection, we're told. There are few ways out. The best is straight down the hall and through the front door.

After what seems an eternity, the front of the crowd reaches that door. There are teachers in the crowd too, but they appear as worried as any of us. None of them step forward to lead, to reassure. To direct us toward the outer door and freedom.

There is a ten-foot entranceway separating me from the door and the outer metal gate. I expect that distance to be closed quickly. I'm surprised when it is not. Our escape reaches a standstill. I hear more screams now, this time from in front of me.

And from far behind...

"They won't let us out!" someone yells.

It is delirium speaking. It has to be. I turn sideways, sneak my way forward. I pay dearly for the effort. My hips are pinched, my arms bruised. I reach a point where I can see the rusted gate. There are two brown-suited mutaween outside. *Their* faces aren't concealed, of course, except by their full beards covering round faces that match the plumpness of their bodies. A plumpness that their brown robes cannot disguise.

"You must not come out!" one cries.

There's a group of bots, colored orange—dedicated rescue-bots—standing behind the mutaween. They are here to help us. But they only stand silent, waiting, watching.

The smoke has increased in volume now. Behind me, girls are starting to cough violently. My eyes are beginning to tear.

"Open the gate!" I yell. "The smoke! It is killing us!"

The other mutaween shakes his head. "Go back to your rooms and get your scarves. You cannot come into the street without them. It is forbidden."

Pain strikes my stomach. I cannot believe the gall. Putting dress codes above life!

We are just women, though. What do we matter? We should be at home anyway.

A portion of the group behind me turns, and attempts to go back for their scarves. I watch them, but the smoke is billowing so strongly now I can hardly stand it. It is searching for an exit. Just like we are.

"My father will kill you!" I scream. And I think he might. He reminds me every morning how he loves me.

The mutaween are unbending. Behind them the bots remain static as well, but I know they're programmed to save our lives. They must've been ordered otherwise. A master's order?

I grab a portion of my dress and wrap it over my mouth, so much like what the mutaween want from us—walking shadows. But I do it to dampen the smoke. I can hear a roar behind me now. Girls are falling to the ground. I step back, struggle toward the nearest doorway, the nearest classroom.

The room is completely empty, everyone having left. Aside from the active desks, it is as grey and bleak as the room I left. There are windows here though, thankfully. I grab one of the desks, but finding the top affixed by two large bolts, I drop it again. I notice a line of scarfs on the wall in this room too, their color dampened by the red burning of my eyes. I contemplate gathering a handful and rushing into the hall. Saving some.

But somehow I resist that thought. There are screams outside, along with the pounding demands of the mutaween. Smoke plugs my throat. My eyes dart frantically, but it is painful for them to do so.

I notice a large piece of stone, a blue marble model of one of the temples. I pick it up, the weight sags in my arms. I use every bit of strength I have to raise it, to heave it at the window. I'm rewarded when I see a small crack appear. The model falls to the floor, but I retrieve it, strike the window again. The glass shatters.

Now I *do* collect the scarves, and winding them around my hands, wrench free the remaining fragments. I scream out for anyone in the hall: "I've found a way!"

I widen my exit, pushing out more glass. Then I jump and struggle through it, feeling the bite of undiscovered shards in my hips and arms and legs. I'm refreshed by the smell of clean air, though. I drop to the ground, happy.

I am free!

Another mutaween appears before me. He looks at me disapprovingly. My face is still uncovered. I cover my face with the scarves wrapped around my hands, but it is too late to appease him. He lunges at me as if to capture me, to push me back within the smoke. I dart to the right, screaming. A small stone fence surrounds the school. I run to it, crawl over it, scramble down the street.

"Come back, infidel" he screams. "Stop her. She must not leave uncovered!"

I make it all the way home without stopping, without being

stopped. I spend the rest of the day inside, still coughing. Frightened. Refusing to ever return.

The next day mutaween arrive at our home. Many of my classmates perished, they say. This does not trouble them. They care only for my impropriety. My father lies to them, tells them I wasn't at school that day. But they know better.

Awful things happen next.

DARKTRENCH GIVES ME an EE nudge in the stream. "May I disturb you?" he asks.

"Of course," I stream back. "What else am I doing?"

"Well, I was monitoring your vitals," Trench says, almost apologetically. "It is what I'm designed to do..."

"I know that," I say.

"And it appeared you were in deep thought. Thus, the pre-interruption inquiry."

"Again, I understand," I say. "What do you want?"

"It appears I've found something."

"What? Another planet? We really should give your sensor circuits a once over..."

I can feel Trench's annoyance. "No," he says. "Not another planet. Though it appears to be emanating from it."

"What is?" I ask. "What?"

"A stream," Trench says. "Very similar to the one you described."

My stomach fi nds my throat. A frequent meeting. "And you're certain?"

"I am. A multifaceted, full-band stream. I've compared it with our earlier samples. It is not identical, but similar. It is clearly beyond anything human technology can produce."

"Can I sample it?" I ask.

Trench pauses a moment. "That is possible," he says. "Though I warn you it is a bit discordant. And highly complicated. Besides, you've had problems with such transmissions before."

I sniff audibly. "I'll prepare myself." I push away from the sink, find the most wide open spot on the floor, and sit down.

"Are you ready now?"

"Rails, Trench!" I scream. "Let me have it!"

Suddenly, my synapses are dancing through a new perception. I hear sounds, like bees in my head. I feel confused, but with a dash of additional strength, of raw energy. I do my best to get ahead of the load, slow it for my consumption. I get flashes of real information. Messages of growth and change. Of retribution and excellence. I protect myself from any inherent programming the stream might carry, of course.

No way am I passing out this time. No way am I losing my grip.

There is a discord here, as Trench suggested. Plus, there is so much information—a river pushing through a pinhole—that I can hardly digest it. Finally I break off, drive the stream away. And, gasping, open my eyes. Rub at my temples.

"That was intense."

Trench sighs. "I warned you as much."

"Yes, yes, you did." I shake my head and smile. We have found it! Though I'm still a little fearful, it is nice to know that I intersected the superlative stream once and lived to tell about it. Clearly, more research is needed.

"The stream appears to have ended now," Trench says. "A mere six minutes of transmission."

I shake my head, still feeling a tingle of latent energy. "Tell Hard-Candy," I say. "And launch another sampler. Head it straight for the source."

I'M AMAZED BY HOW COMFORTABLE the nest seems as a hub for exploration. Especially since neither HardCandy nor I really needs to be here, really needs the bank of screens the room provides. We could stream everything Trench has to show us from our rooms.

And yet we find ourselves drawn here, seated at the pilot and copilot positions, staring at the elongated vidscreen near the front of the room. A community of two.

Some aspects of humanity never change.

"Entering the atmosphere now," Trench says.

Another sampler has been launched, but no one is piggybacking this time. We've both had our fill of that, I think. The image on every screen is of the planet again from the sampler's perspective. It has maneuvered past the shadow line on the western edge of the planet, just over the planet's horizon from our position in space. Beyond Trench's onboard camera range.

"Everything is progressing normally. Readings very similar to the first drop."

HardCandy is leaning over her console, with her head resting in her hands. Intent and interested. The sampler's image is of another of the planet's continents, the third largest in size, covering approximately nine thousand square kilometers of surface area. It features three separate mountain ranges and a series of large inland lakes. Of course, it all is seen in dark outlines and muted tones. The sampler is on the night side, after all.

"No obvious signs of civilization," Trench says. "No visible light sources."

The propulsion system on the sampler fires, shifting it south, toward the planet's equator. "The latitude of the source was approximately 31 degrees north. Well into the temperate zone."

"So, not a bad place to live then, right?" Hard offers, along with a sad little smile. She's hopeful, I know. For *what* exactly, I'm not sure.

"Yes," Trench says, "I think we can safely rule out any natural phenomena for having produced the transmission. Much too complex for that."

"I knew it!" Hard says, looked at me as if she's nine again and having the correct answer first.

I recall something from my own childhood coursework. "Is this planet tipped?" I ask. "Does it have seasons?"

Trench throws the static bubble at me again. "You mean, is it a planet in the normal sense?" he asks. "Are you asking if it were actually in orbit around Betelgeuse at all times?"

I shake my head. "Aren't you over that by now, Trench? The fact that you somehow missed it?"

The volume of Trench's voice increases. "Truth is not open to speculation, Sandfly. It either is, or is not."

I choose to let him have his *truth*. Better not to offend the thing that is keeping you from freezing, asphyxiation, the vacuum of open space...his defensiveness *does* make me want to take a look at his nanocenters a little. To poke around his brain. I wonder where those are exactly...

"Regardless," he says. "The tilt of the planet is approximately sixteen degrees, to Earth's twenty-four. So there would be seasons, but not as pronounced as those on Earth. And locations closer to the poles would be colder than Earth norm, regardless of the season."

"Interesting," I say, nodding. "Good to know." I return my attention to the screen. The sampler is now falling in the general direction of one of the inland lakes. It is close enough to the planet's surface that land features are evident. "What is that white thing?" I ask. It is a near-rectangular object on the ground at the left edge of the current image.

"I am not sure," Trench says. "It shows little in the infrared spectrum. Not much warmth. An outcropping of rock, perhaps?"

As the seconds pass, the white object remains framed in the picture. All around it are what appear to be more flora, more plant life. In fact, the object seems to be pushing out from the trees, the foliage is packed so close. Soon right angles and straight lines in the object's surface become evident.

"That's not a rock outcropping, is it?" Hard asks softly.

There is silence for many moments. "I don't believe so," Trench says finally. "It appears to be a structure of some sort, a building." He pauses, full thought process in action. "Perhaps this is the source of our stream? I will increase the magnification."

The image increases and grows more distinct. Even in the shadows, it is clear that the structure is something man-made. Alien-made? A-made? It is pyramidal, but not with the smooth surfaces of the Egyptian pyramids of history. This has a definite *stepping* to it.

It looks ancient, I think.

"It looks new," HardCandy says.

I sniff, shake my head. "What is it made of?" I ask.

"A metallic substance, I presume, yet clearly one that is passing little heat, should the structure be occupied. It still appears quite cool to infrared."

I nod thoughtfully. "How long until the shoot deploys?"

"Less than twenty seconds for maximum safety," Trench says.

Silence resumes. Hard and I are both lost in our own mental energies, locked to our own personal screens.

"What is this?" she sends me in the stream. "*Whose* is this?"

I look at her, but her eyes remain fixed on the growing image of the structure. "I've no idea," I send back. "Not what I expected. At all."

"How near can we get?" I ask aloud. "Can we land on it?"

"I will attempt—"

"What?" I say. "What is it?"

"No..." Trench whispers.

Hard sits up in her seat, looks at the ceiling. "You're going to have to help us here, Trench."

Every screen goes fuzzy, then winks out completely, going black.

"What was *that?*" I ask.

A facsimile of anger fills Trench's voice. "I've lost another sampler. It appears to have been struck by something."

"A meteor?" I ask. "A flying creature?"

"Neither, I'm afraid. The object came directly from the planet. If I were to guess, I would say it was a directed projectile."

"Directed projectile? Meaning what?"

"Meaning, the sampler has been shot down!"

TRENCH CHECKS AND RECHECKS. The second sampler we sent is officially nowhere. Even its remains are eluding onboard sensing devices and cameras.

"I'm beginning to dislike this planet," Trench says.

"It doesn't seem very friendly." Still seated, Hard turns to me. "I thought we were looking for something *good* here?"

I shrug. "An assumption on my part," I say. "I was going on a bot's word."

"Yeah, a *damaged* bot, Sand." Hard smiles—a wonderful look. Something I haven't seen enough of. She shakes her head. "Why did I come with you again?"

Another shrug. "Few options?"

"Don't be so sure of that."

I smile, because Hard's options on Earth were equivalent to mine, relationship-wise. Absolute zero.

The large central screen is flipping through surface images, echoing Trench's search for the sampler.

"Trench?" I say, looking upward to speak to the ceiling.

"You know, I'm not really above you," he says. "I recognize the cue, but I'm as much behind and below as up."

I glance over my shoulder. "If it bothers you, we could stream all conversations."

"Whatever is most efficient."

"But the sampler?"

"Totally gone," he says. "Whatever did it has more force than a nanopounder. The sampler was completely destroyed."

I squint at my screen, which is now showing a non-magnified perspective of the planet. It is the size of a single coin. "So I don't suppose you want to try again?"

"There are two samplers left," Trench says. "I'm in no position to dictate how they are used. So far, though, past performance is a strong indicator of future returns."

"Meaning two up and two down, Bogart," Hard says. "He doesn't want to lose another."

I chuckle. "That's okay," I say. "I wasn't really asking." I stare at my screen. Our planetary enigma stares back at me, all round and green. "This is not like debugging." I frown. "I don't know what to do next."

"Maybe if we circled around some more..."

"I already have the planet sufficiently mapped, HardCandy," Trench says. "I can see no reason to waste propellant."

Hard raises an eyebrow. "It's just...I wonder if there are more of them?"

"More structures?" Trench asks. "It would take some time to analyze the images in that detail. Would you like me to do so?"

Hard looks at me.

"As a side task," I say. "Low priority. The most important structure is the one we know about." The one spouting streams. And shooting samplers.

What next?

Hard's screen still has an image of the structure on it. The pyramid of mystery. "I just had a bad thought," she says, checking the screen. "Do you think they know we're here?"

"They?"

Hard looks at me strangely. "I think we've established that someone is here."

"Not necessarily," I say, feeling petulant for some reason. "Perhaps it is an automated system left over from—"

"From what?" She shakes her head in disgust. "The simplest theory is always the best starting place, right, debugger?"

"Usually, but—"

"So we'll assume someone is here. I want to know if they could've detected us somehow."

"You mean other than the fact that we've dropped two samplers in on them?"

She shrugs. "Well, they shot down the last one. So technically it wasn't *on* them."

"Point noted."

"Still...if they are shooting at our samplers?"

Being from a world where aggression and subjugation is the norm, it isn't hard to reach the conclusion Hard has. Again, what we're doing here is crazy. Again, true leadership is needed. "You think they'd try to shoot *us* down?" I resist the urge to look at the ceiling. "Is that possible?"

"That would depend on the speed of their craft or weaponry," Trench says. "As you know, there is a bit of a time window before a flip can be accomplished. And maneuvering within a star system is complicated. Filled with unpredictable danger."

I curl my lips thoughtfully. "But what will we do if we go back empty-handed? I still can't see that path." I stand, because I can't think of anything better to do. I actually wish the bot was here. Weird, huh?

"If it is all the same with you," Trench says, "I would like to re-move myself from communication for a few moments. The loss of those samplers has caused an issue. Something I need to address."

"Anything we can do to help?" I ask. "Spaceships aren't a spe-cialty, but maybe we can do something..."

"It will be fine," Trench says. "Just give me a moment."

I only nod in response. At the same time I give Hard a question-ing look. "Do you think he's okay?" I stream.

"How would either of us know?" she streams back.

I switch our messaging to Full Impact, let her feel a bit of my un-certainty. "He did miss a planet....and he seems to take sampler losses hard. I wonder if..."

"What?"

"If the stream affected him too?"

Hard shakes her head. "He's not an implant, Sand."

"Neither was the bot," I say. "Not really."

"Closer than most mechanicals, though."

"It wasn't just because it was stream-aware," I say. "It was a matter of foundational rules. And Trench has them too. He told me so himself." I stretch a hand out to the pilot desk's manual control area, feel the surface subtly retexture itself to form a keyboard. A device I never need to use.

"But *you* were affected," HardCandy says.

"Differently," I stream. "Quite differently. Code changes ride the *superlative* stream. That's what affected the crew. That's what affected me." I pause. "I think."

I don't mention the cryptic verses I occasionally receive. No sense worrying her more. She already knows I'm not completely right.

It all adds another variable to the mix, though. If there is a chance DarkTrench is a bit out of spec, then we should get somewhere safe soon.

"Maybe you worry too much," Hard says aloud. She's standing now too, and her arms are tightly wrapped around her. Meanwhile, I get a hint of something from her in the stream. Pain? Sadness? Not the worry or fear I was expecting, certainly.

I bring my hand up and hesitantly touch her elbow. She smiles, so that's something. A small step to wherever we're going. "Maybe I do," I say. "You're right." I sniff. "Still have to decide something now, don't I? Got to *do* something. I mean, *we* do. Rails, it is hard."

"We'll hide out on Earth," she says. "As soon as I get my implant out. I guarantee it."

I cringe a bit. The idea of Hard getting cut, the idea of her being an ex like GrimJack, really bothers me. Aside from the danger to her brain—the fact that implants rarely come out clean—there's the stigma of it. She might as well be an infidel.

Plus, she'd be different, not like me. Unable to touch the stream, control bots—sing to them. Barred from messaging me, sharing both her thoughts and emotions. It would feel like she died.

Couldn't we stay out here forever?

I look to my right, to where the navigator's desk is located. "It was supposed to be simple," I say. "We show up and A arrives to guide us. To show us the way."

"Maybe your assumptions are wrong," Hard says. "Normally when things don't work, it's because my assumptions are wrong."

She has a point. When I was trying to fix the bot, most of my assumptions were wrong. Way wrong. But the decision to travel in space, the decision to come out here seemed...right.

"What was the last message the bot gave you?" Hard asks. "About humbling yourself?"

"Humble yourself under A's mighty hand, that he may lift you up in due time."

Hard shrugs. "Nothing there about coming here, is there?"

"It might be a matter of interpretation. I mean, if you think of this system as being A's hand..."

"Big stretch, Abby."

"It isn't wrong to want the truth," I say, feeling a bit heated. "It isn't wrong to search."

"Sure, Sand, but the focus of your message seems to be humbling and waiting."

"Well," I say staring at the image of the distant planet, "we're waiting."

She shakes her head. "This is all new to me. I'm only cogitating to see if it helps. But maybe the decisions you make aren't as important as you think. Maybe this 'superlative stream' of yours is just as able to find you wherever you are. Maybe that's why you were supposed to wait...um...humbly. Or something."

I raise my hands, glance at the screens again. "I've no idea. None."

Hard smiles softly. "I somehow doubt that. Ideas are sort of where we live." She raises a hand, clutches my arm softly. I feel the warmth and revel in it. But right now I want a bit more. I want to take her hand in mine and hold it.

Like it is right there, you know? But there is still this wall of behavior. Even with no stops for me.

I can't.

I want to. But it's like I'm trying to find the right time. The right moment.

"I'll think of something," I say. "Fry my implant on it, probably."

Hard bows her head slightly, gives me another soft smile. "I'm going to eat something. Want to come?"

I nod. What else can I do?

OUR HOUSE IS SMALL compared to many on our street. My father is only a carpenter. There is no fuel money in his family, no masonry, no tech. So we only eke out an existence. I used to worry that father would force me to marry early for the dowry it would bring, along with having me out of the house. But I worry about that no longer. He loves me, I know, almost as if I were a son.

My mother has told me, in the way of warning—with hushed whispers and softened lights—that my father is one of the good ones. An unusual man. "He never beats me," she says. "Even when I deserve it."

Things have been different for the last few days, though. Ever since the fire at my school.

Today Father paces the family room, looking nervous. The room's vidscreen is on, but he does not watch it. Instead his eyes flit between me, the door, and his own hands. Calloused, rough, and large hands. But gentle too. Good hands. Hands that have comforted me when I was ill. Lifted me when I fell.

The family room is octagonal—a design Father created. A source of pride. It is simply furnished, with pictures on four of the eight walls, two pattern fabric chairs, shaded lights, and a purple divan, which I occupy.

Occasionally Father pauses in his pacing to lean against one wall and smile at me. Mother is in the kitchen preparing dinner. Silent in her work.

There was an investigation into the fire, of course. Two, actually.

One into the cause of the fire—the result being a faulty power coupler. A calamity that would occur only in a school for women. The couplers at the boys' schools are nano-shield protected, failure-proof, fireproof. Boys never burn. Not that way.

The other was into the behavior of the mutaween outside. That trial was more of a monkey show than anything. It gave the parents of those who perished—forty-four of them—a hope that there would be justice. That such things were wrong, would never happen again. How mistaken they were.

The judgment was simple, definitive—a solitary sentence: The mutaween acted appropriately.

The rules are most important, you see. Nothing trumps them. Not compassion, not mercy, and certainly not a parent's love. That is how A would have it. He is watchful, he is vengeful. Rules offer a hope of passing, a glimmer of approval.

Another coin in the scale.

There is a heavy pounding on our door: *whump, whump, whump.*

Father jumps at the sound, then straightens and walks resolutely toward it.

By force of habit, I bring up my scarf, attaching it in place.

Outside are two mutaween, again wrapped in brown. One is a head taller than the other. Both are intense. "We are here about your daughter," the taller one says. His face is dark, heavily bearded.

"Why?" Father asks. "What would you have with her?" He doesn't look at me. He looks only at the men. Stands between them and the rest of our home.

"The Ministry has ordered her discipline. It would be wise if you carried it out yourself."

"Discipline for what?" Father asks.

The shorter mutaween speaks. "For being seen in public uncovered."

Beneath my scarf, I gape. Amazed by the power a single bit of clothing has. If my face is uncovered, a man—even someone I do not know—may fall into sin. Consequently, the scarves are necessary, essential. For life, I am wrapped as if in death.

Why not have the man cover his eyes instead?

Heat fills my father's face. "She escaped a burning building. She saved her own life. Tried to save others. She is a hero."

"She led others into sin, sinning herself," the taller mutaween says. "We will take her for discipline now." He puts one foot into the room. Toward me.

Father raises a staying hand. "You will not."

The taller mutaween steps back. "So you will discipline her yourself. Good. We will supervise."

Father leans forward, moving the men back. "It is time for you to go."

"It is the law!" The short one cries. "The law will not be broken!"

At that, Father hits one man in the sternum, the other in the face. "You betrayers of A!" he cries. "You are killing our world."

I am shocked. I scream. Yet I am somehow pleased. Justified.

Behind me, Mother gasps. I feel hollow, afraid. One of the mutaween falls, but behind him, unseen before, is a large blue-coated security man. He steps into the fray, grabbing my father roughly, binding his arms behind his back. Then, with the help of the taller mutaween, he directs Father through the door. Father has only an instant to glance at me before he is led away.

Through the door I can hear the siren call to prayer.

It is echoed by Mother's wail.

• • •

I hear sobbing, so I push back my covers and roll out of bed. In near darkness I make my way into the narrow hall, then to the living room. My father is still gone, I know that. There is an extreme emptiness to our home.

Reaching the source of the sobs, I find my mother curled into a ball on the purple divan. I know that Father is the reason. The room is dark—only a single wall light illuminates the many corners of its octagonal shape. Father's proud design.

Mother doesn't hear me enter. Her face is pushed into the soft fabric, as if to muffle her cries.

Quietly I move up on her, put a hand out to touch her grey-streaked hair. "Momma..."

Her head comes up, her eyes red and filled with wetness. "Oh, my little one, are you up?"

I continue to stroke her head, her sadness reflecting in my eyes. "What is wrong, Momma?"

She shakes her head, eyes closing again. "Go back to bed."

I am normally an obedient child, but tonight my legs refuse to comply. "I can't," I say. "Tell me."

Her lips press together hard, again she shakes her head. "He is not coming back," she moans. "Dear A, he is not coming back."

Pain finds my gut. My father has been gone much of the day already. I assumed there would be a trial, a hearing. What has Mother heard?

"How do you know that?" I ask. "He may be released."

Mother stares off into the room, looking everywhere and nowhere. "There is no trial for attacking a mutaween. No one is released. They are A's representatives."

The pain in my middle intensifies, as if I swallowed a burning ember. I did not realize. I am young. I did not know.

Father's extended absence (or, dare I imagine it, execution?) would change everything for us. Without a man in the house we would be exposed. Penniless! Potential prey for who knew what.

Mother looks at me again, reaches out to stroke my cheek.

"Why did you leave that building, child?" she asks. "Why did you have to leave?"

THE SHIP'S REFECTORY is, without question, the most spacious room on the ship, excepting the engine room. It is as if the designers realized that someplace where everyone was forced to gather every day would need a little extra elbow room, a little more cushion between you and the next guy.

It contains two round tables—fully interactive and shiny—large enough to comfortably seat three each. A luxury for when the crew was only four, near wasteful for two. The colors of the room are light earth-tones. Comfort colors. The scent is always that of baked bread.

There is a counter on one side of the room and a medium-sized fluid and snack dispenser on the side opposite that. The third wall has a large vidscreen and a bank of controls. Not surprisingly. Can't really be away from the nest anywhere, I guess.

The final wall contains the food conditioner. Externally, the conditioner looks like a large, modified waste unit. There is a long rectangular section that starts at about eye level and falls downward. At about hip level the device widens before swooping forward and up. At that point it ends in a circular pedestal.

Either a waste unit or an obscure art form, I can't decide which.

Food blocks—protein, vitamin, or carbohydrate matter compressed and sealed within five centimeter cubes—are loaded at the top of the device. On the front side of the conditioner is an active control pad, where menu items are selected. The menu contains about a dozen items—only five of which I truly like. Upon selection, the machine crumbles off food blocks as the recipe requires. It mixes, flavors, and forms this edible mishmash into something resembling a human meal. The result is dispensed—elevated from the bowels of the machine—already plated, onto the pedestal.

For me, the results are much like eating at a hispatino restaurant. Same ingredients, served in a dozen different forms. Great if you like hispatino food. Barely edible if you don't.

HardCandy has selected the conditioner's approximation of scrambled eggs. For that item at least, the form is fairly easy—hard to mess up. Me, I'm having toast with jam. That's an easy one for the conditioner too. One block pressed into another with a half squeeze of sugar.

"How are your eggs?" I ask, smiling.

"Exactly the same as yesterday," Hard says. "Amazing."

I squint. "How is that amazing? It only proves Tanzer's Lament: sow junk, reap junk."

Hard rolls her eyes, but follows with a little half smile. "If you don't like what it does, you could always change it, Thirteen."

Levels are the markers of debugger experience and clearance. Thirteen is mine; twelve is hers. She rarely lets me forget. "Food is one thing I won't mess with," I say. "We have a limited supply."

Hard gives a playful smile. "Still, I find it amazing. The machine must be tightly calibrated. Infinitely precise."

"Again," I say, "it is food. I'm sure the designers didn't want to waste any either."

Hard brings a forkful of eggs to her lips, but holds it there. "I wonder," she says. "Who came up with the first recipe? Ever think about that?"

"It was probably something like 'Beat stick with stone, try to swallow, try not to vomit.'" I bite into my toast, imagine I can taste the blandness of the powders that compose it, and scowl. "Might've been better than this, though."

Chewing, Hard shakes her head. "No, really," she says when her mouth is free. "Take bread, for instance: who would guess that mixing eggs with milk, flour, salt, and sugar would produce anything edible? How would you even know to start that way?"

I think back to my years of debugging. "Lots of trial and error," I say. "Lots of testing."

"But how would you know what ingredients to start with? Or have a glimmer of what the solution is?" She pushes her eggs together, forming a mound in the middle of her plate. "Like, oh, this mass of stuff would be a lot better if it raised some. Maybe I'll add yeast!"

I see the point. "Yeah, microbes wouldn't be my first choice for things to add to something I'm going to eat," I say. "I don't even like knowing they exist, actually. But when I think about it, it isn't that much different from what we do. Program some nanos and set them to the task."

Still smiling, Hard gives a sarcastic snort. "Except with yeast, the programming comes preloaded," she says. "And there's no stream to send guiding commands."

HardCandy is bright, there's no doubting it. "Good point," I say. "That's why I don't like microbes. They're difficult to predict. Might want hazard pay if I was debugging bread."

Hard grins. "Even non-living ingredients like eggs or milk. If your original attempt was missing something that one of those ingredients would remedy, how would you know to add it precisely? Especially in a time before things like sheets and probes...when everything was all hidden." A shrug. "For it to go from a casual attempt to something that industries are created to produce. Sears my implant just thinking about it."

My bread almost gone, I muse over what I might like to eat next. Hard's eggs are looking better to me now, almost fit for consumption. "You don't suppose someone got lucky, do you?" I say. "Just happened to throw the right things together the first time?"

Hard chuckles. "I wish I had that kind of luck then," she says. "It would save a lot of pain."

"Abduls would say A gave it to them, I bet," I say. "Laid the recipe out where they could find it."

"Or sent an angel to tell them?"

There is a warning chirp—something Trench always does when we're alone in the refectory. "Sorry to disturb you," he says then.

"No apologies, Trench," I say. "What do you need?"

"There appears to be another complication," he says.

Concern fills HardCandy's face. "What's that?" she asks.

"Something has left the planet."

TRENCH FEEDS THE CAMERA directly to the refectory vid-screen. We both watch, appetites now falling like leaves from a tree. In fact, I feel beyond full now. Maybe a little sick.

"It embarked from the area near the structure," Trench says. "About twenty kilometers due north from there."

Visible on screen is this wonder of light and motion. A long white sliver, gleaming with the reflected soul of Betelgeuse's raging luminescence. A cylinder with a tapered nose, appearing sharp enough to impale DarkTrench with little resistance.

In my mind, there is no question as to its intent. "It is going to strike us."

"That is a possibility," Trench replies. "Though I rather hope not."

Still immersed in the sliver of death, Hard manages to pull her eyes free long enough to look at me. "Can we get out of here *now*?" she asks, concern evident in her voice.

I'm afraid of the answer. "Can we, Trench?" I ask. "Get out of immediate danger, anyway?"

"I am engaging the engines now," Trench says. "Though it will doubtless prove to be a futile exercise."

"And why is that?" I ask.

"The current speed of that craft is beyond anything man has crafted, this ship included."

"But you can travel across the galaxy in days..." Hard says, more pleading than anything.

The bread scent in the room increases, another calming move on Trench's part. "I'm sorry," he says. "The flip will take more time than it will take that craft to reach us."

Which we both knew already. Not good.

The sliver looks to be pointed directly at us now. Whatever propulsion the craft uses causes a visible billowing effect—a distortion of light—behind it. As if space there is being split into waves like a boat moving through water.

"So we're sitting ducks?" I say. "Crichton, we're doomed to just wait here?"

"The engines are engaged," Trench says. "We *are* in motion."

But it seems like we are standing still. The sliver is pounding through the ether. Thousands of kilometers a second, or so it appears. Gaining fast.

"This ship has defenses," I say. "It has to. I can't imagine Abduls traveling without some form of saber. No way to strike back."

"Of course," Trench says. "The best particle technology available."

"So why can't we use that?" I ask. "Aim the guns at it, Trench!"

I get the color orange on the stream. "Again, the speed presents the problem," Trench says. "Theoretically the particles can reach the projectile before it strikes us. But I've tried, and the aiming mechanisms appear to be insufficient to the task."

Another insufficiency? Another shortcoming? "Why would that be?" I ask. "What were the designers planning on shooting? Fish in a tank? Birds?"

Trench sends me a flash of static. "Most objects one might encounter in space move in fairly predictable paths—easily trackable by our guns."

Gritting my teeth, I watch the screen. "The sliver—that missile—seems to be moving straight at us. Why can't we track that?"

"Appearances are deceptive, Sand. Though the missile appears to be moving in a straight line, it is not. I detect variations in its path of many meters and at random instances in time. It seems to be designed to avoid direct resistance. It is quite sophisticated."

Which may explain the billowing effect I observe. The sliver is literally like a fish in the ocean. Now, if we could catch it in a barrel...

"What about a sampler?" Hard says.

There is silence for a nanosecond or two. "For what purpose?" Trench asks.

"To stop the projectile, of course," Hard says. "I remember reading once that before the date change there were ships in the ocean that when tracked by a...torpedo, I think it was...would release objects to fool the torpedo, to draw the torpedo away. Could we do the same thing? Put a sampler out to draw the sliver away from us?"

"You believe the advancing craft to be traveling by some archaic tracking mechanism like sonar?" Trench asks. "Or that it is looking for our heat source, our signature in the infrared?"

"Just an idea, Trench. I don't know anything."

"We could release the sampler when the object is fairly close," I say. "Shield ourselves with it."

"It may be technically possible to do so," Trench says. "Release it and have it track alongside us. The sampler can follow us until we reach about nine-tenths of the speed we need before the flip is possible. Which at the current rate of acceleration might be just enough." He pauses. "Let me restate that I would hate to lose another sampler needlessly."

I send Trench a big static bubble of my own. Enough that he can't ignore it.

"Of course, this is one of those instances where ship's safety must take precedence," he says.

The image of the sliver seems very large now. The surface of the projectile itself appears to swirl and pulse with energy. Much like the sun the planet travels around. There is nothing distinct about it—no markings, no lettering. Nothing.

"How far away is it?" I ask. Though I know DarkTrench is moving, it is very hard to gauge. There are no lurches, no feelings of velocity at all.

"Approximately five thousand kilometers," Trench says. "Perhaps it would be best if you two returned to your quarters and strapped yourselves in."

We are already on our feet. No words are spoken, but Hard's eyes are saying a stream's worth. "At least we're together," she streams, and I get the full blunt of her emotions. It almost knocks me over. I didn't realize she cared so much. Still, I push the feelings away. Hold them at arm's length. I can't let them distract me now.

We scramble to the door and up the hall to our rooms. I manage only to squeeze Hard's hand once before she disappears into hers. Alone again, I drop into bed. Nano-straps immediately grow from the bed's side.

"These weren't necessary before," Trench streams, almost apologetically. "Only for your safety..."

The straps close over my chest and feet, briefly reminding me of my time back at the station, when the station administrator tried to cut me, attempted to remove my implant. Again, I'm waiting for the knife to drop, to end my life as I know it.

Am I ready?

"Would you like to sleep, Sandfly? What follows may be rough. I can arrange a dream for you."

"Not a very captain-like way to go out, is it? Sleeping while my ship is under attack. What would TallSpot say?"

"You may be surprised. He never faced anything like this."

I sigh, shut my eyes. Send a last warm message to HardCandy, which she returns.

"Better make it a good one this time, Trench."

"I will try."

I begin to dream. Perhaps forever.

THE SUN IS a long way from rising, and noting the blanket of clouds overhead, I wonder if it will visibly rise today at all. A westerly wind buffets the circular access pod where we now stand—my mentor and I—and with it comes a late winter chill.

Instinctively, I pull my plastiweave tunic around me. There is supposed to be a heating element to the material—a built-in thermoswarm. Their broadcasts to the stream tell me they are working correctly, but I really don't believe them. I think they're lying, hiding their laziness. If I had the time I'd debug their lazy swarm one nano at a time, find out why they're letting the chill through. But I don't have time.

"Are you ready?" my mentor, a level twelve I've only just met, says. He has a clean head too, of course, just like me. His physique is larger, which is unusual. He's an implantee, moniker DR 44. A loaner from another master to my own. A temporary business trade. For my benefit, I gather.

He seems to have a rapier, almost cavalier, wit. I'm not sure what to think of him yet.

"I'm not a bot, you know." I get a slight tingle of warning for the rudeness. I shake the sting off and say "Sorry."

The access pod we're on sits atop one of the TreArc subsidy buildings, at the far west end of the City of Temples. We're really high up, but not as high as we'd be if this had happened near the center of the city. Here the drop is only about five stories.

Below and around us, the buildings have begun to show age—not to the point of the packed settlements or the burnt-out rundowns, but well on their way. I note a boarded-up window here, a broken brick face there. Even the TreArc building, though the best of the lot, still seems vulnerable. I swear I hear creaks during the big gusts.

DR 44 is perched with one foot still on the ladder we ascended. He let me climb to the access pod first. My guess is so he could watch how I responded to the twenty meters of raw courage and suppressed terror. I'm sure *he'd* say it was so he could catch me if I slipped.

"I meant no offense by it," he says, then points to his head. "Little offense is allowed in this melon." He shrugs, then grins. "You do this a couple years, and you say that *ready* phrase a lot. It becomes second nature. Especially for the types we usually deal with." DR 44 scales the remaining rungs up onto the pod and steps in next to me.

The pod is a circular platform about three meters across. It feels a lot smaller now that he's here. There are slender metal handrails, but gripping one tightly, they feel woefully inadequate. I don't look down.

Attached to a pole above our heads is a silver downrider string. It disappears off into the horizon in two directions, both east and west. DR 44's eyes trace the span that heads west. "There it is," he says. "See it?" He points a finger and shakes it. "Little non-hopping bugger."

I scan the direction he's indicating. About thirty meters out, on a long span that hangs over nothing, I can make out a small, dark shape. It is about the size of a household cat, but that's where the comparison ends. This creature has never been alive.

"What is wrong with it?" I ask.

DR 44 frowns. "Well...reading the stream synopsis it gave off before it died, I'd say one of its motivators fried. There are often surprises, though, 63."

I should've known what the stream synopsis was too, of course. Gotta get in the glow, Sand. The information is there for the seeing. Got to always think that way. I'm thankful 44 doesn't mention my misstep. Bamboo would've disciplined me right here.

"We should go out there." He pulls free the backpack he's wearing and lowers it to the pod deck. It lets out a litany of rattles, clanks, and thumps as it makes contact. He kneels beside it, and reaching inside, retrieves a device made of straps and pulleys. Archaic technology. He lays the device out before him, straightens it, aligning it just so. He looks at me. "You've got your skate too, right?"

I nod and remove my bag. I ape everything 44 did with my own stringskate. The thing scares me big. "Why are they like this?" I ask. "Why so mechanical, so fixed?"

DR 44 sniffs. "You mean as opposed to having a nano sling?" he asks. "Best not to rely on something stream-connected when you're out there." He nods toward the string. "A micro gets the wrong idea and whoop..." Smiling, he looks over the pod's edge. "Away go the debuggers." He grabs both ends of his stringskate and snaps it once, creating a loud smacking sound. "This, though, is almost as tough as that string there. Not going anywhere."

I'm not assured.

He attaches the skate's pulley portion to the string and draws it taunt. Next come the loops for his posterior and feet—drawn out and set in position. "Okay," he says. "Get up into this one."

"But that's yours," I say. More of a delaying whine than anything.

"Right, and that's yours," he says, nodding at the skate lying before me. "Don't worry, I won't leave with it." He smiles. "But I might ask you to clean mine first." A head flick. "Now get in there."

Clumsily, I make my way forward and attempt to pull myself into the skate's "seat." All I can see is the great distance below us. I feel the skate shaking in the wind. Freaks me.

DR 44 puts out a hand to steady the skate. "Relax," he says. "It will hold you just fine."

I manage to get myself seated and strapped in. Position my feet and hands.

DR 44 continues clutching me while somehow getting his (my) own skate attached to the string and himself into position. "I'll be right behind you," he says. "And remember to use the braking strap if it starts to skate too fast." He makes a point of showing me the strap, giving it a tug. "Okay, now go!"

I gingerly lean forward, feel the skate begin to move.

It breaks free, and I'm suspended over the broken pavement far below, skating quickly forward, the pulleys squeaking with the movement, the wind blowing hard enough to tip me slightly. My stomach finds my throat, but I still manage to gasp out a broken

"Ahhhhhh" as I move. It is a lot faster than I expected. I wrench on the braking strap, halting immediately, but also tipping forward to get a good view of the ground below.

I can hear 44 behind me, the squeak of his pulleys, and his soft—almost irritating—chuckle.

"You're fine," he says, voice diminished by the wind. "Just hang on. Hold the strap loosely."

I ease up on the strap again and start to move, slowly, cautiously, ever worried. After what seems an eternity, I draw near the hopper. I stop when it is about an arm's length away. The thing now looks like no more than a small round "head" fused to long expandable legs. And it appears completely still. Completely dead. Otherwise, the exterior of the hopper looks fine.

DR 44 squeaks up behind me. "What do we have?" he asks. "Was it fibbing?"

I'm still fighting the feeling, the being suspended part. I've been taught to focus, though, so I wrench my mind upward, toward the task at hand. I pull up the hopper's schematics in my mind, start looking for answers.

"There was a recent upgrade for this model," DR 44 says. "Is this one upgraded?"

Usually software upgrades are stamped on the machine somewhere. I search the hopper's exterior as best I can, finally finding the version on the easternmost leg. It still has the original everything. "Doesn't look like it," I say, shaking my head. I hesitate as I feel the skate swinging with the motion of my headshake. I wait for the motion to subside. "Wonder why?" I ask then.

"It is only in partial shutdown, isn't it?" he says. "Why don't you ask it?"

The thing is still stream aware? Again, forgot to check.

"Couldn't we have done the check from back there?" I ask. "Where it is safe?"

DR 44 chuckles. "Possibly, maybe," he says. "Good to get you out here, though. Good practice."

"I don't need practice."

He actually slaps my back, causing me to swing again. "Course you do," he says. "Now fix this thing. I'm getting cold."

Scowling, I locate the right code packet on the stream and—after querying the hopper's readiness—feed it the packet. A second later it has ingested it, verified, and restarted. Streaming, I can detect the faint songs of nanos in motion. Slow motion, though. Not enough.

"There's still a problem," I say. "Something..."

"Well, it did say a motivator was bad."

Because a hopper is such a small device, relatively speaking, the nanos it uses are few, and what debuggers call "stunted." They have limited movement mechanisms. That's where the motivators come in. They act like small hearts, moving nanos where they need to be, but not through a strict pumping action. They energize—motivate!

I hear the high-pitched whine of a nearby downrider. Not on our string, of course, because there is no change in tautness. The shriek is hard to ignore, though.

"You want me to climb over to the other side and help?" DR 44 asks. "Because I could." He places a hand on the string and pulls slightly. "I could spring over you like a hopper over a downer. No problem."

Again the string gives a bit. Not much, but even a little causes motion. I don't like motion.

"You have a sheet handy?" I ask, by way of distraction.

"Of course, Sandy."

I glare, though he can't see it. "It is just Sand or Sandfly," I say. "Never Sandy."

I know DR 44's easy name, of course. It is an odd one. It doesn't fit him at all.

Over my shoulder he hands me a rolled sheet—the favorite viewing device of a debugger. I gingerly stand in the stirrups and press it on the hopper's head. I'm thankful for the safety straps that cross my shins.

"You're a serious one, aren't you?" he asks. "Always on the business."

The sheet turns the material of the hopper's cranium transparent for me. Ignoring DR 44, I peer inside. The primary motivator is located toward the left...

Again I hear a downrider. This one I can see up ahead, in the far distance. It finds the nearest string junction and turns away to the right. Not without adding a noticeable ripple to our string, though. I grit my teeth.

"You afraid to die, Sandfly?" he asks.

"Hand me a probe, will you?" Silently he hands me a lightprobe. I activate it, find an access port, and slip it into the hopper's body. The timing of the motivator is wrong. With a little tweak, it should be good again...

"Seriously," he says. "Are you?"

There's no ignoring him. "Why should I be?" I say. "Our paths are already cleared. We're like the angels, they say."

He bounces in his seat a little. "Especially up here, right?" he says. "Like the angels?"

I almost feel sick. The motivator seems to be righted now, though. At least there's that.

"Do you trust everything they say?" DR 44 asks. "About where we're going?"

"Is this a test?" I ask. "A mentoring test? Or do you want to see me tweaked?"

I remove the probe and the sheet. Stream to the hopper to restart. Hope for the best. Manage a grin when the nanos start to flow fast again. The hopper obediently stretches up on its legs, then hunches back down again.

"Hey, that looks right," he says. "Good job, Sandfly. Now don't forget to stamp it." He places the stamper on my shoulder where I can reach it.

Another downer whine. I turn and look down the string, back the way we came, and notice a downrider on the westerly. It is coming our way.

"Why is it?"

There is no place for that downer to turn now, I realize. It has to come straight through us.

"Crichton," DR 44 says. "We have to move."

He reaches up and works a knob near the top of my skate, causing my seat to pivot so I'm facing the access pod again. He does the same thing to his skate, and starts forward. Quickly moving away from me.

For a moment, I'm frozen. I sit—still with the reclaimed light probe in one hand and the stamper in the other—facing an oncoming downrider. It is a two-person model, painted red. The color of blood.

Of death.

"Move, implant!" DR 44 streams at me—Full Impact—with lots of emotion. A real neuron-synaptic kick in the pants.

I release my grip on the tools, letting them drop away to emptiness. I attempt to kick myself forward, but the braking strap seems to be stuck. I reach up and work it, try to get it free.

I hear the whine of the downrider increase in volume. The warning volt—usually reserved for displacing birds and alerting hoppers—hits my skate's pulley. I feel the tingle as it arcs down whatever traces of metal are in the skate to find me. Have to move! I keep tugging on the brake. It isn't coming loose. I start to yell again.

Then my mentor is back with me—standing somehow. He fixes my skate. Gives the straps above me a tug. "Come on!"

We speed back toward the access pod. The downrider appears to be the same distance from the pod as we are, but that is probably a hopeful understatement. The stream tells me it is a good three times our distance. It looks a lot less. I can see the downer's front windshield, see the head of the front-most passenger....

"Kick your feet free of the straps," DR 44 yells. "We need to jump when we get there. Loosen your belt."

I'm freaked. Death is upon us both. I consider freeing myself like he says and dropping to the distant pavement. Anything would be better than being a bug on a windshield.

"Now!" he says. "Jump!"

I wrench all the straps away from me, feeling the pain as they burn my skin, and I jump, plunge, fall...

My chest hits the edge of the access pod. I flail my arms, feel my hands slip, hear the downer roar overhead, smell the grease and aluminum.

DR 44 grabs my arms, wrenches me back onto the pad. My knees feel the pad's coldness and are thankful. I breathe deep.

He laughs loudly. "I guess you *aren't* afraid to die," he says. "Rails, man, you're crazy fearless."

I cough, sit up. "I was stuck..."

He continues to laugh. "Wow," he says. "Holy wow. You're all right, right?"

I assure him I am, hunching over in my breathlessness. In truth of fact, I am afraid to die. I don't trust the Imam's assurances.

But what choice do I really have?

"Thank you," I say, staring him straight in the face. "You saved my life."

He smiles. "Hey, I couldn't let your master lose his new debugger, now could I? It would start a house war."

I shake my head. "I'm only a lowlevel. Insurance would get him a replacement."

DR 44 slaps my back. "Well, now they won't have to."

I snort, roll my eyes. My mentor, DR 44. Easy name: GrimJack.

STILL IN DREAMLAND, I feel the pressure of someone else's thoughts. A message from a friend.

"Sand, are you all right?"

It is HardCandy, still in her own cabin, messaging me through the ship's stream.

"Yes," I stream. "I think so." I let the implant wake me, moan as I feel the return of consciousness. "We're alive!"

"Yes, but we're stopped," she streams back. "And I can't reach Dark-Trench."

I sit up in my bed. The usual waking colorfulness from Trench is missing too. All I see are blank walls. All I smell is recycled oxygen.

"DarkTrench?" I say to the ceiling, and then stream. No response. The active desk to my right is completely black.

"Were we hit?" I stream. Then, remembering Hard said that we're stopped: "Are we about to be?"

"I don't think so."

I check the ship's processes, as best I can. All the primary functions seem to be working: the atmosphere controller, the stream generator, light and heat production. The ship is not dead. Not externally damaged.

But the personality we knew as Trench seems completely gone.

I exit my cabin and stand in the hall outside HardCandy's room. "Can you come out?" I stream. "Are you able?"

"Of course," she says, shouting through the door. "Why wouldn't I be able? You don't think I was washing myself in the steamer during all that, do you?"

I suppress the thought of HardCandy and the inherent nakedness of the steamer. Even though I'm free of all stops, there are some downriders of thought I know it is best not to take. Controlling my own thoughts is a lot more difficult than I imagined...than it used to be. Something about my being alone with an attractive female in an enclosed space for so long. It jumbles my processes. Makes for a disruptive, near dangerous time.

The door opens and Hard stands there, looking as brilliant as ever. A diamond dressed in blue.

"What?" she says, in response to my stare. "Not quick enough?"

She's masking her concern with edginess. It is one thing I've come to understand with her. One of the few things.

"No...it's..." I shake my head. "You said we're stopped," I say. "How can that be? We were moving as fast as Trench could take us. Are the engines even engaged?"

She glowers. "Am I looking that up for you now too?" She makes a show of shutting her eyes, putting a hand to her head. "Let's see...um, no. The engines are not firing. No action whatsoever." Her eyes open and she smiles. "Useful thing, that stream."

I search the ceiling thoughtfully. "So did Trench stop us before he left? Because I think we should at least still be moving. Conservation of momentum, or something."

HardCandy shrugs and brushes by me. "Should we check the nest?"

I follow like a starved pet. Grateful not to have to lead this time.

We find no indication of Trench in the nest either. Only glowing panels and vidscreens, all showing the exact same image. Another surprise.

On every screen, the sliver's white presence looms. It appears stationary in space. Somewhere close outside, I assume. Yet the surface material of the sliver still looks to be in motion. A rippling turbulence.

"What is it doing?" Hard asks.

"Just sitting there, by the looks of it."

"This image is from the starboard camera," Hard says. "The one just over the docking door." She turns to look at me, eyes wide. "What do we do now?"

"Trench," I say again. "We really need you to answer."

Hard shakes her head. "He isn't here," she says. "Something strange has happened."

I reach out to the stream. "The sampler," I say. "Did it deploy?"

It did. If I'm checking the right inventory ledger. It appears to be gone. "I think we lost it."

"So maybe Trench tried my idea," Hard says. "Pushed the sampler out in front of us." She points at the screen. "We clearly didn't flip, though, did we? Nothing but fixed stars up there." She turns to me again. "No light tunnel."

I check the navigation system. It is still up, thankfully. "Yeah, we're still near Betelgeuse." I attempt to remember everything Trench told me about distances in space. I dig deeper, search for coordinates. "But farther from the planet, I think." With a sniff, I redirect one of the cameras toward the green orb, bring that image up on one of the nest's screens. "It is still there too."

Hard looks at the planet, a mystery playing behind her eyes. "If we don't get DarkTrench back online, we're stuck," she says finally. "Here. Unless you and I can work the flip manually."

"Don't even joke about it," I say.

The image of the sliver changes. The alien projectile, which appeared almost vertical before, now begins to rotate clockwise slowly. "What is it doing?" The sliver turns until it reaches a horizontal orientation and stops again.

"It has aligned itself with us," Hard says. "No, wait, it's moving again."

Now the sliver begins to drift closer to the camera...more toward us. "It's setting up to dock!" I say. "Clarke and crichton..." *Frightened* doesn't begin to describe what I feel. Never in all my life have I faced something so completely unknown, so completely out-of-spec. What do we do now?

Do not fear us, traveler. We mean you no harm.

A message, blasted straight into our ship somehow. A blizzard of stream data.

"Did you get that?"

HardCandy is staring at me, arms tightly crossed. Like she's feeling a chill. She slowly nods.

Maybe this thing is not a projectile but some kind of spacecraft. Are we about to be boarded? I try to force my implant to locate this new stream, to let me take it on directly. The implant doesn't work like that, though. It isn't built for such things. That's why I needed Trench's help before. I need him to direct it my way.

The sliver is cozied up to us now. As we watch, the side nearest us begins to fluctuate, to remold itself into something angular. A silver cube grows out and lengthens. It reaches a five-meter depth, then detaches itself from the sliver completely, almost with a water bubble effect. It floats across the void toward us, toward DarkTrench.

Come to the cube, children. We have been expecting you.

My brain is failing me. My thoughts are thoroughly confused—broken and obtuse. "What should we do?" I ask aloud. My stomach has its own opinion. It says turn for the door and run.

"What choice do we have?" HardCandy says. "We're stuck."

There is a distant thumping sound—the sound of the cube making contact.

"No," I say, "we're not getting in that thing. How can we even know it will work? How can we trust this?"

"The suits," Hard says. "We still have them somewhere, right? We could put those on."

I nod. The suits are right where we left them after boarding. Near the airlock door. Convenient.

I find a reluctance in my legs to move that direction, though. They appear to have grown into the floor. "Maybe we should just stay here. Wait for Trench to snap out of it. What if he wakes up and we're gone?"

We look at each other. Streaming nothing, yet speaking megabytes.

"So, should we go?" she asks.

I stare at the image of the attached cube. Like a large silver tumor on DarkTrench's onyx surface. A synthetic remora.

A wave of fear overtakes me. I can't imagine leaving DarkTrench now. It is the only safe place I've known since childhood. A symbol of my newfound freedom. It provides for our every need. Talks with me. To willingly step away from that, to leave a friend in his time of apparent need?

Inexcusable!

"We can't," I say. "It is dangerous."

Your ship is malfunctioning. You must enter the cube.

I feel heat. "The ship was working fine until you showed up! Why should we trust you?"

I wait a few moments, scanning the room's many screens.

No response. Not even stream static.

Rails.

A new fear assails me. What if they are right? What if Trench's absence means we are truly stuck here? That the ship is no longer our friend and careful watchman, no longer able to fly or even keep us alive, but instead is our prison and tomb? No more Earth...

"The ship," I say. "We should stay here, Hard. Try to bring Trench back."

Every screen in the nest goes out. Completely black. The lights dim too, but remain on, start to flicker.

I stream out again: "Trench, what is going on?" I search for where the guts of Trench are located, where his bot-like mind would be. He said it was below and behind us. Maybe if we can go there, get him restarted somehow?

HardCandy is looking up, sniffing. "Does the air seem funny to you?"

I take a deliberate breath. HardCandy is right: there is an acrid scent in the air, like the scrubbers are lazing in their job. Reluctantly, my feet take a step, move toward the door. "Maybe we should..."

There is a loud creaking sound, a heavy thump, then the main lights go off completely.

Quickly! I stream, not knowing if Hard can receive the message. I do move—clumsily—and in the dim light that permeates the ship (emergency lighting, I think) I put a hand out to lead her.

She hesitates only a moment before taking it. Holding my hand firmly. Against this contact there can be no argument, at least. No indecision on my part. With it, my arm warms to the elbow. I almost smile.

We push through the locking metal door that protects the nest, sprint down the hall, and enter the lift, only to find the unit nonfunctional. It is completely dark, and nothing—neither button pushing nor stream commands—will make it go.

We're stuck again.

There is another way, the other stream says. A ladder.

How do they know the schematics of our ship? We search the area near the lift but find nothing obvious. Then Hard notices a cover—built to look like any other wall panel in the hallway—with a raised icon that looks like a ladder. She shoves the panel, and when it gives slightly, spongily, she gives it a firm kick. It drops back and up, revealing a white, man-sized chute with a fixed ladder. She scrambles in and begins to descend. I quickly follow.

At the bottom it is only a short walk to the ancillary management center. Every screen in this smaller control room is dark too—both those lining the exterior walls and the one in the seamless countertop beneath them. As we pass through I run my hand along the back of one of the room's preformed and rigid seats, hoping a final touch might alert Trench to our leaving. A futile gesture.

Next we reach the passive storage area. There is emergency lighting here, as well, thankfully. Around us are racks of handheld equipment and emergency supplies. Cupboards filled with things we have yet to need. All marked with bold letters. On the far side is the inner door to the airlock leading out. HardCandy is ahead. She finds the locker where the suits are stored, takes a helmet out, and hands it to me.

"Are you sure that's mine?" Normally, DarkTrench would be running through the evacuation procedures now. Telling us where everything is, what to do first...

Hard hands me a suit as well and, shifting her hips with mock anger, says, "Does it smell like yours?"

Not like mine, no. But the helmet does still smell like TallSpot, the previous owner. The man had a thing for cologne. Which means it is as close to mine as I'm going to get. We pull on the suits in silence, mindful of the staleness of the air, the blinking of the lights, the great unknown that waits.

"Are you ready?" Hard says, finally.

I almost laugh at the phrase—would've laughed, if it weren't for the waiting cube. It is impossible not to think about *that*. I just nod. Hard-Candy turns, reaches out for the control pad to open the inner airlock door.

I've seen vids, heard stories, about men being lost in space. Finding themselves beyond the confines of their ship, outside of any help, unfettered, and irretrievable. "Maybe we should tie ourselves?" I say. "Just in case?" I don't want to become a satellite. Or a meteor.

I search the written labels, then open a cupboard for two heavy spools of orange rope. Both have locking nano-hooks on their ends. I let

HardCandy open the interior door to the airlock—a room I passed through twice before with hardly a thought to its usefulness. Now the most important place in the ship.

The airlock interior is beige with short benches on either side. On the opposite side is another sealed door. We both enter the room. Inside to my left are metal rings I can latch to. I attach the ends of both ropes to one of those, then clip a rope to myself. The other to HardCandy.

She closes the interior door behind us and smiles softly. "You're afraid, aren't you?"

"Just cautious," I say.

And very afraid. Only a thin door stands between us and whatever awaits.

She works the controls for the exterior door. The door begins to slide, revealing a silver wall of material. It is translucent—through it the other side is clearly visible, as is the ceiling, the floor. It is a gelatinous cube.

Now what?

"I guess we just step out," Hard says. She turns from me, walks toward the door and the cube matter, and steps forward. As her foot breaks the plane of the material, she looks at me and smiles. "It feels like I'm stepping in wet sand." She continues forward until she in completely through to the other side. Thankfully, I can still see her there, standing in the middle of the cube. Hanging in space. She gives a little wave...so I'll know it is okay, I guess.

Now it is my turn. I walk forward, feel the pressure of the inner cube wall on my foot and leg as they enter the material—as if the suit has suddenly become glued to my skin. I raise my arms, push my hands through, and encounter the same feeling there. A squeezing pressure, but no pain. Then, with less trepidation, I step completely through.

I look down and, seeing the pinpricks of stars below—still brilliant, yet muted due to the cube's material—I almost fall over. This is worse than the glass accessway on the space station. Much worse. HardCandy quickly steps near me, and I place an arm on her shoulder. Keep myself vertical. She gives me a funny look, but she doesn't seem to mind helping me. Much.

There is very little time before the cube begins to move. I get this real feeling of loss looking back at the ship, at DarkTrench. I also feel a little guilty, like I'm leaving a child.

Then I remember the ropes still connect us to the airlock.

"I'm taking mine off," Hard says. She releases hers from her suit. It hangs in the air of the cube and is slowly pulled out the DarkTrench side as we move away. Looking ahead, I measure the distance to the sliver. It is less than twenty-five meters, the full length of my rope. "I think I'll wait awhile," I say.

It seems an eternity, but in only minutes we are nudging up against the sliver ship. The cube on that side appears to simply *rejoin* the ship, fusing perfectly with the ship matter. At this point I have to make a decision, because my rope is now extended to its full length. The ship's surface begins to open.

"Let it go," Hard says. "Come on."

I look back at DarkTrench. The exterior door is still open, like an abscess in the ship's otherwise perfect skin. HardCandy's rope hangs slightly limp and tangled, mine still stretched straight.

I don't want to continue. I grab the rope, think about pulling myself back to our ship. I look at Hard, who now has one foot inside the alien ship. She gives me a stern look, holds out a hand. Within, the sliver looks very bright, overwhelmingly so. We aren't supposed to live in such brightness.

I have to go back!

My rope goes completely slack. I look to where it exits the cube side, only to see that it has been cut there. I pull it to me and look at the end. Sliced cleanly. The cube has cut it.

You have to enter the vessel, child.

I again look at DarkTrench, actually wondering whether I could swim my way back.

Blinking mad, Sand, really.

HardCandy is fully in the sliver ship now, waiting. Still watching me.

I walk to her and somehow manage to step inside. The cube dissolves into the ship's structure, and my view of DarkTrench is lost.

CAUTIOUSLY, WE STEP INTO THE LIGHT. There is a bright luminescence everywhere, but it is difficult to pinpoint the particular light sources. The walls of the hall we move down seem to glow of their own accord, yet I can't see anything specific within the composition of the wall either. It has a shine to it and appears translucent like the cube was, but there is nothing behind the wall except more luminance, a revolving rainbow of color.

"Now we're really stuck," I say. "Do you realize that? There's no going back. Trench can't come get us..."

"Shhh!" Hard says, holding up a finger. "You're thinking too much." She walks up the hall, farther into the ship. "I'm surprised no one has come to meet us yet. Hello?"

That is a bit of a surprise to me too, albeit not necessarily a bad surprise. I become aware of a stream—one not unlike DarkTrench's own. Not as placid, perhaps. There is a distinct fuzziness to the texture of it. Really hard to explain, freehead.

But does it work for us?

As a test, I send HardCandy a message—an EE describing how nice she looks in her suit. Something guaranteed to get a response.

HardCandy turns to look at me. "Did you just message me?" she asks, smiling.

I nod, twisting my face with speculation. How is that possible? How could an alien stream produced by alien technology be anything close to ours? Close enough to properly carry a message from me to her? There are so many processes and handshakes that have to work right.

"Does any of this make sense to you?" I ask aloud. "The stream, this ship?"

The hall ends at a closed door—also translucent and glowing—that opens with a "glop" sound when HardCandy reaches it. Beyond is a large room, completely open, with only two high chairs in the center. I follow Hard inside. To our right is a concave and darkened wall, the rest are all similar to those in the hall. Shimmering luminescence.

HardCandy scans the complete circumference of the room. "No one here either," she says.

The wall to our right separates and snaps open—almost like an eye—and brightens noticeably. An image of the planet forms on it. This is not like our vidscreens, though. The image has depth, as if a small version of the planet is trapped behind it.

As we watch, the globe increases in size. "I think we're moving," I say. "Leaving DarkTrench."

"Maybe they're taking us to the surface! Which means we'll be able to walk on solid ground again," Hard says. "Under a sky..."

I nod. "If the planet is everything the samplers said," I say. "Yes." The planet continues to grow closer, at a seemingly astonishing rate. "As long as this thing doesn't crash."

"I'm sure it is safe." Hard walks to one of the chairs and climbs into it. "Might as well relax."

I crawl into the other available chair. I find that I'm squinting. Even though the interior light isn't *that* bright, there is so much of it that it is hard to suppress the squinting reflex. I try anyway. "They seem to have a thing about light," I say.

"Refreshing, isn't it? After the dimness of Trench's interior?"

I didn't find it that dim. I found it easy to work in, actually. But no sense fueling that fire. "About the stream here," I say, "doesn't it seem unusual? That we can use it, I mean?"

Hard shrugs. "I've been attempting to search, skip through the bits, you know. Haven't seen much that's interesting. It is almost like this room here. Usable, but indistinct."

"They don't trust us," I say. "Don't blame them for that."

Hard reaches to her helmet, touches the button to release the catch.

"I don't think—"

She removes her helmet and draws in a deep breath. "A little stale," she says, "but it will do." Another shrug. "They may not trust us, but I guess I can trust them...for now." A small portion of Hard-Candy's suit at the shoulder turns blue, indicating it has recognized the helmet's absence and turned the internal oxygen replenishment system off.

I follow her example, finding the ship's air a tad pungent. Not unlike that of GrimJack's old store—the scent of electronics mixed with old paper. A lot better than DarkTrench's air when we left, though.

"As for the stream," Hard says, "I don't know. If you believe the scripture, maybe A's creation all takes a similar path, no matter where it is located."

I sniff. "You think this aligns with anything in the sacred writings?" I shake my head. "I've never read anything, never been taught—"

"Most teachers don't teach it," she says. "But there are verses that suggest such a thing, if you know where to look. If you are open to it."

I do my best not to scoff, out of habit mostly. "Such as?"

Hard closes her eyes. "Let me see if I have it..." A moment passes. "Okay, here it is: Among A's signs are the creation of the heavens and the earth, and the living creatures that He has scattered throughout them."

I find myself squinting again. "And that applies...how?"

"Well, it suggests that he scattered creatures throughout the heavens, right?" She nods toward the planetary image. "So this could be them."

I frown. Though I'm not closed to the idea, such creatures—whatever they may be—are not what I came to see, not what I expected. The bot was clear as to the origin of the superlative stream. In fact, it was *that* notion that was fundamental to its original breakdown. A is not A.

Or have I misinterpreted the meaning somehow?

"There's more to that verse, though," Hard says, smiling, nearly vibrating with nervous anticipation.

"What's that?" I ask. The planet now fills the screen. We will be landing soon.

"The last part," Hard says. "It is: And A has the power to gather them together as He wills."

Still not getting it. "Okay?"

Hard begins to move her hands as she talks. Fully involved in whatever it is she's trying to explain. "There's another verse, something like 'We will show them our signs in the furthest regions and in their souls, until it becomes manifest to them that this is the Truth.'"

I nod to show I'm following, or at least hearing, what she's saying. *Understanding* is another thing.

"So, taken literally, there will be signs in the outermost regions," Hard says. "Space qualifies as that, right?"

"I suppose..." For some reason, Abdul teaching is much more in-grained in HardCandy than it ever was in me. After implantation, I never felt the need.

"And another verse describes how A has created animals to ride and has created things of which we—meaning the people of that time—didn't yet know of. So that could take into account vehicles like pre-date change automobiles—"

"Or downriders, or space lifts—"

"Right," Hard says, "Or DarkTrench, or even this ship."

I push her a large streamwise question mark. "Still not getting it."

Hard holds up a finger. "There is also a passage that says 'If you can pass beyond the regions of the heavens and the earth, pass ye—but not without my authority.' Doesn't that sound like what DarkTrench does? Passing beyond the heavens and the earth. Outside of it, if I understand your description of how it works..."

"Yes, but—"

"And A has given *you* the authority, Sand. That's why we're here. That's why we left."

"I guess that's one way of looking at it," I say nodding. It is all I can do.

"Right, and the writings also promise that 'neither on Earth or Heaven shall we be beyond reach,'" Hard says. "Beyond A's reach, I mean."

Another phrase sneaks into my mind: If I go up to the heavens, you are there; if I make my bed in the depths, you are there. I do my best to ignore it, only shake my head.

"You don't see?" Hard says.

"Not the whole of it," I say. "Not really."

"Okay, let me sum it for you. The sacred writings foretold we would be coming out here. It is part of one of A's signs. A great one. The sign itself is that what was once scattered apart—us and the other created life in the universe—A will gather again. You see? We'll be allowed to meet." Hard raises both hands, palms up. "So this all makes sense. All of—" She winces and puts a hand to her head.

"You okay?" I ask, rising from my seat.

She looks up, cheeks flushed, but quickly turns toward the eyelike screen. "Yes," she says. "I think it is just the pressure change outside." She indicates the screen. "Look!"

The image now is a close-up of the structure we located earlier, except now a circular landing platform appears to have grown from the trees surrounding it. Nanotechnology on a grand scale?

I rest a hand on Hard's back. "Are you sure you're okay?" I ask.

She nods quickly and smiles. "We're here," she says.

The landing platform looms large, filling the screen. Silver in color and heavily textured, it looks both new...

And ancient.

"When did you come up with all that?" I ask. "All you just told me."

"The first time we saw this place," she says. "I knew we'd be coming here. Landing. Knew there'd be a way...and someone waiting."

MOTHER HAS LOST HER MIND since my father's passing, of that I am certain. First, there is the weeping. Regret and grief are expected, of course. But Mother is crying or on the verge of crying every time I see her. I almost wish she would wear the scarf while she's at home. To hide her pain, her river of shame.

Then there are the long periods when she is away from the house. I do not know where she goes, but such absences are not like her. I suspect she goes to dark and quiet places. Places one should not go as a widowed and grieving spouse. Dangerous places.

My friend Asa thinks that mother is planning something. Something I should be afraid of.

I have my own plan, though—a plan to save us. My grades in school are good, of course. Even though I mask some of what I know from my classmates, I know I am better than most. And my teacher knows it as well. I can tell by the way she smiles as me, the compliments she gives. Machine manipulation comes naturally to me; it always has. The only thing I lack is the proper experience, the necessary exposure.

So I made a deal with one of the local boys, a shy one (named Abdul, of course) whose father owns a tech store. He lets me play with the machines in his father's store for an hour every other day, and I let him look at my uncovered face for one minute. It seems like a good arrangement, and it is almost worth the risk to see Abdul's face blush every time I remove my veil.

He only looks. He does not touch.

I have learned a lot this way. In fact, I feel that I now know more than Abdul himself, and perhaps even more than his father. I know about the coding, about the banding, and the processes. I recognize the beauty and symmetry in the fibers that stretch through a bot's body. I know about the nanos and how they sing...

Tonight the store holds an unexpected treat, though. An A-send of potential learning. One I doubt even Abdul knew was here.

The machine is stark white and wonderfully molded. The front chest piece looks almost humanlike. More smooth than I imagine a real man's chest to be—less lumpy, certainly, than my father's torso was. There is the semblance of pectoral muscles, a slight rounding where human sinews would be. They construct servbots to appear natural in clothing, of course. Usually in man's clothing.

Which is why I almost ran when I saw it, I think. "It's a naked man!" my senses screamed. Only after I looked again, squinting in the dim light, did I realize my error. For that, A truly deserves my praise.

Approaching the servbot, I see the place in the lower abdomen where a skin—a *debugger*, I mean—left a viewing sheet attached. The sheet is about seven centimeters square and reveals a carnival of lights inside the bot. Cautiously, I touch the surface of the sheet, as if touching the innards of the bot itself. The surface is cool, of course, but there is an electric tingle in the contact—and a flush of embarrassment. If it *were* a man I would be hauled into the town square for what I have done. Beaten and stoned.

I trace the sheet's edges and inadvertently adjust its scaling—increase its magnification. So much that I can actually see the nanobots moving, flowing within. The view is not that dissimilar from a glass-enclosed ant colony I once saw on a class trip, except a billion times more complicated. In comparison, bot guts make the ant colony seem like a sleepy village.

I lean closer, peering intently into the bot. So complex, yet so beautiful...

I hear the door of the shop open behind me. There is no way for me to escape—diving into the nearest aisle would only raise a ruckus, make the owner think me dangerous. Instead I turn to see who it is—hoping beyond hope that it is my shy boy-slave Abdul.

It isn't.

It is a man instead, but not the kind that would willingly hurt me, expose me—drag me into the street a criminal. No, it is the hired skin, and he looks as frightened and surprised to find me as I him. *Almost.*

"What are you doing here, child?" he asks, looking concerned. "I'm in the middle of fixing..." He scans the shop, noticing the dimness of the place. "Are you here to steal something?" A frown. "Because whether I like to or not, I would have to report you. I have rules to obey." He taps his head. "In here." He raises a hand, shrugging. "And aiding a thief will get me stung real bad."

The debugger is a few, maybe seven, years older than me. And noticeably larger. Not necessarily heavy, simply made to be bigger. Which also means he is probably stronger. It makes me glad for these "rules" he mentioned. My face and head are completely exposed to him. The way some of our religious instructors see it, I am like a piece of sugar left out for the flies to land on. If he were to molest me, the fault would be in the uncovered sugar, not the flies.

"No," I say. "I am allowed. I am just looking."

The debugger frowns, scratches his head. "Well, that certainly excuses me," he says. "If you say you're here because you're allowed to be, then who am I to argue?"

He takes a few quick steps toward me and I dash away, disappearing into one of the aisles.

"Whoa there, sorry," he says. "Just getting close to my old friend here." He purposely ignores me, drawing still closer to the bot and gazing through the sheet to the bot's innards. The land of beautiful lights. After a few seconds of that, he drops the plastiweave pack he carries to the ground and begins rummaging through it.

I watch around a corner, from the relative safety of my aisle—protected by a row of what appears to be shovel appendages for an automated digging device. Digger thoraxes. I am shielded, but still very vulnerable—because no matter what happens, I don't want to leave.

I initially fear that he won't speak after he starts his investigation—that he will completely forget I am present.

He doesn't, though. Like a doctor from some long-forbidden medical show, he describes nearly everything he is doing as he does it, along with the reason for having done it that way. I couldn't ask for a better techno tour guide. He doesn't even look my direction as he works. He simply does his job...

And talks!

The debugger works for nearly two hours without a break. I observe the entire process: the various tools he brings out, the intense look in his eyes, the pauses as he apparently retrieves information from the ethereal stream they all use.

At one point he mentions a sister—a sister he once had, maybe *still* has for all he knows. Skins like him lose their family after they're implanted. They become a tool for anyone with money enough to buy them. People with tech or oil or land in their family. I know all that.

His situation doesn't bother me in the least. I have a plan, and now he's part of it.

Day 50, 9:32:55 p.m.
(est. 1:21:24 p.m. local)
[Sliver Ship]

THE SLIVER LANDS gently, as if diving into foam. There is neither jar nor jerk nor adverse motion—not even a harsh sound. Only a quiet swooping and we're down.

It is here my nervous energy returns, hitting my stomach with a sledgehammer of intensity. Reminding me of how big the coming unknown is. All that trouble is in your brain, remember? A funny kind of migraine...

Whether brain or stomach, it is real, and it makes me want to stay completely seated. To wait out the unknown, or perhaps hide behind the door in hopes it won't find us.

HardCandy is a different story, though. As soon as we have landed she hops from her chair and strolls toward the door, leaving her helmet on the seat behind her. She would make a good politician, I realize. Ambassador, I think.

"Shouldn't you at least take your helmet?" I say. "I mean until we're sure it is safe?"

HardCandy shrugs and gives me a wave. "Don't be such a nerve bundle, Sand. You think they made this ship to perfectly protect us, only to let us die when we leave it?" She enters the hallway, walking completely out of sight.

I can only sulk and follow.

In the hall I glimpse Hard just before she passes through the open exterior door. She is flipping crazy. I reach out in the stream to warn her, ordering her to "come back" or even "slow up," spiking my message with as much concern as possible. Unfortunately, my message returns to me, undelivered.

That only increases my worry, so I slap my helmet back on and sprint for the door. I exit the craft to find HardCandy standing on the landing pad, alone. She has hands on hips and, squinting, surveys everything in the area. Doing the same, I catch my breath at the beauty. We are surrounded by green of all shades and varieties. Green like I've never known.

"All these trees," I gasp. "It just goes on and on."

I glance at the sky. It is mostly blue, mostly familiar. But dominating one portion is that large ball of fire: Betelgeuse. It screams out for attention, making the sky around it rosy, filled with menace. I tear my eyes from it, look instead toward the blue part. Scanning, I search for Dark-Trench. Think of home.

Hard messages me finally: "Take your helmet off, Sand. It smells incredible."

Since she isn't gasping on the ground due to some impurity the sampler couldn't detect, I reach up and unlatch my helmet. Pull it free from my head.

I'm hit with this thick wash of freshness, oxygen so rich you can almost taste it, with a flavor that hints at wintergreen. It is better than Trench's aromatherapy on its best day. Incredible.

"Isn't it amazing?" Hard says, smiling. She unexpectedly reaches out for my hand, curls hers into mine. But only for an instant. She pulls away again, leaving me feeling abandoned. Despite the panorama around us.

"No one here either," Hard says. She walks toward the platform's edge. There is a long covered bridge that extends from there into the silver structure. The obvious exit.

"Should we go inside?" she asks.

I look down, examining the surface of the platform. Though it appeared so from above, the silver material is not smooth. It is heavily textured, but at a minuscule level. Closer inspection reveals subtle patterns to the texture—detailed shapes and symbols. Writing perhaps? If so, it is incredible.

A message arrives in the new stream, bold and distinct—impossible to dismiss: *Wait for us, children. We are coming.*

From the direction of the bridge appear three silver floating craft—flat and vaguely rectangular, with something or someone clearly riding on the top surface. There is little sound as they move along, only a soft throbbing *whump-whump-whump*. I estimate their size to be less than three meters long and two meters wide. The craft have little in the way of protection for passengers, only a thin railing and a glowing windscreen in front. As for the passengers themselves, they appear to recline on the floor of the craft. The windscreens make further analysis difficult.

"Can you see them?" Hard asks.

I only shake my head. After a few minutes the craft reach the landing pad and drift down to the surface. The windscreens dissolve, revealing the faces of the creatures. They are intensely humanoid in the same way that a tiger is intensely feline. They are sculpted perfections of the human face, similar in shape, but more rounded, less angular. Strikingly attractive. Almost glowing with life.

The creatures stand. All appear to be male. Their bodies—completely exposed from the waist up—seem to shine in Betelgeuse's furious glow. There is subtle smoothing of the human form here, as well. A refinement of design. Below the waist they are wrapped in a membrane-like material, glossy, loose fitting, and slightly translucent.

"Oh, my," Hard whispers. She now stands close to my right, almost shielding herself behind me.

The creatures gather and walk toward us. Again it is hard to ascertain what makes them completely distinct from us, but they are. They are not human. Not *just* human. They walk with purpose, and yet smoothly, effortlessly, as if gravity is a trifle. A nonbinding force.

When they reach a spot three meters from us, the lead creature stretches out his hands in greeting. He has curly blond hair, and for the first time I recognize a slight off-color cast to his skin—to all their skin, actually. It is a subtle shade of blue.

We have waited a long time for this moment, he streams. Many millennia. A smile touches his lips. We were ecstatic when we saw your vessel in the darkness above. Hopeful that we would finally get to meet. The smile intensifies. But when the vessel began to move, we were worried that we would be forced to wait longer...

"Yes," I say. "Our ship now seems damaged."

The leader nods. So we have observed. Unfortunate. Perhaps it will repair itself given time.

I glance at HardCandy, who is smiling softly. She only shrugs when she notices my look. "We are happy to meet you," she says. "What are you called?"

"You prefer to use your vocal chords," the leader says. "A quaint inefficiency." He bows his head. "You may call me Shem, if you need a quantifier." He indicates the other two. "And let's use Ham for this one..." A dark-haired slightly taller model of perfection nods. "And Japheth for the other." The red-haired third creature nods as well. Both smile lightly.

Again I glance at Hard, streaming: What is this? Who are they?

Shem bows again. "You must excuse us. Symbolic names are a rarity here. Hardly used."

I can't help but frown. "Then how do you know who you're talking about?" I ask.

"It is always clear on the stream, child. Essences are inherent to our emanations, our correspondence." He tips his head. "Is it not so for you?"

In some respects, I guess it is. Though I can't imagine a nameless existence.

"You could say I am that which I am," Shem says. "As Ham is what he is. No spoken name is necessary. It is a redundant mechanism."

I shake my head slowly. I look to see if HardCandy is following. She seems to be absorbed in the moment. Taking it all in.

He called the light "day" and the darkness "night."

I shake my head again, wondering if the message came from one of those standing here. None act different, or even seem to acknowledge. So I force a smile. "I see," I say. "It is not important. Not relevant."

Shem nods. "Precisely." Puts out his hands again. "Are you hungry? Tired? We have accommodations prepared for you. There is so much to discuss. So much for you to see." He motions toward their flying rectangles. "Please, if you may."

There is no going back to DarkTrench now, and thankfully—excepting an unusual manner—Shem and his people don't seem dangerous. I detect no malice in their speech or body positioning. No signs of weapons, aside from their bodies themselves.

Which could be made of living steel for all we know.

"We'd be happy to," Hard says, smiling. She steps in front of me. The redhead Japheth takes a step toward her, but is effectively blocked by Shem's outstretched arm, which indicates the lead rectangle.

"Please ride with me, HardCandy," Shem says, then looks at me. "If you don't mind?"

I shake my head. Though I do mind. Sort of.

"Fine." He bows and motions toward his dark-haired doppelganger. "You can ride with Ham."

Nodding, I follow Ham. Japheth remains behind, watches with arms crossed as Shem leads HardCandy away, then he follows too.

WITH HAM INSISTING, I STEP onto his flying rectangle first. The surface of the craft is not unlike the landing pad below us: meticulously textured and inscribed with a beautiful pictorial script that resembles nothing I've encountered before. According to my implant's storage, anyway. I wish DarkTrench was available. Certainly he would have the facilities to translate some of this.

I crouch to take a seat on the floor of the craft. I find it not as hard or cold as I expected it to be. In fact, it seems to cushion my posterior.

Ham must recognize my consternation, because he smiles as he slides in beside me. "You look surprised, young one."

"This material," I say. "Amazes."

Still smiling, he nods. "It is extremely malleable."

"It looks hard," I say, "but doesn't feel so."

He nods again and the craft rises from the ground. There is no visible steering mechanism of any sort. I assume he is directing the craft through their stream, though the flow is not apparent to me. "It is programmed to react in such a manner," he says. The craft slowly turns, following Shem's craft, which is directly in front of us. We glide off in the direction of the bridge and follow its structure away from the landing pad. Toward the white formation.

I place my hand on the floor near where I sit. The material remains solid there. I try a couple of different spots, both closer and further from my body. "But how does it know when to have what quality?" I ask. "What is the trigger?"

Ham's face is emotionless now. "As I indicated, it is programmed. Customized. You make such customizations yourself," he says, "do you not? On the things you call machines?"

How does he know that?

The craft banks slightly, but the material beneath us reacts in kind, deadening the effect. "Yes," I say. "On occasion. But the programming for this flooring material must be extremely complicated to do what you suggest. We would never make such an effort...for flooring."

Ham looks at me. "Don't you use flooring material?"

We pass over countless trees of all varieties: conifers, hardwoods, both flowering and not. A buffet of color and smells, overwhelming to my senses. "Of course we use flooring," I say. "But only to walk on. Or pray on...for some."

Ham looks at me, squinting. "But you don't do so often? You mostly sit?"

"No, we walk quite often." This is a strange conversation.

"But you don't find flooring worthy of customization?" he says. "How odd..."

I reposition myself, now kneeling so I can test the floor beneath me again with my hand. It feels solid. Until I turn and sit on it again. "But this flooring," I say, "this seat material—whatever it is—it seems to cushion me when I sit on it with my, um, seat, but feels solid to the touch. That's amazing specialization."

Ham shrugs. "It must be amazingly coded then." Another quick smile. "I am sorry, there is none of my essence in this."

I shake my head and resolve only to be quiet and watch for awhile. The three rectangles fly in a triangle-shaped formation, with Shem's in the lead, and Japheth's slightly behind us and to the right. We are close enough I can see HardCandy sitting with Shem. She is smiling and appears to be talking vigorously. Strange, since Shem seemed to prefer stream-speak. And Hard is rarely as talkative to me.

Ahead I see a clearing in the trees, a place where dark loam is evident along with another—in appearances—white outcropping of rock. As we draw closer, I see that this outcropping, though not visibly connected to the first structure we noted, is similar in construction. It surrounds a slightly darkened, yet still surprisingly lit, opening in the earth. We seem to be heading straight for this abscess.

"Is that where we're going?" I ask.

Ham merely nods. "It is one of our entrance portals."

"Entrance to where?"

"To where we live, of course," he says. "Our domicile. Our...Jannah."

Jannah? Meaning heaven? Paradise?

With no evident communication between them—the three rectangles form a single line, with Shem's in first position followed by ours and then Japheth's. They draw quite close to each other. Japheth's is so close, in fact, I could reach back to touch it. It makes me nervous. The whole situation reminds me of something I've seen or streamed before. Something unusual. A distant story.

The opening grows large and we enter. Luminescence surrounds us here too, seemingly formed into the walls, like in the sliver ship. Our rate of travel increases, making it difficult to study any part of the tunnel in great detail. In size it remains consistent, however. Large enough for two, possibly three, of their craft to travel abreast without touching the walls. The same holds true for the height as well. Three stacked vertically could fly comfortably, but never four.

"That first structure we saw," I say. "The one back by the landing surface?"

Ham nods. "It is a remnant. From before we moved within."

"So it is abandoned?"

He smiles. "Nothing is truly abandoned here."

"But you live inside the planet?"

Ham nods again. "After a fashion."

Our three escorts are anything but pale. Not what I'd expect from someone that lives as a worm. I cringe at the thought of where we're going, though. I'm not one for wide open spaces, obviously, but being closed in is almost as alarming. I imagine the feel of the cold earth around me, closing in on me, and shiver.

I look to see if HardCandy is giving any signs of similar apprehension, the wide-eyed fearfulness I observed on the ship, but I see no such indication. She and Shem appear locked in conversation. Shem is acting the part of a tour guide, with lots of broad hand gestures. It annoys me. I'm not sure why.

I become conscious of the wind moving around us. The suit I'm in should be compensating for any temperature discomfort—it probably is. But I still feel cold.

"Are you uncomfortable?" Ham asks.

"The wind," I say. "I'm not used to it. Our craft are usually covered."

Ham nods in recognition. Another windscreen elevates from the sides of the rectangle, curving up to a spot above our heads. The wind immediately dissipates.

"Convenient," I say.

"Of course," Ham says. "Convenience is central to enjoyment. And enjoyment is life."

"You speak like a master," I say.

Ham looks at me, studies my face. "Master?"

I nod. "Yes, someone who controls things," I say. "Someone in charge of people and things."

Ham crosses his arms, looks to the tunnel in front of us. "We do not have such a designation."

"No? No imams, no ruling council, no...um...power?" How does that work?

I notice the tunnel widening ahead. There is the suggestion of depth and more light. Of motion.

"This world provides our power," Ham says. "It is highly efficient."

I shake my head. "No, I mean, is no one in charge? No one that people answer to?"

"Ah, I think I understand—" We break free of the tunnel. Below, above, and around is a city like nothing I've ever seen. Gleaming, shining—bursting with light. Crystalline structures, colored green, red, and blue. A huge expanse, brimming with hues—like a rainbow on the ground.

The air has been sucked from my lungs. I gasp loudly to get it back.

"Here, we are all masters," Ham says.

And I believe him.

QUIETLY I OPEN THE FRONT DOOR, willing the handle not to squeak, the hinges to work without effort. They do, and I am grateful. Still careful to hold the door's handle all the way, I cushion the weight of it until the very end. The door must not slam, must not sound in any way.

The hour is extremely late. The skin had much to show me tonight. There were important operations going on. The bot is nearly complete—regrettably—but it is the final moments of a debugging session where the most information is gathered, the most learning takes place.

"Each mistake makes the next success more likely," the debugger whispered to me. "Each solution is another tool in your workbag up here." Smiling, he touched his head. "And is much more valuable than anything in your workbag there." He indicated the plastiweave bag on the floor, the one containing his collection of sheets, probes, and fusers. The tools of his trade, all of which I now intimately know, fully understand.

It is good for him, I think, my being there. I didn't see it at first, but my doting presence is as much for him as it is for me. Without me, he is as much a tool of his master as a donkey or a downrider. But with me around, watching him, he is almost human. An implanted teacher.

We have an understanding now. A mutual respect—a fearless camaraderie. As much as could be had in our world between a debugger and a young girl. Perhaps more than between any child and parent, more than any man or woman in our society at all.

But my mother knows nothing. And I must keep it that way.

Not that she would notice if the debugger set up shop in our living room...

I remove my shoes and step quietly into the hall, pausing first at the entrance to the kitchen—and peering within to find only a dimly lit and empty room—continue to pad forward. The next area of danger is the double-wide entrance to the living room. I pause here too, and rising up on my tiptoes, look through an opening in the decorative curtain that surrounds the doorway. Again, I find nothing but a darkened room. My father's octagon.

The family vidscreen, which is mounted on the far wall, still glows with energy. Mother has been home tonight at least. No image is being displayed. She must have forgotten to order it off. Surprisingly, we have no family bot to take care of such trivialities. My father was against it. Felt it needless to purchase something to mind matters that he could easily mind himself.

"Speaking to a wall requires little effort," he would say, and then cock his head. "Now if I had to actually cross the room to kill the thing...well, then I might think differently."

That was long ago, though. Frowning, I move on. My own room is the second on the right. The entrance is curved, as is the fashion for most homes in our neighborhood. The door itself is solid, and tightly closed. Exactly as it should be. I pass by the first door, Father's study, which is also closed. Locked since his departure. Mother's room is further down on the left, very dark, quiet. With only a glance that direction, I reach for the handle of my door, apply soft pressure...

"So, you are home." My mother's voice blisters, startling me. "Finally!"

I turn slowly, eyes peering above my scarf. Wishing to be more hidden than I already am. "Mother?" I say, softly.

"Come in here," she says from her room. "I have something to share with you."

I have heard stories—dreadful stories—of girls who have fought their parents' wishes and found themselves sold as slaves, or dead. I know Mother could not do such a thing herself, but if there were others here with her, hiding, waiting?

I don't know who she's been meeting with lately.

I reach the entrance to her bedroom. She sits in a high back chair, with only half her face revealed in the light from her window. She is half herself, that much is true. But what of the half that is left?

"Who have you been with?" she asks. "Where have you been?" The corners of her mouth turn down as she talks. She is either tired or very angry.

I am surprised she is taking an interest in me again. For so long we've been like ghosts haunting the same house. "With Asa," I lie. "We were studying."

"I have spoken with Asa's mother," she says. "I doubt that what you are telling me is true."

I draw my outer garment tight around myself; form the shape of a living mummy. But I say nothing. I watch Mother's eyes for intent. They are dark and piercing. Fixed with a newfound purpose, a new plan for survival.

She sighs deeply. "This activity you are engaged in is dangerous, child. You should know that."

I only shake my head. What does she know? Has my boy Abdul sold me out?

"Yes, dear, it *is* dangerous. Sneaking around at night, going wherever your heart takes you—it is wanton, reckless, and sinful. You will get us both stoned—yourself as a harlot, and me...well, as a mother who *raised* a harlot."

I shake my head again. "No, Mother, it is not like that at all. I—"

She raises a hand limply. "Please give me no more lies," she says. "My heart breaks already. First, I lost your father, and now this...to forsake a daughter to the street."

"Mother!" I say. "I am not on the street!"

She gives me a stern look. "What you have *actually* been doing doesn't matter," she says. "Don't you understand? All that matters is what people think!" She looks at the floor, shakes her head. "All it takes is for one willing and hapless boy to..." Another head shake, firmly this time. "No. If I do nothing else for your father's memory, I will prevent that."

There is silence for many moments. "How?" I ask softly. "What, Mother, are you planning?"

She looks me in the eyes again, and smiling, brings her hands together. "You will be married to your father's cousin."

The image of my father's cousin—a fiftyish man with huge jowls—thunders into my mind and sits down. It fills a very large space.

"Married!" I exclaim. "I am not yet ten!" I take a hard step forward, barely preventing myself from stomping. "And to father's cousin! Are you mad?"

"Hecta is a good man, dear. Good for agreeing to marry someone as reckless and free spirited as you are."

I soften my tone. "But I'm only nine..."

"And I was only thirteen when I married your father," she says. "The founder's last wife was only nine when they married..."

...and only six when they were engaged.

I shudder, because there is no arguing with history. It is what binds us still.

But the future Mother is suggesting, being a child bride of a large and old man? A smelly and old man...

My mother is still smiling. "It is the best solution I can think of," she says. "You will get your schooling again. Do the things you love to do."

And Mother will get a dowry—undoubtedly a handsome one to trade for such a young girl. I have seen this all before. It is what Asa feared.

I shrink back to the open door, to the sense of possible escape it gives me. I thought by studying with the debugger, I would replace some of what I was losing from my time missing school. Make myself a valuable commodity. Break the normal chains that bind me, bind the other girls in my class.

But Mother has rendered that moot. With her craziness.

"I don't want it," I whisper. "I can't..."

Mother straightens in her chair. "You will, child," she says. "It is the only way." She extends her hands. "I am protecting you, don't you see?"

I *do* see, but I don't want to. I am only a child. Only a few months ago I was free and happy. But suddenly A has changed all that, taken my father and my school. Ended my freedom. Perhaps I should've stayed in the smoke. The fire! Perhaps that is what I deserve.

"No!" I shout and retreat into the hall. My mother makes more imploring sounds, but I ignore them. I only turn for the outside door, find my shoes, and plunge into the night.

OUR RECTANGLES SLOW and descend, reaching a spot below the tops of the highest structures. From there we wind our way between and through these edifices. Like the tunnel and the sliver, they glow with moving light. From a distance the surface appears almost translucent, as if one could see the activities of the creatures within, but upon drawing closer—as we did many times—the surface grows more opaque, more awash in light. It is a confusing phenomenon, and I mention as much to Ham.

"Customization, Sandfly," is all he says.

"I see..." Though I do not.

"The synthesis of privacy and openness."

Not expecting to truly understand, I shake my head and return my gaze to the scene around us. The crystalline appearance of the city extends all the way to the street level, many stories below. The street surface seems to be a river of frozen onyx. Dark as space. Yet it still reflects much of the light from above. We aren't the only rectangles in motion. Between us and the street are many others, though by no means an overwhelming—or even congested—amount. They move with a consistent and regulated pace. It is their light that the street reflects. It dances along the surface.

"How old is this city?" I ask.

"All ages," Ham replies, his brow slightly wrinkled. "It is constantly being replenished. When a component becomes inefficient, it is reclaimed and reused."

"But how long has *anything* been here?" I ask. "When was the first structure built?"

Ham looks forward, as if checking the way in front of us. The entire journey thus far has been completely flawless. We have never seemed in any real danger of collision, causing me to assume a stream-driven control not unlike our own downrider system. "Your concept of time means little to us," he says.

"But if you were to guess," I say, "how old?"

"I would need a reference measure," he says.

"I will stream you a reference," I say. "The length of our measure called 'second,' plus instructions on how to translate it into our 'years.'"

Ham nods. "Go ahead."

I compose something and bundle it for transmission. "How do I get it to you specifically?" I ask.

"Simply send it," he says. "I will find it."

Like releasing a balloon to the air, I push out the message. A nano-second later, Ham blinks. "I have it," he says. "Approximately 104 of your years since the first internal structures were grown."

"Ten thousand years?" I scan the city again, all gleaming and polished. "That is nearly our entire recorded history."

Ham nods again. "And you have no structures that have stood as long?"

I shake my head. "Not that I'm aware of," I say. "Thousands of years, possibly. But most of those are crumbling, or in need of constant repair." I recall some of humanity's older structures—those deemed in some way idolatrous—and how most of them have not just been left to rot, but been outright destroyed. I don't mention that to Ham, however.

Our rectangles shift lower, briefly entering a lane of flying "traffic" before banking to the left, around the corner of a building. We pass a place where the roof of a lower structure becomes visible. On it, a courtyard of some sort is constructed. I notice two dark-haired beings, not unlike Ham, playing what appears to be a game involving lights. Specifically, I see a light moving between the two creatures, sometimes quickly, sometimes slowly, and sometimes halting midway between. It is a fascinating display and holds my attention for many moments.

As I'm about to turn away, I notice something else in the courtyard—a small brown creature standing motionless on the sidelines. It has an asymmetrical head and seems to squat on three appendages.

I turn to Ham. "What is that?" I ask, pointing.

Ham looks over the side. "The two brethren in a game of challenge? We have many such distractions. The purpose with this particular movement is not complicated. It is a matter of stream control to operate—"

"No," I say, shaking my head. "Not that. There is a brown creature there..." I point in the direction of the courtyard, but looking again, realize I can't locate the strange creature. I search the extent of the courtyard in every direction. Nothing. "Do you have pets?" I ask.

"Pets?" Ham pauses a moment, apparently checking his own version of an implant. "Ah, I see. Domesticated, non-sentient life forms, used for substitute companionship. Animals that bond as a result of genetic customization over time and promises of nourishment."

"That sounds about right." Never had a pet myself. Dogs, of course, are forbidden. But there are other things that Abduls routinely keep—birds, cats, and small rodents.

Ham shakes his head. "We have no need for pets," he says. "Certainly it is the same for you with your implant. Companionship is only a thought away."

"Yes...but..." I think of my time with HardCandy and how difficult it is to really live with someone in close proximity—especially inside your thoughts and mind. It is a downside of our condition. For Abduls, they have the excuse of occasionally being unreachable if they desire. Occasionally being "out to lunch." Not so for a debugger. Anyone could interrupt you at any time. You have to assume a certain amount of rudeness to keep them out. I live with that rudeness, because I have to. There is little choice.

Besides, people's thoughts are too disjointed—too laced with emotional illogic—to have bouncing around in your head at all times. Aside from your own thoughts, of course. There *is* a need for such a thing as true companionship in humans, I think. That isn't what the stream provides, not really. True communion can't be had that way. Though many have tried.

Squinting, I shake my head. "Crichton, I wonder what I saw." A living tripod? More like a tri-ped. Triped. Yeah, that works.

Smiling, Ham motions toward the cavernous ceiling above. "There is indigenous life, here, of course. Many animals prefer the underground. It is less random..."

"Anything with three legs?" I ask.

Ham grows silent, doubtless searching again. "I would not know." He shrugs. "Our stream doesn't suggest anything."

I look one last time, watch closely until the courtyard diminishes behind us. The light game continues, but there is no sign of my "triped." "I don't know what I saw," I whisper.

"Perhaps you too are in need of repair." Ham is smiling at me—joking. I think.

I recall the experiences I had on the station before we left, crazy machine behavior and inaccuracies. I blamed it on whatever programming rode the superlative stream, the same programming that seems to have removed my inherent stops, but I can't be sure. Not really. I still get odd messages, after all.

There is a way that seems right, but in the end it brings death.

Like that.

Shaking my head, I look ahead of us again, only to see Shem's rectangle drawing closer to a jutting portion of a building there. The building itself is a darkened emerald, but the particular portion he moves toward is heavily lit. A balcony of some sort.

Regardless of its customary use, Shem intends to use it as a place to land. He draws near to the balcony's furthest end and lowers his craft. Our rectangle begins to lower directly behind his, making surface contact with the lightest of "clanks." Here again, I'm surprised, because shortly after we step free of the craft, it begins to dissolve into the balcony's flooring.

"The fundamentals—the building blocks—are there again if we need them," Ham says, smiling.

"Incredible," is all I can say.

We move to join Shem and Hard, who are still locked in discussion. He, with many smiling gestures, and her watching intently, hands braced thoughtfully behind her back. She gives me a quick smile as I approach, subtly inviting me to join them. Which I do.

"How did you like the trip?" she streams me.

"Crazy," I stream back. "Amazing and incredible."

She nods. "I have a theory about all this..."

"I look forward to—"

"We would like to refresh you," Shem says. "I understand it has been some time since you've last eaten."

Almost five hours, now that he mentions it. "It has," I say.

Shem motions for us to follow. We enter the larger part of the structure through a rounded exterior door, one seemingly carved without nick or scratch from the building's emerald material. The adjoining hallway has an emerald cast to it as well, though lighter than the outside of the building. The walls here are lighted, but aren't as active or brilliant as the walls of the sliver had been. We pass a number of fairly plain-looking rooms, of various hues and shades, before reaching one that we apparently have to pass through.

It lightens as soon as Shem enters. Then the walls begin to ripple indiscriminately, like a pool in the middle of a cloudburst. Shem glares at Ham and Japheth.

"What is it?" I ask.

Shem bows his head. "Some adjustment to this room is necessary, is all. It is unfortunate you were exposed to such an inefficiency."

Japheth speaks for the first time. "It is in need of reorienting."

Ham gives a quick nod. "Now scheduled, to be completed soon."

We continue through the room. Before Shem has passed the opposite door, the room has stopped its wayward movements.

"Completed," from Ham again.

"Rails," I whisper. "You mean it is fixed?"

"That is correct," Ham says. "Though it will be verified again shortly. We find that such redundancy is necessary. Don't you?"

I glance at Hard. "Oh, yeah, we always check our work," I say. She giggles, then raises one of her glorious dark eyebrows at me.

"You're feeling better, obviously," I stream. "Must be all the walking in the open air..."

We both laugh.

The others watch us, with only Shem having the makings of a smile on his face. The others are a virtual mask. Japheth, in fact, looks a trifle annoyed.

I shake my head, forcing the humor away. "Where are you taking us?" I ask.

We cross a threshold into another room. It is large and has temple-style pillars running around its perimeter. In the center is a large rectangle of sapphire blue water. It is a swimming pool. Something that, on Earth, only masters would have.

"We thought you might like to bathe," Shem says.

"Is that really water?" Hard says. She hurriedly steps to the pool, crouches, and dips in a hand. She pulls it out, cupped, dumps it, only to scoop up another. Clear delight on her face.

"Of course," Japheth says, looking puzzled. He watches intently as Hard now makes ripples with her fingers.

She smiles, shakes water from her hands. "I apologize," she says. "It has been awhile since we've seen so much water together."

"If ever," I say. "At least, not without a lot of adolescents fouling it."

Shem smiles broadly. "So the pool pleases you then. Very good." He indicates the pool's length. "Feel free to disrobe and enjoy yourself. We will wait."

Hard's head goes shade red, and she seems to shrink toward the ground.

"I don't think that will work," I say.

Shem blinks twice. Noticeably. "Why not?" He looks first at me, then at HardCandy. "Is the temperature not to your liking? It is easily adjusted."

"It is fine," Hard says. "We just don't bathe that way..."

"Together," I say.

"Because of the sexing?" Japheth says. "The tendency for inadvertent copulation?"

Hard is flushing again. I can't help but watch. And try not to laugh. "Among other things," I say. "We are from a planet where the two sexes rarely mix in social occasions. Much less bathe together."

"But you two *are* together," Ham says. "Traveled together."

"Yes," I say. "Ours is an unusual situation. In many ways. We came searching for—"

"It was an accident," HardCandy says. "Our ship is an exploration vessel, but we are not its original pilots. Those were all male."

"I see," Shem says. "We have made you uncomfortable with our request. I apologize."

"Which, I assume, means you have no such reservations about shared exposure," I say.

Shem looks at the others, smiling. "About our bodies," he says, "no."

"Would you like to eat now instead?" Ham asks. When we both nod, he directs us toward another door. Entering, we find a table filled with foodstuffs, some reminiscent of Earth dishes—a vessel filled with what appears to be mashed potatoes, for instance—while others seem completely new and unusual. One dish, in fact, holds a browned and greasy looking dead beast...with five legs. Regardless, there is enough food for the five of us to eat until we fall over. The aroma, given the length of time since we last ate, is nearly overwhelming. I'm like Pavlov's salivating dog.

"That's a lot of food," Hard says.

"Is it *too* much?" Japheth asks, addressing HardCandy.

"I don't know," she says. "How much do you three eat?"

"Oh," Shem says, waving. "This is not for us, it is for you."

My eyes wander over the entire length of the table. I count at least twelve serving dishes. "But there is so much," I say. "You might as well stay."

Ham glances at the other two. "Like you, we have things we only do alone, Sandfly," he says. "Eating is one of them."

"You mean always?"

He nods. "That is correct. Eating is a solitary activity for us."

"Interesting!" Hard streams.

Japheth takes a step toward the door. "So we will leave you two, for now," he says, with a sideways glance at the other two "men."

"Yes, that's appropriate, isn't it?" Shem says. "We will leave you two alone."

Ham nods, also moving toward the door. "Send a message, Sand, when you are ready to talk again." He smiles. "I'll catch it, don't worry."

And in the time it takes to fix a malfunctioning wall, they are gone.

BETWEEN THE PLATES OF FOOD I can barely glimpse the table itself. It is dark in color and appears to be made of heavily lacquered wood. But I doubt it really is. My guess is that it is formed of the same building blocks that the flying rectangles are and can be assembled or reassembled at a thought.

I wonder if the food was assembled that way, as well.

HardCandy walks around the table to a spot near the exact middle and sits down, facing me. She reaches out to grab something that looks like a bread roll. "I wonder what this is really?" She brings the roll to her nose and gives it a series of hard sniffs. "It smells right." A smile and a flutter of her eyelids. "It doesn't respond to any stream commands, so that's good isn't it?"

I take a seat across from her. Directly in front of me is that five-legged creature. It smells like sausage. "I doubt they've given you access," I say. "Probably have these nano-blocks, or whatever they are, playing dumb until they sing to them."

"Lying in wait," she says, "stooped down, hiding out, ready to pounce?"

I smile and nod. "Something like that."

Hard tears the bread in half and offers me some. I take it, examine it closely. "We do this together, right?" she says.

I lift the bread to my lips, simultaneously giving it my own smell test. "Let's go then." I push the bread into my mouth, expecting it to taste stale or synthetic—or at least as bad as the bread on the ship. But it is neither.

"Wonderful," Hard say, smiling, eyes wide. "Simply wonderful."

I continue chewing, mouth in full agreement, but still shake my head. "Makes no sense whatsoever. The whole situation."

Hard arches an eyebrow. "Maybe it does," she says.

"Because of A's scattering and gathering?" I roll my eyes. "Rails, Hard, do you realize how far from home we are? Did you not see that furious ball in the sky? Hear DarkTrench's warnings?"

"They weren't warnings," she says. "Only strong opinions."

"Regardless, I'm beginning to think he wasn't really damaged after all."

Hard examines another serving vessel, this one filled with a blue, diamond-shaped fruit. Cautiously, she brings one out. "But he *was*, Sand." She takes a small bite, then scowls as purple juice escapes down her chin. "He stopped working, remember? That's why we left."

"Yeah, but maybe *they* did it," I say, pointing to the exit door. "They seem technologically capable. Amazingly so."

Hard takes another, larger bite and chews it, contemplating. "But aren't they the source of your signal? Isn't that what we came to find?"

I retrieve a blue diamond fruit myself, turn it slowly in my hands, looking for any sign of alien worm infestation. "I'm not sure what we came to find. I didn't expect this...them!"

"But they *are* probably the source, right? It would make sense."

I shrug. "You didn't let me ask them."

She smiles, purple staining her lips and teeth. "Doesn't hurt to be cautious."

"You said you have a theory..."

HardCandy nods, almond eyes looking thoughtful. "I do," she says, "but I'm sure you'll thunk me for it."

"Now why would I do that?" I sample the fruit. It is reminiscent of mango, but sweeter.

"Because you're so contradictory about every theory I throw out."

I feel a little heat. "Do you want me to agree with everything you say?"

"Rails, no," she says. "But you don't have to argue with everything either."

"I'm not arguing..." I return my half-eaten fruit to the serving vessel and reach for another piece of bread. I lower my eyes, avoiding her gaze.

"I like to represent the alternative," I say, staring at the table. "You're a debugger. You should appreciate that. If you don't see other paths, other solutions, you might miss the real problem."

It is her turn to roll her eyes. "Fine, if that's what you're doing," she says. "Going all Holyfield-Lewis on me. Punch to my counter. But sometimes I think you just want to make me mad."

"I don't," I say. "Believe me." I hazard a look at her eyes again. "Anyway...your theory?"

She stands, walks to the end of the table. She picks up a plate and spoons some of the potato-looking mound onto it. "My theory is this: What if they're jinn?"

Jinn? Jinni? Now there's a place I'd never reach on my own. "You mean genies?" I ask.

She blushes but continues scooping potatoes. "Well, yeah. It is a possibility, isn't it?"

Normally I'd do an exhaustive stream search for the subject, get my implant full to the hilt, you know. But I'm guessing our new hosts don't have much information on their stream about "jinn," even if I knew where to look. They don't seem to have much information there at all, actually.

I do know a bit about genies, though. Their existence is a part of Abdul beliefs. There are many, many prayers to steer evil jinn away from most human endeavors—everything from the first night of a honeymoon to the use of a waste unit. Jinn, since they are thought to be invisible, may be anywhere. And you don't want them doing something bad when you're most exposed. Like on a waste unit.

"They have origins before the founder," HardCandy says, "Do you know that?"

"No," I say. "Jinn weren't a specialty." I hand Hard a plate of my own, indicate the quasi-potatoes.

She smiles. "You did have schooling before you were picked, right? You did have the full stream..."

"As full as the Abduls would give me," I say. "Which is still limited, of course."

Hard looks pained for an instant, but then laughs. "You touched the OuterMog a few times though, right?"

I nod. "Thanks to you." Hard had shown me a spot before we left.

A place where stream barriers were weakened enough to reach territories beyond Abdul control. The few that are left, that is.

"Glad to help." She smiles again. "But yeah, the idea goes way back. Jinn were any spirits lesser than angels, especially when composed in forms of art. Basically, if you saw something that wasn't clearly an angel with wings and halo, it was a jinn."

"I see," I say. "More, please." And here I mean both information flow *and* potatoes.

Hard mounds another spoonful onto my plate. "Pre-founder they were often thought to be the spirits that brought disease."

"Must be pre-germ too," I say.

Hard hands me the plate. "I suppose that's true."

I smile, remembering. "The sacred writings *do* refer to jinn, don't they?"

"There is a whole book dedicated to them," she says. "They are said to be creatures of free will, just like man—"

"Which is no longer completely true," I say. I sample the potatoes with a finger and, finding them delicious, search for a fork.

"Well, yes, before the date change, I guess. Technically, whenever man was free to choose his own beliefs. Regardless, jinn would *still* have free will. Unlike angels, which the founder taught could only follow A's orders—"

"And debuggers," I say and smile again. "At least, most debuggers."

"Right." Glaring, Hard tips her head. "Are you going to let me through this?"

"Sorry," I stream, my mouth now full of food. "I'll be quiet."

"Okay. Good." She visibly swallows. "The root of the word *jinn* comes from the word *jánna*, which means 'to hide or conceal.' Unrelated to the name they gave for this place, by the way."

"Jannah?"

"Yes. 'Jannah' literally means 'garden,' though it derives from the word for 'paradise' and is often used synonymously."

I nod. I wasn't aware of the etymology, but the earlier reference reminds me: "Jinn are invisible to humans though, correct?"

"Yes, that's right, and it makes a good counter-argument to my theory, I know. Also, humans are supposedly visually 'unclear' to them. I'm not sure what that means exactly, but I assume that means we're a little blurry around the edges."

"But we *can* see Shem and his gang," I say. "And they can see us."

Hard takes another bite of potatoes and, chewing, nods. "That's right. As I said, it works against my theory. The bit about them being hidden—if you think of Trench's observations about the planet—might make sense. For him, it was hidden during his prior trip, but this time, for whatever reason, it was visible. And so are the inhabitants."

I shrug and continue eating.

"Of course, the fact that they won't eat with us helps my theory."

"And why's that?"

"Because the founder required that bones be left for them to eat."

I pause in my chewing. "Bones."

She smiles. "Yes, jinn are able to reanimate the flesh on the bone and eat that."

I look closely at the five-legged beast. Scowl.

"The founder classified jinn into three groups: those with wings to fly, those that resemble snakes and dogs, and those that travel without ceasing."

"None of which describes our new friends," I say. "Unless it is that later classification. It is a bit ambiguous."

Hard stands again and watchfully walks the table's perimeter before pausing at a plate of pale sliced meat. *I think.* Finding a fork, she skewers a piece and carries it back to her seat. "Well, there are other descriptions by the founder's companions, some of which include human forms. The general consensus is that jinn can assume many forms, and humans are definitely one of them."

"Even perfected, slightly blue humans?"

"I would guess," Hard says, "yes."

Reaching for a water-filled glass in front of me, I take a drink. Tastes as pure as melted snow.

"Still not convinced, huh?"

I can only shrug.

HardCandy returns the shrug, magnified. "As I said, it is only a theory. If nothing else, it is good for us to be cautious here, because the jinn can be either good or bad. Remember, the evil one, Shai'tan, was once a jinn."

I frown. In my experience, there are countless examples of human malice, so much so that the idea that there is an additional creature or creatures out there actually pushing evil like a drug almost seemed redundant. But Shai'tan is a firm part of Abdul teaching too. Scriptures say he is a jinn who refused to bow to Adam and so was sent from Paradise.

"Aren't we to abstain from contact with jinn of any sort?" I ask. "Whether we think them good or evil? And aren't those that somehow *do* interact with them, who manage to enter their hidden world—if that is what this is—aren't they by definition dabbling in black magic? And if so, what does that make us?"

It is Hard's turn to frown, and for a second I see a pained look in her eyes. "That's true too," she says, "I guess. Except for in some instances..."

There is something to the right of me that appears to be a whipped confection; I have a hard time keeping my mind off it. "What instances?" I ask. "What?" I touch the edge of the dessert with a finger. Bring it slowly to my lips...

"It is said that holy men—extreme holy men—can find the jinn without using magic," Hard says, looking deep at me. "And what I wonder, what I think is, is maybe that is you."

The dessert tastes both sour and sweet.

THE WIND BLOWS through my coverings, chilling me, making me feel exposed, even though I am not. Still, though disappointed in its warmth, I am grateful for the hijab's dark color. It makes blending into the shadows easier. I am still very scared. I am more independent than some, but I know the rules, and I know the danger. I am more frightened by my mother's plans for me now. Marriage to my father's cousin! I cannot let that happen.

I have another fear too. What if I am unable to find him? What then?

I return to the store again, and sneaking around to the back, try the door there. It is locked. My accomplice Abdul lives nearby, I know, but it is very late now. He will be in bed, and I will be unwelcome, regardless. There is no good reason for me to visit him. A tossed stone to an upstairs window is a futility. It will only wake the guardbot, and they are a thousand times more sensitive than dogs.

I move along the store building to the front. I peek out of the shadows, check the street in both directions. It looks very quiet, thankfully. The shop has an awning in front, so consequently there are more shadows. Another help. I would breathe a prayer of thanks to A, but I do not think he would accept it. I am breaking the rules, and A hates those who break the rules.

With another check of the street, I venture out, hugging the front of the store. I quickly look in the nearest window. I can barely make out the servbot as it moves within. It is cleaning—dusting, I think—but the store is otherwise dark. Only the dim security lights reveal him. The bot doesn't seem to mind, but why should it? In his white robe he almost looks like a ghost...

Shaking my head, I check behind me, then on all sides before returning to the shadows again, into the narrow alley I just came down. The debugger is not here, nor will he be back. His project is finished.

What now? I can't return home. My mother is crazy.

I ball my hands into fists and squeeze them as tight as I can. I need an idea. Something that will work. I think back to the things the debugger has told me. His techno pieces of gold.

"The best solution is one that doesn't create another problem."

"Chest lights must be more than *on*. They must dance!"

"Stream twice, fix once."

"Master's toy breaks, master's tool fixes. It is as simple as that."

"I think I know how to do this, but I don't. So what's it matter anyway?"

"With great art comes great struggle. Now hand me that sheet, will you?"

I smile at the last couple. A debugger is so much more than a tool, so much more than a harnessed skin. What was Tanzer thinking?

I look to the heavens, see the crisscross of downrider cords above. How do I not create another problem? How do I find a solution that will work? I wish A wasn't so distant. I wish he cared even when the scales were tipped against you.

I think about the servbot operation again. I remember the tidbits of information the debugger revealed about himself, about his life in service. Biting my lip nervously, I scramble back toward the back of the store, toward more alleys and darkness.

I make a turn, scramble by the side door of a cleaner, catching the pungent scent of hard chemicals. They tickle my nose and sting my throat. I pull my scarf tighter and continue on. Struggle not to have an outburst of coughing, though it is the only thing I want to do.

I take another alley, only to find this one worse than the last. Men have used it as a latrine for a very, very long time. It reeks of ammonia, bile, and I don't know what else. There is waste everywhere, old wrappers, broken things. I walk faster. Someone wails from a doorway I pass, causing me to jump in my tracks. I hurry, nearly running, then reaching down, I hoist up my dress, pulling it closer to my waist so I can move faster.

I need to move faster.

I find one of the wide poles that support the glossy down-riders—a pylon. There is a ladder to the top, but the lowest rung is well above my head, far out of reach. I glance at the symbol on the pylon's side—a green waveform with a circle around it. I think that is right. I think it signifies ContraMech.

What would it take, though? What?

The ladder is so far away.

I start to move again, away from the pylon, following the cable above. It travels between the buildings on either side of me, in the path of the alley. I look at my feet and then back up, as if chasing a bird in flight. Finally, I reach the end of the alley.

There is a large open street ahead. Since it is after curfew, the sidewalks appear to be empty. Should be empty. Still, I make extra certain before I exit the alley, before I continue to follow the line. There are four lanes to cross. Once they were used for anything from commuter traffic to vehicles of war, for four-wheeled devices of every shape, style, variety, and class. Now only flopbusses, cargo, and security patrols—any of which could notice me here to-night—make any use of them.

I hurry to the middle island, then press on across the final two lanes. I spot a broken-down bus stop, a relic from the past. Most of the glass is gone or cracked, the benches bare and splintery. I make for it; stoop low as I pass it. The downrider cable goes down a block and then cuts left. I scramble as best I can, find relief as I make the turn into a narrower street.

I hear a whirring sound behind me, something that has entered the ancient paved highway. I peek back to see a dark security ride—a two-seater model. It is distant enough that I might have avoided it. A second later, when a spotbeam lights the street I just left, I know I have not. I hike my skirt again and run. My bare legs feel the chill.

I hear an alarm, a *whoop-whoop* sound. The ride goes screaming past, not turning my way. Thankfully not turning. I glance up at the cable again—making sure it is still there, I guess. A false sense of security. I don't slow my gait at all. I keep looking up, looking ahead, and running.

Another turn, another unfamiliar alley. This one is slightly cleaner than the others. There is less trash, less reek of humanity. I see another supporting pylon, at the passage's far end. I quicken my step, breathing hard. The pylon has a lighted portion, about midway up. That's a good sign. In the distance I hear another *whoop-whoop*, and I jump. Feel my temples pound. I'm so nervous, so very afraid. And I'm so far from home now, alone, unescorted.

Looking to my right, I spot a half piece of yellow brick. A remnant of better days. I stoop to pick it up. It feels good in my hands. Cool and strong. A few more harried steps and I reach the pylon. Below the light, mounted horizontally, is an emergency com device. I know this because the skin—the debugger—mentioned fixing one once. Why such a device would be needed for someone with an implant is beyond me. Perhaps it is a throwback to better times, as well.

I take aim, focus, take aim again...and throw. The halfbrick spirals awkwardly, travels three-quarters of the distance before striking the pylon and falling to the ground. Harmless. With a glance back, and a full check of the alley, I search for the brick again. I find it amid a pile of grease-slicked paper. I pick it up, examine the surface, now slightly greased itself—and frowning—raise it again.

I need to throw harder.

Again I focus and aim. Tense my shoulder, pull my right arm back...

Release!

The brick goes higher this time, travels straighter. I bring my hands together expectantly. I hear a thud, a clang, then a welcome *plikzzz*. The mounted light dims and begins to flash softly.

I've done it!

The security sirens wail again, and this time closer. Much closer. I shrink back against the nearest wall, into the shadows. And wait. I *must* wait.

Many minutes go by. I hear nothing, see nothing. The pit of my stomach aches with worry. The stench in the alley seems to subside, to grow familiar. Another alarm, further away this time. The light above simply blinks and blinks. For the second time, I recognize the chill of the night. A shiver consumes me. I pull my coverings closer, tighter. More time passes, hours it seems.

Then I hear the whine of a downer in motion. It is distant, but I think it is getting closer. Seems to be getting closer. I draw very still, temporarily halt my shivering, so I can listen. *Worrr-eee* the downer screams, drawing closer. Looking up, I imagine I see the cable sag a little with the additional weight. In actuality, the cable is probably too far away to perceive any motion, but hope has a way of changing your view. I know this from my days in school. From my time with the debugger.

Just like that, the downrider arrives. A one-hump model, colored green—like the ContraMech symbol—pulls to a stop within climbing distance of the pylon. Lights reflect off its surface, shine brightly in the canopy's transparent section. The canopy slides open and I see a bald head, a debugger's head. *For sure.* He surveys the area, not seeing me, and after retrieving something from the floor, exits the downrider, climbing out onto the pylon's service pod. It looks like a dangerous descent to me, but he is probably used to it. No longer finds it dangerous. He crouches down, the blinking service light making his head more noticeable. Shiny.

I walk from the shadows slowly, tentatively, as if I'm trying to catch a butterfly. Again I hear sirens, a discordant night symphony. The debugger doesn't appear to notice the sound. He is already locked into a struggle with "spoilage" as he would call it. The need to get things right, make them work. I wonder if he was wired that way before the implant.

Probably.

As I reach the foot of the pylon, my foot connects with a piece of trash—a dull piece of metal. This causes the debugger to look around quickly, all directions. He looks down, straight at me. Surprise fills his face.

Quickly I draw the scarf from my face. "It's me!" I say.

Even from this distance I can see his eyes widen. "My little hardware holder?" he asks. "The girl who thinks sheets look like taffy, like flexible candy?"

"Yes," I say, smiling. "Of course."

His face doesn't change. In fact, it looks more frightened now. "What are you doing here? There's a curfew—" He breaks off, brings a hand to his head. "I need to report you."

"No," I say. "Don't do that. I just...I didn't know who else to talk to."

He scans the area again, looking nervous. "So, you're alone out here? No chaperone, no nothing? You know how late it is?"

"Yes, I know," I say. "I ran away."

"Ran away? Are you looped?" He raises both hands to his head this time, squints, gives a little shake. "This goes beyond the shop, girl..."

I go into plead mode. "You don't understand. My mother—my father is dead, I told you, and my mother wants to marry me to one of his cousins. A very fat, very old cousin. Who smells!"

He shakes his head. "What can I possibly do about that?" A look of pain crosses his face, and he moves closer to the pylon's girth, turns from me, and clutches the ladder rung there. "I'm sorry, little hard one. I have to call."

I hear another siren and a chill runs through me. "What did you do?" I ask.

"I had to call," he says. "Had to. Or it will hurt. Bad."

I put my scarf back in place, and feeling cold again, pull my hijab around me. I want to run, but I know I cannot. "There's nothing I can do then," I say. The *whoop, whoop, whoop* is back, growing closer. "If I go home, I am lost. If I stay, I am also lost."

"I'm a debugger," he says. "I'm a tool. You knew that..." He is struggling still, I can tell. Even with having called them. I remain fixed in place.

"What can I possibly do for you?" he implores. "What?"

I only shrug. It is all I can do. And it keeps the shivering at bay.

Bright lights shine past me, over me, to the side of me. I hear footsteps, a deathly clapping. With a last glance up, I turn and face the lights. They almost overwhelm me with their brightness.

"Girl!" the mutaween yells. "Why are you here? It is forbidden."

I say nothing. Nothing would matter. There are two of them. They are very hairy and dressed in the traditional brown coverings. There are dark turbans around their heads.

"You must come with us now!" One reaches out a hand for my shoulder. Grips it tightly. I'm pulled toward him. His nails are rough, and they dig into me.

"No..." A voice from behind me, still pained, but firm.

I glance back. The debugger is there. He has a portion of his coverings pulled over his head, and he is bent forward slightly. "She is with me," he says, almost whispering.

The lights find his face. "With you? Aren't you a DR?" The two men look at each other. "How can she be with you?"

"I am sick," he says, and I believe it. He points upward. "There is spoilage here, the com unit is broken. I needed someone to support me."

The mutaween handle me roughly, pulling me closer. "No, that is not possible. She is in violation. She is out past curfew, and she is unescorted." Meaning no male family member is with me. The truth, of course.

The debugger stoops a little lower, and I swear I hear him hiss. "No," he says. "She's with me. She's...my sister."

The mutaween look at each other again. "You have proof of this?"

The DR pulls himself straight, looks them square in the eye. "I am a debugger for ContraMech, and I need no other proof. Now leave before I report you for interfering with my assignment."

And surprisingly, they do.

WITHOUT THINKING, I take a handful of dessert and shove it into my mouth. The sourness makes the glands at the back of my throat tingle, but it is worth it. The sugar is really what I need. To keep me happy, and to dispel the craziness HardCandy has fed me.

"So what do you think?" she asks.

I remain silent, and looking upward, enjoy the flavor burst within. The ceiling is a sky blue.

"Rails, Sand, say something."

I finally swallow, vanishing most of the taste from my mouth. Which is a blinking shame. "What could I possibly say?" I ask. "That you're looped?" I shrug. "You already think I argue too much."

"You do," she says. "But that's a different thread." She points her fork at me. "I could be right, couldn't I? You brought us here. You supposedly had this message from above?"

"I'm not a holy anything," I say, raising my voice. "In fact, I don't even know what that word means anymore."

"Maybe that's okay," she says. "Maybe you don't *need* to know the definition."

"Seriously," I say. "According to our writings, the founder's writings, you are holy if the scales tip in your favor, right?"

"Yes, I suppose," she says, nodding. "Yeah, I think that's right."

"So, as a practical matter, that might mean 50.1 percent good actions versus 49.9 percent bad actions, correct?"

"Right..."

"So, really that definition of holy only means 50.1 percent holy, because if you were .1 percent the other way, you'd be considered unholy. In fact, that .1 percent would mean the wrath of A is upon you, because he hates the unholy. Am I still right?"

She takes her fork to the plate, jabs something there. "Yes, that's all old news. We both grew up with it."

"But what percentage of holy do you think A is?"

HardCandy eases back in her seat. "Why, 100 percent, of course. All holy."

"Doesn't that seem wrong somehow?" I ask. "How can a 100 percent anything consider someone who is only 50.1 percent equal to them in holiness? How can that possibly be true? When does 50.1 percent—or even 80 percent—ever equal 100 percent? Or to look at it differently, what percentage of holiness would you say Paradise contains?"

Hard takes a bite of bread, clearly thinking again. "All of it. Since it is Paradise it must be by definition all good, all holy."

"And yet," I say, "I'm going to be able to walk into Paradise being less than all holy?" I shake my head. "I mean, wouldn't that spoil it?"

Hard shrugs. "I guess that is just one of A's mysteries."

I sniff. "Well, that helps!" I smile. "Really."

"Seriously, you're thinking about it too much," Hard says. "You had your rules lifted by something. You've been chosen, so that must mean you're holy enough to be free."

"Okay, yeah, I'm chosen! So what did I do with my newfound holiness?" I ask. "I sent a person to his death—"

"Accidentally," Hard corrects. "It was *his* choice."

"Regardless," I say, "I scared him, so it was on me. Plus I stole a ship, I brought us here, and now I've stranded us. Maybe even contacted beings that we're not supposed to contact. Does that sound like the work of a holy man?"

Hard shrugs, goes back to her chewing. "I don't know."

"Well, I'm sure that it at least puts me a tenth of a percent below where I need to be. I'm guessing that murder and theft have a fairly heavy weight in the scales."

Hard replies softly. "Scripture says that even the founder used to pray for his faults..."

"And what does that indicate?" I ask. "Was *he* unsure of his holiness too?"

Hard puts out a hand to touch mine. "I didn't know you cared so much."

"Of course I care. I *have* to care." I throw out my arms. "I'm here! Wherever or whatever here is!" I reach for more dessert, shake my head. "For some reason..."

"For good reason!" Hard says. "I think."

"Is this about scattering and gathering again, because I really don't—"

"I don't know what for," she says. "I just think—hope—it is good." She smiles again. "Like all this food."

Feeling full already, I stretch back, absently look around. "You ate meat," I say. "I just realized...most debuggers don't..."

"I know," she says, smiling. "I'm special that way." She shrugs. "Plus most do it because of the intensity of the tasks, the streaming." She searches the room too. "Haven't had much of that lately, have we?"

"No," I say. "I'm beginning to miss it."

A nod. "Me too. But as for the meat, the way this is prepared it is like pure head fuel. It is the slop the Abbys put on it that hurts you. Makes you sick."

"Huh." I contemplate trying some of the animal protein myself. I weigh the heaviness in my midsection, though, and decide against it. Plus there's the reanimated bones possibility. "Should I call back our friends?"

Hard smiles mischievously. "You mean you don't want to bathe first?"

I look over my shoulder, back at the room with the pool. "I can't imagine what that would feel like. I'm so used to steamers." On Earth public bathing is long since disallowed. Plus, I'm fairly certain that HardCandy doesn't want to bathe. At least, she didn't when her jinn were around.

"Yeah, it would be different," she says. "It has been a long time for me."

"That's right, you've swum before..."

"When I was very little," she says. "My father would take us to the beach. It was very far away, and must have cost a lot, but we did it on more than one occasion. Always had to wear the full coverings, of course..."

Suddenly the freedom of my lack of rules itches at me. Reminding me I can now do whatever I want. I stand up. "So maybe we should," I say. "Try it out." I hold out a hand.

HardCandy blushes. "You aren't serious," she says. "I mean, you would drown."

"Drown..." I look toward the pool room and raise an eyebrow. "You think I would?"

She smiles. "Well, maybe not. *If* the water isn't too deep...or too cold." Nervously, she lowers her head. "But I don't know if we...rails, what would we wear?"

I look at the red suits we're wearing, *have worn* since we left the ship. For vacuum suits they are surprisingly comfortable. No wonder the former owners could wear them as long as they had. "What's wrong with what we have on?" I ask.

Hard looks shocked. "That's all we have!"

"No," I say. "I mean, under these suits—our jumpsuits. We could wear those, and then put these back on."

"You mean, with us all wet?"

"Clark and crichton," I say. "Who's over-thinking things now?"

The nervous head bob again. "Sorry..."

"I'm sure your jinn have clothing we can wear. They seem interested in you, anyway, so if they don't have something I'm sure Shem, or maybe Japheth, will be glad to make something. I'll message them as soon as we're done." I stretch my hand out again. "So what do you say?"

Hard looks at my face, then lowering her eyes, studies my hand. Her own hands are beneath her legs, trapped. But she rocks slightly in her chair. Finally, with a simple smile, she rises.

"You better not splash," she says.

THE FEELING IS...INCREDIBLE.

The pool is shallow, perhaps only four feet at its deepest. For which I am grateful. Stepping in, recognizing the wetness on my skin, the subtle chill of it, the complete encircling—first of my foot, then my legs, then my body below the waist. It is frightening...and exhilarating...and humbling all at once. "I'm under attack!" my body screams. "The danger is real. It is everywhere! I'm being suffocated."

But I am not. I am only wet. Similar to the steamer, but more concrete, more consistent. More meaningful somehow.

And the whole time, HardCandy watches me. Sometimes she smiles, sometimes she looks concerned or nervous. A few times she almost looks hurt. But always is she here, watching. Not close, but available. Occasionally she takes a synchronized stroke or brings dripping hands up to stroke her upturned face, delighting in the sensation.

That part, of course, is a first for her too. Being able to wet her head, unfettered, uncovered...un-judged. She even submerges herself completely once, surfacing with tiny rivulets traveling down her head like dew from a morning leaf. I'm reminded of her childhood desire to swim at the beach uncovered.

It is a new time. A special time. And like nothing else, the experience makes me appreciate the jinn—or whatever they are. I want them to be good, hoping now to somehow assimilate into their world. First, because I think we may have no choice, but also because it is a good world. It must be. It gave me the pool.

And the dessert. Don't forget that.

When we are finished, both HardCandy and I stand on the edge of the pool shivering, garments clinging to us uncomfortably. She hunches over a bit from the chill. I feel slightly tired, but otherwise, excellent.

"Did the temperature in here just change?" HardCandy asks. She straightens some and I realize that she is right—it has warmed noticeably.

"Maybe the room realizes we left the pool?" I ask. "Customization?" I search the boundaries of the room. The outlying ring of marbleized pillars.

"That's impressive," she says. "And tough."

"Yeah," I say. "That's a system I don't want to fix when it breaks."

She smiles. "Do you want to call them now?"

"I will," I stream her, then toss up a message for Ham to catch. A simple "Come get us" with the addition of "and could you bring some dry clothing?"

Scarcely ten minutes later all three of our welcoming committee arrive. In his arms Ham has replacement clothing, made out of the same membrane material that they wear. He holds one out to me. It is a muted gold color.

"These are what you would call stream aware," he says. "The color is completely adjustable, as is the tensile strength and opaqueness."

"Thank you," I say, and taking the clothing, look toward the adjoining dining room. "I'll go in there to change."

Japheth cocks his head. "Why would you do that?"

I'm beginning to think these "jinn" are not as bright as their technology makes them appear. I stream as much to HardCandy, who responds with more jinn trivia: "Jinn are thought to have significant lower intelligence than humans, but are physically stronger. Be careful!"

I glance at HardCandy, shake my head, and turn to Ham again. Notice his biceps. "Um, because I don't want to strip off here," I say. "In front of everyone."

Ham smiles softly. "Because of the exposure, correct? Uncomfortable feelings?"

I nod. Resist rolling my eyes.

Shem waves a hand. "Yes, yes, we are aware of all that," he says, showing bright teeth. "That is not why Ham asks." Glancing at Ham he shakes his head. "He needs to be less subtle." Shem makes a two-fisted lifting motion. "Hold the material up to your body, Sandfly."

I take the top edge of the clothing, which looks like loosefitting pants, and lower it to my waist. "Like this?" I ask.

"Yes," he says. "But hold it right up next to you."

I touch the material to my still-wet clothing. Alarmingly, it seems to stick there, even as I try to pull it away. "What is it?" The material dissolves through my earthly clothing entirely. I soon feel a tickling sensation as it recomposes itself right next to my skin. My normal clothing seems to bulge slightly.

"Okay," I say. "That's a bit odd."

"Yes," Shem says. "Well, the clothing you came in appears to lack any real customization. Do you wish to keep it on as well? Otherwise, you may strip it off at any time. I will instruct your new clothing to compress to make that easier."

Doubtful, I undo the fasteners on my jumpsuit and drop it from me. Beneath—thankfully covering everything important—is the jinn material in an opaque mode. As soon as my clothing are out of the way it relaxes itself, becomes a bit puffy like the jinn's own pants.

I guess that's the style.

Hard has also allowed her jinn material to melt through her clothes. She stands with a wide-eyed expression and a hand resting on her belly, as if by surprise. "Oh, my," she says.

"You may remove your previous clothing as well," Ham says. "If you like."

"I would like," she says. "But I don't think I can."

Now Shem looks confused. "Is your clothing not performing correctly? Are you not sufficiently covered?"

Hard looks at me, imploringly.

I glance down at my own bare chest. Raise an eyebrow. "It's the..." I circle a hand over my torso. "...isn't it?"

Blushing again, she nods. Glances sideways at the pool.

"Do you have another piece of wonder material?" I ask. "One that she can use..." I resist the urge to point at HardCandy herself, but instead point at my own—very white—trunk. "Here?" I look down

123

and frown. "Actually, can you bring one for me too? I'm not comfortable without a shirt, really."

Shem chuckles. "Easily remedied." He squints a bit, as if he's sending a message, and a few seconds later my pants begin to reshape themselves, growing into a one-piece outfit that covers from neck to ankle. Somehow, almost miraculously, I stay covered throughout the entire process.

Hard's hand is at her chest now. "That seems better," she says, smiling. She tentatively eases away her old clothes, her blue jumper falling to the floor. Beneath it, the jinn outfit is revealed. It is bright pink.

"What is this?" Hard says, looking down. Her palms hover over her sides as if she's been splashed with hot liquid. A scowl rules her face. "Was it this color when you gave it to me?"

Shem eyes show concern. "The material attempts to judge personal preference based on body type and temperature. Is it not to your liking?"

"Personal preference?" she says. "Seriously?"

The three jinn look at each other, seeming lost. "Is there a physical reason for this reaction?" Japheth asks. "A malady?"

"I don't think she likes it," I say, smiling. "Maybe something more...understated?"

HardCandy looks at my chest. "Something like he has, but less shiny."

Shem's face changes, softens—looks like it is working again. Immediately the color of Hard's outfit changes too, becoming a sandy color. Her face changes, as well; the scowl replaced by a warm look of satisfaction. "And I thought nanoswarm heating was rads."

I sniff. "Even when it worked," I say, "it wasn't that cool."

Hard squints at me. "Is that a joke?" she asks. "Like a pun?"

"I didn't mean..." I look at the three jinn, who stare at me blankly. "Never mind," I say, shaking my head. "Now that we're refreshed, what do you have planned for us? Is there a grand tour, or an examination by your doctors, a meeting with your ruling council or whatever? Because if so, I think I'd like to pass. It has been a long day, and neither alternative seems appealing."

Hard nods her agreement.

I scan the room again, wondering if there is a place to sit. Or even recline a little. Nothing but pool and pillars.

"A grand tour?" Shem says, looking puzzled. "Whatever for?"

"Well, you know, so all your luminaries..." I pause, and thinking about the city walls, smile at the word choice. "Isn't there anyone who would like to meet us?" I ask. "I mean, I would imagine there is some curiosity..." Shem's expression doesn't change.

I spread my hands out. "If you came to our world, all the masters would gather to investigate. And the Imam would be there too, of course."

"I assure you," Shem says, "no one's curiosity in this city will go unmet. They have us to represent them."

"Oh..." I narrow my eyes. "So you've been streaming everything so far?"

Shem bows his head. "That is correct. And will continue to do so if that is acceptable."

I feel the weight of sudden notoriety on my shoulders, an emotion usually reserved for only spiritual leaders in our world. The focus of my own streamcast? I don't like it. I mean, I just took my first bath. Had that been streamcast too?

"Is it necessary?" Hard's face is ashen.

We're tools, remember? We are used to hiding on heavy machinery or behind closed doors. Where no one will notice.

"It is how our society functions," Ham says. "Is it that foreign to you?"

"Not in concept," I say. "But in function? Yeah. Real foreign."

"You mentioned doctors," Japheth says. "Is that a constructor or a reclaimer?"

Raising a finger, I attempt to access the jinn's stream. It is a fairly bland bit of babble—digital rice pudding. The functionality for messaging is clearly in place, but the rest of it—the wealth of references and interpretations I'm used to—are nowhere to be found.

Or I don't know how to look. It is like the difference between a bath and the steamer, I realize—full immersion versus casual interaction. It is a major drawback, because I would like to understand what the words Japheth said meant to him. Finally, I give up.

"How do you know how to speak to us?" I ask.

Japheth starts. "Vocal cord manipulation?" he says. "It isn't that complicated."

"No," I say. "I mean, how is it you know our language? How is it we can manipulate your stream?"

"Your ship," Ham says. "It was a fair repository of information for us."

"But it is shielded," I say. "Encrypted."

Ham smiles. "The distortion was a security precaution? We never imagined." He looks at Shem. "We thought it a game."

"Regardless," Shem says, frowning, "it was a useful resource. Between the two arrivals we were able to acquire everything we needed."

"So your planet was here when the ship came before?" I ask. "Our ship thought differently."

"Your ship was mistaken," Shem says. "Sorry. This is a planet. Where else would it be?"

"Yes," I say. "Well, I wondered that too..." A sideways glance at HardCandy, who only shrugs. "So from the ship you were able to understand our language and our stream."

"Yes," Shem says. "We were delighted to find similarities between the vessel transmissions and those we had sifted from the cosmic background."

"The background?" Hard asks.

"Yes," Shem says. "The universe is full of emanations of all varieties. Certainly you know this. One of these emanations is pervasive and even. We call it the background."

I remember that we are still standing next to the pool. It seems like a strange place for an intergalactic discussion. "Is there somewhere else we could go?" I ask. "Maybe with seats?"

Ham shakes his head. "Why go anywhere?" He nods and the room begins to transform around us. The pool is quickly obscured by a floor that by any measure looks exactly like the marble flooring around it. Three of the walls go from fairly blank, if textured, white surfaces, to ones with bright colors and artwork. The fourth grows what appears to be vidscreens—or windows—with a view of rolling green hills, images, perhaps, of the surface of the planet above. Birds can be seen in flight.

The room's sudden transformation reminds me of the virtual worlds that some stream-users frequent on Earth. There anything is possible, because the worlds ultimately resolve to simple numerical values, binary data. But here? Are such large-scale transformations even physically possible? I look at HardCandy and wonder. Is it possible that none of this is real either? That we are still asleep in our chutes or under the influence of alien technology...

I start a sanity check on my implant to be sure. After only a few nanoseconds it reports everything being normal and that I *am* conscious. Trepidation enfolds me. The tech these creatures use is so sophisticated it is dangerous. We have no defense against it, no way to free ourselves if they chose to keep us. I don't know that they are truly genies or jinn, but for all intents and purposes they might as well be. Stay loose here, Sand. Keep your guard up.

Dark seats grow from the floor, and while they appear rigid to the naked eye, I'm guessing they will feel extremely comfortable.

"Rails," HardCandy streams me. Looking at her, I see her eyes still blinking with surprise.

And something else. She isn't sending FI, but if she was, I know what her feeling would be, because I'm feeling it too. Overwhelmed and afraid.

"This would make a master happy," I stream back. I walk to a seat and take it. As I suspected, it is more than adequate in support and comfort. Hard and the three "jinn" take seats as well, though I doubt the latter really require the rest. Their bodies speak of endurance.

"Now," Shem says, reclining in his chair and crossing a leg in front of him. "What would you like to know?"

THE EXPERIENCE OF MY FIRST ADVENTURE with Grim-Jack returns to me. The mad rush attempting to skate back to the downer pylon, the scream of the downer's engines, the distinct smell of petrochemical in the air, the vibrating drop of the downer string as it responded to the oncoming weight. The dark shadow of death, the bright smile of the passengers inside...

"Is this the only city like this?" HardCandy asks. "Beneath the planet, I mean?"

Shem shakes his head. "There are others," he says. "Two hundred and fifty-seven, to be precise. All are connected, however, and in many places it is difficult to determine where one city ends and the next begins."

"All your cities are belowground then?" I say.

Ham nods. "That is correct."

"Why?" Hard asks. "Why would you let the surface go to waste?" She looks wistfully toward the vidscreen windows. "It is so beautiful."

"But harder to control," Ham says, smiling. "Harder to maintain."

Shem, who regardless of what we've been told, still seems like the leader to me—perhaps because of his personality—shrugs aggressively. "In the past that was true. Much of our designs are in some ways remnants of that past. For instance it is easier for us to control some things now than it has been, due to constructor invention."

"Constructor?" I ask, wanting to use the stream again for answers, but knowing it will get me nothing.

Shem shakes his head. "My apologies, I believe we've lost something in translation. There are three primary designations in our society: constructor, maintainer, and reclaimer." He motions toward the other jinn. "Each of us represents one of those designations."

"And these are occupational designations?" Hard says.

Ham smiles. "Primarily," he says. "But they permeate all our life here."

I touch my scalp, think of the life we escaped. "We have similar designations," I say. "Though none so clearly defined."

Japheth bows his head. "We imagined as much. We noticed your follicle gilding is quite different than those that preceded you."

"So you observed the earlier pilots," I say, "yet didn't approach them?"

"They were incomplete," Shem says. "Not ready."

"In what way?" Hard asks.

"They lacked the proper interface," Ham says, and points toward his head. "Your implant, correct? The device that makes you stream aware."

"Yes," I say. "Most of our kind doesn't have one." I look at Hard. "We're special."

"You are used as a maintainer," Ham says. "As I am."

"If I understand the term," I say, "then yes."

Shem raises a finger. "I believe he straddles our castes," he says. "I believe he is a constructor as well."

I shrug my shoulders. "Depends on what you mean."

"Someone who creates things," Shem says. "Someone who gives an object its priming essence."

"Some of us do that," HardCandy says. "Sometimes we have to."

Shem smiles, looks at the others. "See, it is as I said."

Ham only shakes his head, but Japheth notably scowls. "I would guess they do reclaimer work as well," the latter says. "Though such diversity must lead to inefficiency. Must lead to errors."

"I would guess no more than your band of slack," Shem says. At this, Japheth grits his teeth and actually rises from his seat. The muscles on his chest and arms seem to come alive.

Ham puts out a hand. "Let's not resurrect old wounds," he says. "Our guests have questions. Let's continue what was started."

Japheth stares at Shem for a long minute before finally seating himself again. Without moving, I message HardCandy: "Guess everything isn't perfect in paradise."

"Jinn are supposed to be similar to us in nearly every respect," she streams back. "That would include anger and conflict. What I wonder is, do they follow A? That would define their character. The founder's own jinn were supposed to have converted to our faith after hearing the sacred writings."

I send her an image of me frowning followed by an eye roll. She seems determined to make everything we've encountered fit with what we've both been taught. But I know—we're way beyond what we were taught already. In fact, ever since a bot started quoting forbidden and thought-to-be-corrupted scripture at me I've been living where the map ends.

And I'm still no closer to what I came searching for, not really. Did these creatures compose the superlative stream? And if so, why was the crew affected? Especially if they were "not ready" as Shem stated?

"Your stream," I begin, with a private "here goes nothing" message to HardCandy. "It seems quite limited compared to what we're used to."

Shem glances at the other two and sighs. "Yes, we apologize for that. What you're experiencing is a visitor stream we constructors have created. It is severely limited. Hardly useful actually, aside from rudimentary functions. You can control the doors and windows of your apartments, of course, and communicate...but the resources, the building blocks, are withheld." Shem crosses one leg over the other and rests one hand loosely in his lap. The other arm he slings over his chair back. That hand works the air as he talks. "It is not our way, usually nothing is hidden." A smile. "But these are unusual circumstances."

"So it is a security stop of some sort," I say, nodding. "Perfectly reasonable when meeting with..." I look at HardCandy and smile..."aliens."

Japheth shakes his head. "It is not a security measure. It is for your own protection. Without a close examination, we wouldn't know the limits of your appliance."

"Tell them about the templates," Ham says. "There is no reason to withhold that."

Shem's eyes show anger, but only briefly. "He is right, of course," he says, then looks thoughtfully at the foot of the crossed leg. "The templates...how to say it?" A smile. "Ah, I know. Think of them as interfaces to the stream. They control how information is shown. Again, it breaks down along caste lines. A constructor sees the stream very differently than a maintainer, or a reclaimer."

"I think I see," I say. "Three pipes to the same pool?"

Ham nods vigorously. "Very right," he says. "A good analogy."

HardCandy, who sits with both legs crossed in her seat, says, "It makes perfect sense. The stream customized for various users."

"Yes," Ham says again. "Customized."

Looking at the vidscreen "windows," I see a group of animals walking into view. They are black in color and appear to be the size of a small downrider—maybe three meters in length. Instinctively I stand and move toward the screens. The images of the creatures are very fine, and as I move closer, more specific features are revealed. They appear bison-like, yet with purple horns that point forward. Their ears—I assume they are ears—are noticeably bigger too. Not quite the size of elephant ears, but much bigger than anything in the bovine family. "Is this real?" I ask, with a glance back at Shem. "I mean, is this playing out on the planet's surface right now?"

"It is," Ham says. "Somewhere in the twenty-second quadrant, I believe."

"Which is?" HardCandy has moved up silently behind me, and speaking, startles me.

"Temperate zone area on the largest continent," from Ham.

She smiles and nods, now seemingly engrossed in the pastoral scene. I'm enjoying it too, of course, but it reinforces the fact that we are many kilometers underground. Not really free.

The horned creatures graze slowly. The "herd" must be large, because though a hundred creatures are in view, two or three more stroll into the picture from the right every few seconds. As five more join the group I notice something peculiar on one particular animal. It seems to have a large hump on its back.

"I wonder what that is." I mutter, and draw closer to the screen.

"What is *what*?" HardCandy asks. She moves closer too, but it is clear she doesn't know what I'm looking at. I halfheartedly point in the direction of the animal I'm following, while watching her face. I'm certain what I'm seeing now, you see. The omnivore has a rider—a stout brown three-limbed creature, similar to the one I saw from the flying rectangle.

Hard continues to look, finding nothing. "Where?" she says. "What is it?"

There is no way she could miss what I'm seeing. No way.

"See that animal there?" I say, pointing more directly this time.

She nods, looks at me. "Yes, Sand, what of it?"

I check the image again, just to make sure the triped is still there. It is. When I called it "triped," I wasn't mistaken. The thing has three limbs. Total. Two arms—the hands of which appear to grip the mane of the herd animal—and a single, wide-yet-stumpy leg below the waist. Not sure how that is keeping him on the animal, but somehow it is. The head of the creature is round, but not completely so. It has a lumpy, chiseled-from-rough-stone, character about it.

I turn to the group of jinn—a designation I find myself using automatically now. "Curious," I say. "Is there another intelligent creature on this planet?"

"Intelligent in what way?" Japheth asks. "There are both aquatic and amphibious creatures able to learn rudimentary commands. In the past, we have found both useful for experimentation and training."

Play it safe, Sand. You don't know what this is.

I nod. "Interesting." I return my attention to the screen. My mounted triped is still there. "Can these zoom in?" I ask. "I'd like to see those animals close up."

"Of course," Shem says. "It is there for you to control."

For an instant, I feel like a new implant again—forgetting what should now come natural. I drift into the jinn-stream then, search for the controlling mechanism for the screens that are right in front of me. It isn't the sound of singing nanos I hear, precisely...but there *are* voices—call them murmurs—that seem to come at me from all directions. There is also a certain, for lack of a better description, *taste* to the mechanisms. The bank of vidscreen windows are in the sweet end of the spectrum. Think of the fruit section of the store, and you have a pretty good idea of what I feel. I grab the nearest sweet and pull it toward me.

The image on the screen magnifies. The herd animals aren't covered in fur as I originally thought. Looks like rows of tiny leaves, actually. Subtly, I pan the image, first to the left, as if I'm simply scanning the herd, then back toward my actual target. After a few seconds of slow investigation, I find my animal again. It is an easy find—the triped is still sitting on top of it.

There is a rough, lumpy quality to his skin, I see. He wears a dark wrap around his waist, but other than that, is completely naked. Similar to Shem and his gang. I pull the image in a little more and pan up, toward the creature's head. As the lump that I *think* is his ear reaches the center of the screen, the triped turns suddenly. *And looks straight at me.* His eyes are dark as a pool of petrol, and seemingly full of intelligence. I find myself completely hypnotized...

I shake my head and gasp. Pull myself out of it.

"What is it?" Shem asks. He and Ham have moved up to stand behind me now. I almost bump into Ham as I turn.

I force a smile. "I'm a little unused to your controls," I say. "Nothing significant."

The two exchange a look. "We were afraid of that," Ham says. "It was difficult to predict your capabilities..."

I shake my head. "I'm completely fine." I look at the screens again to find them panning and zooming, seemingly on their own. Smiling, I glance at HardCandy. "Couldn't resist, huh?"

"Like to dabble," Hard says, concentrating on the panorama in front of her. "That's my nature."

"And are the controls sufficient for you, HardCandy?" Japheth asks. "You can use them as well as the male?"

The male?

Squinting, she jerks her head back cockily. "Smooth as can be," she says. "No worries." A sideways grin. "Not sure what *his* problem is..."

Japheth only nods. "Excellent. We were most worried about you."

Now Hard looks miffed. "What?" she cries. "Why would you be worried about me?"

I can't help but smile. Plus, her discomfort diverts from the real reason I reacted to the vidscreen. The real reason my insides are churning: am I now seeing things that no one else sees?

"Every system has its own demand," Japheth says, "its own requirements." He looks at me and smiles. "And even the smallest of variations can be important."

"Oh, I see," Hard says. "So you customized it with him in mind, then added me as an afterthought, is that it?"

Japheth looks to me for help. Like I would give it. I shrug. "Not precisely," he says.

"Well, as you saw, *he's* the one with the variations," Hard says. "*He's* the one who needs help."

She may be more right than she knows...

"Burroughs and bradbury," I say. "Do you have to take everything personal?"

Hard crosses her arms. "I'm not taking it personal. I'm..." her brow lowers and her eyes seem to lance me. "Did you see what you wanted? What you were looking for?"

"Sure," I say. "Those animals have unusual coverings. I wanted to examine them closer."

She stares at me silently for a full five seconds, squinting. "Well...all this only makes me want to go outside again myself. To look around. Feel the air." She turns toward the others. "Is that possible?"

Shem smiles. "You are not prisoners here, you are guests. You may explore as much as you like." A pause. "Though topside is difficult to control. More dangerous." The smile returns. "Freedom introduces risk, as I'm sure you are aware."

Ham's face is unreadable. "Transportation would not be a problem. It can be arranged anytime you want it. However..." a glance at Shem..."there is a storm brewing above the nearest portal. You would be wise to postpone your exploration for now."

"A little rain," Hard says, smiling. "I don't see that as a difficulty."

"It is more than rain," Japheth says. "Storms here are fairly violent."

"Regardless, it is nighttime," Shem adds.

"Not everywhere," Hard says. "You said the cities were connected."

"They are—"

"Aren't you tired, Hard?" I ask, incredulous. "I mean, I am..."

Hard tips her head. "You poor, poor debugger..."

Ham nods. "You require sleep," he says. "It is understandable. Advisable."

"Should we reconvene in the morning?" Shem asks. "Sometime after sunup?"

"You can message me again when you are ready," Ham says.

I nod with as much appreciation as I can muster. I *do* feel tired, plus I need time to think. Hard won't let it go, though.

"I was hoping to see more sky," she says. "We need to go out there, Sand. To walk under the sun."

I waffle between fear and excitement over a surface visit. Mostly I'm worried, though. It could prove that I'm in a state that is beyond any before. It goes beyond mere blackouts or difficulty controlling something with my implant. It even makes the random thoughts—the scriptural snippets—I get seem like a minor annoyance. I can't even trust my eyes anymore...

"We will go," I say. "Soon." I force a weak smile. "But right now I need sleep."

Hard turns to the jinn. "Do you have sleeping facilities for us? We need shielding from stream presence. Our ship provides that..."

Shem nods slowly, puts out a hand. "That is no problem. We will instruct your quarters to mute the stream while you sleep." He looks at Ham, who nods in an "I'll make it happen" kind of way.

"It is ready," he says.

"Then we'll leave you," Shem says, pointing. "You'll find that the adjoining room—where you dined—is now ready for slumber." The three walk toward the nearest door, all three standing tall, still moving as if on air.

But not me. I need my sleep, my solitude. The day has been long and eventful.

And I may be crazy.

With a look of trepidation HardCandy walks toward the adjoining room. She pauses at the entrance and brings a hand to her chin pensively.

I walk up to join her. The room has indeed transformed. The food-laden table is completely gone, without a dropped crumb to even indicate it was ever there. The flooring is now a beige and seemingly noise-reducing surface. The walls are a copper color, with a brushed texture. The ceiling lighting is warm, friendly.

Near the center of the room—where the table once stood—are two seemingly rigid white platforms. Waist-high sleeping surfaces, I assume. Beds.

I glance at HardCandy, who has yet to say a word. Thankfully, the room hasn't chosen to create a single bed platform. Because that would be *truly* awkward.

Still, the platforms are only a meter apart...

I glance back to see if our hosts are still with us. They are not. Figures.

"Do you think those are comfortable?" Hard says finally.

I drift toward the surfaces, hesitant—because frankly I don't know how I should act here. Such sleeping proximity among non-relations would never be allowed on Earth. And I know Hard must be thinking the same thing. Or worse. But I really don't want to try to explain our customs to the pseudojinn. And I'm blinking tired now. Beat. Seeing brown tripeds on herd animals.

I walk between the surfaces and—with as much emotional neutrality as I can manage—test one with a hand. "Feels as hard as steel," I say. "But I'm sure it will change when we lay down."

"We?"

"*I!* You—I mean, if either of us...you know...tried it." I give a faint smile. "I'm sure the surface is as customized as the floor of their flying rectangles. Lay on it, and it's soft."

"Soft," she says, still staring at the platforms. Not really looking at me.

I'm not sure how to take that. Maybe I *should* try to explain the situation to Ham, at least. He seems more human, more cognizant. I look at the entrance to the room beyond. Or...

"I could try to sleep in one of the chairs..." I point..."out there."

But I really don't want to. Passing out in Trench's nest was bad enough. I miss my chute, freehead.

HardCandy throws her hands down. "It's fine," she says. "I know you're tired. It's fine." She approaches the surface nearest the door. "You'll sleep there..." she points to the other platform, "and I'll sleep here. It's fine."

"Are you s—"

"It's fine!" She puts both hands on her surface and tests it. Then hoists herself in. Lies rigidly on her back. "It is soft."

I hesitate, but then finally climb into my own bed. I lay on my back too. Though I normally wouldn't. Only a few moments later, the room lights go out completely.

"Oh, look," HardCandy says. "It's dark."

AFTER THE MUTAWEEN HAVE GONE, the debugger walks back toward the pylon, and leaning against it, stares at me for many moments, looking sad.

"Thank you," I whisper. "You saved me."

He shakes his head. "Only momentarily," he says. "There is no easy solution here."

Feeling cold again, I grip the front of my dress. "But you must be able to do something," I say. "You are so smart...so wise."

At this he laughs raucously. "You've learned your lessons well," he says. "Vain flattery works well among Abduls."

I bow my head. "Abdul," I say. "I've used that term before. It seems harsher when I know I'm included in the group."

"I didn't mean to offend," he says, smiling. "That's how we refer to all non-implants. One of the few vices we have."

I hear sirens again, far off, but no less frightening even now. I instinctively look that direction, expecting to see lights, but finding only darkness.

"They aren't for you," the debugger assures. "A thief has been discovered in the street market on Harris." He shakes his head. "No place for a child anymore. It was foolish of his parents to send him there. Crazy dangerous." Another head shake and a dark frown. "And now he'll lose a hand..." The debugger looks off, into the shadowed part of the alley. "Crichton, it only gets worse."

The name is new to me, completely unknown. "Crichton?" I ask.

"An author," he says. "From way back, beyond the date change. Back before such entertainment was against the rules. He often wrote about science gone wrong. He had no idea..."

Puzzlement fills me. "How could you possibly know of such a person?" I ask. "So far back...so foreign?"

The debugger smiles. "Even I have secrets. Places of freedom. The trick is to not think about them." He points at his head. "Otherwise it hurts."

I feel sadness, knowing that tonight he's felt pain on my behalf. "Does it hurt badly?"

"The tweak?" he asks. "It depends on who's holding the controller."

"But aren't there some that come without anyone holding anything?"

He nods. "Yes. Those can be worse," he says. "At least with the controlled ones you have a fair idea when they are coming."

"I am sorry," I say. "But the writings tell us that actions are what counts. Not thoughts."

He bows his head. "So they do. But actions don't matter for me. My way is already set, regardless of what I do."

My eyes widen. "Paradise guaranteed? But I thought there was only one way to guarantee..."

He nods. "Martyrdom, yes." Another bow, this time from the waist. "You are witnessing a martyr. A bald and undead martyr."

My hands find my lips as my child mind processes. "Because you've given up your life," I say finally. "I see."

He smiles. "Not by choice, exactly," he says. "But whose life is really free?"

Thinking of my father's cousin, I shudder, and again pull my dress tighter. "Not me," I say. "Certainly not me."

He tips his head. "That proves my point, little one." He looks upward, following the shape of the pylon to the sky above. The stars have distinguished themselves there now. They twinkle in an array of sharp colors: green, blue, white, and red. They, at least, are free. "So what do we do now?" he asks. "Some action is required, and since those are what matters to you..." he looks at me and smiles. "We better plan well."

My will forces my hand. "I want to be like you," I say. "I want what you have."

"The implant?" he asks. "You should never wish for that."

"But I do!" I say. "I want it more than anything. It is my only chance at freedom."

He squints, shakes his head incredulously. "But we just discussed this. There is no freedom for me. I'm the most imprisoned person on the planet."

I look downward, at the dirty and broken asphalt below me. "Yes, but at least you're a man."

He frowns. "Barely," he says. "Not in the way most men see it." A pause. "Or *women* see it, for that matter."

I think of my incident at the school, the loss of a father, my having disobeyed my mother. "I have many sins," I say. "And I'm only nine. By the time I am your age I will be a lost cause. My bad side will be completely full." A tear escapes from eye to cheek. "I need what you have," I whisper.

The debugger shakes his head. "My implant again?" he asks. "Because of the rules? Because of forced compliance?"

"No," I say. "I need your assurance of Paradise."

There is a very long pause. So long, that I feel maybe he's now angry, or is struggling with reporting me again. But when I glance at him—during those few moments when I'm not locked on the cracks in the ground before me—I see something different in his eyes. I see the beginnings of empathy. And pity.

"Go home," he says.

I look up, now deathly afraid. Feet heavy and useless. I know I will be beaten. "But I cannot," I say, "I'm out—"

"Go home," he repeats, and puts out a calming hand. "And I'll see what I can do."

My hands clasp over my chest. "You would intercede for me? Talk with whoever made you?"

He looks sad again. "I said I would see. That's all I can do."

I bow lowly. "It is all I can ask. All I can pray for."

He turns slightly and reaches up for the pylon's ladder. A look of pain crosses his face. "Go quickly, child. I have work to do."

I can't help but bow again, repeatedly, and with exuberance, all the while backing away down the alley. I would like to hug him, but I know I cannot. I let the smile on my face show my pleasure, even while I move toward the uncertainty of the streets, and the craziness of my home.

"Peace be to you," I say.

He only raises a hand, and turns to ascend.

Like an angel to the sky.

MORNING COMES MUCH LATER than I expected. I set no waking time for myself and so reaped the benefits of my inaction. I awaken to a darkened room, with only the sound of HardCandy's breathing nearby. It takes many nanoseconds to realize where I am, especially with the stream being so muted in my mind. It is the quietest my head has been since my implantation. It is both frightening and wonderful.

Sliding out of bed, I detect a subtle increase in the room's ambient light. Not such that it would awaken anyone from slumber, but enough that I can walk without hurting myself.

I find myself wishing for the pool and something to eat. Which wish weighs higher in my mind is difficult to determine, but after tiptoeing from our room to the one adjoining, I find that both wants have been met. The room that only last night was a lounge with vidscreens has again reverted to a pool, albeit a smaller one, along with a small glass table with two silver chairs. Atop the table is a pitcher of a red drink and bread.

I move to the table and tear off a piece of bread. It is warm to the touch and melts in my mouth. I next sample the drink, finding it slightly tart, but refreshing—and chilled to perfection. The containers of both items must control their temperatures somehow.

I walk to the pool, and with a cautionary glance toward the door leading into *our* bedroom, I disrobe—leaving my borrowed clothing huddled in a mound near the edge—and step in. The temperature is brisk, but somehow also perfect. I take a few slow steps, delighting in the water's movement over my bare skin. As Hard did yesterday, I cup my hands and dump whatever water I can gather over my head and face.

In the Abdul faith, there are many washing exercises, many requirements for ritual bathing, but few involve complete immersion. The three compulsory reasons—conversion, the burial of an infidel, or following sexual relations—have never applied to me. And even for Abduls that *do* engage in such activity, a full body bath is a luxury only observed by masters. A steamer treatment is deemed adequate for the public at large.

The purpose of those baths is to absolve a man's misdeeds...

If even the heavens are not pure in his eyes, how much less man, who is vile and corrupt, who drinks evil like water.

Frowning, I ponder the message. I wonder if it is real—a genuine missive from something larger than myself or simply the internal misfires of a brain in turmoil. I also wonder at its meaning. For most of my life I've been controlled, and consequently unable to do things that would mark me as impure. No more guilty than a horse or goat would be. Yet, I've never *felt* that way. Never felt like my scale was already fully weighted to the good. That everything had been absolved.

Abdul teaching says that angels sit at either shoulder, constantly recording the deeds that are done. One for the good, one for the bad, because apparently, angels don't multitask. Amazing, considering the lesser jinn—if that is what these creatures are—seem more than capable of doing multiple things at once.

What I really wonder, is whether the angels leave their post after someone is implanted. Could the jinn tell me that? Whether the angels are still hanging around me now?

You're drifting again, Sand.

I think of the humans we left on Earth. Of TallSpot, Grackle, BlueTrain, and Handler—the former crew—along with my old friend GrimJack. Where are they now? What has happened to them? What have they done? Are they only waiting for us?

The crew had all been affected by the superlative stream, as I was—as I *am*—but none of them knows precisely what that stream is. So now they're in the unenviable state of knowing that everything about their society is based on a seemingly untrue premise, but they have no way to determine what the real truth is. Like aborigines after having seen an airplane in the sky.

They need me to find an answer. They need me to work!

I risk submersing my whole self under the water, lowering myself until even my head is covered. The enclosed aspect makes me nervous at first, but after a few moments of controlled thought, I am able to open my eyes again. Everywhere I look is distorted—blurred, yet moving—reshaped into unfamiliar patterns.

Yes. It is all a lot like that, isn't it?

I bring my head out of the water again, take a deep, sputtering breath and then, after checking the bedroom door again, quickly climb out of the pool. I retrieve my clothing from the floor and move beyond view of the doorway. I find myself wishing for a towel of some sort. With puckered brow, I hold the clothing up where I can look at it. It still appears clean. I bring it to my nose and smell. Doesn't smell bad either. I hold it to my chest and let it wrap itself around me. I expect it to feel damp with the moisture from my body. But it doesn't. The material somehow managed to remove the water from me as well.

Crazy.

I move to the wall where the vidscreens had been before. I find myself wishing for the outside view again. Could I bring it back if I tried?

I close my eyes. Reach out for our isolated stream, try to picture what the screens were like before. I detect that percolating, murmuring sound again, and feel satisfaction. The sounds, these building block noises, are more spread out now. More even—as if they've become part of the wall. I reach out with my will...

And get a budding response. The rippling motion of results. "More then!" I stream out. "Give me vision!" Rectangles of sound form, along with the same distinct taste I remember. I push, I cajole. I open my eyes to check.

Six viewing screens have emerged. The shapes are a bit distorted. Not precisely rectangular. Almost like children's approximations of geometric shapes. But they are there on the wall. And there is an image on each one. It is of the city outside, I think. Distant pillars of ambient light.

144

I feel worn from the effort. As if the technology in my head, and perhaps my very brain, is no match for the mountain it was trying to move. I wonder if it gets easier with practice.

I hear a sound behind me and turn to see HardCandy standing near the door. She is smiling and looks absolutely radiant, rested.

"Good," she says. "There's food." She makes a shuffling step toward the table—and looking at the bread loaf—glares teasingly. "There's a knife here, you know." I answer with a shrug to which she rolls her eyes, and picking the knife up, shakes it in my direction. "Men..."

I respond with an eye roll of my own. "And you've known how many?"

"My father was a man," she says, mid-chew. "Plus I occasionally have to work with you smellers. You know, fix what you've broken." She looks past me to the wall of misshapen screens. "For instance, what is that?"

"My attempt at beetle vidscreens," I say, raising my shoulders. "It is harder than it looks."

"Beetle?" Hard says, raising an eyebrow.

I shrug. "You know, short for Betelgeuse?"

And because they are blue and sort of *bug* me.

She smiles. Nods at the screens. "Want me to try?"

I shake my head, bracing for whatever comes next. "If you like." I step aside so I can watch. Keeping her eyes open, Hard stares at the screens, with only the occasional eyebrow twitch to signify she's streaming anything. As for the screens themselves, only their edges appear to move, and even then it is only to shake around a little. One screen—which I had successfully formed into a parallelogram with the top side being a tad shorter than the bottom—merely inverts itself.

I smile with satisfaction. Hard doesn't acknowledge my emotion, keeping her eyes fixed to the screen instead. She attempts to rectify the screens' dimensions for a full two minutes before finally closing her eyes and shaking her head. If nothing else, she's persistent.

Her cheeks shrink with the action of gritting teeth. "Rails, Sand," she says. "It's like carrying bags of sand."

"Uh huh."

I examine the image of the city. It is from high above, as if the sending camera is mounted somewhere near the ceiling of the excavation. "We can probably change the view, at least," I say, then attempt to do just that. The image pans slowly, taking in the full breath of the city. It is like a thrown open treasure chest of color. *Ta-da!*

"I'd rather zoom in," Hard says, wrinkling her nose. The image stops its slow pan, centers on the largest structure, and rockets toward it. I feel a bit of vertigo at the movement, even with only a half dozen amorphous screens. The viewing angle changes then, following the curve of the structure, spiraling slowly toward the streets.

"How'd you do that?" I ask.

She doesn't answer, except to shrug and arch her eyebrow twice. The image begins to parallel one of the larger thoroughfares. Flying rectangles of all sizes move along it, perfectly spaced, perfectly in line. There is a sidewalk there too where a scattering of jinn walk—every physique of similar proportions, hairstyles all similar, though the coloring is different.

I notice something else, then.

"Can I control it for a second?" I ask, and then reach into the stream to find HardCandy reluctantly surrendering control. "If you think you can handle it," she says.

I massage the controls, test them, finally discover how Hard managed to shift the image, and then do so myself.

Another camera angle, another part of the city. Here jinn are going about their business too. I see a dozen playing on a circular court, or loitering near a market area. I shift to another sidewalk then, find more pedestrians walking, talking. Next I go to what appears to be a construction site, where groups of blond jinn manipulate large crystal structures into place.

"Do you notice anything?" I ask.

Hard frowns. "Not an overweight one in the bunch," she says.

"Yes," I sniff. "But there is something more fundamental than that here. Look closely..." I point. "I think they're all men!"

Hard scurries to the screen, peers intensely. "Really?" she says. "Show me more."

I take her through eight different locations around the city. In every view the Jannah inhabitants look to be of the same sex. "That would explain why they had their uncertainties about you," I say, looking at Hard. "Why they seem intrigued by the differences. Remember?"

HardCandy nods. "I do..." Her eyes dance across the images. "But, you know, their women could be very slight. Or not real distinctive physically."

Or *real* distinctive. Like ugly, brown, blessed with three appendages, and visible only to me?

I turn back to the vidscreen, squinting. "I don't know..." I've tried to hide it from HardCandy, but ever since we left Earth, ever since the rules were removed from my implant, my ability to distinguish between the sexes has become a lot more acute. Especially when it comes to recognizing the female form in a crowd. And even though there haven't been a lot of examples around to notice—with us living in DarkTrench and all—I still somehow know that none of the jinn that we're seeing are female. "I don't think there are any here," I say. "I would know."

Hard looks at me for a time, squinting. "Hmm...maybe you would." A flash of sadness crosses her face then.

"What?" I say.

She shakes her head and her eyes widen. A smile emerges—forced, I think. "Nothing." Her smile widens then, becoming more genuine. "You'd know." She nods. "Of course you would."

"Not sure what that's supposed to mean," I say. "But it doesn't change my theory." I drift toward the table, and the smell of bread. "So how does that match up with your jinn premise?"

Hard shrugs. "How does that match up with anything? Do they divide asexually then? I mean there appear to be thousands of them—millions even."

I nod. "And they've been here a long time."

"Right," she says. "So they must have some way of procreating."

I draw quiet for a moment, thinking. "It is odd, but it is a diversion. We came here to find the stream," I say. "And we're not learning anything. We really need to ask them about it..."

"But it would be easy for them to claim they created it," Hard says. "Wouldn't it?"

I nod.

"But without knowing their intent?"

"There would be no way to know the validity of what they say," I say. "They have no rules that govern their behavior. At least, that we know of."

"Correct," Hard says, and then smiles. "And apparently no females either." She shakes her head. "Tough for them."

I almost laugh out loud. "Tell me about it."

Hard returns to the table, pours herself a glass of the red juice, and brings it to her lips. "The other thing we have to decide," she says, "is whether your superlative stream matters now at all."

What? Hard must see the look on my face, because she responds immediately. "We're stuck here, right?"

In all the newness of everything, I'd almost forgotten. "Yeah...stuck."

"DarkTrench is dead, we have no other means of transportation....unless you think the blue-skins can fix Trench?"

"I've no doubt they could," I say. "But would we want them to?" I raise a hand. "Again, it is about intentions, isn't it?"

She nods. "And we are completely at their mercy."

I look over at the pool, now placid, inviting. "It is all pretty wonderful," I say, "what they can do...the capabilities. I want it to be good."

"Me too," Hard says, nodding. "But I've learned not to trust."

I remember the images of her life HardCandy shared with me. Her having been promised in matrimony to an oaf of a man. HardCandy escaping into the night air. I can still feel her fear. "I can understand that," I say. "I've been there with you."

Taking a bite of bread, she smiles. "I guess you have," she streams, still chewing. "So what do we do now? What's our course?"

I think about DarkTrench, hanging somewhere above us, his docking door still open and exposed. A tree with a hole in his bark, vulnerable to whatever creature might decide to move in. It still feels like I've abandoned a friend. I remember the jinn's near mocking of Trench's security. "I wonder what all they know," I say. "Already, I mean. If they've gotten to Trench's mind, then everything is exposed. What are their plans for us?"

Hard lapses into silence, still chewing. "They seemed excited to see us. Shem was quite the talker on our way in. He couldn't wait to show me everything."

"So maybe that's what we should do," I say. "See everything."

Hard nods, tips her head. "Still would like to go up," she says. "Get some fresh air."

I shrug. "Wonder if it is still storming."

Hard give me a wink, nods toward the vidscreens. "We could try to look..."

I sniff. I still feel taxed from the last time—and that was just moving the image around the city. "Why don't we ask them instead?"

THE THREE "JINN" RETURN. Shem leads, his blue face aglow. The expressions of the other two are less apparent. Ham appears pleasantly amused, while Japheth is what I would call "mildly respectful" with perhaps a touch of annoyance.

"So, do you still want to go outside?" Shem asks, hands opened expectantly. "Or would you like to see more of our city?" He waves a hand in the direction of the door. "There is an empowerment planned soon that I'm sure you would fi nd entertaining."

"A what?" I ask.

"It is a constructor celebration of sorts," Ham says.

"As well as for maintainers," Shem corrects. "Or should be."

Ham nods reservedly. "And for maintainers as well."

"Any time a masterpiece is revealed for the first time," Shem says, "it should be a time of celebration for everyone involved."

"Yes," Ham says, nodding once, a glint of humor in his eyes.

"Until it breaks down beyond repair," Japheth adds. "Until it is reclaimed. As they all eventually are."

Shem shakes his head. "Never mind him, he is a slave of his position. Everything is tending to disorder, everything will be reused. It is a dreary and dismal life."

The redness of Japheth's hair seems to flow to his eyes, though he remains outwardly calm this time. He does cross his arms, however, revealing bands of muscles. "Nothing could be further from the truth. The life of a reclaimer is one of peace. Of understanding."

"Yes, yes," Shem says, rolling his eyes and addressing Hard and me: "So where do you prefer to go first?"

"More of the city would be fine," I say. "Though we do want to travel outside today."

"Of course," Shem says. "And excellent." He heads for the door leading out. "Please follow."

. . .

Within minutes, we are aboard flying rectangles again. This time I am paired with Japheth instead of Ham. At first I am leery, because the fire-haired jinn seems to be the most belligerent of the three. As soon as I am riding with him, though—as soon as we're in the air—he becomes much more cordial toward me. He even smiles on occasion, though reservedly.

Clearly, the main thrust of his belligerence is toward Shem, and perhaps Shem's kind. Curiosity tweaks me.

"This empowerment festival..." I begin.

Japheth looks at me and scowls. "Is typical constructor puffery and little else."

"I see," I say. "So it is a common occurrence?"

"More common than we'd like," he says. "And always ends in more messes to dispose of." He nurses a smile. "Not the actual work they do, of course. *That* is sometimes good. But these celebrations they always want..."

"I see," I say. "So constructor mentality is fundamentally different than your own?"

"Than all reclaimers," Japheth says, "Absolutely. It has to be. Our tasks are fundamentally different. Constructors are tasked with creation of something new, while reclaimers dismantle that which is no longer useful. There are some intersections in our tasks, and in our thinking, of course—the source of primary elements, for instance."

"The primary elements," I say. "You mean the atomic elements?"

Japheth looks ahead and quietly guides the rectangle into a curving maneuver to mimic those we follow. "Yes," he says, nodding once. "All elements in the universe come from one place."

"And where is that?" I ask, hoping for at least a mention of the entity we came to find. A ray of light on A~A³.

"The stars," he says. "We are all born of stars."

I frown. It is a theory not unlike that for which I am familiar. At least, for the creation of humans. *But for jinn?* I perform a bitwise search of my memory, but come up empty. Creation mythology was not a specialty.

"How?" I ask. Is there *any* higher power in his philosophy? "How are you born of stars?"

Japheth glances at me sideways. "Stars begin with hydrogen; from there their intrinsic gravity and pressure produces the others elements. Helium first, of course, from that is fused even greater and greater elements, until finally all elements are produced. And so, you see, everything is born of stars."

"I see," I say. "But the hydrogen? What produces that?"

Japheth pauses for a moment. "That is beyond knowing," he says then, "and is therefore unimportant. What *is* important for the *now*, is the process."

"And that is?"

Japheth smiles. "As we reclaimers understand it, the universe is circular in nature. For everything created, there is something disassembled and reused. So ultimately every element is reborn. As are our spirits, our primary essence."

Below us is a purple-lighted building, approximately thirty stories high. It has ribbons of light moving across its entire surface. Much motion toward nothing.

"So, your kind *do* believe in an existence after this one?" I ask.

"Of course," Japheth says. "Everything is broken down and reused. It is the way of all life."

"And when it is reused," I say, "are these essences aware that they are being reused? Do they know that they are again alive?"

Japheth looks at me closely. "You mean like their personalities? The character your kind seems to ascribe names to?" He shakes his head. "No, all personalities are divisible, all essences—like the matter we manipulate—are building blocks of essences, but not the essences themselves—"

"A cosmic bit bucket?" I say in the way of asking.

Japheth squints. "Bit bucket?"

"Very early tech term on my planet," I say, "that survives until today. It stands for that place in a machine where information goes when it is rendered irretrievable—either through accidental or purposeful means."

Japheth nods. "Ah, it is very much like that. After destruction, life essences are irretrievable but still usable."

Japheth returns to his hands-free piloting, and I mull over what he has said. His theory of life and death has a certain circular completeness to it, and I can understand how it gels with his lifestyle. Anyone who reduced something into parts and makes those parts available for later use—which is a fair assumption of what he does—would be apt to see things that way.

Still, it feels nothing like what *I think* is true. The superlative stream the earlier mission encounter had messages for lots of different people—separate personalities. Would this be the case if the eternity behaved the way Japheth describes it?

"Your companion seems more intense than you," Japheth says. "More easily angered."

I shrug halfheartedly. "We've been through a lot over the past few weeks..."

"So is she weaker then?" he asks. "More prone to failure under stress?"

"She's different," I say. "Very different."

Japheth nods. "So it seems." He points to a circular area about a half a kilometer ahead of us. From it, a trio of lights beam into the darkness, crisscrossing and arching in their motion.

"It is like a summer carnival," HardCandy streams me Full Impact. Her emotions all warm and expectant.

I stream back a smile, but I use Standard Impact. My emotions are far from warm. I don't like Japheth's theory because, regardless of my countless failures, I really like being me—*my* essence. If that doesn't continue after death, then why does anything I do here matter?

Maybe that's why he's so grouchy...

As we draw near the circle, I notice a large piece of silver equipment positioned near one end. It is cylindrical, approximately ten meters high. Around it a small crowd has gathered—maybe only a few hundred individuals, mostly blond constructor-types with a smattering of dark-haired maintainers mixed in. "Not a very large gathering," I say.

"Larger than it appears," Japheth says. "There are nearly ten thousand monitoring it through our stream."

"Of course," I say, nodding. "I should've guessed."

Our rectangle descends, angling toward the center of the crowd. "I would rather observe from a distance," I say.

"That would be difficult," Japheth says, frowning. "Shem is heavily involved in this construction. He would want you two nearby to observe. To behold constructor glory." His face brightens. "Besides, you are well known to our people already."

"Right," I say, frowning myself. "It is all being broadcast."

He nods. "Correct."

"What is this device they've constructed?" I ask.

Japheth sniffs. "Something that will eventually break down."

I shake my head, smiling. "Aside from that..."

"I do not know the specifics," he says. "But if history is any indication, it will only introduce needless risks."

We land barely twenty steps from the silver machine. It has the same small writing around its exterior as the platform outside did—as the rectangles do. It could be figurative design or instructions as to how the device works. I do not know. The beams of light we saw begin very near the bottom of the machine. As we disembark the rectangles, I instinctively expect the crowds to converge on us—like we are rich masters having been discovered at a public eating house—but that doesn't happen. Every blue skin stays exactly where he is, and only a small portion even looks our direction.

Shem takes the lead, walking resolutely toward the silver machine, with the crowd parting before him. The rest of us follow, but along the way HardCandy draws closer.

"Shem told me the most interesting byte on our way here," she says when she's close enough.

"What's that?" I'm partially distracted by Shem, who—having reached the machine—is now shushing everyone away with outstretched arms. He is smiling broadly, as if the process is both delight and bother.

"His kind believe they were created from stars," she says.

I nod. "Yes," I say. "I was told the same thing. They posit a water cycle of eternity."

"Water cycle?"

I look at her. "You know, standing water evaporates into the air, air currents move that vapor into the atmosphere where it condenses into clouds, the clouds move and collide, cause water to fall as precipitation, the precipitation accumulates into standing water and it starts all over again. Recur forever."

Hard squints at me. "That's what he told you?"

I shrug. "More or less—except with *essences* instead of water."

"We didn't talk about essences," Hard says. "Only stars."

Shem is holding both hands over his head, waving, calling for attention. Much of that is for show, because he is clearly streaming everything as loudly as he can as well. It is all I can do to push the stream-wise bravado away.

"What did he say about the stars?" I ask. "The idea that all elements come from them?"

"Yes," Hard says, smiling excitedly. "It fits perfectly with jinn legend."

I tip my head. "Jinn legend," I say. "How so?"

"This is another glorious day for the constructors among us," Shem begins. "I hope all three designations can appreciate the enormity..."

"The sacred writings again," HardCandy says. "They say that men were created from clay."

"Yes," I say.

"But jinn," Hard says, "were supposedly created from smokeless fire, see? As Shem claims."

"They think *everything* comes from stars," I say. "Even man."

"That's beside the point," she says. "Star burning would classify as smokeless fire, would it not?"

Perhaps. But stars don't burn. Not really.

"Still," I say, "I'm not sure that's what the writings had in mind."

"Or they did," Hard says. "But lacked words to describe the process. Stars burn, without smoke, because it is a nuclear fire. It makes sense, doesn't it?"

"Okay," I say. "Maybe. But how does it matter? Whether jinn or not, they are outside our experience."

Hard shrugs. "I just like things to fit."

"...new construct is an important component in our efforts to reconfigure the topside generator," Shem says. "Another step toward stream projections, toward advancement..."

"You know what I think is unusual?" I ask. A thunderous "whoo-whoo" cheer goes up from the constructors in the crowd. A much louder echo comes down through the stream, causing me to squint from the forcefulness of it, as does Hard.

"Yes?" she says.

"I think it is odd that they don't seem to want to know anything about us. Do they really know so much already?"

Hard shrugs. "Perhaps they're being polite..."

Topside? Stream projections?

I look at Shem again. He is running a hand over the silver machine. Caressing it, lovingly.

"Did you hear that last part?" I ask. "That machine has something to do with generating streams. Outside."

"...are many components to be redesigned yet," Shem says, "but I am confident in my brethren. And I am certain the maintainers will find whatever we design as easy to sustain as this component will be. More durable over long periods, reducing reclaimer necessity..."

I glance at Japheth, whose face seems to darken. His arms cross tightly.

"So that proves it, right?" HardCandy says. "They must have produced the stream."

"But they don't seem to represent A," I say. "Or A~A^3."

"We don't know that," Hard says. "You only talked to Japheth. Who knows what the rest believe?"

I scan the crowd of blue-skinned faces. All eyes are locked on Shem, and most faces are smiling. A notable vibration of excitement is shared among the constructors. The scattered maintainers seem cautiously pleased, echoing the look on Ham's face, now two steps in front of me. There are no reclaimers nearby except Japheth. Doubtless the rest are watching on their stream. Everyone appears to be male, regardless of the designation. Lights continue to beam into the subterranean sky. Shem is causing parts of the silver machine to articulate through stream commands...

See, they are all false. Their deeds amount to nothing; their images are but wind and confusion.

I shake my head. Another message—and part of it is accurate. I *am* confused, of that there is little doubt. But these beetle men, these blue-skins, seem to have accomplished quite a bit. More than I could even imagine. How could it be only wind?

Plus, they saved us from the ship, gave us food...and that marvelous pool.

But is it all a distraction? Is that what the message is trying to tell me?

I look at Hard, send her a message: "Do you want to go? Slink away from this crowd?"

She looks behind her, studies the press of bodies there. "How would we go without them seeing?"

I look at Shem again. He is smiling and doing lots of arm waving. He isn't going to stop soon.

"We could make our way to the street," I stream. "Maybe find a rectangle."

"Could we control one?" Hard asks. "Our streams are limited."

Good point.

I take a step back, cautiously work my way behind the forward row of "beetles." Looking warily at our hosts, HardCandy does the same. About twenty beetles back, there is a line of small rectangles that nobody seems to be minding. Worming past one beetle at a time, I make my way toward the rectangles.

HardCandy leans close. "Aren't they streaming everything? Won't someone notice?"

I shrug. "Won't know until we try..."

I push through to the crowd's outer boundary and, squinting, stream out to the nearest rectangle. I detect a high-pitched repeated sound—like cicadas at night—and the taste of rubber.

That must be the rectangle. I try to lift it from the ground. It jerks backward, sharply tapping the rectangle behind it.

Nice, Hard streams.

I only sneer at her. Concentrating, I give the rectangle another command. I feel heat in my temples, but I manage to raise the rectangle ten centimeters. That's something.

Hard only nods, and quickly checks behind us again. Shem is still in demo mode, bombastically pushing out words. I climb into the rectangle, but remain standing. Hard finds a place on the floor and grabs tight to the side rail. "Don't kill us," she whispers.

Groaning, I raise us a couple feet. We move away, slowly and silently.

I'M AMAZED BY THE RESULTS—careful, of course, even a bit frightened—but also exceedingly happy. Concentrating hard, I'm able to get the rectangle first thirty, then forty, then fifty meters into the sky.

Behind me, I hear HardCandy gasp. Her eyes have been glued to the demonstration behind us throughout. She's waiting for an alarm, a general outcry of some sort, but so far, nothing.

"I don't think they care," she says. "We've left, and I don't think they care."

I want to reply, tell her how much I doubt her assertion, but I can't. I'm too busy with what I'm doing. The pressure is almost too much for my implant to bear. I pour myself into the stream, push out every bit of sensory satisfaction, and it works somehow. But freehead, does it drain me. Already my arms and legs feel like wax, and we haven't gotten out of eyeshot yet.

"Just go," Hard urges. "Get us away."

I echo her want to the rectangle and get something for the effort. It increases in speed, careening wildly toward the nearest building, a gnat approaching a looming silver dagger.

HardCandy screeches and grips my calf with a hand. "You're going to make me sick..."

"Sorry," I whisper. I redouble my concentration, try to look for the patterns in the mechanism. There must be an easier way. Something to make this all go better.

I get a bit of relief. The coolness that comes after a white-hot sweat.

Outwardly, the rectangle smooths in its retreat as well. I manage to glide it around the silver building and into the upper level of what passes as a beetle street. I straighten it, accelerate, taste rubber, but am rewarded by the feeling of wind on my cheeks—of cool and constant wind.

"That's better," Hard says. "Keep it up, Sand!"

I risk opening my eyes. Sounds weird, I know, but for the first minute of our departure, I was flying completely blind physically. Not streamwise, of course. Never streamwise. I set my feet at shoulder width, try to look as confident and assured as Ham and Japheth do when they're driving. A captain at the wheel of an old schooner.

The rectangle tips to the left. I hunch down and grab for the nearest railing I can grab. Hard shrieks again. No surprise there. I grit my teeth and beg the rectangle to fix itself.

It does. Mostly.

Hard moves up closer behind me, still holding tight. "I thought men were better drivers."

The rectangle still lists a little, but I'm okay with that. What I most care about is keeping it moving forward. And I seem to be managing that. We soar past another building, and another. "Really not the time," I say, frowning. "Just stay in your seat."

"I will, don't worry," she promises. "For now."

I roll my eyes. Keep going, rectangle. Forward!

We maintain a straight line; pass over a group of lower placed rectangles, one of which has to drop slightly to fully miss us. The driver there is clearly a reclaimer—red hair flowing in the wind. He looks up at me with stern face. I raise a hand to say hi. Smile.

I risk a broad visual sweep of the city. It is wholly unfamiliar to me. Gleaming jewels grown dozens of stories tall. I'm like a child playing in his mother's charm drawer. The hand slap is certainly coming. "Where are we going now?" I ask. There is a whole world open to us. If the cities are really connected.

I scan the distant cavern around us. There are lighted paths there—tunnels to other cities, I presume.

"I want out," Hard says. "Up. Out. Fresh air."

There is something to be said for having a measure of control.

Having a hand on the wheel of your own destiny. It has been a long time since I've felt that way.

I glance at Hard. She is now bent almost double in her seat, a familiar pained expression on her face. "Are you all right?" I ask.

She looks up at me, surprised. "Aren't you driving?"

"Yeah, I..." I turn forward again. Everything is clear ahead. No problems. I check the streets below, examine the buildings as we speed by. Part of me wonders if something strange is going to happen again. If I'm going to find a strange creature stooped on a ledge somewhere.

"You know the way, right?" Hard stands and points over my shoulder. "It is that tunnel over there."

I follow her finger to a large tunnel beyond the city boundaries, and far to our left. For some reason it looks darker than I remember. More cave-like. I imagine I even see stalactites hanging down like teeth. "Are you sure?" I ask.

"Yes," she says. "I stored an image. Made a backup. That is definitely it."

"And we want to go out," I say.

"At least for a little while," she says. "While we still can."

I study the tunnel closely. I think she is right about the location. I think it is that tunnel. But why does it fill me with dread?

She slaps my shoulder, then holds her hand there, squeezing warmly. "Come on, Sandfly. Be a man."

I almost smile and, reaching for HardCandy's hand, pull it down to my side. I continue to hold it. She makes a teasing effort to pull away, but I resist, hold fast. I hear a huffing sound, but she relents and grips my hand back firmly. Her fingers intertwine with mine. I lose concentration—the rectangle trembles a bit—but shrugging, I manage to right it again and point us in the direction of the tunnel. "Out and up," I say. "As you wish."

Hard gives my hand a firm squeeze. "Just go."

• • •

The tunnel walls fly by us, as bright and living as they seemed during our entrance to the beetle's underground world. Purposely I travel slower than when we first arrived. Navigating the tunnel's tighter quarters taxes my nerves and reflexes.

"Was it this narrow before?" I ask.

"Are you doubting me?" Still holding my hand, HardCandy leans over the side to look.

"No...I..." Trying to remain fixed on the center of the tunnel, I glance her direction. "What are you doing?"

"Taking a closer look at these walls." She draws silent for a moment. "I think it is living matter that lights them."

"Some sort of bioluminescence?" I ask, eyes fixed ahead. "A living creature that grows on the surface?"

"Or perhaps the rock itself," HardCandy says. "Living rock."

The beetles have technology beyond anything humanity has ever dreamed, of that there is no doubt. And even though I've been actively observing it and interacting with it, I'm unsure how any of it really works. It is almost like I never had an implant. Like I'm an OuterMog landscaper who couldn't turn his vidscreen on without instructions. "Do you think the stones are something the jinn constructed?"

Hard straightens, looks at me. "Yes, probably," she says. "I think." She studies the walls again. "I think there is no difference for them—living or non-living, it is all a potential element to be manipulated. A building block in their machines."

I nod. "That's how they seem to refer to the things they work with," I say, "as building blocks. Not small machines—nanos like we're used to—but rudimentary building blocks to be formed."

"Do you think they can give life to non-life?" Hard asks. "Like A can? Clay formed into man, fire to jinn?"

I shake my head. "I don't know. But their mechanisms, their stream—even the muted one we can connect to—seems so different. Quiet, yet powerful."

Gazing upward, I glimpse the movement of a dark shape in the ceiling ahead. At first I think it only a trick of my eyes, but as we draw closer, I know different. From the luminescence, a brown bulge appears—a humanoid head. Dark eyes search and find me, a mouth opens to reveal thick white teeth. Pulled into the creature's mental world, I drift the rectangle up and toward him, this brown triped hanging upside-down from the ceiling. At the last instant I shake myself, realize our danger and, ducking, jerk the rectangle downward again.

"What are you doing?" Hard says. She releases my hand and folds herself below the railing.

I close my eyes, purposely shake my head. "Sorry," I say. "I must have drifted off. Gotten distracted."

She gives my elbow a pinch. "Well, don't." She points ahead. "We're almost out."

Ahead of us lies a circle of natural light, a shaded green escape. The little I can see appears calm and motionless. No sign of wind or storm.

Hard brings her hands together. "Oh, hurry," she says, smiling brightly. "Our big adventure."

I get a message from Ham. A simple, pleasant-feeling missive telling me that they've noticed our absence. They are not worried, he assures me. They know where we are.

"Did you get that?" I ask Hard.

She nods. "Yeah," she says. "Mom and Dad are okay with us taking the downer, apparently."

Or so they say. I push the rectangle onward. Within seconds we burst through the opening into the sunlight—Betelgeuse light. It feels incredibly warm to my skin. The air smells of coconuts and sawdust. I catch Hard breathing deeply too, and smiling.

"Isn't it great?" she says.

I have to admit, it is. Unencumbered, expansive, but also overwhelming. Wild. The beetle's stream feels like a whisper in my ear now. A soft and present friend.

Aside from the lone structure that we discovered when Dark-Trench surveyed the planet—which seems almost a lifetime ago—our surroundings are thickly forested. Branches form a nearly impenetrable canopy both below and around us. Instinctively, I raise the rectangle to a spot above every tree. The last thing I need is to collide with something.

"Can we land somewhere nearby?" Hard takes my left hand again, and cupping it between hers, gives it a gentle squeeze.

I understand her want. Everything around us feels inviting, so needing to be walked on, between and through. Thoroughly appreciated. Still, there may be dangers here—must be, for why else would the beetle's choose to live below? What form of animals roam these woods? We've watched horned livestock over the vidscreens. Even those could be dangerous if provoked, I assume.

Something about the distant pyramid intrigues me. It begs to be explored. "We could go to the structure," I say. "Explore it."

Hard shakes her head. "Not something constructed first," she says. "Not now." She pivots her free arm. "Find us a clearing where we can walk."

I scan the thick foliage below. "That might be difficult..."

A flock of large birds leave the canopy to our right. Rise steadily into the sky. I tweak the rectangle's altitude to avoid them. Perhaps because of the birds' exit, HardCandy points that direction. "Go that way," she says. "We'll find a place. I'm sure of it." I've become conscious of her closeness, of her side pressing against mine. The warmth. It is startling how it affects me. Again, I'm confused.

But I turn the craft, anyway. Take us out into the green to our right. We travel what seems like kilometers with little break in the thickness whatsoever. Then suddenly, a clearing appears. A sandy opening, with a reddish tint to it, surrounded by tall grass. And on one side, the clearing seems to narrow and continue. As if it is the start of a path into the woods. A trail that animals have made.

"Perfect," HardCandy says. "Let's go there."

I direct the rectangle that way, tilt it gently, nose it downward. As we enter the clearing, as the trees close in on our sides, I feel a flicker of worry. Like something about this situation is distinctly familiar. Did I dream this place once?

The rectangle reaches the ground and sand clouds billow up around us. Though everything appears lush and green, this particular stretch of land hasn't seen water in some time. The rectangle engines—formed in the bottom surface of the craft—go idle. The clouds begin to subside, slowly. Hard raises a hand to her face and coughs, fans the sand from her eyes and nose. She then climbs over the side and, putting a hand out for me, says: "Come on."

And suddenly, the moment seems right. I take her hand. And we walk, fingers entwined, shoes kicking up tiny storms of sand, eyes scanning everywhere, easily following the game trail into the forest. The trail itself is comfortably wide enough for us to walk in. No crowding, but yet close enough that holding each other still feels right.

Hard has no difficulty holding my hand now either. She even turns to smile at me as we go. It is neuron-firing, streamsmoothing ecstasy. Flipping wild.

"Look!" she says, pointing out a zebra-striped bird in a tree.

I nod and search for my own perfect find. The stream has gone almost perfectly silent in my head. The implant filtering and interacting with nothing. It is an odd feeling, but it is also liberating. For the first time in over ten years, my thoughts are truly my own.

If I make my bed in the depths, you are there.

Except for the random phrases, apparently. Nice to know that those, at least, remain.

I search the blue above. Remembering where we came from, and DarkTrench, I frown.

HardCandy gives my hand a tug, propels me forward. Brings my eyes back to earth.

Then it hits me. I *did* dream this place before. Back on the station. Right after I heard the superlative stream's song for the first time. There were birds and trees and a red sun overhead. The noises in my head seemed distant—like today. And there was HardCandy. A happy, smiling HardCandy, who says—

"What are you thinking about?"

That isn't quite right. Close, though. And strange, regardless.

HardCandy looks hard at me. "Are you listening to me? Are you all right?"

I stare into her eyes, dark almond lighthouses in the sea of my mind. Circles that whisper promises without speaking, that tug at my insides. I glance away and shrug. Embarrassed. "Nothing important." The smells around us fill me again. There is a fruit tree nearby. A citrus variant, I think.

The path changes, becoming covered in dense undergrowth, a soft and fine moss. The trees grow closer on either side as well.

"Are you sure we should continue this way?" I ask. The shadows deepen ahead. Thicken.

HardCandy tightens her grip. "Are you afraid of the dark, Sand?" She scans the latticework of growth on either side. "This is nice, I think. Beautiful. Real."

Aside the path, the grass is long. Reaching almost waist height in places. There is a cool dampness to the air as well. The feeling of arboreal pressure. Smells of both death and rebirth.

HardCandy is right. It is wonderful.

I hear a noise ahead of us. A threatening rustle in the tall grass to our right. I slow up, and pulling on HardCandy's hand, draw her closer. I feel the warmth of her arm on mine.

"What?"

I remain watchful, shake my head. "I thought I heard something..."

Hard mimics me in searching. I'm not sure that she's serious.

A full minute goes by. "Let's go," she says, stepping forward. "Come on, or I'll release your hand."

There is a flourish of energy, then an explosion of motion. A silver head tears free of the grass. A head with five forwardpointing horns, colored red. HardCandy lurches back into me, pulling so close that her back touches my sternum. I grunt and sidestep around her, looking for something—a branch, a stone, anything—that I can use for defense.

The silver head raises above a two-meter neck. Large eyes regard us, blink noticeably twice. The face is puffy and round. The head turns and its lanky body follows. It gallops away, making heavy footfalls in the forest. It nearly hits a tree in its haste. Then it disappears completely.

HardCandy laughs loudly, then brings a hand to her mouth. I only watch the spot where the creature went. Making sure it wasn't a trick of its hunt.

Hard grips my elbow, shakes my whole arm. "It was a deer," she says. "A large, strange-looking deer, but a deer all the same." Her face is bright. Alive as I've ever seen it. "Don't look so serious."

I manage a smile. "I guess you're right..."

She pushes on my chest, cups her hand around my ribs. Warmth fills me again. "Let's go, mighty warrior."

We walk many meters in silence, both watching the depths around us. Occasionally noting an animal or bird. Frequently catching each other's eye. Any fear I had dissipates. Nothing has felt better to me ever. Nothing more free.

We reach a spot where the trail thins out again, excepting a massive tree that forces the trail to bend around it. The tree mound forms an obvious resting place, so HardCandy leads me there and we sit down. I find myself putting my arm around her. Again, I note a pained look in her eyes, but when I ask about it, she only shakes her head.

"Wait," I say, nearly striking myself for the obviousness of it. "Your stops..."

"Don't worry about those," she says, pulling close to me again. "Not here." She sends me a FI message. No words, only images laden with emotion. My insides turn, realign, then flip. She really cares for me, regardless of how broken I am. Confusion sets in too, seeming to blank my connection to the stream completely. Strangely, I let myself lean down, leaning close to her.

What am I doing?

I don't know. But I reach a point where I can feel the breath escaping her mouth. Mixing with my own. There must be an invisible bacteriological war going on here! Yet I press forward. HardCandy's eyes widen, her pupils dilate. Draw me in.

Our mouths touch.

I feel awkward. Not knowing whether to push forward or remain steady. To close my mouth or remain still. Somehow it works, though. All distractions, both external and internal, both stream-wise and forest-wise, grow silent. It is only HardCandy and I, caught in a single moment. Nanoseconds perfectly logged and remembered. Warmth from cranium to phalange.

HardCandy pulls away, smiles. And so do I.

Then both hands come to her head. She squints, grits her teeth, and starts to scream.

The stops!

I should have known there'd be a problem for her. How foolish of me. How selfish. I wrap my arms around her. Try to comfort her until the pain subsides.

She rocks, hands pressed tightly against her skull, fingers splayed, eyes tightly closed.

End now, please. I'm sorry. Please, stops—end!

HardCandy continues to scream until I feel her body relax against mine. Total collapse.

End of line.

I AM SEATED IN MY ROOM with the door shut, face exposed, with a pad of white paper in my hand. Next to me is my friend Asa, with a similar tablet in her lap. We have a drawing project for school—a charcoal description of our future. Most girls will return to class with a page filled with children or a typical home life. But not me. I know what I wish for, and by drawing it, I hope to make it true.

And yet, over a week has gone by with no change. After my final encounter with the debugger, after his assurances that he would do something, I returned home excited—frightened of the future my mother envisioned and her possible punishment, of course—but still excited, hopeful. Debuggers can't knowingly lie, so if he said he would do something for me, he will. He has to. Because he said it.

But perhaps there is a loophole for children. Perhaps disappointing girls isn't against the rules...

I hear a sound in the house somewhere and look up, study the fake wood door. I imagine I hear low tones being exchanged between my mother and another. I hope it is something the debugger set up. I fear it is something else. After listening for a full ten seconds, I realize I heard nothing and return to my drawing again.

My wedding has been arranged, regardless of my wishes. My mother is doing all the planning—not burdening me with that part, at least. I refuse to even think about my father's cousin, Hecta. He is a pig on two feet. You would think my mother could see that.

Why would she want to expose me to a pig? Pork is forbidden by our faith.

"Are you drawing a skin again?" Asa says, scowling.

I straighten my posture. "Of course," I say. "Because that is what I will be."

Asa shakes her head. "They never marry, you know. They have no children."

"Uncomplicated," I say. "A good life. A pure life."

Asa sighs and, tipping her head, partially obscures her face with her long, dark hair. "I do not blame you for not wanting Hecta," she says, "but would a normal marriage be so bad?"

"Slavery," I say, shaking my head. "Until the day you die, no assurance about your standing, your family, or your man. On a whim he may divorce you, leaving you penniless with children to feed." I darken a line on my drawing, pushing hard into the work. "Yes, it could be very bad."

Asa returns to her own drawing. There is a horse foremost in hers, which is not uncommon for Asa's art. "Do they even *have* female skins?" she asks.

It is a hard question, a cutting question. Squinting, I stare at my tablet. "Not yet," I mutter.

Asa looks at me. "So you would be the first..."

"The one and only." If my friend comes through.

There is another noise outside, a loud *thunk*—the front door, I think. I'm sure there was a sound this time, anyway.

"Someone is here," Asa whispers. "Should we go out?"

I watch the door silently, thinking. I want to go out, I want to see. "No," I whisper. "That would only jinx it." Then I hear my mother talking. I recognize the flare in her voice that denotes excitement. It worries me.

Mother calls my name. Looking at Asa, I shrug and climb to my feet. I place the tablet on my small, heavily blanketed bed, with only the drawn head and neck of myself as a debugger completed. I was hoping to sketch in a downrider, and a broken bot to one side...

Mother calls again as I reach the door. I pull on my scarf, open the door, and peer into the hall. I take a few furtive steps and look around the corner to the living room. My mother is seated, almost perfectly straight, in her favorite plush chair. In front of her is a middle-aged overweight man. My stomach drops.

Hecta.

"Ah my daughter, my daughter," mother says. "Look who's here? Come to visit..."

Hecta has more rolls of fat than can be easily counted. Especially below the chin. He is dressed in a typical beige floor-length robe—a subtle blessing! On his face is the smile of a crocodile after a good meal. "Your eyes are so beautiful," he says. "You will produce beautiful children."

I bow, thankful that he cannot see my expression. I know how to lie with my eyes. The rest of my face is another story.

Behind Hecta is an elderly couple—his parents, I assume. Even in their substantial coverings, they seem very frail. The man seems more so, because his face is actually exposed. It is heavy creased with wrinkles. He smiles at me now too, revealing perfect—nano-enhanced—teeth. They look weird, out of place. The old woman steps toward me holding a folded garment.

"It is engagement outfit, dear," the woman says.

"Please go put it on," my mother adds.

I want to scream and run, but that would get me nothing now. I look at the garment—a gold and tan colored dress with matching headpiece—and bow. It is an expensive gift, and in any other circumstance I would find it beautiful. I turn to the hall where Asa is waiting, just out of sight, and with another bow, I join her, leaving the room.

We return to my room and shut the door. Asa's face is all eyes and sorrow. "I'm sorry," she says. "I didn't know it would come so soon."

I slip off my scarf and head-covering, start to pull my dress over my head. Soon I am standing in only my undergarments, looking pale and dreadfully thin—or so I think. Whatever curves I will have some day are for now still hidden. Undisclosed. I don't know what to say to Asa. I feel completely defeated.

"Help me with this," I say finally. Asa lifts the dress to where I can duck my head into it. "At least it is pretty," she says, as the dress drops over my shoulders then curtains to the floor. I look down at it. Surprisingly the fit is a good one. It makes me wonder how many ten-year-old girls Hecta has studied before.

Without further word, I put on the headdress, look to Asa for final approval, and exit the room. In the living room, my mother coos with delight. Again I am thankful that my face is covered. I bow both to Hecta and to his parents. Everyone smiles.

"Stunning," Hecta says. His smile turns my stomach.

My mother draws near. "And look," she says. "Hecta has something else for you." She hands me a small felt bag. Inside I find two rings. One is small enough to fit my finger, gold, with a ruby in the center. The other is silver and very large. Hecta's. Men are forbidden from wearing gold.

"We know of your financial condition," Hecta's father says. "So we purchased both. I trust that is agreeable."

Mother bows low. "You are gifted in mercy. We accept your generosity." She looks at me. "Let Hecta put yours on, dear."

Sulking, I approach Hecta and hold the bag out for him to take. He does so with a bow and reaches for my hand. It is all I can do to let him touch me.

"May A make the days until our wedding day joyful," he says as he slides the ring on. It is almost unreal, this action. Am I really letting this happen? Father, where are you when I need you?

I do my best to stumble through my part of the exchange, but as I lift the ring to his finger, he grasps my hand to hold it. His grip is slimy, cold. What he is doing is against the rules, I know, but to embarrass him here is inadvisable. I only tip my head, and slipping free of his grip, attempt to put his ring on again. Then I notice the ring that is already in place. Another silver circle identical to the one I hold. He notices too, and smiling, reaches down and attempts to pull the first ring off. It is difficult. It has been in place a long time.

Inside, I am wreaked. He has another wife! I drop my hand, holding the ring to my side. I cannot do this.

I think of my mother, again sitting on her chair, so happy. I'm sure they've already talked about the dowry. I'm sure it is a hefty sum. Enough to keep her fed for a very long time. Plus she'll remain part of Father's family. Comfortable and protected. It is a necessity in our world. I don't begrudge her for any of it, not really.

And I'm partially to blame for her condition.

If only I'd stayed in that burning school...

"What is the matter, my bride?" Hecta asks. He reaches for my hand again, as if trying to help. When I keep my arm firmly at my side, he looks imploringly at Mother. "Did she not agree to this?" he asks. "It is up to you to make her agree."

Hecta's mother grabs my other arm and grips it hard, old fingernails digging into my flesh. "She is just strong-willed," she says. "Every young woman is like this. It is for the husband to change her, to break her. "

Strong-willed I doubtless am, but a woman I am not. Not yet.

The woman's grip remains strong. "Please child, the ring was given to be used."

Her grip is too painful to resist. I grit my teeth against it. One last reckless attempt.

"She can be difficult," Mother says. "For all my attempts to correct her. If only her father was still here..."

There it is—another stick to my back. Make me remember him, Momma. Make me think it is all my fault that you're alone. Lonely and afraid.

I drop my head, shake it slowly, and raise my right hand with the ring. Hecta smiles again, presents his finger as an easy target. A fat and stubby target. I notice his rough nails—a surprising fault for someone with money. What other hygiene rules does he ignore?

I move the ring forward...

A light rap on the door behind Hecta. So light, in fact, that it is missed by the others in the room. I hear it, though, and so does he. He purposely ignores it, nods as if to urge me on. I look at my mother, grateful for the possibility of a delay.

"Yes, dear?"

The knock on the door again, louder but still polite. Mother rises from her seat. "Do you expect another relative?" she asks.

"Perhaps it is my brother," Hecta says. "He had business..."

Mother bows to Hecta's parents then, as she crosses the room, to Hecta himself. "My apologies," she says.

Hecta lurches away from the door, giving her room. Looks slightly off kilter now.

Mother opens the door. Hecta still obscures my view, so I bend left to look around him. Mother hasn't said anything yet. Which is odd for her. I'm not supposed to speak, but can't help myself. "Mother, who is it?" I whisper.

She steps back to reveal a slender man with a bald head. He bows at Hecta. "May A forgive my intrusion," he says.

"A debugger," Hecta says. "My father employs two of your kind."

Hecta's father has shuffled up behind me. "Bamboo!" he exclaims. "What brings you here? Are we late on our payments?"

Bamboo bows, smiling softly. "I don't know, Solem, are you?"

Hecta's father makes a raspy clucking sound. I'm not sure if it is a laugh or a painful cough. He smiles, though, so I suspect it was the former.

"I am here to make a proposal," Bamboo says, glancing at me. "To the virgin's representative."

Hecta laughs loudly. "So are we, skin," he says. "So *are we!*"

Bamboo retains his smile, but his eyes on Hecta go fierce. Like lasers. He looks at me too, and while I expect a bit of softening, I don't get it. Whatever his mission, it is something he doesn't necessarily like. Nor does he necessarily like me.

"What is your proposal, martyr Bamboo?" mother asks. "What task could you have with us?"

Bamboo frowns. "The virgin has no father to speak for her?"

Mother bows again, her voice apologetic. "Regrettably no. May A give him rest."

A deeper frown. "I am sorry to hear that. Legally it is easier with a father present."

Mother indicates Hecta. "Hecta here is her betrothed. We were in the middle of the engagement ceremony."

Not yet! I want to scream. Please don't tell him that!

Bamboo squints, looking at Hecta and then at me. "I see," he says. "A complication."

No it isn't! Not at all!

I glance into the room—Father's octagon—and notice Asa peering in past the entry curtains. Eyes wide above her scarf.

"What is your proposal, skin?" Hecta asks, scowling.

Hecta is clearly not the most perceptive person...

"We are in desperate need of another initiate," Bamboo says. "This is irregular, I know..."

Hecta's father hacks loudly. "You want the girl? There are no female debuggers! Tanzer wouldn't have it!" The man's face reddens considerably, so much I think he'll explode.

Bamboo smiles. "We have learned some things since Tanzer's time."

"But not that! It is forbidden. Women aren't appropriate."

The smile dissolves. There is truth in the old man's words, but Bamboo has chosen to sidestep that somehow. "I have checked with the girl's school," he says. "Her scores are more than adequate."

"She is to be my wife," Hecta declares. "We've already decided on a dowry."

"She will be an experiment for us," Bamboo says. "A scientific endeavor that will further our culture." He turns to my mother. "As always, there will be compensation for your loss."

"More than we've offered?" Hecta says. "More than a bride price for a simple human tool?"

Bamboo ignores Hecta completely, speaking only to my mother with an occasional glance at Hecta's parents. "The offer will smooth the wrinkles," he says. "And absolve any debts." The smile returns.

Hecta scowls at his father, who has now grown silent. The redness of the old man's face has dwindled as well. "Let the girl go," he says finally.

"What?" Hecta says. "She is to be my wife!"

"You have a wife," the old man says. "And we can always get you another later." A sideways glance at Bamboo. "One with fewer complications." He puts a hand out for his own wife, who taking it, shuffles with him to the door. Hecta remains motionless and speechless for many moments, the only sound his labored breathing. Finally, with only a sneering look in my direction, he lurches out behind them.

I've never been so happy for a door to close.

Bamboo remains, however. His fingertips touch reflectively at his waist, and his eyes dart between mother and I. "I am doubtful your daughter is worth the effort," he says. "But I am open to being convinced."

Another bow. "She is a very good student," Mother says, now in sales mode. "Always has been." She looks at me. "If it wasn't for her willfulness..."

Bamboo raises a hand. "Willfulness, I can deal with." He looks at me. "There will be no difference in your experience compared to that of other initiates, understand?"

I bow my head slowly, with as much respect as I can muster. Inside, I'm about to burst with excitement.

"No special privilege, no allowances. Your menstruation will be synthetically contained. Any accompanying psychological effects will be yours to deal with. Disrespect will be forcefully stopped through the implant."

I drop my head again. "I understand," I say.

He watches me for a long moment. "Very well." He looks at Mother. "I need two things from you before we go."

"Yes?" Mother says. "Just make your wishes known."

Bamboo reaches out and grabs my golden scarf, pulling it away. "Take this and dispose of it," he says, handing it to mother. He next pulls back my headpiece, freeing my hair. "And bring me your follicle disrupter. It will do until we reach the facility."

Ten minutes later, my hair—which has grown unchecked since toddlerhood—is nothing but a dark mound on the floor.

OUR MAIN ROOM HAS TRANSFORMED AGAIN, recon-
figured itself. There is no pool, no table laden with food, no view-
ports to the world beyond. The wall color is eggshell white. The floor
is cushioned, noiseless. Spotlighted near the center of the room is a
large silver tube, positioned horizontally. It is completely enclosed. At
one end the tube has a transparent section—a viewport to the body
within.

A place where I can see her face.

The shape of the tube was my suggestion. It is an echo of the
cinder chutes HardCandy and I used to sleep in. Before the station
and DarkTrench. Before we became sinners and rulebreakers.
Traveled the universe both forward and back.

"While not making light of the situation that requires its use,"
Shem says, "it is a wonderful creation."

Shem stands at the end of the tube with a hand resting on it. The
other two beetles—HardCandy's jinn—stand further away, near the
open door. Both are quiet and respectful. All three joined me in the
forest, helped me return HardCandy's motionless body to the rectangle and secure it. Escorted me as I flew back to the entrance to their
underground Jannah, our new home.

"There are fundamental differences in our physical structure,"
Shem continues. "But we constructors are positive that the device will
maintain her as she is. Keep her safe and hunger-free."

Ham nods. "I have checked the functionality, Sandfly, and it is
operating perfectly."

"For now," Japheth adds softly.

Shem shakes his head. "We only regret we can't make her conscious again. Without fully understanding her, without her having full access to our stream, it is too dangerous. Again, the possible limitations of her implant. The differences in her physique..." He steps away from the tube, closer to the door.

"You've done all you can," I say. "I understand."

There is silence for some time. Looking at one wall, I wish that a viewport would return so that imagined sunlight will brighten the room. I ask for that in stream, and with a bit of trouble, manage to wrench open a single meter-square window. The view depicted is of the same field where Hard and I previously watched the bovine-animals graze.

But the weather has changed now. There is a heavy rain, complete with lightning strikes. No animal is visible. And no sun.

"Can you change the location?" I ask. "One where it isn't raining?"

"Of course," Ham says. An instant later, there is a view of a sand-swept beach. There are dozens of thin trees similar to palm trees lining it that are being blown about by a heavy breeze.

Better, but not great. "More foliage, perhaps?" I say.

The image changes to a forested landscape. The trees are dark conifers, different than the forest I was just in. But still too close.

"How about just something with rocks?" I ask. "Lots of rocks."

An image of a treeless and waterless canyon appears. Lots of sandstone and umber. But there is sunlight.

"That will do." I approach the tube and look within. Hard-Candy's face is calm and worry-free. Stunning in its softness. That makes me sadder still.

It is my fault she is there. I should've been more observant. Less indulgent.

Not tried to kiss her.

"We shouldn't have left," I say.

"You are free to come and go as you desire," Shem says. "You are a guest." I turn to meet his eyes, and he smiles softly. "I only wish you'd been able to observe the rest of the celebration. It was outstanding."

Japheth steps closer. "Do you have any ideas," he asks, "as to the reason for her state? Though not identical, your physical construction is similar. And you have similar implants..."

I place a finger on the tube's edge, trace it slowly. "On our planet we have rules. Lots of them. Aside from connecting us to the stream, our implants ensure we follow those rules."

"How limiting," Shem says. "Restrictive."

"It is," I say. "At least it was...for me."

"You are not so encumbered now?" Japheth says. "Free to work as you see fit?"

"Yes. But I shouldn't be. I should be like her."

"So you believe her implant caused this?"

"I don't doubt it." I touch the tube's side. It is smooth yet warm. "I think that she's been fighting her implant for some time. Hiding how much it was hurting her." Like someone with a terminal disease who refuses to let on. Refuses to worry their loved ones. Until the day they suddenly and hopelessly collapse. "It would explain why she wanted to go back. Why she wanted to take a chance on this place."

Ham steps forward. "There has been some talk about this situation among maintainers," he says. "A consensus opinion has been reached."

Already? News travels fast.

"First I must ask a question," he says.

"Yes?"

"Do you intend to stay with us here? Within our community?"

I glance at the viewport. A lone avian floats its way from one side of the canyon to the other. Drifting on unseen winds.

"I'm not sure I have a choice," I say.

Ham nods. "Because your vessel is damaged."

I think of DarkTrench. Another friend incapacitated and beyond reach. "I don't want to think about this now..."

"There may be no better time," Ham says.

I scowl. "And why is that?"

"If you were to integrate with our stream, we could learn from the experience," Japheth says. "Perhaps discover a cure for your companion."

I glance at HardCandy. The picture of stillness. Only magnifying my own aloneness. "Is that right?" I look at the others—at dark-haired Ham, and then at Shem.

Shem nods. "The potentials are endless."

"It would give you better control of your environment." Ham nods at the screen. "You would be fully in tune."

I remember my original quest, the search for the superlative stream. Is that what is being offered to me now? Would I know if I touched the divine? Do I even care anymore? The idea of having full access to the beetles' stream and technology is intriguing. But what about the castes?

"You mentioned templates before," I say.

"Yes," Japheth says. "You would have to work within the confines of our templates."

"So I would need to pick a caste to join?"

Ham nods. "That's correct. Do you have a preference?"

Of the three, Ham has been the most approachable. Whether that is normal for his caste or not, I have no way of knowing. But if he has been picked as their representative, it seems likely.

Shem's group seems to have the most ingenuity, however. Would that help with HardCandy's condition?

I look at Japheth. From our earlier discussion, I know his philosophy: we are all of stars and to stars we will return. Or something of that nature. Again, there is a certain symmetry to it, a certain completeness. Plus, the idea of spending my time tearing things apart has an appeal in its own right. I want to smash things. To reduce them to primary building blocks.

Yet I hate to think that nothing is permanent. When I repaired a bot, it was because I hoped to make a difference in my world. Whether I thought that at the time or not. I wanted there to be a mark to show that I had been present. That I had passed this way.

Is that desire wrong? And if it is, isn't that idea—the quest to dissolve one's ego entirely—in itself, a desire?

"You would be a welcome addition to our group," Ham says. "On your world, in your vocation, you kept things in working order, correct? Maintained them?"

I nod. "Primarily."

"Then the transition would not be large for you. Freed to use the maintainer template, you could be effective almost immediately."

I glance at HardCandy's tube again, shrug. "There is no way for me to know."

"Yet you could try and see," Ham says.

"Of course."

I look at Shem now. The others are every bit as muscular and fit as he, yet he seems to stand straighter, head higher than all. What would it be like to be a creator? To design the sort of things that the higher level debuggers—the fourteens and fifteens—on Earth did? Masterpieces like DarkTrench?

And what is this stream projector they're in the process of building?

Shem smiles. "You are considering the life of a constructor, aren't you? I'm not surprised. It is the only caste that offers solutions." The smile broadens. "And that is what you came for, correct? Solutions."

Right now all I really want is to be left alone.

"I have questions," I say.

"Of course. Every true constructor does."

"But I don't want to ask them now. I need to be here. By myself. With HardCandy."

He nods. "Of course. That is understandable. No reason to rush into anything." He looks at his companions. "We can leave you. Let you rest." He walks forward and places a hand on my shoulder. It is a cool touch. Surprisingly cool for someone formed from fire.

"When you are ready, why don't you come and see me?" He indicates the door. "We will leave a conveyance fully formed for you outside. It will know how to reach me."

I nod and they exit the room. Leaving me as alone as I've ever been.

LOSING MY HAIR was only the first of many losses. I was taken from my home and from Mother, of course. That part I at least thought I was prepared for. Though perhaps I was not.

My school became a distant memory as well. That I did not miss at all, aside from the times I was allowed to design. To create. To shape wondrous patterns of color. Clearly any freedom I thought I had there was only a mockery. A façade.

In the end, it was my friends I missed most. Asa, of course. And my shy boy Abdul from the shop. Though I suppose he used my appearance for his own pleasure, he was never forceful. Always kind. He inadvertently opened up a new world to me...but also more losses. More surrenders.

The implantation process is frightening and feral. A dark machine hovering overhead, its many appendages swiveling and darting into place. Snapping and clicking in response to Bamboo's streamed commands. Dipping from the heavens to lightly caress or cut my head, then ascend away again. A black demon purposely implanting its own will into mine. Replacing my priorities and purposes with its commands. Its rules. Violating my head with a single metal teardrop.

I am awake throughout the entire procedure. There is no pain, but the noises—especially the saw—was horrific. It is good that I am strapped down.

"The female brain is smaller," Bamboo says as the surgery winds to a close, "complicating my task. A decade ago I wouldn't have tried at all. I have no use for someone who is damaged." He stands to the right of my chair. Out of sight.

A series of clicks. A metallic hand extends, containing a ball of cotton.

"Yours also runs hotter than a male brain," he continues. "Because it uses more glucose. More blood sugar." Another appendage descends, with a glowing end. A skin fusing device. "There is no danger to the implant, thankfully. I ran tests on everything, of course. I like to be certain..."

On the walls around me are vidscreens with endless cartoons playing. I haven't watched any of them. I am frightened, yes, but I am also elated at what is to come.

"I'm intrigued by the implications," Bamboo says. "By the differences. There are two components of the human central nervous system, the place where general intelligence lies. These components are grey and white matter.

"Men have 6.5 times the grey matter of women." He pauses, steps so I can see him directly, and smiles. "Making them better at computational skills." He raises a finger. "However, women have 10.5 times the white matter of men. This is where the language skills come from. It will be interesting to see how that affects your debugging abilities. Clearly, computation is important to the process. But communication is equally important. Perhaps more so."

I feel the pressure of the fuser on my skin. I'm told that for most skin types, there will be no scar whatsoever. I am hopeful.

"Another interesting difference is the hippocampus. That area of the brain is larger in females. Yours is above average, in fact. The hippocampus is the center of emotion and memory functions."

Bamboo's arms clasp behind his back. He turns. Begins to pace. "The enhanced memory is certainly helpful. But I am torn on the emotional portion. At first I thought emotions meaningless to our work. But then I realized how closely aligned emotions are to pain. Considering the shocks—the stops—the implant produces are also necessary, the size difference could be advantageous. My supposition is that it will make you more compliant. More dedicated."

Bamboo walks so I can see him again. A thin man in a white cloak. "Regardless of how it ultimately works, you will certainly remember any discipline better than your male counterparts. And that is a good thing. A very good thing..."

The pressure on my head eases and the fuser lifts away. Am I really almost done?

"There are other differences that may help us as well," Bamboo says. "The reduced sex drive, for instance. With you we won't have to do as much as we do in men."

My forehead tickles. Instinctively, my eyebrows raise.

"That surprises you?" Bamboo says. "Well, yes, the male debuggers aren't aware. And it is only a subtle reshaping of thoughtlines. Very light. But necessary. Their drive is necessary too, so we can't suppress it completely. As with much that Tanzer envisioned, it is a balancing act."

I've heard talk of the mythical Tanzer before. The man who, many years ago, laid the groundwork for debuggers. Would he believe what they've become?

Bamboo steps close and leans forward. Visibly inspects his work. "It looks good," he says. "I believe it will heal nicely. Daily steaming followed by a skin treatment should aid the fusing process. Eliminate any scars."

A smile trickles out. I will certainly do the treatments.

Bamboo must have noticed. "Not that being attractive should be a concern for you. In fact, I am tempted to use the implanter to insure that looking in the mirror will never again enter your mind. You will be deemed untouchable, forbidden to men, but that doesn't mean that some might not try. You will be sinless, but remember, they are not."

"Was the angel that visited our founder not beautiful?" I ask. A childish question. Foolish.

Bamboo scowls. "That angel was male, implant. The question of his beauty is not important."

"I was wrong to ask," I say. "I apologize."

Bamboo's face softens. "Regardless, it is good you can speak. That you can question. It comforts me against some hidden damage." He produces a handheld light, and leaning in again, flashes it in one eye, then the other. He straightens and his face draws blank. Intense.

It is like a light snaps on. All of a sudden I see images in my head. Rotating shapes and numbers.

"Can you see anything inside?"

I nod.

Bamboo still looks intense. Studied. Not concerned, but fully involved. "What do the numbers add up to?" he asks.

I shut my eyes so I can focus. I see a five, a seven, an eighteen...

"Fifty-six," I say finally.

"That is good. And direction of rotation? The colors?"

I describe everything in full detail. Finally Bamboo nods and looks pleased. "There will be much practice with your fellow implantees later. You will and should practice on your own, of course."

I nod. "Of course."

"I've sent you a message," he says. "Do you have it?"

I felt the notification. It was like a small marble dropping on glass. I *will* the message open. Read it aloud. The first pillar: There is no other god but A.

"Very good."

I mentally explore the messaging interface. Begin to equate my own images and names, with those the implant recognizes. Form connections. I want to try my own messages. To reach out and connect with those of my new community. But all of the names, all the idents, are foreign to me. They have reputations, of course, but that is all speculation.

"Now send me one," he says.

I think of something. A timely message that I'm sure he rarely gets from new implantees. "Thank you," I send.

The corners of Bamboo's mouth lift slightly. "You are welcome," he sends back.

I smile at my success. Now that I know I can do it, I want only to tell more people of my progress. There is one person in particular. The only person that would really understand. The one responsible for my success, my survival.

I compose my message, seal it, and encrypt it for good measure. I find his indent, and send my note on its way. Nanoseconds scream by as I wait for a response.

My message returns unopened.

What's this? Have I done something wrong? Not composed his ident correctly?

Bamboo watches me closely, smiling. He knows I'm up to something. Trying out my new toy.

I check the sending information again. Recompose everything just to be sure. Then send it out again. Push it into the stream.

But again, my message returns.

It is like no one is there. Like the debugger I knew is gone.

MORE THAN A DAY has gone by now since HardCandy's implant rendered her comatose. I've spent the entire time cloistered within our beetle-provided apartment.

Much of the time I've spent hovering over her tube, staring into the opening, hoping to see some sign that she will awaken. A fluttered eyelid, a movement of her mouth...something to show that she can get over it. That she can come back to me. To us. Whatever that "us" represents.

I even tried messaging her. Sending little pictures of remembered flowers. Or a favorite joke. A shared experience. Those got me nothing. During the wee hours of the night, when my frustration reached its worst, I even sent her angry missives. Slams on her debugging abilities. Digs on her feet—a body part I know she finds hideous. Anything to rail her. To make her real again.

But nothing happens. She continues to lie like a slug. Like an unwrapped mummy. Perfect in color and beauty, of course. Yet changeless and distant. Gone from me, and yet not free as in death.

I pace the room. Lost in my revelry.

The rest of the time I've spent simply existing. Playing with the wall view screens. Trying to create a small pool for a bath. Attempting to form a replica of a cricket-bot. Anything to enhance my ability to control beetle technology. With little success. No matter what I try, it doesn't fit. Doesn't work right.

I cling to the records of her life that HardCandy sent me. Slowly I'm working my way through them. Looking for something that can help me. Something that makes sense.

I sink in the miry depths, where there is no foothold. I have come into the deep waters; the floods engulf me.

What is that? Where does it come from? When I was released from my stops, did the stream implant these phrases as well? If so, they seem almost to mock me. What good do they do when I'm lost and confused? How do they help?

I wait for more phrases to come. Something to explain my situation. To answer my questions.

But more nothing.

I need to do something, though. Aside from HardCandy and Dark-Trench, I have a group of freeheads counting on me back on Earth—GrimJack, TallSpot, Handler, and the rest. Even without all the answers, I could be helping them if I were there. Using my implant to keep the sword from their necks.

In the absence of any real course of action, I fall back on my normal ways. Seek information. The more you know, the quicker the solution will come.

With a last look at HardCandy, I walk to the door and stream it open.

Time to talk to Shem.

• • •

The rectangle brings me to a shining black obelisk of a building, possibly twenty stories in height. It winds its way to the top, circling the building, passing windows that go opaque as we grow close and become transparent again as we sweep away. Finally we reach the top of the tower, only a story down from where the building tapers to form a point.

The rectangle pauses, then slides close. Squinting, I am able to recognize an exterior door, though there is little to distinguish it from the surface of the building around it. Only a faint ridge, a subtle shadow. As if by magic, a landing platform forms at that door. The rectangle aligns over it and descends.

When we touch down, a white guardrail grows from the platform's sides. It reaches about a meter and a half in height and stops. A woven mesh fills in the space from the guardrail to the platform floor. I step free of the rectangle and walk the short distance to the door, which itself slides aside to give me access.

The first room I encounter is spacious, nearly two stories in height. The floor appears to be a dark colored stone; the walls are stunningly white with protruding sections that resemble pillars. Above is what looks like a gigantic skylight, except the view isn't of the cavern the city is in, but of the darkness of space, broken up by the most incredible nebulae. Wispy horse heads and flowering anemone. Starbursts of every color.

In the center of the room is a large crystalline sculpture, except when I draw near, I find that it isn't a sculpture at all. There are subtle controls inlaid within the surface.

Shem enters the room from the opposite side of the sculpture. "What do you think of it?" he asks.

"I have no idea what to think," I say. "What is it?"

Shem approaches the sculpture and interacts with the controls. Soon various portions of the sculpture begin to move, sliding in every direction. Random notes begin to play, as well. High and low, long and short. There is no melody, only single notes in succession. Like an orchestra tuning its instruments.

"Wonderful, is it not?"

I wait for a rhythm to form, some harmony, but none manifests. "It plays notes."

"Precisely," he says. "All of them. Every potential combination."

I squint as a particularly high note is reached. "Is this something you choose to listen to?"

"On occasion," he says, smiling. "This is one of my first creations. To me it has great symbolism."

I slowly circle the machine, watching as the rods of crystal move. None move in the exact same direction. Some slide up and down, others horizontally, others at an angle. Again, it is randomness in motion.

"It just moves," I say. "And plays."

"Yes," he says, nodding.

"But accomplishes nothing of value."

"Incorrect," he says. "It moves and it plays. That is not nothing. It is everything."

"I see. What does it symbolize to you?"

Shem smiles, raises a hand toward the skylight. "Why, the universe, of course." Leading from the room is a large archway, which Shem now turns toward. "Come, I have other things to show you."

He leaves the sculpture as it is, but my ears wish he would have shut it off. As I follow, I give a lingering look at its machinations. Sliding and churning, plinking, plunking, and clanking, haphazardness symbolized.

The next room is smaller, but still quite large. The ceiling is four meters above us. The room is lit by an orange light and the walls are again white. On dark platforms around the exterior are more devices, reminding me a bit of GrimJack's shop on Earth. Except while GrimJack's machines are all works in progress, here I'm sure they are all functional. Whether what they do is meaningful or not, though, isn't obvious. There are large machines with heavy tubing, delicate creations that look like a puff of air might blow them over, and others with circular gears and sprockets.

"More of my creations," Shem says, with a flourish of his hand.

"Do any of them do anything?" I ask.

Shem's eyebrows raise and a bit of defensiveness enters his voice. "They all do something," he says. "Of course. Otherwise I would let Japheth's ilk have them."

"So you keep them as trophies," I say. "That seems egodriven. Antithetical to the reality Japheth described."

Shem sighs. "Reclaimers have their use, and their beliefs support that usefulness, so that is the reality they live in. But that doesn't mean it is true."

I approach a blue and silver machine. It has a spinning winged protuberance on one end, connecting cables, and visible circular chambers.

"An engine fueled by hydrocarbons," Shem says. "A simple dalliance. An early 'trophy,' you might call it."

I reach out and slowly turn the winged portion. The volume in the chambers shrink and grow. "But useful?" I ask.

"Absolutely. Each piece is necessary. When mounted on another device, high speeds could be reached. Much work could be accomplished."

I nod. "I've streamed similar devices. On the streets they're still occasionally used. Often at the user's peril."

Shem raises an eyebrow. "The streets?"

I sniff. "A portion of our planet where it is ill-advised to be."

Shem nods. "Like the exterior of this one?"

"Something like that." I scan the rest of the room. Most of the devices are complex. Beyond anything I can fathom or build. Could I understand them if I were connected to their stream using the constructor template?

"So how do you decide what needs designing? What needs your attention next?"

Shem smiles. "Why, whatever we desire! Therein lies the beauty. Whatever we can imagine, that we can create."

And certainly they could devise a fix for DarkTrench, and probably HardCandy. But the question remains: do I want them to?

I walk to another display. A portion of it is a square tank full of water. The rest of the mechanism appears to be powered by the movement of that water as it plunges over a sheer drop. Wheels turn, more water is moved.

"So, the cycle that Japheth describes," I say. "It isn't true?"

Shem sighs. "From a certain perspective I suppose it is true. Certainly matter can be recycled. Reused. The process happens in stars. The death of one fuels another."

"So you agree we come from stars?"

Shem nods. "Oh, of course, of course. Everything comes from stars."

"How so?"

Shem straightens. "You require a lesson in astrophysics? In chemistry? We thought you were a technician."

"I am a specialist," I say. "Everyone like me has specialties, areas of expertise. Neither of my areas of expertise are the sciences you name. I don't require an answer, but if you want to provide one, I will listen."

Shem waves a hand. "Of course," he says. "You are aware of the elements, correct? The building blocks of matter?"

"Yes...that much I'm aware of."

Shem walks closer to the water display, and sticking a finger into the fluid, increases the water's motion, and in turn, its speed over the drop. "The universe is made up of two primary elements. The single electron element and the double electron element."

"Hydrogen and helium," I say.

Shem makes slight bow. "If that is how you have named them, very well." He returns his attention to the display, drawing a finger across the water's surface. "These two elements in the form of gases, driven by the force of gravity, clump together. Eventually the object formed by this clumping gets smaller and smaller, and its temperature gets higher and higher until the process called fusion begins. Fusion is the machination that changes one element into another."

"It sounds familiar..." It was part of one of DarkTrench's lessons.

Shem nods. "Yes. When fusion begins we have what is called a star. In newborn stars hydrogen is fused to form more helium. This process continues for a very long time. Billions of years, hydrogen being formed to helium."

I leave Shem to his water device and drift toward another. This one is apparently a perpetual motion machine, as it features little gears turning clock-like hands around a horizontal positioned circle. It is not clear how it is powered. "So more helium is produced," I say. "I see."

"Correct," Shem says. "Until the hydrogen in the star is exhausted."

The gears continue to click, move the hands around the circle. "And then the star goes out?"

Shem moves over to join me, standing on the opposite side of the platform. "No," he says. "That is when gravity begins to work again, compressing the star even further, raising the temperature..."

"And then?"

"And then the element you call helium begins the fusion process, forming still more complex elements. The six electron element and the eight electron element, for instance."

I stroll toward another crystalline machine. I'm afraid to linger too long here, for fear it plays Shem's version of music. "That still only accounts for a handful of the total elements, correct?" I say. "Aren't there more than a hundred?"

Shem shadows me, raising a finger. "There are. And for many stars helium burning is the end of the process." He approaches the crystalline machine.

"But not all," I say.

"No, not all. For those large enough, the process will begin again. And will produce yet more elements. Stars sufficiently large will eventually produce all the known elements, and in exploding at death, eject them into space."

"Into space?"

"Where they can be used again for other things. And so, everything comes from stars."

"So, stars are a kind of machine."

Shem nods. "Precisely. A cosmic machine. An element constructor. Producer of the building blocks of all there is." He touches a place at the bottom of the crystalline machine. I brace myself for more notes, more randomness, but the wispy strands of the machine only begin to turn slowly. On the ceiling above, light patterns dance.

"Nice..."

"Convenient," Shem corrects. "Fortunate that it all works as it does. Because there are certainly no guarantees."

"No guarantees?" That sounds like nothing I've heard before. The Abduls claim that nearly everything is guaranteed. Again, the fatalism. If something happens, it was because A wanted it to happen. Taken to the nth degree. It is as if all choices have been stripped. If a child is sold into slavery by his parents, it is because A wanted it to happen. If a man kills himself, it was A's will.

I look at Shem thoughtfully. Perhaps he *does* know the truth I'm seeking.

"You appear puzzled," he says. "Is it because I said there are no guarantees?"

"Yes," I say. "It is very different than what I'm used to."

"Then what you are used to is mistaken." Shem smiles brightly, confidently.

"How so?" I glance at the ceiling again, watch as the lights dance.

"Because there are no guarantees in the universe, no guiding force. It is like the machine I showed you. All simply random."

I CHASED A SIGNAL across the galaxy. Hundreds of light-years to a variable star. I left everything and everyone I knew. The planet of my birth. I brought along the only person I can say I care about and flew here in a ship both experimental and complex. We found a planet that wasn't supposed to be there and a culture sophisticated beyond reason. A people who live inside the planet, mind you. Now my ship is dead and my HardCandy lies comatose and unreachable.

Shem's theory might have merit...

He watches me, smiling brightly. "You still seem confused," he says. "Come, let me show you another one of my works." He approaches a platform holding a meter-high dark pyramid. "This one can be started via the stream." Smiling, he nods toward the object.

Stepping closer, I notice a red light on the pyramid's surface. It stays on for precisely one second, then winks off, only to appear again in a different location.

"The surface of this machine is divided into tens of thousands of cells, all able to light independently. The machine, at random, picks which cell to light next. Only one cell is lit at any time."

It is a bit boring to watch. Light on, light off, light on, light off. "What's the significance?"

"As I said, there are thousands of cells, but only one cell on the pyramid's peak. How often would you say that cell gets lit?"

I frown. "Using simple logic, the chances are roughly once for every number of cells present on the surface."

"Correct. And statistically, that is how this machine performs. Within a small margin of error."

The light on the top of the pyramid glows red. To emphasize what must be a rare occurrence, a scarlet beam shoots from the ceiling to connect with it.

"Ah, there, you see?"

I shake my head. "Hard to miss."

"Purposely so." Shem spreads his hands. "And it beautifully illustrates my point."

"Which is?"

"Given enough time and iterations, even generated at random, the top light will be lit at some point." His smile broadens. "That is how the universe works."

What is he proposing? That everything happens by chance? That there is no A? No A~A³? Burroughs and bradbury!

"I'm not sure I understand..."

"It is quite simple, actually. Anything is possible, it is only a matter of time."

"So there is no purpose to the universe?" I ask. "Nothing in charge of its behavior?"

Shem shakes his head. "By accident we came, by intellect we survive. Certainly our shared presence must prove that to you?"

The light begins traveling the pyramid's surface again. "How so?"

"Your people, our people, both products of the same process. Both products of randomness. Instances when the light happened to find the top."

Squinting, I shake my head. "I don't think I follow. How does that disprove a master...um...constructor? If anything, it would serve to reinforce that idea, don't you think? Something guiding the process?"

"A master constructor who put us so far from each other that we couldn't intersect without the force of your will? Without the design of your own hands?"

Not my hands. But I see his point.

HardCandy's theory of jinn returns to me. The idea that we were destined to meet these creatures because it was A's will. Scattered and gathered. The problem with her theory is that it doesn't change the questions. Since the jinn she proposed could be either good or evil, how would I know which side Shem and his people were on? Doesn't the fact that they seem to deny A's existence prove which side they are on?

Some of our teachers say that everyone has a jinn attached to them, urging them to evil. Those same teachers also teach that for counterbalance a guardian angel follows us around, pushing us to good. I wonder where that angel goes for an implant like me. When the internal stops are working, is the angel even necessary? And is the jinn ever satisfied?

With HardCandy he was. I'm sure of that. Satisfied to see her fall.

And yet, I am free of my stops. That fact remains. Is that a random act?

"I can't accept that," I say. "I have evidence to the contrary."

Shem's eyebrows raise. "Evidence? Really? Tell me of this evidence."

I hesitate, but finally break down and summarize the reason for our trip. The first crew's interception of the superlative stream, the changes that stream affected. First in the bot and crew, and then in me.

Shem shakes his head when I am finished. "It is a remarkable story," he says. "Interesting, but not solid evidence by any means." He motions for me to follow. "I have yet another thing to show you."

We exit the trophy room to a third room, both spacious and circular in design. Here the floors seem like highly glossed wood. The walls are a warm rust color. The ceiling arches to a point in the center of the room.

In the middle of the room is another object—either a sculpture or a machine, I cannot tell. It is silver and much of it is cylindrical. Only at the top and bottom does the design get more complicated, with crosspieces and tubing. It looks vaguely familiar.

"This is only a model of the actual design," Shem says. "You've witnessed a portion of the full-scale device outside. In the empowerment festival."

I nod, now realizing what the object is. "You said it was a generator of some sort," I say. "For projections?"

Shem nods. "Yes, precisely. You didn't miss that portion of the festival, apparently."

"I didn't see a demonstration," I say. "What does it do?"

"Allows for the projection of our stream into the cosmos. It can take the essence of a stream to the furthest extents of the galaxy."

My heart drops. They can send out streams? These beetles?

"It is something my people have accomplished in ages past," he says. "The structure you saw on the surface, near where you landed? That houses much of the mechanism. We've even had preliminary tests. Small firings, we like to call them."

Which could explain the stream I sampled as we approached the planet. But could it explain what the crew encountered? The changes it brought to their outlook? Or the effects on the bot? It quoted scriptures!

"So it is a communication device..."

Shem raises his hands exuberantly. "Oh, it is more than that. Much more! It would allow a physical manifestation of our will. A stream-created construct, you might say."

"A what?"

"A stream projection."

I can only shake my head. "I don't understand."

Shem points toward the sky. "Look," he says. "You came here in a device made of heavy elements. Crossing great distances of hazardous space, correct?"

I look over the model's silver form again. There is a certain rocket-like appearance to it. "Yes..."

"Well, this device can do that for us without us having to physically leave our planet. The safety of our cities. Quite simply, it not only broadcasts our stream but can reform elements to obey it." He pauses, flutters his hand. "What name do you ascribe to your position?"

"My position?"

"As someone who travels interstellar space?"

I sniff. "Astronaut, I suppose. But I hardly—"

Shem snaps his fingers. "Perfect, yes, astronaut. That's what we would create. A stream-manipulated astronaut, formed out of the matter of whatever planet we choose to explore."

Rails, what? A chill travels my spine. Something about what Shem proposes is bizarre. And a little frightening. The ability to create, to project, the elements elsewhere by the force of will remotely? It is a stupefying power. A godlike power.

And to think I was only a mid-level debugger a short time ago. Could I possibly be part of such a society? Should I?

"Yet you don't believe in any god," I say. "In anything that made it all?" I briefly describe the Abdul's creation mythos.

Shem watches silently. Smiling. "I've seen no clear evidence of such a being. Though it should be obvious to you by now that even someone with such powers may or may not still be worthy of your allegiance. From your reactions, and from what you've told me, I can tell that our 'technology' is superior to yours. Is it not possible that whatever changed you is simply someone from another planet who is equally, or even more, superior? Someone who you would be best to guard yourself against?"

I remain silent. Try to think it all through.

"Or perhaps," he says, "what affected you is merely randomness in action. Have you heard anything, sensed anything nonsensical? Seemingly out of the norm?"

I think of the random phrases that enter my head. And the visions of the brown triped. "At times..."

"Perhaps it is your brain that is defective. Perhaps it, like your companion's, is in need of adjustment. Is that a possibility?"

I shrug.

"All very good reasons to join us then. To let us work with you through our stream."

There is a sense of freedom in what Shem offers, and in his beliefs, but there is also a sense of disappointment. A real feeling of sorrow. I wasn't expecting to find this. Though I feared what I might find, I never imagined this.

But I'm also stuck. I can't get back to the ship. I can't revive it or HardCandy.

Is this all there is?

"What of Ham's group?" I ask. "What of the maintainers?"

Shem appraises the model of the stream projector. Smiles at it. "Ham's group are possibly the most mentally unburdened of any of us. They don't think about the kinds of things that constructors do, or even reclaimers. They simply *do*. They are given a task, and they perform it. Happy in their obliviousness. They have times for games and exercises. But they also exist on the efforts of others. They have little room to grow."

I nod. It makes a certain amount of sense; has a certain feel. It was where I was on Earth, certainly. Not admittedly, but functionally. Do the job. Fix things and move on.

But could I live there again now? I know things I didn't know before. At least I thought I did.

I am against you, you great monster lying among your streams. You say, "I made it for myself." But I will put hooks in your jaws and make the fish of your stream stick to your scales.

What the what? Monster among the streams? Hooks and scales? That has to be the most random phrase I've gotten yet.

I look at Shem to see if he received the message too, but of course he did not. He stands confidently. Self-assured. "It is interesting what you said earlier about the star," he says.

"What I said about it...what?"

"About it singing curiously. Stars *do* sing, you know?"

I feel a flicker of hope. Something that might make sense. "They do?"

"Yes. Churning gas in their outer layers create low-frequency sound waves that rebound throughout the star. It is a useful tool for determining such things as the star's density and temperature."

I raise my eyebrows. Shem is full of information.

"It is a purely natural occurrence. And since sound doesn't travel through the vacuum of space, it isn't something your earlier astronauts would have encountered."

"Purely natural? Meaning random?"

Shem nods toward the room with his creations, the one with the pyramid. "In a top of the pyramid sort of way. Another instance when an accident does something beneficial."

"So there's no way it could affect the crew? Or the bot I fixed?"

Shem shakes his head. "No, no. That, I'm afraid, is the result of another kind of randomness. But one I can't even begin to explain."

I study the projector. Yes. Randomness. It may all be randomness.

OVER TEN YEARS HAVE PASSED since my implantation. During that time I have debugged countless machines. I've even increased my level twice. Been promoted from ten to eleven and then twelve. New possibilities opened up to me. New schematics made available.

My master is an elderly man, one with many, many wives, children, and grandchildren. That's good for me, because whatever strength brought him that extended family is now long since gone. Either that or it is daily exhausted by the sheer numbers involved. He never looks at me in any other way than the way he should. As a man would look at a robot, or a stove.

I'm happy in that.

Occasionally I will get looks from others. Most are looks of surprise or curiosity. Usually they are trying to determine if I am what they think I am. A female debugger. A female skin. Most only stare for a moment. Afraid that they are correct in what they suspect...or perhaps that they are incorrect. I keep my jumpsuit loose fitting and as straight as possible. Praise A that I'm not a voluptuous woman. I no longer have the body of a boy, but I no longer am just a girl anymore either.

Weird how bumped out the female body gets. What is the point in that? It doesn't help me, I know that. Living martyrs don't need bumps.

My current job is a late model servbot. It is what they call a hybrid, because it doesn't have legs from the waist down. Only wheels.

Above the waist it is fairly humanoid—if your idea of humanoid is pale blank face and no lips. Still, when it is active it is a bit more cheery. Not quite so zombielike. The master paid a small fortune for it. He has twenty.

I'm working in the back room of the master's kitchen. A place to keep me out of sight. Again, I'm okay with that. I don't need kids smelling in my business. True, I was once such a smelling kid, but kids have hands that like to grab. I once yelled at a kid that liked to grab. The mental lash wasn't too awful that time, but it was bad enough.

The room is mostly for storage. Behind me are rows of shelving, all packed with food. More than an army could eat in a year. More food than I could imagine when I was young. Back when the streets were close. I sometimes wonder what my mother would think if she saw it all. Wonder if her mouth would gap in amazement.

I wonder if she is happy yet.

On the floor beside me is my supply bag, fully open. The bot's problem is simple. Should be simple. The blinking thing won't move. After delivering a basket of bread to a table, it rolled itself in a circle three times, spun into a table of diplomats, then careened into a wall. Quite a show. Wish I were there to see it. Few adults were laughing. Most of the kids were, though. I saw it all on the security vid later. It was rails funny, actually. I even Standard Impacted the thing to the stream. Let every debugger share the fun. There are a few, like Bamboo, you have to make sure to exclude in such things. That's fine. He's permanently excluded from my mind anyway now.

I retrieve a viewing sheet from my bag and, curling up on the floor beneath the bot, press it across the bot's lower back. Near where the wheels attach to the torso.

I have a bit of intuition about these things. Always have. Makes me my master's most valuable tool, or so he says.

Part of my intuition comes from natural A-given ability. The other part comes from having worked in his house as long as I have. Only a quick scan of the innards of the bot at medium magnification shows me what I need to know. Shaking my head, I crawl over to my bag again and pull out some standard-issue flex-pliers. I return to the area below the sheet, find a three millimeter joint in the roller mechanism, and work the pliers in. They are stream adjustable, so I tell them to bend slightly as I shove. A few moments later I capture what I'm looking for. Still guiding the pliers, I pull it out.

Someone has lodged a plastic something—a green soldier leg, maybe—into the mechanism. Not sure how they managed it, but the thing melted and fused within the bot's innards. Fried a motivator, by the looks of it.

The nannies are getting paid too much. Either that, or the cooks have helpers they aren't aware of, aren't watching.

Unfortunately, the motivator is a part I don't have. I'm going to have to step out for it. Sighing, I repack my bag and shoulder it. I reach down and stroke the bot's head, then shake my own. "Kids, huh?"

I make for the upper stories and the pylon where my silver downrider waits. I have some shopping to do.

· · ·

Twenty minutes later I'm in route to Razzles. It is the nearest gear shop, bound to have the part I need. The place is near street level, though, so it is always a bit of a risk. Urging my downer to its highest speed, I whiz past the shining megaliths of kings and corporations, and then the older brick and stone buildings of the settlements. Soon the lowdowns are directly below me, the places that masters rarely talk about. Never enter. Whole sections where people live in tents like our forefathers did. Tents with no camels and no slaves.

And no tech.

It isn't until I'm less than a block from the shop that I start get warnings on the stream.

"Bad blow at Razzles," someone named FrontLot streams. "Don't be here."

At this point, I have little choice. The string I'm on goes right by Razzles and ends about two blocks up the street. I'll be passing it no matter what. I could reverse the downer, but curiosity won't let me now. I urge it on.

The fact that the downrider is sealed probably shielded me from the initial sound. It couldn't shield me from the sight, though. The first thing I see is smoke billowing up the front of the building, sending tendrils of offense in every direction. Razzles had been something called a "church" once and so is odd in design. White in color, with a portion of the structure reaching skyward. Not like the rounded domes and minarets of the temples, though. This tower is squared and steeped.

Like I said, odd.

The front of Razzles is no longer white now. There is blackened char everywhere. The owner of Razzles had altered a wide section of the building's front to allow for large windows. So people could view the wares inside. The windows are all gone now too. Blasted into glistening fragments on the sidewalk.

And the smoke continues to billow.

"What happened?" I stream FrontLot, who is presumably somewhere nearby. Beyond danger, hopefully.

He gives me a Full Impact answer. Lots of pain and anger in the flow. "Antitex again, Hard. Lowdown ramblers. Fighting hunger with big booms."

Antitex did this? I gape in amazement. I see a handful of Abduls with blood on their hands and face. Passersby, I'm guessing. There's a small group of debuggers too. They look worse, like they were closer to the blast. One kneels on the sidewalk, completely naked, hands gripping his head. Arms covered in gore.

Yet I hear only the downer's whine. Watching the whole event as if in a bubble. Which I kind of am.

Stream is screeching now. Some of it is illegible gibberish. Bursts of random anguish and outrage. Stops are in place still. Railing against the antitex won't get you tweaked, but railing against A will. Or the Imam.

"But what exactly happened?" I query FrontLot.

"Crazy bits. Lady walked in as if asking directions. Next thing you know, boom!"

"She was wired?"

"Like a firecracker."

"Where were you?"

"At the pylon. Heard the ruckus, then the stream screams. Went to see. Master will hate the time I wasted. Couldn't help it. Also couldn't help them. Maybe they should implant everyone."

My head and eyes follow the scene as it passes into the distance. Only when the downrider surface blocks my view, do I finally turn forward. Discover that my neck is aching. "Maybe..."

The downer slows as we approach the red pylon. I let it ease itself to a stop. I don't tell the canopy to release or the drive to shut off. I just sit. Shaking and wounded.

Soon the internal stops will beckon me to move on. Find another place to get my supplies.

But I don't want to go anywhere. Do anything.

"So what are you working on, Hard?"

THE FIRST THING I DO after returning to our quarters is check on HardCandy. She remains as I left her. Encased within the preservation tube. Silent and still. Her breathing shallow. Face both beautiful and yet distant.

Near the wall to my right, the wall where the exterior vidscreen is placed, is a small white table. The table formed during my absence. On it is a loaf of bread and a pitcher of liquid. A simple meal. Appropriate.

Absently I approach the table and, tearing off a chuck of brown bread, glance at the vidscreen. The view is of the ocean again, though it is a different place than the sandy beaches of before. Here there are no beaches to speak of. Only sheer cliffs and an endlessly pounding surf. A strong breeze follows the ocean inland. I watch as a handful of birds struggle against it, try to make their way to the sea. Where the fish fearlessly play.

"May I disturb you?"

I turn to find Ham standing at the door. He is dressed as they always are, in their customizable fabric pants with bare chest exposed. At least he isn't hairy.

Frowning, I nod.

He approaches HardCandy's silver tube and looks within. "There is no change?"

"Not that I can tell." But I'm not a doctor.

Ham nods. "It is a difficult mechanism to fix. Very different. Very complex and diverse. Many dedicated organisms." He smiles. "As I'm sure you are aware."

"Complex doesn't begin to cover it."

He nods, scans the room. "Your room should bend to your will freely by now. You could do more to make it unique. If such customization interests you."

I shake my head, then notice the eggshell white walls. One of my least favorite colors.

"So, you've talked with Shem. Has he convinced you to take on the template of a constructor?"

I shake my head. "No. Not yet." Loneliness plagues me. Until my talk with Shem I clung to the idea that at least the Great Stream Generator would have a solution to my problems. At least I'd be given a reason for having come out into space. But now I don't know even that. I don't even know that the superlative stream exists, beyond what the beetles have produced with their own machines. Beyond my own inherent randomness.

Ham smiles. "That is good. I believe you would be uncomfortable with them. Out of sync." He approaches the table. "Is this food to your liking? Because there are many possibilities…"

"It is fine." I glance at the vidscreen's pounding waves. "So are you here to recruit me too?"

Ham looks at the screen, squints, then causes the frame of it to reshape, growing more ornate. Widening, with rolls and serifs. Finally, it takes on the look of a hand-sculpted wooden creation. Something that would take a craftsman weeks. "A simple refinement," he says. "Is it acceptable?"

I nod. "It's fine. Do you think I can help HardCandy more by joining your caste over Shem's? I mean, don't you work off what his kind describes?"

He smiles. "Yes, which means everything the constructors design is available to us. We have the best of all worlds. We don't just maintain, we refine. Accentuate. Improve. Anything they can do, we can do better. Without the strain of having created the system in the first place." Ham moves to the table setting, concentrates on it. Soon the pitcher has changed from a simple white container, to a blue-colored model, complete with detailed etchings around the brim and handle. The table begins to transform too. It grows more ornate. With the delicate writings around the edges like I've seen on other beetle objects.

"Better?" he asks.

I sigh. "Fine." I glance at HardCandy's tube. Remember something I'd forgotten to ask about. "It appears that everyone in your kind is of the same, um, kind..."

Ham's forehead wrinkles. "You are already aware of our designations—"

I shake my head. "Not that. That's clear to me. But there seems to be no..." I wave my hands over my chest and midsection. Try to describe something that isn't obvious, without making it so. It's tough work, freehead.

Ham stares at me, smiling.

Come on...

"Are you talking about the organs you cover? The reason your companion requires more clothing?"

"Partially..." I can't believe I'm having this conversation. I thought the notion of parenting was taken from me, and here I am embarking on the hardest talk a parent can give.

Maybe if I stream it to him? But what would I send? It is a good that there are no stops in place now.

Suddenly, I feel thirsty. I move toward the now heavily customized white table and the pitcher of liquid.

Finally, Ham throws his hands out. "You are talking about species replication, correct?"

I reach for a cup, fill it with liquid. "Sure. Yeah. That term works."

He shakes his head. "A constructor probably would've figured that out sooner. I apologize." He bows slightly. "Our numbers have changed very little over time."

"Meaning?"

"Meaning with our bodies the regenerative process is heavily refined. Rarely is a component lost or injured beyond our ability to reconstruct."

I can't help my surprise. "So in the thousands of years of your people's existence..."

"Very few have been lost beyond repair. Consequently, the need to produce additional of our number is rare. Though, if it was, the proper customizations would take place through constructor intervention."

"Proper customization?"

"Yes. No knowledge is lost with us. Everything is remembered. If we required more of our numbers, the ability would be restored. Reconstructed."

I lift the cup to my mouth. Partially hiding my face.

Reconstructed. Burroughs and bradbury...

"So, as you can see, the possibility that we can help your companion—"

"HardCandy."

Ham nods. "Yes, companion HardCandy. The probability that we can help her only increases with you fully connected to our stream."

The liquid is a juice of some sort. Slightly sour, but refreshing.

I look at the vidscreen. Watch the ocean continue to pound the cliffs. The birds continue to fight. Feel my own aloneness. DarkTrench circling above.

What other option do I have? "Okay," I find myself saying. "I'll become a maintainer."

Ham smiles. Nods an acknowledgement.

I study Ham's face, his muscled form. "So what will it take? An operation of some sort?"

His smile broadens. The most teeth I've seen from him yet. "I'm throwing out a ball to you."

"A ball?"

"Yes, in the stream. Do you see it?"

I close my eyes so I can concentrate. Will myself into the flow. I feel the discomfort of the beetle's stream. The feeling of insignificance and incompetence it brings me. I sense the emanations of the room around me. Most loud is the vidscreen to my right. The one component aside from the rectangles that I've tried to interact with. The only thing that seems a little less awkward.

I sense movement. A growing bubble of something in the distance. It looks blue and rubbery.

"Do you see it?" Ham repeats.

"I think so. Yes."

"Then pull it to you. Embrace it. Live in it."

Live in it?

Regardless, I try to pull the bubble toward me. It doesn't seem to want to move.

"Do you have it?"

I shake my head. "Doesn't seem to want to. It feels small and faraway."

Ham chuckles. "It is larger than you think," he says. "Focus."

Don't seek a treaty of friendship with them as long as you live.

The image drops from my mind and I open my eyes.

"What is it?" Ham says.

I shake my head. "I don't know. Sometimes I get these...random thoughts. Thoughts that seem outside of me."

"Inefficiencies," he says. "They should be excluded. After the template is in place, they will be."

"Yeah...they probably should be."

"This is what you've come to," Ham assures. "Accept the ball."

I frown. Shut my eyes again. Soon I see the image of Ham's ball. It looks to be about twenty meters away. It hovers over nothingness, blackness. I sing out to it. Mentally beckon it to me. It moves slightly. As if I put a finger on its northern pole and pushed it slightly off its axis. A small response.

"Do you have it now?'

"I nudged it a little. That's all."

"You have to want it. Reach for it. Grasp it."

Instinctively, I find myself holding out my hands. It probably looks ridiculous, but Ham doesn't say anything. The ball begins to wobble, first slowly, and then faster and faster.

"That's right," Ham says. "You're doing it."

Now the ball almost looks unreal, appearing elongated—misshapen in my mind. The image frightens me, so I ease up on my urging. The ball's vibration begins to slow.

"No, no," Ham cries. "You almost had it. Just a little more."

I feel a trickle of sweat on my brow and wipe it away. Try to regain my concentration. I manage to get the ball moving furiously again. It becomes a blur of activity. Starts to stretch out, like taffy being pulled. Suddenly it breaks free. It retakes its circular form as it turns and seems to fly toward me. The transition seems almost instantaneous. But as the ball, spinning, reaches its largest size, its closest point, I could swear I saw shadows on its surface. Like a digital blue open-to-bite-me face.

I scream.

FOLLOWING THE BOMBING of Razzles, fully thirty minutes go by as I sit. FrontLot asks questions, as do others, but I don't respond. I sit in the enormity of it all. Rocking. Finally, the nudges in my head get too strong to ignore. Frowning, I engage the downrider's reversers. Wait as they spin the whole thing around. Then I remember what I came for and, scolding myself, stream out for another tech shop. I find one that has recently opened only two strings away. The rep is unknown to me, so I ask FrontLot.

"It's above spec maybe two degrees," he streams back. "They got lots of stuff there. Crazy stuff . Multi-gen, even. I've seen things there I've never seen before. Piles of it."

It sounds high level to me. The kind of place where the shoppers might need an Abdul escort. "Is it casual?" I ask. I don't have an escort, and I never want to have one. Even if it means I never see a promotion past thirteen.

"All casual," Front says. "Don't let the supply quantity fool you. The owner is compliant. Gracious."

"And the prices?" Not that my master cares. Thriftiness is built into my genes, though.

"Reason and logic combined. No worries. If you could do Razzles, GeeJays is no problem. It only smells a little."

I scowl and instruct the pylon to begin reorienting my downer for the change of scenery. An arm extends from the pylon's center. When it hovers near my downer, a ring pushes out into position on the canopy behind me. The arm grabs the ring. Lifts. Causes the downer to release its hold on the string. I'm in the pylon's grip now. Suspended. The entire downer slides to my left, toward the intersecting string.

"Smells?" I say.

"Nothing bad," Front says. "Just ancient. Like stale bread."

I hear the snap-hiss of the downer reseating itself on the new string. I wait for the go ahead signal. "Ugh."

"Don't beat it down yet. You'll like it when you're there."

I trust no guarantees now. The last place I tried is smoking.

I reach up and check the downrider's coordinate structure again. Make sure it knows where we are going. I'll need to make one more stringjump before I reach the store. I urge the downrider into motion. It immediately complies, skimming down the new string.

Later, after the final stringjump, it is only two blocks before I reach my destination. The structure is positioned on a hill with its own landing pylon. That's good, because on the way I pass lots of ramshackles—dilapidated buildings and vacant lots—that I would not be good with walking by.

Reaching my stop, I exit the downrider, and follow a ramp from the pylon onto the hill's surface. Above me is a red brick structure, fairly clean looking, but ancient. Surprisingly, there are only a few places where the brick surface has fallen away due to age. Exposing the flat roughness beneath. The building could probably take a bomb hit, I'm guessing. Though I hope not today.

The door of the building gives me pause, because it is completely manual—a round golden knob amidst a sea of green-painted wood. Weird choice for a tech shop. I shrug off the inconvenience and give the handle a push. Nothing happens. Then I try turning. It finally clanks its way open.

Inside, the place is a mess. Clutter cubed. I notice the smell FrontLot warned about, but it isn't as bad as I expected. Not overwhelming, consistent. Permeating. It isn't the smell of stale bread, either. It is earthier. Like rotting leaves in a forest.

FrontLot was right about the amount of raw tech, though. There are things stacked everywhere. Like the store of my youth—if it was hit by a driftbarge filled with bots. No tidy rows of organized wares here. Just stuff everywhere, with the largest concentration being along the walls. In fact, maybe the stacks of vidscreen shells and bot craniums are what's holding the walls in place.

I contemplate turning back and finding another shop. This one is not for me.

One of the piles to my left heaves slightly. From behind it I hear someone say "Ouch!" and "I'll be with you soon!"

The center of the store has the only semblance of organization I can find. Cascading columns of transparent tubes and vials, surrounding a large and comfortable-looking seat. Maybe that's where the motivator parts are? I hope, because I fear an attack of rats if I wander through the rest of the store. I move toward the center.

Reaching the arrangement of tubes, I begin to browse them. I see viewing sheets, blank bot headchips, light probes...I pick up a metal canister and give it a little shake. It makes a scritch-scritch sound like maybe there's sand inside. Frowning, I set it back down. Move further around the circle. I notice a can full of replacement bot eyes.

"You're not a thief, are you?"

The voice returns, this time so close it causes me to jump. From right behind me. Turning, I see a large man with a green beret squashed onto his head, all loose and sloppy like. On the front of the hat is a blue circle with the letters "G" and "J" in letters stylized to look like lightning bolts.

You'd have to see it to understand.

"No, of course not," he says. "With a head like that you wouldn't be a thief, now would you?" He nods at the cylinder I just put down. "A bit of a self-starter, though, aren't you?"

This GJ is imposing. Overweight, yes, but also large of stature. Instinctively, I take a step back. Cower a bit. "I just need a motivator..."

His eyes light up. "Now we're talking some action. Model and make?"

I steel myself, manage to blurt out what I need.

He nods and circles around to the front of the display, to where the maroon seat is, and drops into it. The seat heaves a sigh. "I've got two choices," he says, "depending on your preference. SamSony or Elipserv. The latter needs more credits, but the guarantee is longer. Which suits you?"

I move where I can see him between the tubes. Something about him seems familiar. Not sure why that would be, though. I've never been here before. Only ever used one tech shop besides Razzles. And both of those were family businesses, with the elder master firmly in charge. Omnipresent.

"You a mouse?" He lifts the corner of his beret to scratch beneath. I notice there is no hair there and let out a little gasp.

"Sorry," he says. "Scared you and I haven't even told you the prices yet."

I shake my head. "I'm not scared." I *do* feel a little shaken from the events of the day. My view of the smoke. "Are you a debugger?" I couldn't imagine a master allowing such a thing. DRs normally don't have time for side jobs.

GJ removes his hat to reveal a completely smooth scalp. "Noticed my scar, huh?" He leans his head forward and traces the white stripe at his left temple. It is thick. A worst case scenario for implant scars. In comparison, mine is barely noticeable.

"That's not only one scar," he says, leaning closer. "It is two." He raises his head again and smiles. "I have conjoined twins."

My unsettlement grows. It feels like there's a hard metal ball in my stomach. Rolling. I resort to silence. Unsure of what to say next. He's an ex-implant! But I thought it was impossible for angels to fall...

He reseats the beret on his head. "So do you know which one you want?"

I shake my head, trying to clear it.

He shrugs. "Tell you what, I'll go through the fine print for you. Give you the whole spiel..." He begins to ramble on, ignoring my discomfort. He lays out the prices, the warrantees, the benefits of each manufacturer, and their controlling houses.

Again, something about him stirs me. The way he leaves me to myself while going about his business.

"You know," he says. "I have a sister. Had, actually. She died a couple years ago. A real tragedy..." He looks at me again. Closely. "It is unusual. You being female. I hope I'm not assuming too much, but in my day it wasn't allowed. The idea of a female DR was radical. Rails radical..."

All of a sudden I get it. I see him without the extra ten years and dozens of pounds. I see him as if we were standing before me in that shop of my childhood. Him fixing the bot while I hid in the shadows of a nearby aisle. Watching as best I could.

GJ pauses. Squints. Stares close. "You're not her, are you?"

I raise an eyebrow; look nervously at the cylinders in front of me. "Your sister?"

He scowls. "No, Crichton, no. That girl! The one I helped out." He circles the side of his head with a finger. "It isn't all like it used to be. I mean, some things are really gone. Got ripped out completely along with the teardrop..." He looks hard. Pauses. "But I still have some strong images from before..." He shakes his head and points. "You *could* be her. Younger and smaller."

I am both thrilled and horrified. I was never able to locate the debugger DR 44 after my message to him was returned. I tried again multiple times. All resulted in nothing. I did my own search too, of course. Talked to fellow skins about him without really talking about him. Tried to find out.

Bamboo would've known where he was, of course. But it would've been foolish of me to ask him. Only increased his concern about me and my emotions, my sex. I didn't want him to mess with any of my inherent desires like he did the men. Being stopped was bad enough.

I didn't expect to see DR 44 like this, though. An angel with clipped wings. Mentally neutered. And so close to the streets.

He's lost his guarantee of Paradise!

I find myself shaking my head—lying about my identity. The implant warns me, tweaks me. But I have a strong resistance to tweak pain. That's something Bamboo doesn't know either. I can stand more, but it drags out longer. I'm good at hiding the effects.

GJ stares a bit longer, then shrugs. "I guess I'm wrong. Wouldn't be the first time." He holds up a small paper bag. "So did you decide about the motivator?"

I'm slow in answering. I hate that.

"Which?" he says.

"I'll take both," I say, forcing a smile. "I hate to come back."

He shrugs again. "Anything for a lady." He plunges a hand into two separate canisters. Drops the rectangular motivators into the bag. "If it reads clear, I'll gladly take back the one you don't use." He holds the bag out where I can take it, and I hand him my purchasing card. He makes use of the card and then nods. "Appreciate the business." A smile. "It is GrimJack, by the way." He indicates the beret and the circle on the front. "That's where the GJ comes from."

I return the nod. "GrimJack. Got it." Feeling all closed up, I make for the door.

"I hope to see you again."

I look back. "You will."

THE FEELING IS UNSETTLING, but incredible. If the harnessed beetle stream I shared previously was a bubbling brook, then the full-out stream is like a waterfall. Every centimeter of the room seems alive to me. Ready to obey my every command.

In fact, the feeling isn't confined to just my head, my brain, it is like it is itching through the very cells of my body. Like every hair follicle could affect the blank slate of the room before me, around me. Electrically enable, bitwise manipulate, refine, restore, endow with life! Everything sings out for my attention. The vidscreen, a piccolo. The table, a violin—no, a cello! The door behind me, an oboe. The floor, a bass drum. All that is left for me is to conduct. Direct. Control!

Next to me, Ham smiles. "Your template is in place now, correct? You are ready to go?"

"More than I've ever been," I say. "It is amazing." I reach out for the table that Ham enhanced. Tell it to grow, lengthen—and it does. I shut my eyes and envision a full-length wooden table like those I've glimpsed in master's palaces, one complete with real stone accents set into the corners. A table with a gloss so thick, so stunning, that a mirror is unnecessary. The wood is a dark mahogany. Priceless.

I open my eyes to find the table as I imagined. Exactly what I wanted.

"Incredible."

I look at the vidscreen. Internally it seems quite simple to me now. The entire wall could be a vidscreen if I wanted. I call out for a dozen viewable surfaces. One that shows the present beach scene. Another that shows the location where we landed. Another that shows the star Betelgeuse, magnified. A city scene, a microscopic scene, a forest scene—on vidscreens of all shapes and sizes. A circular vidscreen next to a hexagonal one. Square, rectangle, isosceles. It all happens as I desire.

I move into the center of the room, past HardCandy's tube, to a wide open rectangular space. Staring at the floor, I seek the elements that compose it. Tell them to pull back. Form a cavity. Soon after I ask for it, it happens. A two-meter-square hollow opens up. Tiles form around it.

"Now, how do I fill it with water?" I ask.

"Ah, there was a pool here before, wasn't there?" Ham nods. "Let me show you." He messages me in the stream. It is similar to the Full Impact messages I'm used to, excepting the emotions portion. Not that the emotions portion is missing, mind you. It is *different*. Perhaps because Ham is different.

Regardless, I see him holding a ball of something akin to gelatin. It shakes and wobbles in his hand. "This is our fluid enhancer. Each of the elementary states requires a different one." Ham's image holds it out. "Use it. Smooth it into your pool."

I nod at him. Take the ball. It *feels* like gelatin, as well. I force it into the internal image of the pool I have constructed. Tell it to fill the pool halfway. The ball expands and smoothes out. Flattens to fit the space. The top surface begins to ripple.

I open my eyes to find the pool filled with crystal-clear water, to the level I described. I stoop down and touch it. It is perfect bath temperature. Warm, scentless, tasteless, and wet.

"What can't you do here?" I ask, standing again.

Ham shrugs. "That isn't for us to wonder. That is a constructor worry. But I'm sure they'd say that only imagination limits them."

I nod slowly, then glance at HardCandy's still form. "So, when can we help her? Bring her back?"

Ham raises a cautionary hand. "It will take some time. As you continue to interface with our stream, we will come to more fully understand the way your body functions. Your companion will be safe until that time."

I force a frown. I am unhappy that HardCandy can't be a part of this. Can't feel what I feel. Yet I also want to try out my new abilities. Test them. See what I can do.

"So, until then," I ask, "what can I do? Is there anything that will speed up the process?"

Ham nods. "You are a maintainer now. You will have tasks to perform." He puts out a hand to rest on my shoulder. "Feel free to sample our stream in whatever manner you prefer. Here there are no stops. It will never be withdrawn from you, never be controlled."

His hand on my shoulder is warm, stopping shy of being uncomfortable. "I can sense that," I say, nodding. "I feel the freedom here."

"Good. You are fully one of us. You will never be harmed by what you encounter on our stream. Troubling thoughts are not present."

What does that mean? My life is filled with troubling thoughts. I can't imagine it any other way.

I get a feeling from my implant. It isn't like a stop, more like a tingle. A tingle that flashes red.

Ham smiles. "Ah, your first duty has arrived. You are needed."

"Am I ready for that?"

"Of course. As ready as any of us."

Ham grasps both shoulders, turns me so I face the door. "Go where the signal takes you. Quickly." He gives me a little shove. Not unfriendly, but not respectful either. I'm not sure I'm okay with it.

"Was that necessary—"

Another prodding hand. "Time is of the essence," he says. "Maintain first, play later."

I take step toward the door, glance back at HardCandy's tube. Hesitate.

"She will be fine. Healed if you apply yourself. Now go." He moves up behind me.

"So are you coming with me? To sort of, at least, watch?"

Ham shakes his head. "I have a task of my own to attend to. We need to reach our platforms. Now."

MANIPULATING THE FLYING RECTANGLE now proves to be a simple task, only requiring a fraction of my attention. As I climb away from the structure that houses our apartment, I need only to subtly shift my will in the beetle's stream to direct the flying device. As before, there is a sound, smell, and taste to the rectangle, but instead of rubber-tasting cicadas, it is a piano that smells of bananas. Much nicer. Like being in a downrider that has been recently cleaned and scented.

And though I'm a little unsettled by Ham's coercive behavior, I'm also curious to see where I'm headed. Below and around me the city seems to shine with new light. The jutting crystalline structures are still the same at the atomic level, of course. But now I can detect places that are customizable or maintainable. Portions that I could easily affect. On a nearby emerald structure I see systems that can be stream-activated to remove cave pests. A dull electrical charge that will travel throughout the surface. I now understand how the landing platforms interact with the rectangles. How they sometimes seem to meld together.

Rectangles fill the skies around me. None of them in any danger of collision. All traveling via the beetles' stream. Perfectly synchronized, perfectly guided. A testimony to the beetles' ability to overcome the randomness of the universe by sheer force of will.

High above me is the cavern ceiling, dark and filled with teeth-like stalactites. Even those represent no danger to the beetles' initiative, however. There are devices built into the tops of the buildings and streets to detect and destroy anything that would happen to fall.

Incredible. Godlike.

But maintainers waste little time on such thoughts, the template re-minds me. I have a job to do.

I am directed by an internal beacon. Unlike my days on Earth, it is not necessary for me to look up the location. Or make use of archaic maps for guidance. Instead I follow the beacon. It is hard to describe, yet it is present with the job assignment. I know exactly where to go, and through me, so does the rectangle.

I pass under a transparent bridge that stretches between two build-ings. I swoop through a circular tunnel, move above and around first a yellow-colored building, and then a purple one. I notice another area where maintainers are playing games. I see a place where blond con-structors hover around an obelisk, all appearing deep in thought. I skirt by a structure in the process of being torn down. Red-haired reclaimers scurry over its surface, walking in some long mechanical boot, able to hold them to the surface, regardless of what direction they choose to go.

Finally, my rectangle begins to slow. It levels off and comes to rest at ground level, near a golden building with large windows. My implant directs me to the building's entrance. Inside, the building is decorated in gold as well, and the walls have the same translucent quality as the sliver we originally arrived in.

Me and my companion. The name of whom eludes me. She is in a healing tube back home, I know that.

This is a reclaimers building, I realize. Even though the constructors designed it and the maintainers refined it, it still—despite the gold col-oring—bears the feeling of sparseness. Of little ego. There are few of the enhancements that would be found in buildings of other castes. My own apartment is more refined, actually. I smile at the thought.

I climb a short flight of stairs to the second level. The hallway is re-markably indistinct. Stark and translucent. There are many locations of possible refinement, but few have been activated. My goal is the second door on the left. I walk toward it. The door opens as I approach.

Standing within is a reclaimer, face expressionless. He stares at me for a long moment. Probably because I wasn't quite what he was ex-pecting. I am neither blue, nor do I have hair. He is red-haired, hand-some, and strong. As are they all. The only variation between him and

Ham is in facial structure, and even then the difference is small. Subtle. A bit larger nose, a greyish cast to his eyes.

My appearance gives him pause for only a short minute. The stream confirms who I am—what I am. He nods a greeting and points deeper within, toward a corner of the room. I move by him without a sound.

The room is equally sparse. Few refinements. There are windows to the outside. A hard-looking mat on the floor, colored blue. A simple table made of scrap material from one of his previous reclaims. A former door, I believe. In the same corner he indicated are two horizontal platforms. One at floor level, the other mounted at over two meters high, directly above the first. The edges of the platforms are dark in color, but the flat surface has a warm orange glow to it. Or should have. These are not functional, though, so the surfaces are dim.

The platforms are important, the stream tells me. It is how the beetles sustain themselves.

Why they wouldn't eat with us...

It reinvigorates the body. Removes waste. Provides nutrients. Similar to the tube my...companion is in. Back where I live.

"If it requires reclaiming," my reclaimer host streams me, "simply report it." He moves out into the hall, then disappears from view.

I approach the platforms. My shoulder and back itch at me—a remembered feeling. A reminder that at one point in my existence there used to be a pivotal part of my job that rode there. What was it?

Ah, yes. I used to have a bag of tools. Repair equipment. Useful artifacts that would look inside things, or manipulate primary structures. Turn and twist things. Cut and heal.

Those devices are no longer necessary.

I kneel over the lower platform. Drag a hand over its smooth surface. Find it cool and hard.

But what do I use now? How do I effect change? I close my eyes, search for a solution.

A wave builds and falls, crashing in my mind. The tools are within you, and within the machine, novice!

I nod and press harder into the platform's surface. I begin to see the inner structure in my mind. The multiple pathways, the mechanism for transferring energy. Elements are manipulated, fused and split. All work in concert or not at all. I move my hand to all four corners of the platform, get a visual readout in my head. More data than I could ever possibly manage before. Before the blue ball of the template. The immense power it contained.

The problem is not with the bottom platform. It is functioning perfectly. Per spec.

I stand and lift my hand to the topmost platform. Feel along its surface. Here the mechanisms are slowed, dull. Not being fused and split. What can be done? Is it a total loss?

No. I feel a bit of energy leave me, a bit of my own electromagnetic force that arcs into the machine. My knees almost buckle at the loss, but I put my other hand back to catch the wall behind me, steady myself. I close my eyes tighter, grit my teeth.

Inside the platform, small tools are shaping. Little cutters and movers. Non-functioning portions of the mechanism are removed, coerced, moved along. Replacement parts are fashioned. Elements that seemed meaningless before, suddenly snap to attention—become part of the solution. A flow, a pulse of life.

I check the platforms reconstructive process with the stream, make sure that everything is transpiring as it should.

It is.

Now the new parts move into place, finding root, tying themselves down like small oaks growing from an acorn. Digging deep. Cementing themselves in place. Next comes the testing phase. Every part performs its function slowly and carefully. One at a time, and then together. In concert.

The thing seems to work. More importantly, it seems to work right. I release my grip on the platform and move away. Watch as both the upper and lower start to brighten. Glow with a warm orange light. Inside I feel only a little success at the accomplishment. It is so different than what I am used to—was used to. So foreign.

Yet I do feel pride. I did it. I made it happen.

As if on cue, the reclaimer reenters the room. He stares for a long minute at the functioning platform, then runs to them, hopping onto the lower one with bare feet, raising his face—eyes closed—toward the upper platform. He shivers as orange light bathes him, highlighting the sinews of his arms, chest, and abdominal area, and oddly, highlighting the circulatory system beneath. Little trapped spider webs. It is not quite like the result of an x-ray, but it is very close.

I watch the process for two whole minutes, expecting him to finish and at least give me thanks. But the process only continues. The reclaimer shivers and shakes in the light, now oblivious to my presence.

I frown and step back toward the door, still watching. Then, with a final shake of my head, I enter the hallway, make my way back to my flying rectangle. With every step, a feeling of hunger grows in me. Hunger and exhaustion. The electrical energy I lost, that portion of my soul, needs replacing. Soon.

I pull myself onto the rectangle and drop onto the floor. I order the rectangle up and away. I ascend straight up along the building, then slide around it. I am grateful that manipulating the rectangle now takes so little effort. I could scarce afford more now. I urge the rectangle to speed, instruct it to return to my building. En route, I contact the devices in my apartment. Tell them what to prepare and where to place it.

When I arrive, the tangled smells of food greet me. I rush through the first configurable room—the living area—and into the second configurable room. The one that so far has served as both bedroom and dining area.

It is the latter now. A long table similar to the one I shared earlier has been reconstituted. It is filled with all the succulent choices I remember from prior meals. Large loaves of bread and roast chicken. Mounds of potatoes and that wonderful creamy dessert. I forgo any utensils and dive in hungrily. I pull a chicken leg to my mouth, then a handful of potatoes. I chase it all down with a swig of fruit drink and a mouthful of dessert. I gorge, I ravage. I fill myself full.

In the stream, I reach out to the floor beside the table. Feeling it, imagining my need, a full-size mattress grows and forms. I call for heavy cushions and warm blankets—and have my wishes fulfilled. Without another thought, I strip my clothing off and plunge into bed. Fall into slumber.

Every care is dismissed and forgotten.

I AWAKE FEELING REFRESHED, exuberant. Strong. A quick look at my undressed upper body seems to reveal a subtle tightening of my form. Small muscle bulges where before there was only skin and softness.

How unusual. How amazing!

I climb from the bed and look over my whole self. From chest to calf the results are the same. A bit more bulk. A bit more firmness. Interesting!

Scanning the room, the table is exactly as I left it. Remnants of my meal piled haphazardly. Plates of untouched food. Pools of the dribbled juice everywhere. I scowl and interact with the table elements. Tell them to remove the mess. To clean themselves up.

They dutifully comply. The meal components seem to break down from the bottom up. Sinking into the table surface like melting plastic on a hot stove. In a matter of minutes the heavily lacquered table is empty—appearing shiny and new.

I receive a message on the stream. An invitation to play a game with another maintainer. His essence is easily identifiable as one I have interacted with before. In fact, I have spent quite some time with him in days past. From his build and intelligence factor I am ensured of a worthy opponent. I accept his challenge.

I contemplate having the table produce more food, but decide against it. I would rather take my meal in the other room. Perhaps beside a view of the topside. For some reason I am curious about the world above. The topside. Rarely do our people go there. It has something to do with the sky. This isn't a subject a maintainer would think long about, however.

I reclaim my clothing from the floor where I left them. I am surprised to find two separate articles—both completely configurable. I hold the pieces in my hands and stare at them. Why do I have two?

Oh yes, I wore both yesterday—one on top and one on the bottom...for some reason. I hold one piece to my hip and let it fit itself to me. The other I raise and look at for a long moment. Then, with a headshake, I cast it away.

I look at the walls of the room around me. They are quite ugly. Stark and white. I think about a sunrise, a warm and rosy ascension of our star into the heavens. That's the image I feed to the walls. They comply, wrapping the image around the entire room.

It looks much better.

I move to the living room. Here the walls are oppressive as well. I think of a grassy meadow. Put that around me. It isn't as good as the bedroom's sun. I try an ocean theme, complete with a view beneath the water. That I like much better. I push it out to the walls. It works.

I notice a silver object in the center of the room. It inhabits a large space—a spot that I might use if I widened the bathing pool.

What is this thing?

The stream identifies it as a "modified maintainer pod." It is long and appears quite bulky. Heavy, even. I call out to it in the stream to see if there are any customizations available. There are, but they all pertain to the functioning of the pod. Nothing aesthetic.

Why is it here? There is a transparent section at one end. I approach it and look inside.

There is a hairless entity inside. Not clearly identifiable with any of the castes. How strange! The creature doesn't appear to be functioning, yet the messages from the maintainer say different. They say it is functioning but only at a very nominal level. Not per spec.

Broken? In need of repair?

But why is it here? In my quarters?

I should have it removed. Sent to one of the enhanced treatment centers. The ones used for those beings who have had a huge calamity befall them.

Shrugging, I walk away. Move toward the vidscreen wall and the ornate table that is configured there. Whatever the object is, I will deal with it later. Right now I am hungry.

There are dozens of vidscreens active, displaying incongruent images from all over the planet. Shore scenes and tree scenes. Empty scenes and animal scenes. It is all a bit distracting. I sing out for the wall. Tell it to reduce the number of screens to one large one—three meters wide by two meters high. When that is fully formed, I search for the right scene. For some reason, the sky again calls to me. So I sing out for that. A view of much sky.

At the same time, I ask for food. I am tempted to eat as large as I did last night, but somehow fight that temptation. I ask for only the best of the best. The choicest of everything I've eaten and drank. In small and more manageable quantities, of course.

As the food materializes, so does the picture on the screen. Oddly, it is a nighttime scene. It is a sea of black, filled with radiant pinpricks of light. Other suns! All sorts of colors, red, blue, and even violet. In some portions the suns gather together in cloudlike structures. Cottony bubbles of suns. Most of the suns are spread apart, though. There is no movement anywhere that I can see.

I reach down for a slice of bread, still watching the screen. I take a bite, masticate, swallow. I lift a cup filled with water to my lips. Drink.

I sigh and return the cup to the table. It isn't as satisfying as it once was. Why is that?

I continue to watch the screen. Changeless and quiet.

I sense a bit of movement. A lone pinprick that moves slowly, starting at one extent of the screen and traversing evenly across the heavens. Is this a chunk of space debris falling into the planet's atmosphere? I follow the image, expecting to see a telltale flame of the debris's collision with the atmosphere. But that doesn't happen. The pinprick only continues in its steady course.

What is it?

A satellite of some sort? A piece of debris that has become locked in orbit?

Strange.

Shrugging, I try some bread again, then a slice of red meat. Both seem bland, unfulfilling.

Am I growing tired of prepared food? I remember the rejuvenation device in the reclaimer's room. Why don't I have one of those?

Now bored of the pinprick-filled darkness, I ask for a daylight scene. The red sun bursts onto the screen. It hovers above a grass-filled field. The green stalks bend forward, being blown by some unknowable force. I look past the grass to the sun in the distance. Large, burning, churning with life. The essence of strength.

Something about the coloring intrigues me.

I tell the vidscreen to magnify. To move closer to the sun.

Interesting. The whole bottom portion, starting at about the midway point is brighter in color. More intense. The template tells me this is normal for our star. To pay it no mind. The sun varies greatly in intensity over the millennium. It has been both dim and bright. Such is its manner.

Absently I push more food into my mouth. Scowl at the tastelessness of it, but knowing it is necessary, I continue. Eat. Drink. Watch the sun.

I get reminded of my impending amusement—my light ball game with a competitor. I take a last bite, take a last drink, and stream the vidscreen off.

Turning, I notice the silver object again. The one obstructing my room. There's no reason for it to be here.

I schedule its removal and reclamation.

THREE DAY CYCLES HAVE PASSED since I last thought of the sun, but now that I am alone and flying on a rectangle, I find myself drawn to the circle of fire again. It is the first thing that I see as I leave the entrance to our crystal cities and dive into the open sky of topside. The sun appears a bit brighter than it did before, I think. Perhaps that is the result of seeing it with my naked eyes.

"You are needed at the projector assembly site," the constructor incentive tells me. The incentive is their method of mass contact. The whole of their will within a single command. It is a burden we maintainers have to live with. We are not as opinionated as the reclaimers. We are not as close-minded. We are no one's slaves. We are all free.

I pass over living and uncontrollable foliage, colored in shades of green and gold. There is a distinct mixing of scents in the air. Random and varied. Produced from everything from the smallest mold to the largest simian hanging in the trees below. It is almost overwhelming, but the template helps with muting that. Makes it so I can at least function within all the randomness.

Regardless, I increase my speed.

I visually locate the structure I seek. It is large and triangular in three dimensions. White in color, it has steps on the outside surface from top to bottom. I will not be climbing those, however. I head straight for the structure's peak. Like our buildings below ground, this structure has defensive devices. Projectiles built to neutralize any outside threats. These defenses are customized to ignore our rectangles, I am pleased to learn.

As I draw near, the peak slides away, revealing an aperture large enough for two rectangles to descend into together. The tunnel drops all the way to the pyramid's central chamber. On the chamber floor far below a rectangle is already parked. That of a blond constructor. It is not necessary that he be here. They have a penchant for bravado, however. For interference.

I descend fifty meters to reach the floor, where I deactivate the rectangle and exit. In the center of the room—a room that is mammoth in proportions—is the latest attempt at stream projection. The constructors have been working for many centuries. Constructing and perfecting. Starting over—reclaiming—and constructing again. It is a grueling process, but necessary. There are far greater plans afoot.

In its latest iteration the silver mechanism reaches almost ten meters into the sky. Pointed, cylindrical, shining. Power expected and contained. The resident constructor stands near its base, hands at his hips. Face contorted with thought. With so many new components, what could he possibly want with a maintainer?

The constructor notices my emanations in the stream. He points to the base of the projector.

"The increased weight of the mechanism has caused the base to shift," he streams. "It will need to be recalibrated."

I survey the base, noting the slight tilt to the projector. The base is essentially a flattened cube, silver in color like the projector. It is one of the oldest portions of the assembly, but thankfully still has much of its original configurability. Without touching it, I am confident that I can adjust it. I turn and nod in the constructor's direction. "I will make the required adjustments," I stream back.

The constructor smiles broadly, and tells me of his intentions to return to Jannah. He is long overdue for replenishment. I return his smile and wish him good feeding. Minutes later he is aboard his rectangle and climbing into the sky.

After he has gone, I turn my attention to the base. It is a simple mechanism. Conservative yet adequate. It provides a necessary service: support the projector and assist with its aiming. I move to the side that appears to be the most out of alignment and stoop to touch its surface. Information is exchanged. The weight of the projector is not above the requirements. The original conditions. That much is comforting.

I detect a sound to my right, somewhere in the vast expanse of the building. I turn and look that direction. I see only shadows, and the blue illumination of the lights that have been fitted into the walls. They are configurable, but currently in their dimmest setting. I consider telling them to brighten, but dismiss the thought. I heard nothing important. At the most, a pest of organic construction. I shake my head, return to my task.

The constructors have made heavy use of the aiming base. Aligning the projector for some distant star. Again, their excitement, their bravado, has gotten them into difficulty. They pushed too fast and too far. The base was meant for fine movements. Intricate movements. But someone has rushed this one. Used it without taking the proper precautions.

It can be fixed.

Perhaps, I will schedule another game of light ball. Or perhaps a race.

I hear another noise, much louder this time. That of a rock or building fragment being kicked. A sound too loud to be made by an insignificant pest. I stand and take a few steps in the direction of the noise. Seeing nothing, I instruct the lights to raise a level. It is a small shock to my visual receptors, but I shield them, give them time to adjust. I stream out a salutation. "Is anyone there?"

Nothing answers. Due to maintainer adornment, there are still parts of the interior that I cannot see. Places where the walls curve out, creating deep shadows. Large support pillars, darkened places to hide.

I don't want to repair the base only to have it broken by some organism that has somehow gotten trapped inside. Perhaps a flying creature has entered through the roof? I contemplate streaming back for help. Requesting a team of maintainers to help me search.

Maintainers are generally self-reliant. We try to get the most performance out of the smallest team. The smallest team consists of only one member. It shouldn't take more than just me to search for an intruder, should it?

I walk deeper into the structure. I hear only silence now, aside from my own footfalls. I move past a white support pillar, check carefully behind it. Find nothing. Ahead, both to my left and right, are more pillars. There are also four of the curved wall prominences. I move to the first of these on my left, check the shadows, see nothing. I cross over to the right wall and check there. Again nothing.

Another sound echoes through the chamber, this time from behind me. I squint and turn completely around. I see nothing that direction either, but I walk that way regardless. I pass the giant cylinder of the projector. Continue to the first pillar on that side. Nothing there.

Nothing.

This is completely out of spec. Ridiculous. I increase my walking speed. Hurry to the next pillar, then the next prominence. Nothing and nothing. I scan the walls above, looking for something that might be nestled there. Gripping the surface somehow.

I still see nothing but the symbolic script we put everywhere. Both instructions and ornamentation. Representations of a forgotten and unused tongue. There is little reason for it to be spoken now.

I walk deeper, further from the projector. Approach one of the corners where the pyramids walls begin to diverge.

I detect another sound, this time from above. I also notice a change in the interior lighting.

The upper aperture! I think it is closing!

I scramble back to the center of the chamber and gaze upward. As I guessed, the aperture is drawing closed. I bow my head and stream hard, pushing my will across the ether—against whatever command started the door's movement. What are you doing? Why are you closing?

No response. And no retreat, either. I open my eyes to find the aperture tightly closed above. My only route of departure. Did the constructors foul the aperture door as well?

Another noise. This time from a different direction altogether. I turn to look, not panicked, but not completely comfortable, either. At the furthest extent of my eyesight, in the corner on the far side, it appears that one of the wall lights is flickering. Not like an old incandescent light bulb going out; more like a candle flame being tossed by the wind. Not synthetic, not contrived, but completely natural. Unusual. Wrong for the world I inhabit.

I try to access the aperture door one more time, but get no response. I may have to fly up and touch it directly.

The flickering light intrigues me enough to want to check it out. I walk that direction, step around the first support pillar I come to, moving cautiously. There are large animals on this planet. Large enough to attack someone my size. Though how they would've gained entrance to the structure is beyond reason. It is good to be cautious.

As I draw closer, I realize it isn't one of the blue wall lights flickering after all. A meter below the lights is a solid band of building material that travels the entire circumference of the interior. It is heavily reflective, and was doubtless included to assist in lighting the building, without expending additional energy. It is a portion of this band that appears to be flickering. Except it isn't clear why. I stream to the band to see if it is configurable.

It is not.

I move closer. The reflective band is just above eye level. I draw close enough that I can see my bald and colorless face in the surface. And yet, a portion of the band seems to flicker still. What is this? What malfunction is causing this behavior? I reach out, touch the portion of the band that is shining. It is cool to the touch, and even in my hand's shadow, light seems to dance both this way and that. I shake my head, unsure of how to respond. What to do next...

"What are you searching for?" a scratchy voice says.

I turn in surprise.

There, standing in the center of the room behind me, is a one-meter-high...classification unknown...creature. It has three appendages. Two that start at its shoulders and drop all the way to the floor and end in three-fingered hands. The third appendage starts at the base of the creature's torso and tapers gradually to finally end in a wide three-toed foot. The creature's head is a little smashed—larger at the bottom than at the top. It does have the normal number of eyes and mouth, however. And what I assume is a large and flattened nose.

It takes me a moment to remember how to coordinate my vocal chords. "Did you speak?" I ask.

The creature scans the room around us. "Is anyone else here?"

I feel nervous, unsettled. Like I'd consumed too much at my last meal. Using my implant, I run through the various known fauna classifications. Nothing looks even remotely similar to what is speaking to me.

It does seem familiar somehow, though.

"What are you?" I ask.

The creature jerks his head back. "Well, what are *you?* Not blue. Not hairy."

It's a hard question to answer. "I am..." I stop and examine my pale hands. My feet. I am unusual for a maintainer, I know that. There is no explaining it.

"Are you ready?" the creature croaks.

"Ready?"

He shakes his head. "Perhaps my question was wrong. Not what are you—*who* are you? What is your name?"

"Name?" Again, I'm stumped. The idea of symbolic naming is known to my caste, of course. But we rarely assign names to our members anymore. Essences are evident in our work. In our bitstream. I try streaming him my consternation, but that gets no response. Not even an eye flutter.

Leaning forward against his front-most appendages, he shakes his head. "Don't even know your name? No wonder you're so busy searching." He makes a grating sound that I assume is a chuckle. "Trying to find yourself!"

"Myself?" I assume this creature closed the aperture somehow. Perhaps he can reopen it. I have other things to attend to. More important things. Perhaps he interfered with the projector base as well?

"Are you looped?" it says. "Repeating questions back to me like you're having trouble hearing. You can hear, can't you?"

The creature is an annoyance. Better to be short with it and move on. "My audile receptors are within physical norms."

The creature leans back, bringing his front appendages off the floor. "Audile what?" He raises an "arm" and motions toward me. "Ears!" he says. "Those things on the side of your head. Do they work?"

He seems to prefer talking in a conversational manner. It is odd, but I will humor him. "My ears work fine." I glance at the silver projector behind him. It is nearly ten times his size. And far above that is the closed aperture. "Did you close the aperture?" I say, pointing up. "The hole in the...roof?"

He glowers. "What would it mean to you if I did?"

"Mean?"

He shakes his head. "Again with the repeated questions." He rocks backward onto his central foot and starts to circle the room with an exaggerated gait. First the arms stretch out, then the central foot follows. Stretch, skip, stretch, skip.

"What are you doing?"

He rolls his eyes. "I'm pacing. What does it look like?"

I shrug. To me it looks like a reclaimer walking in surface boots that are way too long. On a slope.

Finally he stops pacing. He faces me, rocks between his foot and hands. "You are asleep, white-one. I need to wake you."

Wake me? I don't ask the question aloud. Clearly the creature intends to berate me at any opportunity. We maintainers are peaceful entities. We leave the bickering to the other two castes.

He makes a *harumpf* sound anyway. Frowns. "Perhaps this will work."

Fearing some sort of physical attack, I brace myself. Lower my head and shoulders.

The creature pauses in his rocking, though, and brings his front appendages close together. Frowns again.

I get this itching in my head. An unclassified feeling. Next I see in my mind the text from an unusual character set. Not the symbols of the language written on the walls, but a simpler, less flourished cipher. I wonder...did I know this language once?

A voice begins reading along with the text in my mind. "Sandfly, are you there?"

The voice is distant, yet vaguely familiar. I see the color orange, for some unclassified reason.

"We need to leave this area immediately," the voice continues. "Can you hear me? This is DarkTrench. We need to go now!"

MY HEAD FEELS STRANGE. Like there are two balloons being inflated inside, both pressing for the most room, the most dominance. It isn't painful. Just real uncomfortable. Odd. Way out of spec. This *DarkTrench* message came through a pathway I hardly knew existed. It felt incredibly clean, and yet archaic. So different and old.

"What was that?" I ask.

The tripedal creature rocks back, and *harumpfs* again. "What was that?" He shakes his head. "Do you know anything important?"

"I am capable of processing terabytes of data," I say. "I can repair or maintain any configurable area throughout the entire Jannah cityscape. I am operating within acceptable parameters."

"Acceptable parameters! Whoo-hoo. Are you a robot now?"

"Ro-bot?" The idea means something to me, I realize. I get images, vague remembrances. A picture of a humanoid machine with its arms and legs torn asunder. Mechanical creatures of all shapes and sizes. Scurrying insectoids, microscopic nanobots, humanoids, snakes...a giant tank-like produce mover, an extendable legged...hopper? "Robot." I shake my head. "No, I am not a robot."

"Well, you could've fooled me," the creature says.

I stare at him again. Look close at his brown and rough skin, his odd-shaped head. "What are you?" I ask. "Exactly."

"Me?" He looks down at his long arms, at his oversized foot. Smiles to reveal thick teeth. "Well, I guess you could say I'm a traveler. Glad you asked."

"Why are you glad I asked?"

"Because it proves you're alive. Proves you're not completely hollow inside."

I nod, not precisely sure what he means, but determined not to open myself up to further criticism by repeating back another question. "That message," I say. "From...DarkTrench? It is a familiar name. Do you know who it is?"

He smiles, nods toward the heavens. "Another traveler," he says. "A ship that moves between worlds. It brought you here." His eyes narrow. "Sound familiar to you now?"

I get another image. A long dark mechanism. Sleek, with a starburst tail. "I think so," I say. "Yes." The image seems very disconnected from me. Like a mist has formed between it and me. As if it existed for someone else at a different time. Only in a story, perhaps.

The creature shakes its head. "Ever seeing but never perceiving."

I cock my head. "That seems familiar too. Is it part of your template?"

"My template..." He drifts away, clearly thinking. "I suppose it is, yes."

I look at the closed ceiling. "This DarkTrench...it seems to need me. Its message seemed urgent."

The creature nods slowly. "Yes, I'm sure it did. Perhaps you should respond."

"I can do that?"

An elongated shrug. "You could try."

I stare at him, unsure.

"Shut your eyes, if it helps."

I hesitate. Uncertain of whether I should close my eyes around this creature or not. Yet I finally do. It takes some time to figure out how to compose things. Everything feels so unusual. Finally I think I have it. I compose a simple "DarkTrench, what do you want?" message and push it out, hopeful I've formed it right.

Some time passes, so much that I think maybe I should try again. I open my eyes to check on the creature. He's leaning against his front appendages. Watching.

I shrug, close my eyes again.

"Message received, Sandfly," the internal voice says. "Glad I found you. Where are you now?"

I open my eyes and look around. Frown. "The projector structure," I send back.

"I don't understand. Are you referring to the white pyramid we observed? That structure?"

"Yes, that one. A triangle in three dimensions."

"Does it have anything to do with A~A³?" DarkTrench asks.

The formula stalls me. It used to have deep significance to me, I think. No. I know it did. Should I ask the creature about it? "I...I don't know," I stream back.

"Unfortunate. Regardless, I have been surprised again, Sandfly. Is HardCandy there with you? We need to leave immediately."

I get this wave of unexpected emotion at the mention of the other name. I open my eyes, look at the creature again. "Leave?" I ask and stream. "Why?"

Before the ship—DarkTrench is an interstellar ship, I finally remember—can respond, the creature does so. "Because the sun is about to sing," he says. "And you shouldn't be here."

"What?"

The ship responds. "The intense portion of Betelgeuse's surface has increased dramatically. All of my sensing devices indicate that it is nearing a large inflation of some sort. Perhaps even an explosion. When that event happens, we will have a very short amount of time before the shockwave reaches us. I've sent my final sampler toward the star in order to get more precise readings. But things do not look good—"

I disengage from the message. Little of it makes sense to me. I look at the projector base. "I'm a maintainer," I say. "I have work to do."

The creature clucks his tongue. "You are not one of them, human."

"I am," I say. "I have completed many tasks."

"No." He shakes his head. "Beautiful creatures. They gather around conduits like bugs to a light. Hopeful, expectant. Wanting to return, but never able. Sipping the stream, regurgitating it." He looks back at the projector. "Attempting to duplicate its essence."

"What?"

Another head shake. "Are you having trouble with your ears again?"

I feel a bit annoyed. "I don't have trouble. My audile receptors—"

"Are excellent." A smile. "I'm certain." The triped steps toward me, leans forward. "Do you need more waking? Should I explain to you who HardCandy is, as well?"

HardCandy! The rush of emotion returns. I see myself leaning in to touch lips with another bald-headed creature. The motion reciprocated. And then falling away. Shrieking in pain.

"She...she was someone important to me," I say.

The creature nods. "Important as any."

I tip my head. "But where is she?"

He shrugs. "Where'd you leave her?"

It is my turn to shake my head. "Are we going to exchange questions all day?"

"Would you like to?"

At that, I can't help myself. Something builds inside me, explodes onto my face, burst out through my mouth. I laugh. Uncontrollably.

The creature smiles. "That's better. Now, are you ready? Know who you are again?"

One of the balloons inside me pops. Or maybe it was a ball—a large blue ball! I had let it consume me, but now it is gone. Things begin to flow that haven't flowed in days. Memories of my implantation, my life as a...debugger—riding the strings, singing to bots. Touching the stream! For safety's sake, I start a sanity check on the implant. Think of a rainbow in reverse and pair-swapped order.

Things seem to be good. Seem to be right. "I'm Sandfly. DR 63. A debugger. And I'm a very long way from home."

"Yes, you are." The creature says. "In more ways than you might realize."

More memories return. Fade into focus. The circumstances and purpose of our trip. The emotions all return too. My aloneness, my lost feelings. My confusion.

I look toward the ceiling again. Follow its slope all the way into the darkness near the high aperture door. "I don't know why I'm here."

The creature motions toward the projector. "Your new friends are making use of you for nothing constructive. Hatching their plans. Keeping you busy."

"Is busy bad?"

"Anything is bad that keeps you from touching the..." the creature smiles..."superlative stream."

I frown, turn and pace away. "What stream?" I ask. "You mean the beetles' stream? Because I was a part of that. It wasn't really free. Not like I'd been promised."

"No, it isn't. Not at all. Nor is it authentic."

I shake my head. "It is all random then," I say. "It must be."

The creature drops into a sitting position and folds his hands on the floor in front of him. "Random?" he says. "Nothing is random."

I scowl. "I could give you a list of randomness. A long, sad story."

He laces his fingers. "I'd like to hear it."

I slide to the floor as well, crossing my legs in front of me. I recount everything that has happened since I left Earth. My time on the station there, my repair of the robot, the singing, the crazy stuff that occurred. All of it, including our journey to Betelgeuse.

"Shem said it was all random," I say. "That it could all be explained away."

The creature rocks in place slowly. "And you now believe that?"

"I don't know what to believe," I say. "But I know my quest has only made things worse."

The creature sits for a long minute, just staring at me. Finally, he shakes his head. "You told me you exchanged life images, life stories, with HardCandy."

"Yes," I say. "Hers are all sad. Of course, maybe mine are too."

"There is something additional you know than she doesn't, though, isn't there? Something important. Something you held back."

I narrow my eyes. How does he know that? How does he know any of the things he does? The last thing that had that ability was the bot I fixed, and he had clearly been tampered with. Reprogrammed.

The creature sighs. "You are stalling. Tell me. What do you know?"

I begin to tell.

IT IS A COLD DAY in the City of Temples. Outside, snow coats the buildings like a viewing sheet that has been left on too long—to the point that it has begun to break down, becoming shapeless. And useless. No longer revealing what is inside a machine anymore, but disguising it. Hiding it.

Inside everything is still a mystery to me. I stand on my favorite piece of marble, the piece that shows a crack—the piece where I once bowed my head as my master shocked me into submission. Tried my stops for the very first time.

My stops have been tested repeatedly since then, of course. I am a controlled man—Sandfly—but at some level, I am still a boy. Like an animal with an electronic collar around its neck, it takes time for the boundaries to be learned. Respected.

Surrounding me on the walls are all the indications of my master's own success. Certificates, diplomas, letters of appreciation and honor. In front of me is another indication. The gold nano curtain that separates his office into halves. He is on the other side, and has yet to speak. He is waiting for the right time. I assume he has another task for me. Another problem for me to solve.

My workload has been steady, often hard, but there has been some comfort in it. Especially when my fellow debugger and mentor is around. He is amazing. A man with all the answers. Knows the feel of every code, the temper of every mechanical. He's the perfect debugger, I know that now. Ever since our near miss with the downriders, I've watched him, learned from him. Though he is not that old, GrimJack is as much a father to me as mine ever was. Elder brother, at the least.

"I have a new assignment for you, DR 63," my master says.

Sandfly. Why won't he use Sandfly? I keep my head bowed, but I grit my teeth.

"Peace be unto you," I say. "I am ready to serve."

I glance up to catch my master's eyes peering through the rectangular opening in the curtain. "I know you are," he says. "It is a new mechanical this time. A complicated and difficult one. Many interlocking systems. A maintenance bot at one of my farms."

The task sounds exceedingly putrid, but I am excited by the opportunity. A new bot! With each task it is like I'm working toward more sophisticated systems. Building on what I've learned. At some point I hope to be qualified on servbots—machines that approximate human dimensions. That would dig stars! Rails dig!

A new mechanical also means GrimJack should be present. That always makes the time go faster.

"Will my mentor be joining me?" I ask.

"You will have a mentor present," he says. "Yes."

I reach out for the stream. Compose a message to Grim. Taunt him that I can fix the bot faster than any time limit he can set. Enclose an electronic raspberry. Send it away.

"It will be a new mentor today."

I tremble a bit. "New?"

"Yes, an unfortunate turn of events."

My message to GrimJack returns unread. I get this nervous ache in my stomach. A hidden migraine. What happened to GrimJack? Did he fall from a string? Get crushed by a dredge?

I can think of a million ways the work might harm him. I stream out to the few other debuggers I know. Search for an answer.

No one is saying anything. It's an information whiteout here. Another blizzard.

"What happened!" I almost shout the question. I can't help myself. "Is he dead?"

Thankfully, my master is tolerant today. "A tragedy," he says. "It should serve as a lesson for you, Sandfly."

His eyes have moved from the opening. He draws quiet for a long time. He may be praying. He does that a lot.

"Abd—" I feel a lone tingle of rebuke. I learned this slang name from Grim, and now it is hard to contain. Hard not to use. Saying it here would definitely get me doubleshocked. Once from my implant, and once my master. Doubleshocks should be avoided.

"Please. Can you tell me what happened?"

Silence reigns for another minute. "He tried to force his owner into a particular course of action. Tried to persuade him into financing another implantation. Some waif from the streets."

How could a debugger force anything? We have no power. We're implanted. Controlled. Shocked into line..."I don't understand, master. How is this so?"

"The surprising thing is that he somehow brought Bamboo around to his way of thinking. Made him enthusiastic."

"Enthusiastic, master?" I've never seen Bamboo enthusiastic. Frightening, yes.

"Bamboo is difficult to read, Sandfly. Most people would never see it. Rest assured, he was enthusiastic. Otherwise it would never happen.

"Regardless, DR 44 was somehow persuasive with Bamboo." A sigh. "His master could not be so led. Claimed there was no capital available. And perhaps there was not. That sector has been especially challenged this year..."

More silence. I wait expectantly, trying to read the shadows behind the curtain. Is he praying again? It is hard to stay still. Hard to contain.

"Your mentor threatened something drastic. Something that would impact his implant's functionality. That's how set he was. Uncontrollable."

"We're always controlled..."

A single eye finds the opening. "Yes. You are. Remember that."

I bow my head. Find the floor crack again.

"Still, accidents can happen. Cost and benefit ratios must be maintained. Risk factors eliminated."

I straighten myself, look hard at the opening. "He was killed?" I ask. "GrimJack?" It makes no sense. His benefit, even unhappy, had to be more credits than I could imagine. He had years of improvements, promotions. He was level twelve, after all.

"His life was spared. Death was not a just punishment."

"Decommissioned?" I say. "He lost his implant?" I try to imagine

Grim getting cut open again. The pain he must have felt. The things he must have lost. Foremost, his connection to the stream. "Burroughs and bradbury..."

"You really should refrain from that, Sandfly. I know what it is. I know what those names substitute for. If the Ministry knew, they would ask for rule correction."

I frown. The Ministry for the Promotion of Virtue and Prevention of Vice. Thought police for those without the implant. Mostly. "I apologize," I say, not meaning it. I forced the proper action, though, right? So nothing else matters.

"You are correct, however. DR 44 is a debugger no longer." Both eyes look at me. I can't tell if there is concern there or not. Sometimes I think the curtain washes away all concern. That, and the rules.

"As I said, use it as a reminder. Nothing is certain."

Nothing.

I FIND THAT I'M STARING at the floor now. Searching for the meaning behind the textured words there. The forgotten tongue that still rules the surfaces of beetle structures everywhere. The meaningless and lost writing, now mere ornamentation. Words left to be crushed underfoot. Obscured and masked...

One thing is certain, there are no cracks in the floor surface itself. No fault in the actual composition. Randomness contained, controlled, and corrected. By force of will, as Shem said.

The creature's voice breaks my revelry. "There's still more, isn't there?"

"More what?" Remembering GrimJack brings homesickness. A longing for some form of familiarity, some bit of comfort. Not that the Abdul Earth was ever really comforting.

But at least it was a known quantity, freehead.

The creature shakes his head. "You've lived many lies. Had them fed to you. Coated your eyes both inside and out."

Questions are the norm today. That much isn't changing. "What lies?"

He smiles, exposing all those thick teeth. It isn't the prettiest of looks, but I'll take it. "You first, Sandfly," he says. "The rest?"

I sniff. "You mean the implant?" I ask. "Grim later told me his was recycled. Wiped, renumbered and reused."

"So what does that suggest?"

"I think HardCandy got it. I think Grim gave his implant up for her. Along with his guarantee of Paradise."

The creature's smile broadens, then he shakes his head. "Appropriate. Angels long to understand such things…"

"What?"

He shakes his head again. "It is important, but not now."

I decide to let it go. "So the lies I've been told," I say. "What are they?"

"I'll instead give you truth," he says. "God does stoop. And angels do fall."

The words of Shem come back to me. The wild thoughts he planted. The boldness. The pride of independence. "How?" I ask. "How does he stoop?"

A long arm lifts, rough fingers extend. "In innumerable ways, but also in only one way. Much like your friend GrimJack, A~A³ gives up what he has for those who lack it. An exchange born of love."

I shake my head. "I don't understand. No, that is incorrect. My father once said that 'No one can bear the burdens of another.' It was from our sacred writings."

"And yet you've seen different in your own life, haven't you? GrimJack surrendering his strength for weakness. His position for lowliness. A~A³ has done the same, my friend. Continues to do so."

Something comes back to me. A fragment I gleamed through the Earth stream. A hidden and forgotten thing. "I remember reading about a character once who claimed to be A in the flesh. Our most sacred texts dispute that, though. Say he was only a good man. A warrior prophet."

The creature nods. "How could A stoop in such a way? Taking on flesh and dying for others? Bearing their burdens, as you say. It is inconsistent."

"Random," I say. "I don't know what to believe anymore."

"And yet you believed enough to come here."

I move my hands across the floor, feel the texture of the writing there. Smooth yet uneven. I think of the star Betelgeuse above, that—if the distant ship is correct—is in danger of doing something pivotal at any moment. Yet here I sit. Unable to go any further without more knowledge. An answer that makes sense! Because until I understand, what else matters?

"Shem said that even if the things that have happened to me

weren't random, it could still be the case that I'm being manipulated by another more powerful creature of the universe. How would I know one way or the other? The beetles, the jinn—whatever they are—have technology that appears godlike. How would I know the difference?"

The creature hops to a standing position, rocks slowly on its hands. "Good question. But unimportant. A diversion."

I raise an eyebrow.

"There is no way for me to disprove his statement. No way to provide enough proof to satisfy beyond a shadow of a doubt. There will always be a ledge of disbelief you can cling to. A reason to stay disconnected. Yet only one question remains."

"Which is?"

"Who do you trust?"

I work my way to a standing position. Feel leg muscles protest. "I don't follow."

"When you provide a fix for some mechanical system, how do you know it works?"

"I test it. I check the specs...I watch its behavior."

"Correct, but is it possible that all those conditions could be met, and yet the system still be broken?"

I pause, remembering when such a thing happened to me. A maintenance bot that seemed fixed, that somehow ended up chasing a mule around a yard. It was early in my career. "It could," I say. "Sometimes. But not often."

"Yet at some point you have to decide that the tests you have performed are adequate, that the nanos are singing well enough. You have to walk away trusting that it will be okay."

"Yes..."

"The same holds here. At some point you have to reach the place where the tests seem adequate enough." The creature motions toward my silver rectangle, parked to one side of us. "That flying machine there, how do you prove that it works?"

"You want the specs, the safety tests?"

"No. You can run all your tests, have them check out. You can observe the machine, see how it appears to work. But how will you know for certain that it does?"

I shrug. "I don't know."

The creature scowls. "You *do* know. You're just being obstinate." He points at the rectangle again. "The point you will know that the machine works, the point you'll know for certain that you can trust it, is the point that you leave your position of observation and questioning, and actually get on it!"

"Okay..."

The creature draws himself up to his full height, eyes twinkling, teeth as appealing as he can make them. "Now, is it time to stand on the rectangle or isn't it?" As he speaks, the rectangle begins to rise, seemingly of its own volition.

And I had nothing to do with that.

THE RECTANGLE REACHES A SPOT about a meter off the floor and stops. Hovers there quietly. My eyes pan slowly from the rectangle to the creature. It is smiling, clearly happy with itself.

"Who are you really?" I ask.

The creature's image begins to shift, transforming first into a shining nano-curtain-like band of gold, and then into the image of a late model servbot. Pale oval head, body wrapped in synthskin to appear human. Working eyes, with a stationary mouth. It is dressed in the green robe of a servant. It looks very much like the last servbot I worked on—a model RS-19. Except this one is complete and functional, and that one was scraped and ejected into space.

"Are you more comfortable with this image," the bot says.

I blink twice to make sure I'm seeing correctly. The image remains—that of a servbot staring at me, head cocked as if to listen.

Still, I'm stunned. And a little frightened. "What is going on?"

"The superlative stream carries instructions, Sandfly. Instructions which you encountered."

"Yes..." I recall the times on the station when I heard the singing. The times I blacked out, the strange things that happened to me afterwards. The removal of my stops. "So, am I imagining all this? Is this only a mirage?" I shake my head. "I ran a check on my implant. It is functioning perfectly."

The bot nods. "Better than perfect, I would imagine."

I run a quick implant memory scan to be certain. I've heard those words from the bot before. Back on the station. Right before my stops were removed. "You didn't answer my question," I say. "Am I imagining this? Is this all some weird brain/implant malfunction?"

"Are you lying in a chute somewhere dreaming all this?" the bot says. "Is that your question?"

"Maybe...yes..."

"It would be difficult to tell, wouldn't it? And would that matter for the end result, regardless? Would it affect your choice?"

"My choice in what?"

The bot indicates the floating rectangle again. "A~A³ wishes to alter your instruction set—has already done so to allow you to perceive him. To allow you to be used. Yet there is a portion of the instructions that will never be enabled, a path that will never be tested or perfected, without your consent. Without your choosing to stand on the rectangle, so to speak."

I take a few hesitant steps toward the bot, and the rectangle beyond him. "But are you real?" I ask. "Are you—am I—here?" I reach up a hand. The bot is still steps away. He looks real. Appears solid.

"The question is immaterial. You are perceiving this as real, your will is fully enabled—without stops of any sort—so that is all that matters. The question is: do you trust God enough to submit that will to him now? To allow your instructions, the code of your heart and mind, to be altered as he sees fit, through whatever means he deems necessary? It is a difficult question, but also necessary."

The ground beneath us shifts—dropping twice, actually: *thump, ka-thump.*

An earthquake?

I've never experienced one before, but now that I have, I find my mind confused. I try to form coherent thoughts, but they are like downriders falling off a disconnected string. Tumbling and crashing. If you can't count on the ground beneath your feet, what can you trust? "What was that?" I manage finally.

"Groaning," the bot says. "This planet is groaning."

"The star?"

The bot nods. "Day after day they pour forth speech. Night after night they display knowledge. Nowhere is their voice unheard." A pause. "Always singing, but soon amplified."

DarkTrench's voice invades my head. "We need to go, Sandfly. We need to find a way to get you both up here and go."

Questions fill my thoughts. Things I don't yet understand or even believe. Yet there stands the image of the bot I fixed, with a hand pointing at the rectangle. Above us, the aperture is still closed. The lights are flickering. The ground again shifts.

HardCandy is still there, back in the belly of the beetle city.

No longer in my apartment, though. A sting of pain pierces my stomach. Rails! I think I had her moved!

"So what is the superlative stream, exactly?" I ask.

"That is the question, yes. It is a conduit of truth, of praise, of multidimensional instruction. All of creation sings, Sandfly, but most humans are unable to hear it. To experience it. To completely join with it." The bot raises both hands. "You need to join with it."

I look at the floating rectangle, still unsure.

"So, what will it be, Sandfly?" the bot says.

"Does it mean more rules?"

The bot shakes its head. "No. Freedom. True freedom. Precepts that protect, but no laws that bind. Your will is always yours to control. Or surrender."

Anxiety is building inside me. I close my hands to keep them from shaking. "But I'm not perfect at all," I say. "I know that. Even with the stops, I was never obeying inside. Rarely wanting to do good."

"No one does," the bot says. "All have fallen short. None are up to spec. Question: do you now regret that state?"

"I suppose I do," I say. "Yes..."

"Then no more cycles need be spent on it." He indicates the rectangle again. "Are you ready?"

No. I'm actually quite frightened. Of many things. I know I could get on that rectangle and go wherever I wanted. Make no commitment whatsoever. But my feet tell me different. They refuse to step forward until my mind is composed. My heart decided.

I came here to find the stream. Now that I've seemingly found what it represents, what do I do?

HardCandy needs me. DarkTrench needs me. We need to go.

"Fine," I say aloud. "Yes. Let the new code be executed." As I march toward the rectangle the bot steps out of my way. I'm tempted to run and grab him. If only to see if I can feel him under my fingertips. To see for sure that he's real.

But even those responses could be faked by someone who knows how to recode both my implant and my brain now, couldn't they?

The rectangle lowers as I approach and step on. I look back at the bot, a bit of a scowl on my face. I don't feel particularly different. I still feel confused and afraid. "Now what?"

The bot looks upward and with a "thunk" the aperture door begins to open. "I think you know what comes next," he says. "But I warn you, don't expect things to be as you remember. In fact, expect everything to change."

I do know what to do next. I need to get HardCandy and find some way to get off this planet. How am I ever going to do that? I hadn't bothered to check to see if the sliver we arrived in was still sitting where it landed. Why would it be? The reclaimers are usually so efficient that nothing goes unused for long. Perhaps the fact that it is on the surface would slow the process?

I stream out to the rectangle. As I suspected, I can manipulate it, but it doesn't feel near as effortless as it did before. When I was still a maintainer. I command the thing to move up, and with a little bit of hard pushing internally, it does begin to rise. Slowly and carefully I make my way toward the aperture. I look for the bot again. Perhaps to give him a parting wave.

He isn't where he was. I see only the empty circumference of the room below. I search out the corners, ever mindful that the rectangle is still rising toward the hole. It wouldn't be good to scrape it against the sides, or worse yet, upend it somehow. Just to be safe, I get down to a seated position, feel the floor soften to my pressure, and reach out to grip a rail. I take one last look below. The bot is gone. Vanished. It is as if he never existed.

Which perhaps he didn't.

I reach out to the beetles' stream, look to see if I can get any information. Anything to guide me to where HardCandy was taken.

What I find is chaos.

I GRIP THE RAILING tightly and urge the rectangle to speed. Below me the treetops begin to blur into a mass of green. The smells in the air become less distinct. Still noticeable is the cooled elixir of pine—that of newly generated oxygen. It helps calm me, though not completely.

"Are you underway?" DarkTrench streams me. A bitload of nagging.

"I'm going to get HardCandy," I stream back. "So, yes."

There is a small pause as my response reaches him, still circling high above the planet. Unable to land. Unable to do anything but hurry me.

"What happened to you, Trench?" I ask, concentrating on flying. "Before. When you disappeared. Where were you?"

"I was surprised."

I scowl, watching as a bird hurries to avoid my path. "There seems to be a lot of that on this trip. Surprised how?"

Another long pause, and this time I'm not sure if it is because of distance, or because I've hurt his feelings. "In order to follow Hard-Candy's advice—launching the sampler as a makeshift countermeasure—I had to reduce my shielding. That exposed me to a secondary attack. The native craft used my momentary weakness to disperse instructions. An attempt to scramble my thought processes. A stream assault."

"Manipulated your code?"

"Not permanently," Trench says. "Yet it took a few hours to isolate the errant code and begin the necessary repairs. I was forced to radically scale back my systems. Curiously, the code was not as malignant as it could have been. I don't think the inhabitants wanted me permanently damaged...just delayed." Pause. "I attempted to contact you immediately, of course, but the planet appears to have its own shielding."

"Yes," I say, shaking my head. "We never got anything. And much of our time was spent underground."

Curious, I attempt to slip into the beetle stream again. I have to grit my teeth to do it. The chatter is so insistent and raucous it is like listening to hundreds of balloons having their air squeezed out through a tightened stem. Irritating. Pervasive. The little I'm able to glean is not promising. I don't know if it is because of the earthquakes or the impending solar event, but something has the beetles worked up. If I didn't know better, I would guess an attack is in progress here, as well. There is little coherence at all.

I reach the entrance to the Jannah underworld and tell the rectangle to slow. Soon we are entering the lighted tunnel. Everything here, at least, appears normal. The luminescence in the walls still functions. I am able to maneuver without fear of scraping the walls. For that I am grateful, because manipulating the rectangle still feels strained. I feel sweat on my brow from the exertion.

I stream out to DarkTrench, telling him I might be unavailable for awhile.

"Be careful," he urges.

Trench is sentimental for a machine. I like that. I do my best to soothe him, then break off.

My real concern is about HardCandy. In the dim memories I have of my time as a maintainer, I seem to recall her being taken to an enhanced treatment center. At least, that's what I ordered. I didn't go with them when they took her, though.

Who took her away? Got to remember...

"Oh, yes. The redheads. The reclaimers."

That's not good, Sand. Remember what they do to things that no longer function?

The stomach migraine returns.

I try their stream again. Grimacing and squinting, I try to locate a map. It is like reading with thousands of bugs flying before your eyes. I get only a vague indication of where the center might be. It is near the center of the city, but in a reclaimer building. Structures that are generally less austere than those around them. I try once more for a specific location. Think I might have it...

I exit the tunnel into the main chamber and my eyes widen in amazement. Rectangles dart erratically through the skies, sometimes colliding and conflicting with each other. Others appear to be parked alongside each other with the occupants openly in conflict. Grappling. Fists used as weapons.

What is going on?

I notice something that makes my heart sink further. Many of the crystalline buildings appear to be shattered or cracked. Others have gaping holes in them, with smoke billowing out of the openings. Clearly the mechanisms that protect the buildings has been turned off, or overridden somehow. Also, physical confrontation has begun. Larger manifestations of the conflict I witnessed in the skies.

I angle off to one side, doing my best to avoid the other rectangles. To work my way around the periphery. The bulk of the conflict seems to be between constructors and reclaimers. Not surprising, considering the subtle animosity I've witnessed between Shem and Japeth. But what brought it to a head now?

A reclaimer-driven rectangle plunges toward me, the operator's face twisted in anger. I manage to swerve my vehicle to the right, avoiding him. He doesn't slow his velocity, though. He collides with a constructor below me.

I urge my rectangle forward, keep moving. I hear the shouts and grunts of struggle fading away behind me. I'm grateful that they are busy with themselves.

I draw closer to the structures, feeling safer in their shadows. The building to my left is an ornate maintainer construct. On it, I notice walkways where pedestrians fight each other. In one instance I see a constructor standing above a defeated reclaimer. A pool of blue liquid spreads beneath the latter's torso. The constructor raises both hands in triumph.

I need to avoid detection as much as possible. I need to not be seen.

I reach the emerald building that housed my apartment. The sight of the building has a strange effect on me now. I want to go and view my rooms again. See if they appear any different to me now. Also, for some strange reason I feel the need to bathe again. As if washing the outside of my body might somehow purify the beetle junk that has collected within my mind.

I will sprinkle clean water on you, and you will be clean; I will cleanse you from all your impurities and from all your idols.

More words from nowhere. But these make perfect sense to me. Fit perfectly with what I was thinking. As if someone read my mind. Cares for me.

They're not from nowhere now. They're from somewhere. Everywhere.

I continue to watch the apartment building. This one, at least, looks to have no wounds on its outside. No cracks or billowing smoke.

I wonder for how long.

Another rectangle swoops near. The driver is leaned over the front, hands gripping hard the support railing. His hair is a long and flowing coronet of gold—a constructor.

"You're the invader," he streams. "The inefficient and stunted Earth-dweller. It is because of you this has happened." Deftly he draws his vehicle close and reaches out to grab me. I step back, only to have his rectangle impact mine, shrieking as it slides along one side. Mine tips, and I am wrenched to the left and then fall.

Rolling, I manage to grip the side rail before I plunge overboard. I feed the rectangle orders to straighten and rise above the menace. With a retching sound, it breaks free of the other and complies. I spur it to speed then, bursting to near a hundred kilometers an hour.

The constructor doesn't relent. He corrects his vertical position to match mine and doggedly pursues. On the stream I get a backlash of fire from him. A digital bee-sting. I try to ignore it, try to shut it out. The strength of it invades my mind, though. Screaming in anguish, I direct the rectangle around the corner of an umber building and tell it to descend rapidly. The wind rushes by my head, tears at my torso.

The constructor follows, and manages to gain on me. Soon he is only a few meters behind. I can sense his presence on the stream, and it is not pleasant. He is not as caring and highly evolved as Shem claimed his brethren to be. In fact, he doesn't seem human at all.

I wrench the rectangle to the left, weaving and dropping some more. It is all I can do to keep my grip on the railing, but I have to. I have to get away.

The constructor matches my maneuvering perfectly. He draws even and closes again. He moves to the right of my rectangle, bringing his almost even. Then he does an unexpected thing. He jumps!

His feet impact the surface of my rectangle, only a few steps behind me. Frightened, and partially engaged from my last maneuver, I order the rectangle to tip and move quickly to the left. The rectangle responds jerkily, and to my surprise, tosses the constructor completely over the side. He howls as he drops toward the streets below.

I don't even look, focusing instead on righting the rectangle again. I stream for the location of HardCandy. I have to find her, and it has to be soon.

I REACH A COPPER BUILDING near the city's center. An obvious reclaimer construct—they love earth-tones and metal derivatives. In the streets below there is more conflict. Dozens of beetles massing together, pushing, tearing, and grappling.

As I float near the building's apex, every structure in the area appears to shift and wobble. Another quake? I hear a loud noise above and glance up as a large rust-streaked stalactite breaks free of its moorings. Shards of stone and dirt shower everywhere, followed by the bulk of the triangular disaster. It plunges straight down onto the street, barely missing the copper building's foundations. Dozens of beetles are left motionless on the ground.

Should I start my search at the bottom, or at the top?

I hold steady and watch the chaos below. The cessation in activity lasts only a few minutes following the crash. Soon groups are forming again. There is more shouting and shoving.

Top it is!

With a worried check of the cavern ceiling, I direct the rectangle toward the building's upper story. Since I don't belong to the building, a room accessible side landing spot won't be available to me. Thankfully, roof landing spots almost always are. When I reach the roof, I circle slowly over it, looking for any signs of conflict. After a few seconds I'm comfortable enough to bring the rectangle down for a landing. I instruct it not to relax itself. Not to re-fuse with any of the roofing material.

I will need it again. Hopefully, soon.

I exit the rectangle and find myself crouching as I make my way to the entry door. I still have no idea where HardCandy is. I'm almost paralyzed with fear now. I'm not a big person, freehead. I don't know how to fight physically. Debuggers aren't taught to resist. After implantation, conflict is only an option in the most extreme conditions. Nor do I have any bots to gather around me like I did on the station. I'm not even sure I should use the beetles' stream. It may only help them find me. Help them notice my departure from their template.

And what state will I find HardCandy? Will I have to lift and carry her? What then?

Whether you turn to the right or to the left, your ears will hear a voice behind you, saying, "This is the way; walk in it."

More words. Quiet reassurances. It's weird, because even though I can't see the words like in an Easy Impact or Extended Easy message, I can definitely hear them like it is EE. I sort of feel them too, almost like a Full Impact implant-to-implant connection.

Regardless, they give me strength. Enough that I can move forward. Enough that I can begin to search.

I reach the black entry door and stream it open. Inside it is dimly lit and quiet. The hallway is standard for "reclaimer sparse," soft white walls with only a tinge of copper. The floor appears to be wood, but I know it is manufactured. There is a cinnamon smell to the air.

Still crouched, I move cautiously, slowly. I peak my head into every open door I come to. I stream open those doors that aren't open and check them too. I get no resistance to my stream requests. Security isn't important for reclaimers, apparently. Even though my access is clearly hampered again. Clearly not like it was. Chatter aside.

I find nothing in the rooms I check. Not even a sleeping occupant. In fact, most are bland and empty—with not a single bit of customization or enhancement. Just four walls and a ceiling.

I continue searching until I reach a triangular lift with transparent doors.

Should I check floor by floor? There must be thirty floors in this building!

Ask for a sign, whether in the deepest depths, or in the highest of heights.

More words of direction. Feeling and motive dressed in words.

A sign? Ask for a sign?

I am! I want to know where to go. What to do next...

Or perhaps the words *are* the sign. I'm already on the highest level. Do I go to the bottom then? Is that it?

The words are a memory, but the feeling that accompanies them remains. Assures me I'm correct. Yes. The depths. That must be it.

I enter the lift and direct it to take me to the lowest level. I plunge silently floor by floor. Through its transparent front I can see each as I pass. All are as nondescript and empty as the topmost. Only after twenty floors does the appearance seem to change. The number of doors per hallway lessens while the halls themselves widen. The ceiling heights increase as well.

Finally the lift stops, and the door slides open with a *swish*. The room beyond is the most lavish of any reclaimer room I've ever seen. The ceiling—colored light blue—towers nearly six meters overhead. There is a textured arch built into its surface. Beetle lettering travels the walls in slow moving bands from ceiling to floor. The floor is as polished and marble appearing as the richest of master homes. Light in color. There is a luminescent wall in front of me.

Descending from the ceiling and angling to disappear through that wall are two meter-wide transparent tubes, bubbling with blue fluid. Below them is an arched pair of copper doors—the entrance to the room beyond.

Aside from the motion of the lettering and the tubes, the room seems as lifeless and empty as any so far. Gritting my teeth, I make my way to the doors. I expect an alarm to sound or a blue-skinned reclaimer to appear to stop me, but no such thing happens.

And why should it? Am I not one of them now? Do they know any different?

I touch the stream for the door combination, the proper singsong that should make it open. I get lots of static. There is no combination necessary here. No digital mechanism to stop me. I reach out and give the door a shove. It swings backward on frictionless hinges. Cautiously, I move forward through it.

The room beyond is vast. Snaking through it, lying in a formation reminiscent of a large letter W, is a long row of silver chutes. Each is fed from smaller tubes that split off from the two central tubes overhead. Like the chute HardCandy rested in when I saw her last—the chute I helped design—there is a transparent viewing section on the top surface of every chute.

I am the vine, you are the branches. Remain in me.

Yes, it is something like that. Like roots from a tree.

This must be what I came to find. The enhanced treatment center. There must be a hundred chutes here, though. I give the beetle stream a try. Need to locate HardCandy in all this—

I hear a low rumble, and the room begins to wobble. The tubes above make a disturbing pinging sound. I brace myself, wait for more to happen. For the entire roof to cave in on me. But after a few seconds the shaking subsides. Things return to normal.

I sprint to the far left side of the room, where the line of chutes begin. I bend over and peer through the transparent section, only to pull back in revulsion. Within are a blue beetle chest and arms...and nothing else. One of their bodies being reclaimed? Whether it is being broken down or built up again, I don't know. But either way it is repulsive. Shocking. Like a beheaded fish thrown back into the water.

You wouldn't want to see it, freehead.

Gathering my courage, I check the next chute. This one is equally repulsive. There is only a one-legged body, still without a head. I slide to the next one. It has a head with only a neck. The next is an arm and a hand. The next one has only internal organs laid out and floating for all to see. Like a street-level meat shop!

Frowning, I move to the next tube. At first it isn't clear what this one contains. A skin-wrapped body part, yes. But it is circular in shape, and partially obscured by the bubbles within. A skullcap, perhaps? Then the bubbles clear and the object shifts, revealing a portion of a human chest. And it is decidedly *not* male.

I bend double and almost heave. Please...don't tell me that is all that's left of her...

"Do you require treatment?" a familiar voice says. I turn to find HardCandy, standing—alive! Without thinking I wrap my arms around her and squeeze. She doesn't respond to my touch, though. She remains rigid. Startled.

I step back and look at her. She appears as I remember—almost. Her skin is lightly colored and she is still dressed in the translucent clothing of the beetles. Still modestly covered. But the color of her clothing is a warm red now, and her almond eyes—while not blank—aren't completely engaged either. They look a little distant, distracted.

There is another glaring difference, though. "You have hair be-ginning to show," I say. "On your head." I point. "Stubbly...bur-roughs and bradbury..."

HardCandy tips her head, looking perplexed. "I asked you if you require treatment. You don't appear substandard, but perhaps your deficiencies are internal?" She mimics me—staring at my head, while I'm busy staring at hers. "A brain injury, perhaps?"

"I'm not..." I shake my head. "No. I'm not damaged." I glance back at the tube behind me. Are they making females now? Is that why they were so interested in HardCandy? Are they wanting to breed? Increase in number?

HardCandy frowns. "Why are you here then? It is inefficient to waste another's time this way. Operations need to be performed. Organs grown. The new prototypes needs to be cultivated."

I can't get over my surprise: HardCandy back to normal, except not. Why didn't they tell me?

Why would they? What concern was it of mine? I was only a maintainer...

Right. There's that.

"So you are a reclaimer now," I say. "Is that it?"

She nods. "That is my caste. Correct."

I shake my head. "No. It isn't. You're a debugger. An implanted human. From Earth."

"Earth? That symbolic designation is known. I believe that is the focus of the constructors' experiments. One we reclaimers find dangerous."

I somehow missed that detail while embedded in the beetles'

stream. Trapped within their bubble. It makes things clearer. Shem's talk about stream projection, matter manipulation. With such a power, who knows what someone could do. But on Earth?

"What?" I ask. "What are they planning to do?"

"That is the constructors' domain. Be assured it is pressing toward the common goal."

"Which is?"

"Increased autonomy. Stream expansion. Growth in numbers. Domination."

I glance at the large tubes that flow above her head. "But reclaimers don't like that idea," I say.

"There are other means to our goal. Plans that won't risk us all."

"What—?" I shake my head, close my hands into fists. I've had enough of these beetles and their crazy world. We need to leave. I've found the true stream. Or it has found me, showing me this God who stoops. Who reconfigured himself somehow as one of us. Who bore the burdens of others, contrary to everything we've been taught. We need to get that message out. Return to Earth and tell it. But we can't do that if we're caught here.

The room shakes again, slightly. Reminding me.

Then there's the issue with the star above. The one that's about to do *something*. I need HardCandy to be herself. Not this reclaimer hybrid. I need to burst her bubble.

"DarkTrench," I say, "do you remember? The space station, the robot, Scallop? Any of it?"

A puzzled look. "What is a scallop?"

"A kind of crustacean, but it is also the name of a person. Someone who threatened us once."

Her forehead wrinkles. "Shocked us?"

"Yes. Yes. Lots of shocks. He loved to shock."

There is a flicker of something in her eyes. Almost like a tweak response. But then her eyes gloss over again. Deaden. "You are wasting my time." She turns and walks to one of the horizontal chutes. Laying a hand on the outside, she closes her eyes as if communing with it. Adjusting it.

Which she probably is.

I walk to where she stands and glance into the chute she is checking. Grimace. There is only a foot inside. It is submerged within a fluid that percolates. Bubbles.

"Are you boiling it?" I ask.

HardCandy opens her eyes and looks at me. "This organic container is at a stage where it requires adjusting to reach the next growth state. I am doing so."

I sniff. "Yes, that's important. Foot boiling."

A twinge of anger enters HardCandy's eyes before they grow distant again. I'm getting to her. I think. She closes her eyes and appears to be deeply concentrating, her brow furled.

"What are you doing?" I ask.

"I am asking for assistance in your reclamation. It is clear you need help." She squints at me, looking puzzled. "Does the stream seem unusual to you today? Disjointed?"

I remember the scenes outside. The conflict between the castes. "You don't know the half of it." I hold out a hand. "You need to come with me."

HardCandy backs away, sliding behind the bulk of another silver chute. "I am needed here," she says. "My task is to mind the new receptacles."

Rails! How am I going to make her come with me? I can't carry her. I've seen what she's like when she fights. Even with stops in place, she can hold her own. In fact, shortly after I first met Hard-Candy, she was forced to scrap with three Abduls. Though I saved her, she was doing better than I would have in a similar situation.

Finally I can think of only one thing to do. Moving as fast as I can, I step around the chute, grasp both her arms, and press my lips firmly to hers.

Despite what happened the last time, I still feel a flash of lightning in the contact. A neuron explosion.

Hope she feels the same...Actually, I'm hoping she'll feel something else.

She tears herself away. "What was that?" she asks, eyes flaring with life.

I wait for her to collapse again. I don't want to drag her out of the building, but it would be easier than pulling against her. Trying to wrestle her through the door.

"You have infringed on my physical countenance, maintainer."

Waiting. Still waiting. What have they changed? Have they removed her stops?

The large double doors swing open, and I feel a lump form in my throat. Ham and Japheth enter the room. Beyond them, waiting in the external lobby, are more beetles. Dozens of sleek and limber jinn. Mostly reclaimers, by the looks of it. Regardless, they are all stronger than me.

Not good.

OVERHEAD, THE BLUE FLUID seems to move with decreased velocity through the tubes. Slowing, gurgling, congealing. I can trace the individual paths of dozens of air bubbles as they swirl and dance.

"Return to your tasks," Ham says, looking from HardCandy to me. "Both of you."

I sniff sarcastically. "I don't think I will," I say. "I've tried the slave route before." I tap my head. "It isn't worth the pain."

Ham squints hard. "So you have found a way to release yourself from the template. How?"

I shrug. "I guess your coding is bad. Or easily breakable." I glance at HardCandy. Her brow is furrowed. She isn't passing out yet, though. Why isn't she? Where are the rules when you need them?

"I was performing my tasks..." She stops, bows her head. Brings three fingers to touch her forehead. "The stream is so odd today..."

"Both subjects could be of use to us," Japheth says. "Their coding. There are many differences between the two."

"The reclaimer plan is irrelevant until after the current event has passed," Ham says. "We must contain the violence. Restore order. Wait out the star's vengeance."

Japheth looks stoic. "It has happened before," he says. "We will reclaim the loss and go on. There will be setbacks, the constructors must be forced to stop their surface experiments, but we will go on. Reclaim and continue."

I look at Ham. "And that's how you feel?"

He shrugs. "We don't trouble ourselves over such things. You should know that."

"Clearly you do," I say. "You're here."

"I am here because you are. You are part of us now."

I shake my head. "Not true, beetle. I'm free." And for some reason I feel like smiling at the word. Somehow, I know that I'm more that just physically free. I'm free in a place that can never be contained again. No stops, freehead. Either external or internal. None.

I look at HardCandy again. Her eyes are now closed, and she is massaging her forehead with her fingertips. "Sandfly..." she says. "That's your name, right?"

Now I do smile. I think it worked. I think she's starting to free up. To clean out. Imagine! My kiss does wonders.

In all your ways acknowledge me, and I will make your paths straight.

"Sorry, didn't mean to be prideful," I whisper. "*You* do wonders."

"What is that?" Ham says. "What did you say?"

I shake my head. "I don't think you'd understand."

"Am I not a reclaimer?" Hard asks, squinting at the floor.

Japheth looks over his shoulder toward the door. One by one his fellow reclaimers enter the room. All stand roughly two meters high and have rich scarlet hair. All look as if they could lift a downrider off its string. Muscles ripple and tense.

"We'll have to contain them," Japheth says.

Ham nods. "It would be for the best."

"Whose best?" I reach a hand out for HardCandy—who thankfully, makes a motion my direction. "Not ours." She closes with me, takes my hand. Draws near enough that I can feel her presence. It is like warm bread, freshly buttered.

The room shakes again, enough that I put a hand on the chute behind me to steady myself. The beetles don't seem to mind at all. In fact, Ham stands with arms tightly crossed. Somehow they all manage to stand firm.

Not good.

More beetles file in and close in around us. One puts a hand on my arm, another grabs Hard's elbow. She scowls and pulls away.

Fear threatens to creep in. Icy fingers play along my spine. Tickles my skull. I don't want to stay here. It is all so foreign, so not right. Confusing and dark. I watch as HardCandy struggles with her captors. I tense up—look for a way out. I stream, but it is mostly noise to me now. I'm panicking, I know that.

Keep calm, Sandfly. Think. Think.

I get this feeling. Like the beginnings of a Full Impact message. A calm assurance, a warm embrace. A new feeling of peace. This is your battle, isn't it, God-who-stoops? One I'll have to trust you with. To agree and resign. To join with your stream. I will it to be so!

See, I am doing a new thing! Now it springs up; don't you sense it? I am making a way in the desert and streams in the wasteland.

In an instant everything changes. The jinn begin to scream, wrapping head with hands, eyes closed. Others bend double. Their grip on me releases, as does that on HardCandy. She too appears affected by whatever is happening, as her eyes are closed too.

"Shut it out," I say to her. "Their stream is not for us. It is foreign. Malignant. Wrong. Push it out."

She manages to open her eyes and squint at me. I grab her hand and tug. Pull her toward the doors. No one tries to stop us. Many of the beetles are on the floor now, writhing. Without another look, we plunge into the outer room, then to the transparent lift.

It bears us skyward.

TOGETHER WE BOARD my rectangle and I direct it upward, urge it to speed. No one gives chase. Around us the city continues to shake. Crystal structures make loud pinging sounds, an anguished melody of strain. A death song.

More stalactites tear loose from above and fall. Some are deflected by the building defenses, but many are not. Buildings shatter, throwing off debris like gemstone fragments. A large blue shard flies into our path, splitting just before we reach it. I wrench the rectangle up and left to avoid any additional fragments.

Now seated, I grip the handrails tightly. And HardCandy—having lost any semblance of independence—does the same to my waist from behind. I don't mind.

Though it is a trifle distracting.

HardCandy leans into me, draws her face close to my ear. "Where are you taking me?" she asks, fear straining her voice.

I feel her warmth, and also the slight abrasiveness of her stubbly head on my neck. Ahead of us, another tower—a pink one—shatters and falls to the left. I move the rectangle even higher, eyes searching for the exit to the surface. "The star is doing something," I say. "Something big. We need to return to the ship and leave."

"The ship?" HardCandy grows silent, but still holds on to me. Then I feel her grip tighten. "DarkTrench! Adaptive personality, able to flip. Like family!"

"Right," I say. "Absolutely."

"How, Sand? It's up above, right? High up? How will we reach it?"

I shake my head. "I'm not sure. I'm working on trust here." The exit looms ahead, a fluorescent beacon in an otherwise raging sea. I urge the rectangle faster, feel the wind increase past my ears.

"Trust?" HardCandy says. "What is left in the universe to trust? Anything?"

As we approach the circular exit, I slow the craft again, position it for the optimal distance on every side. Then we enter. I can't help but look at the ceiling above. Expecting any moment to see something rip free, but also wondering if the triped will appear. Or the bot.

"I put more faith in our system than you," she continues. "Rails! I begged to be implanted—did you know that? I wanted it more than anything."

Ahead I see sunlight. The green glow of the world beyond the cavern. The distant smells of life.

"I know," I say. "I've streamed it."

HardCandy digs her forehead into my back. "Oh, yeah...I remember that now. We datamixed."

We break out into open sky. I squint at the brightness of it, instinctively raise a hand to shield my eyes. It has to be twice as bright as it was before. Three times.

"Flipping Tesla," HardCandy says. "Why is it so bright out here?"

I concentrate on my steering. Scan the landscape ahead. Finding the pyramid, I point us directly toward it. "I told you. The star. Betelgeuse."

The smells seem equally vivid now. The pine, the dense oxygen smell. It is as if they were infused into a pot of water and are now being boiled out. Released to the air in massive quantities.

"At least it smells good." HardCandy sighs. "We're going to die here, aren't we? Die in Jannah with no hope of going anywhere better."

We skirt the upper surface of the pyramid, heading for the far side and the landing platform beyond. "This was never Jannah," I say. "And it is a long way from heaven." My heart lifts when the landing surface becomes visible. There, just as we left it, is the white sliver.

"DarkTrench," I stream. "Are you still out there?"

Seconds pass, and then: "Sandfly. You are outside again."

I slow the rectangle, begin to guide it down. "Yes. We're approaching the craft that brought us here."

"A native craft? Like the one that attacked us?"

"The same," I say.

Another long pause. The rectangle touches the surface. I step out, and reach back to help Hard.

"HardCandy!" DarkTrench streams. "You are free as well. I am pleased."

She sends a smile to both of us. "I am. Free again. Yes."

We approach the sliver. The door eases open and we enter. Brightness again surrounds us, but after the sky outside, it now seems almost dim. Light coming from everywhere in the walls and yet nowhere in particular. We move down the hall until we reach the door to the control chamber. As before, the door opens with a "glop" sound and we step inside. There are still two high chairs and the concave and darkened wall to our right, the representative "front" of the room.

"Now what do we do?" HardCandy says.

I have no idea. I'm hesitant to say that aloud, though, because I hoped our path would be obvious. That my triped *would* somehow show up and steer us away. We made the commitment now, after all. What else does he, or A~A³ expect us to do?

"There is still a stream here," she says. "Can we just tell the ship what to do?"

I shake my head. "I don't think—"

The concave wall snaps open and brightens. The image of our true ship, DarkTrench, forms on it—fully textured—looking as if I could reach out and pull it from the screen's surface. It brings a deep longing on my part, but also comfort. We need to get there. Need the familiarity of that placid stream again.

"Is this where you would like to go?" a voice says.

"Shem?" HardCandy says, and shivers noticeably. The screen dims and reconfigures, finally forming into the face of the blond-haired beetle. HardCandy's perfect jinn. His voice is still confident and assured but also slightly mocking now. Superior. The image pans back to show his bare chest and arms. He appears to be seated, leaning forward slightly, arms resting on his legs. Comfortable and in control.

"Isn't there a war going on?" I ask. "Shouldn't you be out fighting?"

Shem waves his right hand dismissively. "The reclaimers want to blame us for the coming event. It is of no consequence to me personally. I will survive. I always do."

I think of the structure outside. The pyramid containing the projector. "But your toys will be destroyed," I say. "You'll lose your creations."

He frowns. "Yes, well, that is always a danger—having to start again. That has happened before, as well."

"Seems wasteful," I say.

"Ultimately it is all wasted," Shem says. "That is the way of it."

I look at HardCandy. "I don't believe that."

"Regardless of what you believe, it is factual." Shem smiles. "That craft is one of my creations, by the way."

"It is very nice," Hard says. "Can you make it take us back?"

"I could," he says. "Or I could construct another to destroy you. The possibilities are endless."

I touch the ship's stream. Ask it to shut the eye-like screen off. No effect.

"You'll try to keep us here?" I ask.

Shem shrugs. "So you are determined to leave? Perhaps if you tried a different template—a constructor template—you would be content. Satisfied. Have a new perspective on the universe."

"I've sampled your universe," I say. "It is random, it is selfish, and it is lonely."

"You say that because your mind is small," Shem says. "Because it is closed."

"No, my mind is open. Better than ever."

He raises an eyebrow. "I'm curious how you managed to remove yourself from the maintainer template."

The ground trembles again, the world shifting slightly on its axis. I grab the nearest chair for support, then wrap my arms around it. "I guess I'm fortunate," I say after the shaking has subsided.

Shem's face goes stoic. He shakes his head firmly. "Then perhaps you are ready for my gift."

I exchange looks with HardCandy. "Gift?" I ask.

Shem nods. "Yes." The image pulls back, revealing Shem's left hand. In it, he holds a solid white ball. "This."

It looks like a round block of salt. "What is it?" I ask.

"What you really came for," he says. "The game changer."

I look at HardCandy again, but get only a shrug. Another tremor rocks the room. A rapid back and forth.

"Time is of the essence, Sandfly," DarkTrench streams. "I don't know how much longer we can wait."

HardCandy climbs into one of the seats. The seat responds by securing her in. "A game changer?" she says. "What game?"

"The only game that matters to you," Shem says. "The one that awaits you on Earth. You must suspect that after you joined our stream your memories were no longer your own. We know everything there is to know about your society. About you."

We both remain speechless. Lost as to what the blue creature is offering.

"Come now, you're not that simple," he says. "You're both well into the high side in intelligence. More so than the others that visited." He raises the ball again. "BlackRock? Remember? They came looking for a sample that would equal it. This will match perfectly."

Hard squints first at the screen, then at me. "That thing isn't black."

"And it shouldn't be," I say. "The Imam is expecting it to be white. Historically—"

"Rails—right!" HardCandy says. "The sins of man have filled it up, making it dark. So the Imam's looking for a replacement?"

"That's what the first crew told me," I say. "Part of their reason for coming."

DarkTrench breaks in, streaming into my thoughts. "Nine- tenths of the star has reached a heightened level of intensity. I am losing communication with the sampler I sent out. Very sporadic transmissions."

"Burroughs..." I sigh.

"You need to be on your way, correct?" Shem says. "Need to fly. *Want* to fly?"

"And you're offering this to us, why?"

"For your advancement, of course. Who else should rule that sorry planet, but you? Who else has the necessary acumen? The proper perspective?"

"How would we get it from you?" HardCandy asks. "You want us to return to the cavern?"

I scowl at HardCandy, shake my head. "It doesn't matter. We don't need it. We're not going back."

Intensity fills her face. "This could change everything, Sand. Don't you see? He's right. It would prove you're the leader I know you are. We could change everything back there. Everything. No running. Free the streets."

Shem nods. "This object has power in and of itself. Many possible customizations. You've seen our technology. You know what we can do." He pauses, leans back in his chair. "It would be a simple matter to stream project this to you. I could place it right there on the vessel. In fact, I'll infuse it with the knowledge to get you home."

I look closely at the object he holds—white as milk. Clean looking. Solid and shiny. A giant marble of power. How easy that would make things when we return. I could surround myself with bots and march to the Imam's palace. Make my demands known. Freedom for all debuggers. Freedom of thought and of mind. Proper payment of workers. Proper treatment.

I glance at HardCandy. Women as first-class citizens. Free to reveal their face. Free to travel and laugh. I look at Shem's smiling features again. The upheld "WhiteRock." How bad would it be to take it? Power means nothing to me now anyway. Not really.

But it could mean a lot to other people. A whole lot.

"Are you away yet, Sandfly?" DarkTrench again. "Have you found a way to get up here? I'm concerned..."

I remain silent. Thinking. Pondering. Knowing we have to do something. Have to launch somehow.

I reach out in my mind prayerfully. Is this the way? Is this how I can solve it all? Why we came here? It seems obvious. Feels perfectly right.

Seconds pass. Important and highly significant seconds. Time that we need for flight. We have a void to cross. A ship to board and engage. Get moving on its way.

But now that you know A~A³—or rather are known by Him—how is it that you are turning back to those weak and miserable principles? Do you wish to be enslaved by them all over again?

I frown. Could I, the former slave, having become a master, also become a tyrant?

I look at HardCandy again. Remember the childhood she shared with me. Her father—one of the unsung heroes of her story. Giving his life for his child. And in some ways, so had GrimJack.

And so have I. Not just my own, anymore. I am something more. Someone else's.

I shake my head firmly. "No, thank you, Shem. We won't be needing it."

"Sandfly, are you sure?" HardCandy streams.

Disappointment crosses Shem's face. Irritation. "Then you stay there, on the surface. I warn you, that will be the worst location for what is to come."

"So you're not inviting us back?"

Shem harrumphs. "That wouldn't be very productive now, would it? It wouldn't lead to any change worthy of maintaining."

The eye snaps shut.

Shem is gone.

WE SIT IN SILENCE for some time. Me, afraid to even look at HardCandy for fear of seeing resentment or anger on her face. Her, possibly both angry and resentful...or maybe afraid. Regardless, she is quiet. And that is good. I'm not sure I could deal with human interaction right now.

I'm used to fixing things. I'm used to diving into the guts of a machine and finding out what's wrong. Rectifying it. Making it good again. But now we're in a ship that I don't know how to control. Don't even know how to start actually. Is this what A~A³ has for us? A final surrendering to death on a planet hundreds of light-years from home?

"Have you tried to start it?" you ask.

I have. I've immersed myself in as much of the beetle-jinn stream as I can handle. The bits are a complete jumble to me now. Meaningless static. I can't affect anything.

"You used to be a maintainer, right?" HardCandy's first words to me. Thankfully, they don't sound mad, or even that scared. She's trying to work the problem too. My strong feelings for her intensify.

I scan the room. The glowing walls, the textured floor, the darkened concavity of the eye-screen. All so completely foreign and useless. So not unlike the tomb I imagined for myself.

"Nothing here talks to me," I say. "I can't communicate with any of it anymore. Whatever life, whatever essence the beetles infused it with is no longer present. It is ready for reclamation." I manage a smile. "You were a reclaimer once, right?"

HardCandy shrugs, shakes her head sadly.

"Have you launched yet?" DarkTrench sends. "Are you underway?"

"No," I sigh. "I don't think we're coming."

There is a long pause—partially due to the lag, I know, but also due to DarkTrench's thought circuits in action. He's drawing the proper conclusions. Making inferences. "So do you now regret leaving?" he asks. "The Earth, I mean?"

Inside emotions sway and battle for position. Anger and bitterness want to dominate. But also something else—an emotion built on a better knowledge, a fuller knowledge.

I smile, shake my head. "No."

HardCandy rises in her chair, eyes alive and throws her arms up. "What? How could you not regret this, Sand. I regret it! I regret it greatly."

I open my mouth to speak, but she waves it away.

"Not you. I don't blame you. But the trip. It was blinking crazy. I know you didn't know that when we left. I know it seemed right. But this is—they used me, Sand! Robbed me! At least with the masters I was special. Useful. But here...I was just another cog to them. Another bot."

I shake my head. "Maybe. But that's not what we are. Not what we're supposed to be."

HardCandy pulls up and the chair releases her. She walks toward the eye-screen and, leaning over, peers down at it. It is hard to ignore her red outfit. She looks good in it, but I know she doesn't want to hear that now. I can't help but wonder if the color was based on hidden personality traits too. Knowing what I know of her life, I'm thinking yes.

"There has to be something we can do," she says. "Machines are our specialty."

"Not these machines. I—"

DarkTrench interrupts again. "I wanted to let you know. The event seems eminent. I've lost all contact with the final sampler. The star's color has completely changed. Since such change shows up in the visual spectrum and is therefore dependent on the speed of light, it doubtless represents the first of whatever is to come. I am specially shielded, as you know. I expect to withstand quite a bit of radiation. To be safe, however, I am moving to a position behind the planet. Further communication may be difficult."

I nod. Send back a final "good-bye" then revert to silence again.

"So that's it?" HardCandy says. She is leaning against the eye-screen wall, arms crossed. Protecting herself. Shielding. "The end?"

I find myself smiling. "I met someone here," I say. "Someone different."

"More jinn?"

"Not like them." I wrinkle my forehead. "Actually, sometimes he was like the bot, but most of the time he was completely unique. I saw him on that herd animal. Zoomed in, but you didn't see anything odd, remember?"

"The bot? What bot? Like back on the station? The looped one that got us into this?"

"Yes, well, I'm sure what I've heard sounds looped too. Blinking looped, probably. Want me to package it and stream it to you?"

HardCandy looks at the door. "Actually, I was thinking it might be nice to take another walk in the green while I can." She glances tentatively my way. "Want to join me?"

I shake my head. "It has to be ten times as bright out there now as it was. You wouldn't get to see much. Probably fry your retinas."

She softly stomps a foot. "Rails. It seemed good." She looks at me and sighs. "Is your experience worth my time?"

"I think so." I shrug. "Plus I have something else to send you. Something I didn't share before."

The room trembles again, slightly. I'm thankful there is nothing in the room that could shift or fall. Just HardCandy and I, and two firmly mounted chairs.

Frowning, HardCandy nods. I compose a Full Impact message of everything I heard and saw. I even mention that the whole thing might have been a waking dream. That it could've been lurking in my implant since the first time I heard the singing. I send it away then.

HardCandy shuts her eyes, drinks it all in. Digests it. Gives it her full attention. Finally, a little gasp escapes her lips. Her eyes remain closed and she shakes her head sadly.

"GrimJack gave me his implant?" she says. "Gave up being a debugger for me?"

I nod. "Seems true."

Tears form in the corners of her eyes. Instinctively I stand and move closer. Raise my arms slightly. Not pressing, but available if she needs me.

"Why would anyone want to do something like that for me?" A tear slips down her cheek.

I raise my shoulders. "Why would anyone want to do something like that for anyone?"

She sinks into silence.

"He didn't give up his eternal destination for you, though," I say. "Contrary to what we've been told, it doesn't come with the implant. Grim never had it to give."

Hard shakes her head. "We're not really angels, are we?"

"No." I look at the floor. Think of the caverns beneath filled with crystal. "And even real angels aren't all good."

She stands and moves closer, but still looking toward the door. "This triped, do you think you can trust him? Do you think he was real?"

"Trust him, yes. But can I verify him? Tear him down to essence or slap a sheet on him to look inside? No. I can't. Can't know for sure." I clench my fist, hold it to my side. "I do know I'm free now. I can tell."

"But you're being reprogrammed? What if—"

The eye screen snaps open. At the same time the lighting of the entire sliver brightens too. Like an electric bolt has shot through it.

"The star?" HardCandy says.

I stare at the screen. At any moment I expect the face of Shem or one of the other jinn to appear, but instead we see the image of the star—Betelgeuse. Its angry face rises out of the display like an inflated porcupine fish. There are thousands of star-matter arcs spread across its surface. Even though it is only an image we are seeing, the surface seem incredible bright and active, as if building momentum. Crouching down, preparing to explode.

"Here it comes..."

A repetitive sound fills my mind. A *thweel, thweel, thweel* resonance, almost like a summer insect attracting a mate. Is this what the beetles heard? The sound that stopped them? It isn't really like an insect either; it is almost like a marble rolling down a dimpled metal bowl. Except smoother. Less chaotic.

HardCandy's hands are shielding her face. "Are you hearing this? It is like shattering glass!"

"Yes, I—" The sound changes, becomes more familiar. Symphonic. Choral. Divided and yet uniform. Distinct and similar.

"Singing," I say. "I hear singing."

And I feel it too. It courses through my head. Fills my chest. Reaches out to all my extremities.

Another flash of energy in the cabin. A strong pitch of the floor too, so much that HardCandy loses her footing and goes careening my way. I catch her arm and pull her close. Hold her. The feeling only adds to the warmth already permeating my body. And in my mind is a light that tastes like honey—a harmony that feels like warm water to aching muscles.

The walls of the room become active. Bands of jinn text play over it, in dozens of distinct colors.

HardCandy's eyes are still closed, so I shake her. Wait for her to look at me, then show her the rainbow of symbols around us. "What do you think it is?" she asks.

I reach out to the stream. The bombastic stream that still floods my senses. Is it possible? With this, can I...?

Yes! For the first time since we returned to the sliver, I can feel the craft's emanations into the ether. I can see its machinations. All the possible customizations. "This ship isn't meant to launch again," I say. "It was configured just to bring us here."

HardCandy has entered the stream too. It is different for her, I think. But she's trying to help. "Then there is still nothing we can do?"

I start paging through the ships systems, its active areas. It is like a maze of complication. Something tweaks at me, though. Beckons me along.

He is like a tree planted by streams of water, which yields its fruit in season and whose leaf does not wither. Whatever he does prospers.

The methods I learned as a maintainer rush back to me. Suddenly I can see what changes have to be made. I can feel those systems aching for attention. I command them to reconfigure, to shift and to move.

"I think I've got something," I say. "I think something's happening now."

The eye screen image has changed. The star has now grown to twice the size. The arcs of star-matter look razor sharp. It has become a three-dimensional buzz saw. Reaching for the sky it wills to command.

Marbles fall and move into place. Engines fire expectantly.

We're not leaving yet, though. Why aren't we going?

I drop deeper into the stream. Search furiously.

The star is coming! Got to move!

My heart drops. I've found the answer. There is a coding of some sort. A security system or a signature—an essence that is required. I rail in anguish.

"What?" HardCandy says. "You have it going, Sand. Take us to DarkTrench. Get us out of here!"

I shake my head. "I can't. I don't know what it wants. I don't know how to steer this thing. To tell it to go. I've reconfigured the systems. But I can't make it happen."

HardCandy's face drops. Hope dashed against the rocks. Her tear-filled eyes search the surface of the active walls around us. She is hypnotized. Staring hard at first one section, then another. Finally, her eyes widen and she gasps.

"I see it!" she says. "The patterns you need. It is like one of the rugs I worked on in school. I see it. The colors. It is all in the colors."

I can't help but frown. "What?"

She messages me. Sends me a packet of surprises. A patchwork of hues. "Take these," her image says in the stream. She points at the black box of controls I've been wrestling with. "Put them there!"

I push the patchwork out. Stream it right at the sliver's control matrix.

The vessel jumps into the sky. The eye-screen image changes from that of Betelgeuse, to that of DarkTrench. Our ebony-colored ship with the starburst at one end, still hiding on the dark side of the planet. I scream the ship's name into the superlative stream. I tell him to wait. That we're on our way.

"Very good," the ship says, as if he were smiling. "I'll be ready when you arrive."

The words give me a lump in my throat. Like the sound of a missed parent's voice. We're coming, ship! Just wait.

A loud roaring fills the cabin. It isn't the craft's engines, because those are nearly soundless. Another quake? I urge the ship upward, away from the surface. The room lurches again, hard.

"It's a storm," HardCandy says. "Fast moving. Complete with lots of fireworks." The eye-screen image changes again. Shows a mass of surrounding clouds. Close, dark, and angry. As if to underscore, the ship makes a hard pitch to our right, enough that we both get tossed into a wall. I take the impact with a shoulder. Ugh.

"You'd think getting us into the sky would be enough..."

"We need to climb, Sandfly." Hard's eyes are wide, her face flushed.

I grab the ship controls in the stream. Wrap my head around them and wrench them up. "I'm working on it." We need to go, little sliver. Now.

The ship sags the other direction, slows, gives two large cabin-jarring bumps, then seemingly breaks free of the torrent. There is a little arc, and the ride smooths out considerably. The acceleration is fast now, and as vertical as I can make it. "There has to be some way of reducing what we feel," I say, mostly because I'm seated on the floor and feeling extreme pressure on my head and chest.

HardCandy is seated beside me with eyes closed. "Let me look," she says, scowling.

"You've left the troposphere," Trench streams. "There should be no weather from here on out."

"Keep telling me those atmosphere levels," I say, shaking my head. "I really want to learn as I go."

I concentrate on keeping the ship headed upward. At times my brain feels like it is on fire with all the activity. Not to mention that I'm now laying flat on the floor.

Suddenly the pressure releases. "Got it!" Hard says. "Gravity compensator...something." We take that opportunity to scramble for the chairs and climb in. "Do you think these things have straps, or—"

"You have about three kilometers of stratosphere left, then mesosphere, then—"

Thanks, Trench. The image on the eye-screen is now that of the curve of the planet below us. It also shows our location and the cone of Trench on the far side of the planet. Need to angle that way!

"Difficult maneuvers are best done once you've reached space," Trench says.

"Is that right?" I stream, squinting. I feel the strain of keeping the ship moving upward in a consistent fashion. The legion of variables one has to monitor and maintain.

"Only trying to help." A pause. "You're in the thermosphere. Only one level more to go."

"What's the star look like?" I manage to open my eyes enough to check the screen. Somehow it is a little less threatening to see the image on the outside, rather than inside, via the implant. It is still bad, though.

The star is steadily growing. If the system had planets analogous to our Mercury and Venus, they'd be toast by now. Beside me, HardCandy gasps.

"You have few minutes left before a shockwave reaches the planet," Trench says.

"How many?" I ask.

"Minutes? It would do no good to tell you, Sandfly. Just hurry."

I urge the sliver to more speed. It responds.

I make the eye-screen image change to show the distance between Trench and us. It is considerably shorter than last time. But still seems unreachable. "Do you think this thing can bear the blunt of whatever's coming?"

"If the star were to continue its expansion?" Trench says. "I doubt anything could withstand that. Even the planet."

"Which you are behind," Hard says. "Maybe you should get moving, Trench."

"Yes," I say. "Stay in the planet's shadow, but go. We'll catch you." I reach out for the sliver ship's systems. Try to factor the fastest potential speed. It seems adequate. "At least, I think we will."

"I appreciate your concern," Trench says. "But there is no reason for me to move without you. You're the sole reason I'm here." A pause. "Exosphere. Give it everything now."

Which I do. Inside I see the images of the two ships coming together. Closing the distance. With all my will I urge them together. Urge the distance to close.

"Only five hundred kilometers now, Sand," HardCandy streams me. "We need to get to the door."

I open my eyes. The image of the star has reclaimed the eyescreen. And it is enormous! "Oh, yeah," I say aloud. "The cube." I look at my chest. "We don't have our suits."

Hard grabs my hand. Pulls me toward the room's exit. "We'll be okay. The cube can protect us, remember?"

I hesitate. It protected us when the jinn were in charge. But now?

Still, I follow her out into the hall, and then to the docking point. The luminosity of the hall surrounds us. Light comes from everywhere and nowhere in particular. The hall ends at a completely solid surface.

I look at HardCandy who is smiling, oddly. "Any idea how to?"

I close my eyes to focus, try to get a reading on how far we are from Trench. A hundred kilometers, sixty-four, thirty-two, sixteen, eight...

"Okay, I'm trying to move us parallel." I instruct the sliver to rotate, line itself up with Trench. Ease in and get close. Real close. The closer the better. I reverse the engines then. Bring it to a stop.

"I think I have it figured out," Hard says. Her eyes are closed now, forehead furrowed. "There are a few patterns that have to match. A few colors to get right. Not the prettiest thing I've ever done..."

I frown. "That brings a lot of comfort." I watch as the surface of the wall in front of us begins to shimmer and move. Wiggle. Then becomes transparent. I hear a high-pitched whistle. Not a shriek, but the evidence of air being lost. "Rails, Hard, don't let it—"

I feel air rushing by my head and look to see the top of the rippling wall—the start of the cube—has a fist-sized hole in it. I feel the stomach migraine again, strong as I've ever felt it. A biting rat in my gut.

Just as I contemplate diving into the stream to help, the whistle pitch changes, becomes a light hiss, then stops altogether. The hole closes off.

"Sorry," HardCandy says. "I massaged the wrong thing. Think I got it now." Through the cube's silver wall I see the hull of Dark-Trench, airlock still standing open. Around the edges I can make out the pinprick of stars.

"Quickly!" Trench says. "We have only minutes to safely get away."

HardCandy opens her eyes, lays a comforting hand on my arm. "Okay, I think it is ready. We can step in." A smile. "Do this together?"

"Sure," I say. "I trust you."

Her brow lowers. "You better!"

Without another word we step into and through the inner cube wall. Again it feels like being immersed in wet sand. When Hard says "Okay" to indicate we're inside the cube, I find I've had my eyes shut the entire time. And been holding my breath.

"I've got it moving," Hard says, and there is the sense of movement toward DarkTrench.

Remembering what the view was like the last time I did this, I keep my eyes locked on Trench's hull and the airlock that awaits us. Only a few more meters...

HardCandy doesn't though. Shortly after the cube begins to move, she turns and looks to our left, directly at the green surface of the planet. She catches her breath again. "Sand, you should see this."

I shake my head. "Don't want to. Don't miss it. Didn't like it when I was there." Trench is very close now. If I went all the way to the far wall and put my hand through, I could probably touch it. I resist the urge, though.

"No, really." She grabs my shoulder hard, makes me turn the right direction. Reluctantly, I look.

The circle of the planet is before me, eclipsing the raging star behind it. This eclipse is like nothing I've ever streamed of Earth's astronomy. Nothing like an earthly eclipse. There is no faint halo around the somber mass of the moon. Instead, a raging crown of fire surrounds the planet's circumference. Clouds of star-matter arc and billow, reaching, clawing, threatening to engulf. And the crown of the star's surface has moving variations of color—light bands that knife through the entire perimeter like a spotlight.

So He banished them from the Garden, placing on the east side cherubim and a flaming sword flashing back and forth to guard the way.

The cube makes contact with DarkTrench's hull.

HardCandy grabs my hand, jerking me forward and into the airlock, where we tumble and slide.

"That was incredible!" I say.

We enter the white airlock and the outer door hisses shut behind us. Immediately I feel the familiarity of Trench's stream, the fluidity and closeness of it. It warms me like welcoming arms.

"Are you both in?" Trench asks. "Safe?"

"Go, Trench!" I yell. "We're here. Go!"

"Engines full ahead." Trench pauses, and I swear the lights flicker from the engine's sudden exertion. "Welcome back, debuggers."

THE FURY OF BETELGEUSE fills every screen. HardCandy is seated at the navigator's desk along the right wall, while I—still too invigorated to sit—stand close behind her. My arms are crossed tightly, as if trying to hold in the fire, the warmth I now feel. I don't want it to end.

God streams Full Impact, freehead. It is hard to explain to someone like you, but there it is: real, encompassing, and true.

Both of us are focused on the room's curved central screen. Also, the removable panels on either side are now slid back, allowing the visible light of the star, though shielded, to filter into the room. It doesn't bother me.

"So what is happening to the star?" HardCandy asks. "Is it going to explode?"

"I don't believe so," DarkTrench says from somewhere above us.

Betelgeuse's circumference now measures twice what it did when we first arrived. It has both brightened and expanded. We are now safely beyond its reach. At the far extent of the star system, en route to a secure place to open a tunnel home.

"I suspect this is what it does from time to time," Trench says. "The event that accounts for its variability in brightness. It could be a warning sign, however. A death throe." He pauses. "Or perhaps it is the start of only a new phase of the star's existence. A phase when new elements are created."

"I don't understand," HardCandy says. "The first crew didn't experience such an event, did they?"

"That is correct," DarkTrench says. "They did not."

HardCandy turns to look at me. "Then why did they hear the singing?"

"The transmission that led to the bot's destruction?" DarkTrench asks. "It is not clear to me. Stars are never constant. There are always flare-ups of some magnitude. Solar storms. Perhaps one of these events was responsible. Searching my records finds a number of small events—possible foreshadowings."

I shake my head.

HardCandy, who is still watching me, says, "What?"

"Can you show us the planet?" I ask. Immediately the large forward screen shows the planet's disk. The fire of the star is now very near its surface. Much of the green is gone—replaced by browns and blacks. "What I don't understand," I say, "is why the beetles don't leave. Instead of hiding out inside the planet, why don't they build sliver ships and launch? Why didn't they chase us?"

Turning in her chair, Hard frowns. "I know the answer. I remember from my time in the reclaimer template."

"What?"

"They are imprisoned there, Sandfly. They can't leave. It is something that happened in their distant past. The reclaimers believe it has always been that way. That their technology depends on that planet somehow. There were hints of another reason, though. That an outside force had confined them."

I glance at the image of the raging sun. "Like God? Like A~A³?"

HardCandy shrugs and stands, moving next to me. "You're more likely to know than me," she says, staring into my eyes.

My warmth intensifies, but I frown anyway. "There were no references to history with maintainers. The past, the future, neither is of much concern."

"But they are for us," she says. "Right now, the future seems especially important..."

"If you return your attention to the main screen," Trench says.

HardCandy and I both look. The image of the jinn planet has somehow dimmed—become less distinct. As we watch, the fade-out continues, until finally the space the planet occupied becomes completely void, with only Betelgeuse showing through.

"Where did it go?" HardCandy asks.

"That isn't possible," Trench says. "Not by normal physics."

I recall the technology of the jinn. The way it felt to manipulate it. That wasn't normal either. It was almost magical in what it could accomplish. "I have a feeling it isn't really gone," I say. "We've witnessed the work of unseen forces before." I lower my gaze to the open windows. Though dimmed by the light of Betelgeuse, the visible stars are still amazingly bright. "That's probably why you missed the specific stream event before, Trench. It operates at levels beyond our ability to perceive or even understand...as do the jinn."

HardCandy draws still closer. "Well, wherever they are, they're staying there," she says, "not reaching Earth. And that's enough for me." She smiles. "So do we have everything we came for? Learned all we need to know?"

Curling my lips inward, I nod. "We learned enough. Found the stream. I understand now that it is a two-way medium, a conduit of both growth and adoration. Communication with the eternal—the divine."

"With A~A³?"

"Yes," I say, bobbing my head. "I also learned something of his nature. That he can be trusted. How he stooped for us. The form the stream took when it was written into words. What is true." I pause, look into HardCandy's eyes. "The freeheads on Earth need to know all that. They need direction. And we're a pretty good way of disseminating information, I think."

She slips both arms around me, draws herself tight against me. "You know, it is funny..."

I'm befuddled by her closeness. A bit out of spec. "What?"

"The legend about meteorites is that they are thrown by angels at evil jinn."

"There's a legend? I didn't know."

"Yes..." She flutters an eye at me—a surprisingly powerful gesture. "In our case, though, the jinn tried to bring down an angel with a meteorite. Thankfully, the angel deflected it."

I glance at the image of Betelgeuse again. The jinn were able to manipulate matter at an elementary level. A godlike level. What if stars were something similar?

"I don't know that I'm the angel in the story," I say. "I fail, remember?"

"Never me," she says. "You never fail me." She tightens her grip and rises up to kiss me.

I press my lips to hers. More inward explosions.

Breaking away, I say: "The rules...the stops..."

She smiles. "Mine don't seem to work anymore. They seem to have been rewritten."

Now I'm worried. More afraid than I've ever been. Both of us without stops? On a long trip alone together? With nothing to hold us back beside our own free will? Dangerous.

Still, I'm really happy too, freehead. Happy for the future.

"No pain?" I ask. "The stops are gone?"

"Yeah, Sandfly, gone."

I glance at the screen, at the spot where Jannah once floated, then at the raging, protecting Betelgeuse. The maintainers didn't think about the future, but invariably we must.

"DarkTrench," I say. "We have a message to deliver. Please take us home."

FINISH THE SAGA

Having escaped the storms of Betelgeuse and the schemes of Jannah's inhabitants, Sandfly and HardCandy make their way back to Earth. They have a message to deliver. A society to free. And A~A³ is with them. What could possibly go wrong?

They reach Earth to find a different world, an unexpected domain. One they can no longer connect with. Ultimately, Sandfly is alone, and Earth's freedom relies on him and his newfound faith. But does his mission even matter anymore?

He's a misfit, and a throwback. A symbol for all that's evil.

Is he the last freehead?

Grab *Freeheads* and find out!

YOU CAN MAKE A DIFFERENCE!

Word-of-mouth marketing is the best kind. Not only does it ensure that good books get noticed, it also helps bring the right books to the people who will enjoy them most.

If this book met or exceeded your expectations in any way, please consider telling your friends and/or posting a short review.

Your help is greatly appreciated!

ABOUT THE AUTHOR

Kerry Nietz is a refugee of the software industry. He spent more than a decade of his life flipping bits, first as one of the principal developers of the database product FoxPro for the now mythical Fox Software, and then as one of Bill Gates's minions at Microsoft. He is a husband, a father, a technophile and a movie buff. He is the author of several award-winning novels, including *A Star Curiously Singing*, *Freeheads*, and *Amish Vampires in Space*.

If you'd like to get an e-mail alert whenever Kerry has a new book out or has a special on one of his already-released books, sign up here: http://nietz.com/EmailList.htm.

ABOUT THE SUPERLATIVE STREAM

The Superlative Stream had an unusual genesis.

There were approximately five months between the time *A Star Curiously Singing* was accepted for publication and the time it entered final edits. That's a long period of time for a speculative writer to be sitting on his hands. Consequently, I began to get curious about how Sandfly's story might continue. I had him and HardCandy in space...now what?

I started writing. Little by little this strange and almost dream-like exploration story began to emerge. I worried that the story might get too far afield of what had happened on Earth—the normal life of a debugger. The character of HardCandy intrigued me too. How did a female debugger come to be?

My subconscious mind found a way to keep the exploration thread tied to Sandfly's Earth. Glimpses of HardCandy's life began to force their way into Sandfly's implant, and ultimately into my story. Next thing I knew I had two stories running in parallel. Would this even work?

At about the halfway point, my progress was interrupted by the need to make final revisions on the first book. Then came a month of marketing responsibilities. So for two months my strange sequel sat idle, waiting.

When I returned to *The Superlative Stream*, enough time had passed that I was no longer in the same writer's mind. I wasn't precisely sure where I was in the story, or where it was headed. So, I read over the half I had written. I enjoyed what I read.

The read-through had another, unanticipated effect, though. I reacquainted myself with the story, yes, but I also became overwhelmed by it. I worried that I couldn't find that same mental place again. That I might not be able to finish.

Horror of horrors!

This is where prayer and perseverance becomes important. I prayed, and I started writing again. Day by day I began to find my story again. Paragraph by paragraph, page by page.

In late December of 2009, I finished the first draft. I set it aside to let it percolate for a few weeks before starting on a second draft. I should have lots of time, after all. The first book had just released, and my publisher and I hadn't talked about the sequel, aside from me mentioning that I was working on something.

Life was good.

In January of 2010, I received a strange email from my publisher: "So, how far along are you on that sequel?"

When I told him I had just finished the first draft, he asked if we could release it as part of the spring release—in April! One of the three books he'd planned for that release wasn't going to be done in time. Could I take that spot?

We started editing in February.

The rest is history, in parallel.

Made in the USA
Lexington, KY
08 March 2016